So Long, LA

By

H. P. Oliver

MYSTERIES IN HISTORY

HPO Productions
8698 Elk Grove Boulevard
Suite 1-271
Elk Grove, California 95624

Cover art and design by Steve Eitzen

Back cover author photo:
1937 Chrysler Imperial Business Coupe owned by Camela and Dave Labhard and displayed at the California Automobile museum in Sacramento, CA. Photograph by Tim McCoy.

Printed in the United States of America

ISBN-10: 0-9888331-8-2
ISBN-13: 978-0-9888331-8-0

DEDICATION

For good friend and valued associate,
Gary Weisenberger.

ACKNOWLEDGMENTS

The author wishes to thank the SFO Aviation Museum and Library, the *Los Angeles Times* archive, the Southern Pacific Historical & Technical Society, and the Mills-Peninsula Medical Center for their assistance in researching background for this novel. The author is also grateful to his many associates who contributed historical anecdotes and additional period color that help bring this story to life.

PLEASE NOTE

This book occasionally refers to individuals and groups with terms that are considered inappropriate in today's society. These terms, however, were in common usage during the historical period in which this story is set and are included here solely for the purpose of accurately depicting the attitudes and customs of the era.

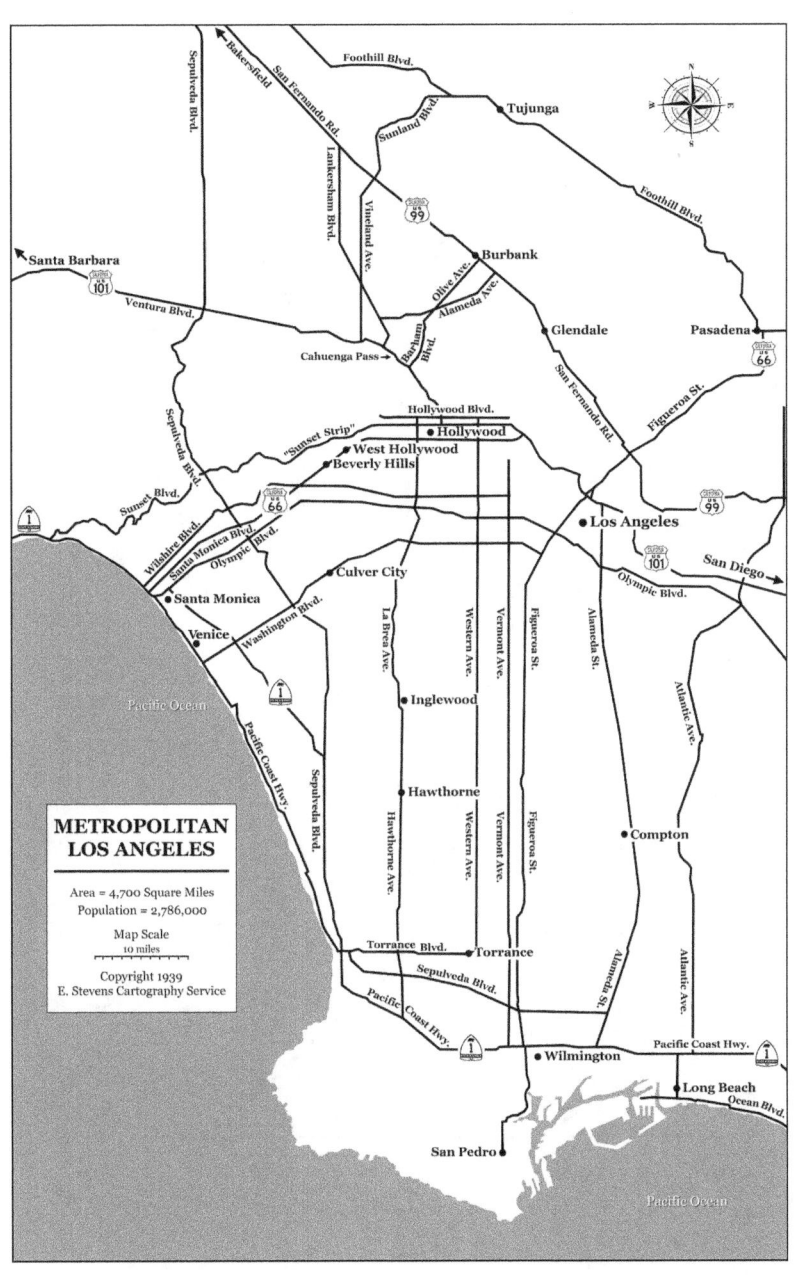

METROPOLITAN
LOS ANGELES

Area = 4,700 Square Miles
Population = 2,786,000

Map Scale
10 miles

Copyright 1939
E. Stevens Cartography Service

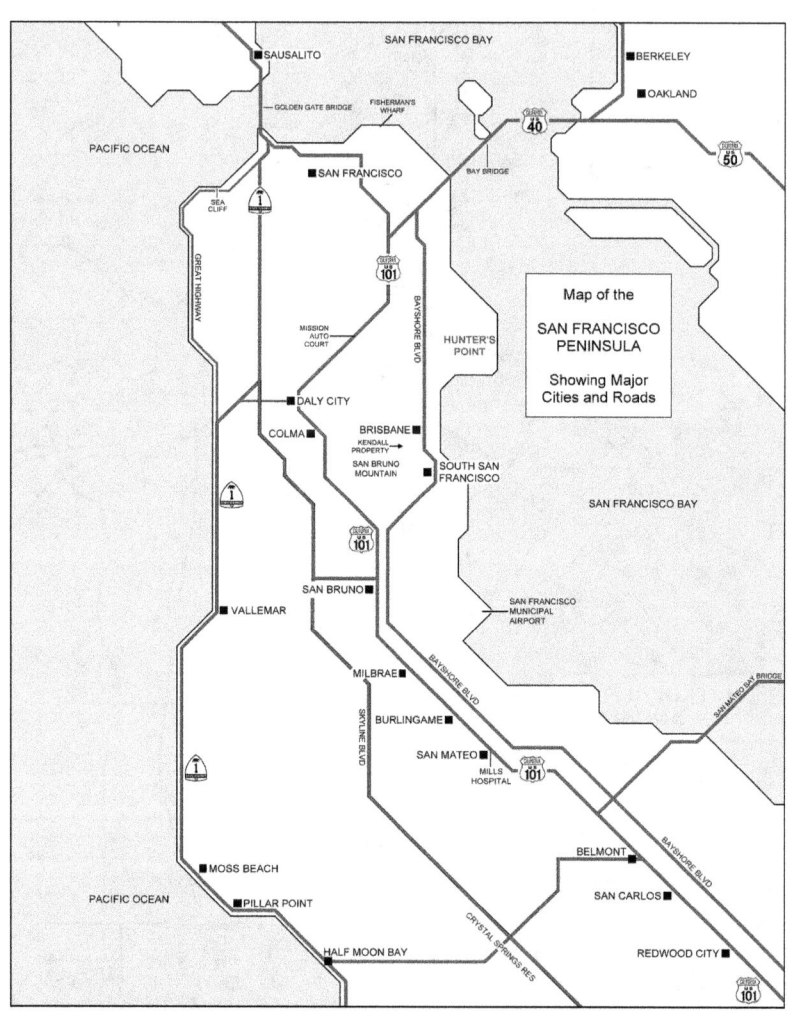

So Long, LA

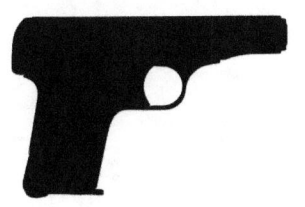

One

While it is a generally accepted fact that dead people tend to remain in that state, whoever was responsible for the two bodies in room 12 of Winchell's Motor Court wasn't taking any chances. There were enough bullet holes in them to make Swiss cheese jealous.

The guy in the seersucker sport coat next to the door was short and stocky with one of those thin little moustaches that are so popular these days. There'd been a lot of Latin in his blood, but he didn't have much of it left. Most of his blood was soaked into the room's threadbare beige carpet.

The other fellow was on the floor across the room with his back against the wall. He'd left a dark smear of blood on the faded pink and blue wallpaper as he slid to the floor. This one was much bigger than the first guy and was dressed to the nines in a classy white dinner jacket that was no longer very white nor very classy.

I took all this in during one glance around the dingy little room, after which I turned around and walked back out into the bright mid-morning sunshine. There, I gulped in several lungful's of more or less fresh air to flush out a death stench that was so strong you could taste it.

The two dead guys weren't my problem, and there were more than enough cops around to handle the situation. I figured they could get along just fine without my help, so I walked across the parking lot, which was filled to overflowing with Culver City Police Department squad cars, and leaned against the lone vehicle representing the Los Angeles Police Department at this morbid little gathering. It was the car I arrived in and I intended to continue leaning on it until Detective Lieutenant Don Chambers finished his business in room 12.

Chambers was once my boss, but that was a long time ago. Now he was just a friend who agreed to help me out with a feature story I planned to broadcast about the gambling ships anchored off the southern California coast. That was why I spent most of the previous night on a train and why I was back in southern California for the first time in nearly two years instead of behind a microphone at radio station KDG in San Francisco. The trip seemed like a good idea when I called Chambers a few days ago and asked him to help me out, but now I was beginning to wish I'd never set foot on the Southern Pacific San Francisco Lark streamliner that brought me here.

It wasn't just the stench of death in room 12. It was also seeing the old Central Division Headquarters on First Street again and hearing radio calls directing squad cars to familiar locations as we drove around in Chambers' black unmarked Ford sedan. Most of all, it was knowing that for every honest, hardworking cop like Chambers on the LA police force there were two or three guys supplementing their pay checks by looking the other way every time they passed a whorehouse, backroom bookie joint, or some other criminal operation under the control of local and east coast mobs.

All those things were fixtures from a part of my life I once drank into hazy oblivion, but encountering them again proved human memories aren't nearly as fragile as most of us think. Mine were perfectly capable of withstanding repeated soakings in eighty-proof bourbon.

I lit a Camel and watched the traffic go by on Washington Boulevard, an area thoroughfare that ran more or less northeast to southwest from downtown Los Angeles to the coast at Venice. Culver City is about halfway along the route, and like most of the little communities dangling from LA's coattails, it began life as a real estate development during the land booms of the teens and twenties. But Henry Culver's burgeoning metropolis has something none of those other towns have. It has the mighty lion of the film industry, Metro-Goldwyn-Mayer, which we'd passed a block or two before reaching the motor court. For that matter, Culver City also has the Hal Roach and Selznick studios, along with a few smaller lots. In fact, it is said that as many motion pictures are made in Culver City as in Hollywood.

I glanced back toward room 12 and was surprised to see Chambers weaving his way in my direction through the maze of squad cars. He hadn't been in there nearly long enough to do justice to a murder scene. I guessed that was because we were out of the LAPD's jurisdiction, and even though he had a professional interest in one of the stiffs, his hands were tied until the local cops wrote up their reports and the county coroner did his business. Chambers' invitation to the party was merely a courtesy extended by the Culver City cops. Don got a radio call about the shooting just before he picked me up at Southern Pacific's Central Station an hour ago. Since Culver City was more or less on the route to our intended destination, we were making a slight detour.

Watching Chambers approach, I was struck by the notion that the man hadn't changed one iota during the five years since I left the force to begin my somewhat less than meteoric career as a crime reporter at the *Los Angeles Times*. For me that was two careers ago, but Chambers was still carrying the same gold-plated badge and wearing the same wrinkled sport coats that, even draped over his chunky frame, looked like they were at least a size too large. His thinning hair was still combed across the top of his head to hide a bald spot, and he still had the sort of pleasant features that remind you more of a favorite uncle than a tough veteran homicide cop.

The first words out of his mouth, however, quickly shattered the kindly uncle illusion. "Still ain't got no stomach for blood and gore, huh?"

"Hell, no. Blood doesn't bother me," I lied, "But those mugs are your problem, not mine. I was just takin' up space in there."

"I see." The sarcasm in Chambers' voice made it clear he wasn't buying my story. He added, "Ya know, Park, you were one of the best homicide detectives I ever knew. If it weren't for that squeamish gut of yours, you'd have made Lieutenant by now. Hell, I'd probably be workin' for you!"

"Yeah, wouldn't that be fun?"

With a gesture so familiar it seemed as if he last did it five minutes ago instead of five years ago, Chambers stuck a big paw inside my jacket and pulled the Camel pack from my shirt pocket. Putting a cigarette between his lips, he stuffed the pack back in my pocket and said, "Light me, will ya?"

I spun the spark wheel on the brass trench lighter my old man kept as a souvenir of the Great War and held up the flame. He puffed a couple of times to get the fag going and mumbled, "Thanks."

We climbed into his Ford and Chambers turned right onto Washington toward the coast. There was a frown on his face as he shifted into third. Knowing Don as I did, that meant one of two things. Either something he saw in room 12 was puzzling him or his breakfast wasn't sitting well. Guessing the first of those two possibilities was more likely, I let my curiosity get the best of me.

I said, "Which one was yours?"

"Huh? Oh, you mean back there? The big guy in the white coat. Name was Arturo Bellaguisi. How's that for a moniker?"

"Sounds like he should own a spaghetti joint with red and white checkered table cloths."

"Yeah, he shoulda. He'd have lived longer in the spaghetti business."

"What was his business?"

Chambers looked over at me. "You sure ask a lot of questions for a guy who don't want to be a cop."

I smiled at him. "Just curious."

"Yeah, well my old pal Arturo was in the mob business."

"Chicago, New York or local?"

"New York. He was one of Bugsy Siegel's boys, which means he was workin' for Charlie Luciano. Kind of a jack of all trades—bagman, enforcer, whatever needed doin'."

"What got him killed? Did he cross Bugsy?"

Chambers thought for a moment, and then said, "No, I don't think so. Crossing the mob ain't very healthy."

"Well, in case it escaped your notice, Mr. Bellaguisi isn't exactly in the pink of health at the moment."

"Yeah, but if he was crossin' Charlie Lucifer, they'd have handled it different."

"I don't know about that. What I saw in there sure looked like a professional job. One with a message attached."

"That's what's botherin' me. Arturo really upset somebody's apple cart, that's for sure."

There was something in Chambers' tone that said we'd reached the end of the discussion, so I dropped the subject and watched the scenery roll by. We were coming into Venice, or what was left of it.

I had good memories of Venice as a kid. The place really had canals then. And gondolas. I remember going there on outings with my folks and watching guys in colorful Italian costumes pole boatloads of tourists under the arched bridges. It all seemed pretty terrific then.

Venice, the way it was when I was a kid, had been the dream of a guy named Abbot Kinney. The way I understood the story, Kinney made a lot of money in the tobacco business and came out to restful California in search of a cure for his insomnia. Like just about everybody else he fell in love with the place, and just like everybody else with a spare buck or two he got into the real estate business.

But Kinney went about it with more imagination than most. He had an idea that Los Angeles was the perfect place for America's cultural renaissance. All it needed was the proper setting. To his mind, the proper setting for a renaissance was a recreation of Venice, Italy, so he built one, complete with canals, Italian facades, and a pier with a midway grand enough to excite any kid and most adults.

Unfortunately, from Kinney's point of view, Venice of America attracted more fun-loving tourists than culturally stimulated artisans. Still, the place made enough money to offset the high cost of digging all those canals even if it didn't live up to Kinney's aesthetic expectations.

The big problem was the water in the canals. It was supposed to circulate naturally with the tidal action of the Pacific Ocean, but it didn't. Instead, the water just sat there and got stagnant. When the tourists stopped coming and the locals got tired of the stink, the town filled in most of the canals and the gondoliers went back to drivin' taxicabs.

Washington Boulevard dead-ended at the coast road and Chambers swung right. A few miles north, about halfway between Venice and Santa Monica, he turned left onto a sandy road that led down to the beach.

Pulling over to the shoulder, Chambers pointed out toward the ocean and said, "Okay, there's what you came to see."

We got out of the Ford and I scanned the horizon for some sign of gambling ships. When I finally spotted them, the scene was disappointing to say the least. I'm not sure what I expected, but the two low gray hulks Chambers pointed out certainly didn't inspire visions of glamorous folks living the gay life.

Two

Pacific Coast Highway, North of Venice

While the gambling ships were big news at the moment, they weren't new. The ships were around when I was on the force and even before that. We just never paid much attention to them back then.

According to a feature story I found in a back copy of the *Times*, the first of their breed, the *Johanna Smith*, appeared off Long Beach ten years ago. The article said the *Johanna Smith* once plied California's coastal waters as a lumber carrier. In twenty-eight her engines and superstructure were replaced with a roulette wheel, three crap tables, three blackjack tables, two chuck-a-luck cages, and twenty-three one-armed bandits. Thus equipped, the *Johanna Smith* was towed offshore and became the first of several gambling ships seeking their owners' fortunes in the waters of southern California. The problem of getting customers and their money to the action was solved with a fleet of water taxis. Twenty-five cents buys high-rollers a round trip from Long Beach or Santa Monica to the floating casinos lying at anchor just three miles off the coast.

That three-mile distance is significant. For the most part, gambling is illegal in California. There is, however, no federal prohibition against gaming, and since the state's jurisdiction extends only three miles from its coast, the *Johanna Smith* and her sister ships are technically legal operations. Or are they?

That question has been asked before—actually, several times before. It seems like every few years some politician or other develops a severe case of moral indignation at the hot beds of sin anchored off the coast and launches another campaign to shut them down. Of course, cynics question whether the motivation behind these crusades is really moral outrage or just greed. As long as the ships are legal, there is no reason for their owners to pay off authorities for looking the other way.

One of the earliest assaults against the gambling fleet was directed at the *Johanna Smith* shortly after she dropped anchor. Federal officials towed her back into port and inspected all the gambling paraphernalia in hopes of finding that it was rigged so they'd have a reason to shut the operation down. To the dismay of those federal authorities, however, all the equipment was working properly and the ship was back in business within a day or two.

The fact that the *Johanna Smith* came through that federal raid unscathed did not go unnoticed by those who found separating the sporting crowd from their money a lucrative pastime. Gambling is just like any other business and when it appeared the operators of the *Johanna Smith* had themselves a gold mine, other entrepreneurs were eager to get in on the act. Over the years, at least nine casino ships have operated off the coast at one time or another. And, why not? It's a great racket—just like having the keys to the bank, except for one minor detail.

A lot of cash changes hands aboard those ships—on some nights as much as a hundred thousand dollars. Any time there's that much money floating around, you can count on some bright guy looking for a way to walk off with it, especially since the ships were relatively isolated with no cops for at least three wet miles in any direction.

Anticipating the problem, ship owners employed bouncers and guards to discourage opportunists, but their precautions weren't always effective. Several successful hold-ups have been pulled over the years. And a couple of ships, including the *Johanna Smith*, were actually burned and sunk during robberies.

Such goings on, however, have had little effect on the ships' steady stream of customers. The most popular of the current fleet, the *Rex*, operates twenty-four hours a day and seldom has fewer than a thousand gamblers on board at any given time. During peak night and weekend hours those figures often soar to three or four thousand. But the robberies, sinkings and other such unpleasantries, including the occasional rough handling of unruly customers by bouncers, gave politicians more ammunition in their war against the ships' owners.

Not long after the Feds' unsuccessful raid on the *Johanna Smith*, the Long Beach City Council enacted an ordinance making it illegal for a taxi to convey anyone to a place where immoral acts were performed. Of course gambling ship owners challenged the law in court, arguing there is no difference between a water taxi carrying people out to their ships and a land taxi taking passengers to Las Vegas or Tijuana. The judge agreed.

Now a new broadside had been fired at the off-shore gambling industry by LA District Attorney, Buron Fitts, and it showed some promise of being successful. That's why I was here in the land of sunshine and oranges, instead of toiling in my usual fog-bound vineyard four-hundred miles to the north. If Fitts' plan for shutting down the gambling ships once and for all was as fool-proof as he so eloquently proclaimed to the press, it would be big news that effected the entire state of California.

Fitts' legal eagles came up with the argument that the crescent shaped body of water between Malibu and Palos Verdes was actually a bay—Santa Monica Bay, to be specific—thus making activities on that body of water subject to local, rather than federal, jurisdiction. Since the gambling ships were anchored three miles from points along the curving shoreline, rather than from an imaginary line drawn across the opening of the bay, Fitts claimed they were subject to state anti-gambling laws and he, by God, was going to bring the evil-doers to justice and put an end to their nefarious activities.

Fitts chose the *Rex* to test his case. Yesterday he presented his arguments before the LA Grand Jury and convinced that august body to hand down an indictment against *Rex* owner, Tony Cornero, and two unnamed defendants.

Cornero responded to the indictment by offering to turn himself in today and agreeing to cease operations aboard the *Rex* at midnight, tonight. He even seemed eager to face the charges, and with good reason. If he lost and the California Supreme Court decided the *Rex* was actually anchored in a bay, Cornero and the owners of at least three other gambling ships were out of business. Sure, they could move further off-shore, but that would result in longer water taxi rides through rougher water for their customers. Since it was reasonable to assume seasick gamblers who were tossing their cookies at the rail wouldn't be nearly as eager to participate in games of chance, the fate of a highly profitable business rested on the outcome of Fitts' case.

Leaning against the fender of the department's Ford, Chambers looked bored as a tour bus driver waiting for his passengers to finish clicking Kodaks at the La Brea Tar Pits. I said, "Don, you ever been out on those ships?"

"Sure. Haven't you? I figured a poker player like you

would've been a regular customer."

"Not me. I prefer friendly games without the house taking a cut out of each pot. You go out there on official business?"

"Yeah, sort of. The vice guys visit the ships a couple of times a month just to keep an eye on things. I've gone with 'em a time or two just to see what's what."

"The ship owners don't mind cops snooping around?"

"Mind? Hell, they treat us like long-lost kin! It really gets the vice guys' goats. Those bums, especially Cornero, know we can't touch 'em and they love to rub it in. Last time I went out to the *Rex*, they knew we were comin'—I think the water taxi outfits tip .em off somehow—and Cornero himself greeted us at the gangplank . . . offered us drinks on the house, the whole works."

I grinned. "Of course you politely declined his hospitality."

"You know damned well I did. I don't drink with gangsters."

"Gangsters? I thought those gambling ships were one hundred percent legal."

Chambers grunted, "Yeah, well, we'll see about that. Besides, word has it that Bugsy Siegel is a silent partner with Cornero. We can't prove it, but Siegel's brother-in-law is an officer in Cornero's company. That makes it a pretty sure bet Bugsy is involved one way or another."

"You thinkin' Fittsy will shut 'em down this time?"

"He might. It depends on what kind of defense Tony Cornero comes up with. He's got some real high-priced shysters workin' for him. He can afford 'em."

Then, looking at his watch, Chambers added, "We'd better get movin' if we're gonna be there when Cornero shows up to turn himself in at the Hall of Justice."

We climbed back into the Ford and Chambers got us headed north on the coast road again. As we sped up the two-lane highway, I glanced across at the gray hulks on the horizon and realized that, if I wanted to see what all the fuss over the *Rex* was about, I'd better get out there tonight. If DA Fitts got his way, it would be my last chance.

Three

Los Angeles County Hall of Justice—211 W. Temple Street

The Hall of Justice was right about where I'd seen it last, downtown on the north side of Temple between Broadway and Spring. On the other hand, imposing thirteen-story buildings that look like they were carved out of a single, gigantic block of granite do tend to stay put, even in earthquake-prone California.

A small crowd of about a dozen guys were already gathered on the sidewalk and front steps when Chambers pulled into a parking space under a sign that said, "Reserved for Sheriff's Vehicles." A uniformed deputy standing nearby gave us the eye and pointed to the sign. Chambers flashed his LAPD. shield and the guy gave us a nod in the spirit of professional courtesy.

Most of the group in front of the Hall of Justice were men carrying either notepads or four-by-five press cameras, and Chambers observed, "I guess we made it. The news vultures are still here."

I was about to point out that he was with one of those vultures when a little guy in a salt and pepper tweed sport coat near the edge of the crowd glanced in our direction. He did a double-take, and said in a loud whiney voice, "As I live and breathe! It's the *Times* ex-boy wonder, Park Atkins."

It only took me a second to place the guy's pockmarked face and the sarcasm that went with it. The pinched features and big mouth under the oversized black fedora with a press card stuck in its band belonged to a *Tribune* reporter named Ebert. Needless to say, there was no love lost between us.

I said, "Hello, Tommy."

"Still hangin' out with LA's finest, I see. And sober, too!

Where you been keepin' yourself, Atkins?"

A large black Cadillac saved me the trouble of answering. It pulled up to the red curb directly in front of the Hall of Justice steps and Ebert, along with the rest of the mob, crowded in close. Cameras were pointed and clicked at the three well-dressed men who stepped out of the Caddy. I'd seen pictures of Cornero, but I'd have recognized him anyway because he looked exactly like a gangster boss is supposed to look. Tony was wearing a sharp black suit and tie with a narrow-brim hat and dark glasses. He was a good-sized guy with some gray showing around the edges of his hat and a confident way of moving that clearly said he was used to being in charge. Questions immediately began flying at Cornero.

"Tony, you gonna beat this rap?"

"Does this mean the end of the gambling ships?"

"What's your defense gonna be?"

Cornero raised his hands in a gesture meant to stop the questions and said, "All I got to say right now is we ain't doin' nothin' illegal. The *Rex* is outside the three-mile limit and Fitts ain't got nothin' to say about it."

Tommy Ebert yelled, "The DA says you're in Santa Monica Bay. What about that?"

Tony put on a broad grin and said, "You fellas know as well as I do there ain't no such thing as Santa Monica Bay. You ever seen it on a map? Hell, no! That's just a lot of hogwash Fitts cooked up to look good in the headlines, but he's gonna end up with egg all over his mug again."

That was followed by another barrage of questions which Cornero waved off as he climbed the Hall of Justice steps flanked by the two men who arrived in the Cadillac with him. The crowd followed and I asked Chambers if he knew who the other two guys were.

"Shysters. The guy on the left is a hotshot by the name of Newt Cavendish. I don't know the other one, but he's gotta be a lawyer, too. He don't look dumb enough to be muscle."

We tagged along behind the reporters and watched as a Sheriff's Captain met Cornero just inside the double doors and proceeded with the ritual of officially arresting Tony on multiple charges of felony bookmaking. The growing entourage, which now included the Sheriff's Captain and two uniformed deputies, then moved through the Hall of Justice and out the back entrance where a sheriff's patrol car was waiting to haul Cornero to the county jail for booking.

Sounding bored to tears with the whole spectacle, Chambers

said, "You want to see the booking or have you had enough of this circus?"

"I've seen enough. I just wanted to take a look at Cornero and see how he handled himself."

"Okay, let's go. If you want, I'll call over later and see what bail was set at."

I told Chambers I'd appreciate that and we headed for his car. In it, he turned and asked, "Where to now?"

"My hotel, I guess. I've already shot the hell out of your morning and I need to get my notes together for tonight's broadcast."

"Tonight's broadcast? How you gonna do that from down here?"

"On the telephone. I call in and they hook me up from the switchboard so my voice goes out on the air."

Sounding a lot more awed than he looked, Don said, "Now ain't that somethin'."

"Yeah, but don't ask me how they do it. I haven't got the slightest idea."

"You gonna come by headquarters this afternoon?"

"If you've got the time. I'd really like to interview someone from Vice about the ships."

"I've got all the time in the world. Ain't nothin' but a foot-high stack of homicides sittin' on my desk waitin' to be solved. They can wait."

"Look, Don, you know I appreciate your help, but if you're behind the eight ball . . ."

"Oh hell, don't go gettin' sincere on me, Atkins. Another hour or two ain't gonna make much difference. Besides, if I treat you right, you might tell all those good citizens up there in Frisco what a great guy I am. I'll be a celebrity!"

Grinning, I said, "That's 'San Francisco' to you, Chambers. The good citizens up there don't like foreigners calling it Frisco."

With an exaggerated expression of exasperation on his face, he muttered, "Oh, brother!"

Two blocks later, as Don pulled up in front of my hotel, he said, "Come by about three. I'll have someone from Vice for you to talk to."

I got out, grabbed my suitcase off the back seat, and thanked Chambers for his help. He waved a big paw at me and gunned his Ford away from the curb. I turned and entered the New Brunswick Hotel.

The one thing you could tell right off was that, despite its name, the New Brunswick was anything but new. In fact, it's been right there on the southeast corner of First and Spring Streets for as long as most Angelinos can remember. There are several other hotels to choose from close to Central Division Police Headquarters in the Civic Center area, but they're mostly classy places with elevators and doormen. The New Brunswick had neither, but it did have one thing going for it the others lacked, It had room rates low enough to fit the limited expenses Bill Kastner authorized for this trip.

Kastner is my boss at KDG—actually, he owns the station—and he was more than a little skeptical about this project from the beginning. He couldn't see why I needed to be traipsing off to Los Angeles when there was plenty of news going on right there in San Francisco. It took all my powers of persuasion to finally convince him that the Cornero case had the elements of a great crime report—gangsters, a crusading district attorney, and the depraved lure of gambling ships on the high seas. Even after convincing Kastner the story had local interest, he made me give up a week of my accrued vacation in exchange for financing the trip.

After registering at the front desk and paying for three nights in advance, I climbed two flights of stairs to my room and considered myself lucky to have talked Kastner into letting me make the trip at all. It isn't just that Kastner is tight with a buck. Oh, he is that all right, but in fairness I had to admit that KDG isn't exactly the biggest money-maker on the dial in San Francisco. With no network affiliation and a minuscule talent budget, KDG mostly aired recorded music. About the only bright spots on the broadcast schedule that attracted any advertising revenue were a cooking program conducted by a well-known local chef and my nightly news broadcast.

Without Chef LeBlanc and me, KDG wouldn't bring in enough to keep the lights on. So I did have some leverage with Kastner, but not enough to get me a room at the Mayflower or the Biltmore on Pershing Square. On the other hand, I wasn't staying at the YMCA, either.

And I really didn't mind giving up a week of my vacation because this trip was as much for my own benefit as KDG's. I needed a break—time to think about some choices I had to make very soon. The dilemma I faced centered around a job offered me by the big Mutual Broadcasting System. It was a swell deal with a salary high enough to give me the jitters just thinking about it. But there were other considerations, like moving to Chicago and a little brunette cutey named Dandy Harrison who was, among other things, the love of my life.

Four

New Brunswick Hotel—First & Spring Streets, Los Angeles

I tossed my coat on the bed and settled myself at the small writing desk thoughtfully provided by the New Brunswick Hotel. There, I lit a Camel and put the telephone handset to my ear. There was no dial tone, but the phone didn't have a dial anyway, so I just sat there patiently hoping the instrument was actually connected to something.

About the time I was ready to hang-up and go down to a public phone in the lobby, the desk clerk came on the line. "Front desk. Whatcha want?"

"I'd like to make a collect call to San Francisco."

"Sure," he said. "What's the number and who do I tell 'em is calling?"

I told him and did some more patient waiting while he got the long-distance operator on the line and she, in turn, did whatever it is that long-distance operators do to get you connected with distant places. Finally a familiar voice said, "Good afternoon. Radio station KDG."

The operator said, "I have a collect long-distance call for anyone at this number from Parker Atkins in Los Angeles, California. Will you accept the charges?"

Sally, the station's daytime switchboard operator said KDG would be simply delighted to accept the charges—or words to that effect—and the long-distance operator said, "Go ahead with your call, please."

I asked Sally to hook me up with my assistant, Charlene Blanchard, known less formally around KDG as Charlie, and a moment later I heard another, even more familiar voice say,

"Newsroom."

I said, "You mean news closet."

Ignoring my reference to our less than spacious office, Charlie said, "Hi, Park. How's Los Angeles?"

"Full of oranges and nuts. What's going on at that end?"

"Not much. Mr. Kastner was in earlier and wanted to know if I'd heard from you. I told him I expected you to call any minute. I didn't know they grew nuts down there."

"They do, but I was referring to the human kind, kiddo. Don't worry about Kastner. He was probably just making sure I'm not having any fun at the station's expense."

"Well, are you?"

"Not yet, but I've got plans for a big night on the town."

"Not until after your remote broadcast, I hope."

"Of course not. Work before pleasure and all that."

"How much air time do you want?"

"Oh, let's say four minutes. Or do you need some fill?"

I heard paper rustling four hundred miles away and knew Charlie was skimming over long yellow sheets of wire service copy she probably just tore off the Associated Press teletype. "No, we don't really need any fill. There's quite a bit going on. Hitler's still shaking his fist at Czechoslovakia, they had a big earthquake in Athens, and the Irish government is returning Wrong-Way Corrigan's airplane after he promised not to try flying it back to New York."

"Sounds like a wise decision. Okay, save me four minutes. How did Stewart do with the broadcast last night?"

Dick Stewart, KDG's evening announcer, was doing double duty this week by filling in for me on my nightly news broadcast. Charlie said, "Not bad, but Dick sure sounds bland compared to you. Do you want your four minutes at the beginning or the end?"

"At the beginning. That way I can do my usual opening. Maybe that will spice things up some."

"Okay, Bea will be on the switchboard by then. I'll tell her to put your call straight through to the control room. What time?"

"Five before six. That should be early enough."

"Okay, Park. Have fun down there. Don't do anything I wouldn't do!"

"I thought you said to have fun."

"Park!"

"Calm down, kiddo, I'm just pullin' your leg. Talk to you tonight."

I put the handset back on its cradle and glanced at my watch.

We managed to get everything worked out in just a little over two minutes of long distance time, well within KDG's three minute limit. I wondered if the Mutual Broadcasting System had a three minute limit on long distance telephone calls.

I dug a yellow legal tablet out of my suitcase and wondered if Mutual had anybody as efficient as Charlie around to keep their newsrooms running. Back at the writing desk, I picked up a complementary pencil that had "New Brunswick Hotel, Los Angeles . . . a place to write home about," printed on it and scribbled roughly three minutes' worth of deathless prose about the events so far in the gambling ship caper. That left a minute for my opening and whatever information I might glean from the vice cop interview Chambers promised.

After that I donned my coat again and walked six blocks south and a block west to Clifton's Brookdale Cafeteria on Broadway. There, I let Bill Kastner buy me a modest lunch.

It was almost two o'clock—well after the lunch hour rush—and the only other folks in the huge dining room were a hen party of three gals with a pile of shopping bags around their table and a guy in the back corner who looked as if he might be trying to memorize this morning's edition of the *Times*. I munched my chicken pot pie amidst a fake forest of towering redwoods, complete with babbling brooks, and felt restless.

Once upon a time this was my town. As a cop, and then as a reporter, I covered every sprawling inch of it from Anaheim to Encino. Back then I knew every head waiter and newshawk in the county. To a cop or a reporter, head waiters and the guys who sell newspapers on the street are the really important people in any city. They see things other people don't.

But LA didn't feel like my town anymore. It wasn't that I'd been away that long or that the city changed. It was me that changed, and Los Angeles was part of a life I watched go by through the bleary eyes of a drunk. Not a passed-out-in-the-gutter drunk, but a mostly functional boozer who needed frequent stiff belts to keep going, or thought he did. With just the right amount of liquor in me, I was brilliant, and when the stiff belts got far enough ahead of me, I stopped functioning entirely.

I don't do that anymore, but being here reminded of those times. I finished my coffee and decided to wrap up the story I was here to cover as fast as I could and get back to San Francisco. Bill Kastner would like that idea. The sooner I got back, the fewer chicken pot pies he had to buy.

Beyond the double doors to Clifton's cool, pseudo forest, the

17

thin morning overcast had finally burned off and things were warming up. Whatever is in concrete sidewalks that makes them sparkle in the sun was sparkling, and all but the stuffed-shirts on the street left their coats wherever they came from or they were carrying them slung over their shoulders. I slung my coat in a similar fashion and hiked north on Broadway.

Crossing Sixth Street, I looked two blocks west past Pershing Square toward the massive Biltmore Hotel, and decided whoever said big cities were all the same was full of beans. Los Angeles was different from San Francisco in every way I could think of, from the size and style of the buildings to the expressions on the faces of pedestrians, and in the relatively short time I've been a resident of San Francisco, I've come to appreciate the qualities that make it different than any other place I've been. I wondered how Chicago stacked up against those qualities. If I accepted the Mutual Broadcasting System offer I would find out, but by then there would be no turning back.

What city they live in might not matter to some people, but it mattered to me and I knew it mattered to Dandy. My life began in San Pedro, not more than twenty-five miles west from where I stood waiting for the traffic signal to change at Fourth and Broadway. Dandy was born less than five miles from where she lives in her parents' home in the Pacific Heights district of San Francisco. If I took the Mutual job and if we decided to get married, it would be one hell of a change for both of us. The question was would it be a change we could live with?

What if I didn't take the Mutual job? A news job at a bigger station than tiny KDG might eventually come my way in San Francisco, but if I wanted a top job with one of the four national networks, I would have to go elsewhere because all the national news broadcasts originated in New York or Chicago.

Rounding the corner at First Street, I forced my thoughts back to the task at hand. Central Police Headquarters was a block away. If I was going to interview a vice cop who could give me some straight answers, I needed to think up some straight questions. Of course, I wasn't sure where Chambers was going to find somebody in Vice who was straight about anything. In this town the vice beat was paved with gold.

Five

Central Police Headquarters–First & Hill Streets, Los Angeles

Chambers was alone in the small second-floor office he shared with two other homicide detectives. He looked up from the clutter that was about to overflow from his desk onto the floor and waved a sheet of paper at me.

"Can you believe this shit? I gotta march in a damned parade Friday!"

"In front of the horses or behind?"

"Where the hell do you think? Sheriff Biscailuz and his damned drugstore cowboys are gonna be right up front with the Boy Scouts for crying out loud!"

The LA County Sheriff, a fellow named Eugene Biscailuz, was an avid horseman and prided himself on his mounted posse. Of course, the posse was for strictly for show. These days the only place bad guys got chased across wide-open country on horseback was in the movies, and there were a fair number of folks—mostly in the cop business—who thought the Sheriff ought to stick to his horses and leave sheriffing to those who knew something about law enforcement. Still, Biscailuz looked good in newspaper photos and the voting public of Los Angeles County apparently thought a good looking mug in the paper was more important than catching crooks.

I asked, "What's the occasion?"

Chambers scowled. "It's Law Observance Day or some damn thing. They're throwing a parade and a big shindig at the Coliseum."

"Can't get out of it, huh?"

He waved the paper at me again, "Hell no! This is a command

performance from the Chief! Uniforms and the works. Hell, I haven't worn my uniform since the last police funeral and that was three years ago. I don't even know if it fits anymore!"

I sat in the scuffed straight-back wooden chair alongside his desk and gestured toward the half-eaten doughnut holding down a stack of papers in front of him. "Then you better start cuttin' back on those."

Chambers picked up what was left of the glazed old-fashioned and took a deliberate bite. "Screw 'em," he said through a mouthful of doughnut.

The guy who leaned in the office door about that time made me think of Harold Peary, the radio actor who plays Fibber McGee's neighbor, Gildersleeve. He was big and broad-shouldered with a full head of dark, curly hair and a mustache that stretched wide across his upper lip like a big fuzzy caterpillar as he grinned and said, "That's telling them, Don. You wanted to see me?"

Chambers said, "Yeah, Ed. Thanks for stoppin' by. Come on in and meet Park Atkins. Park, this is Detective Ed Poole from Vice."

I stood and Poole still towered over me. With the wide caterpillar grin still plastered across his face, he stuck out a mitt that was twice the size of mine and said, "Pleased to meet ya, Atkins."

As Poole tried his best to pulverize my right hand, Chambers filled in the blanks. "Ed, Park was on the force a while back. Now he's does one of those radio news shows up in Frisco." I caught the smirk on Chambers face as he said, "Frisco."

He continued, "Park came down to do a report on your buddy Tony and the gambling ships. I thought you might be able to help him out with some information."

Poole scraped another wooden chair across the floor and sat. "Sure. Be happy to help. What do you want to know, Atkins?"

Pulling a notebook and pencil out of my pocket with an aching hand, I said, "Mostly just background stuff. Like, are the games legit?"

He was still grinning. I wondered if he ever stopped grinning. "Oh, they're on the level, all right. In fact, the odds aboard the *Rex* are better than what you get in Tijuana. Cornero and those guys run on a one-point-four percent profit. That means they pay back almost ninety-nine cents on every dollar bet. You can't beat that deal anywhere.

"Tony even buys newspaper ads offering a cash reward of a

hundred Gs to anybody who can prove his games are crooked. Hell, Cornero doesn't have to cheat. Even legit, those ships are gold mines. The suckers line up around the block every night, just waitin' to get out there and throw their money at the slots and tables."

Still writing, I said, "So the ships really do make money? Enough to make it worth Cornero's while to fight Fitts on this thing?"

"Hell yes, they make money! Look at it this way: let's say the *Rex* takes in four-hundred G's a day. That's about right. Out of the four hundred, Cornero keeps around six grand and pays the rest out in winnings. Overhead runs him, maybe, thirty-five hundred tops, so he's clearing two-and-a-half grand, pure profit. That adds up to a cool million going straight into Tony's pocket every year. And some guys who should know say he's doin' even better than that."

"Yeah," I nodded, "a racket like that's worth fightin' for."

Poole's grin got even wider, which I didn't think was possible. He said, "You bet your life it is. Old Fitts has met his match this time."

"Think the court will shut the ships down?"

His expression got a little more serious, but the grin was still there. "It's a toss-up. The DA's got a good angle, but Tony's got the best shysters money can buy. You can bet those mugs will put up a good fight. I wouldn't bet either way at this point."

"Okay," I said, "Anything else I should know? I'm planning a trip out to the *Rex* tonight."

Standing up, Poole said, "Nope. Just have a good time and say hi to Tony for me if you see him."

I stood, too, and without thinking about it, offered him my hand. "Thanks for the info, Poole. I'm glad for the help."

He did his hand-mashing trick again and said, "Good to meet ya, Atkins. Call me any time."

I noticed that Chambers didn't offer to shake hands with Poole. After the vice detective left, I flexed my hand few times and said, "I bet he doesn't need a nutcracker to eat walnuts. And he's sure happy about something."

Chambers laughed. "Yeah. Well, he's got a lot to grin about. I wondered why you shook hands with him a second time. Most guys are smarter than that."

I caught the oblique reference to a reason for Poole's elevated state of jovialness, but let it drop. Instead, I said, "That was habit. But I won't make the mistake a third time."

He nodded a little absently and said, "By the way, I called a buddy over at the county slammer. Cornero's already sprung. Bail was set at five hundred and Judge Kincaid scheduled the arraignment for Monday morning."

I added those tidbits to my notes and put the notebook back in my pocket. Leaning back in his chair, Chambers said, "You got everything you need now?"

"I guess so. I'll take a look-see at the *Rex* tonight and maybe try to get an interview with Cornero."

"You gonna head back north after that?"

"Probably. There's not much point in hanging around for the arraignment. Say, have you heard anything from Culver City about that motel shooting yet?"

"Naw. And I ain't holding my breath waitin' to hear from 'em, either."

"I gather you don't think they'll find the killer?"

"If we can't find him, it's not likely they'll do any better."

"I didn't realize you were looking for the guy. The shooting wasn't even in your jurisdiction."

"Yeah, but I wasn't talking about this one."

"There've been other killings like it?"

"Yup. Arturo is the fourth mob scumball who's died from lead poisoning in eight months, and I'm not counting the other guy who just happened to be in that motel room at the wrong time last night. Bellaguisi was the target."

"If somebody's out to get Lucky's boys, it must be Nitti."

"Nope. The first guy that got it was a Nitti goon."

"Then you've got a mob war on your hands. An eye for an eye."

"You'd think so, except for one detail."

"What's that?"

Chambers stuffed the last of his doughnut into his mouth and chewed for a minute. "The punks on the street say neither Luciano's nor Nitti's guys know anything about it, and both sides are screamin' for us to find whoever's killing off their boys. It's kind of ironic when you think about it."

"You saying somebody out there is playing Lone Ranger? Killing off mob guys one at a time?"

"That's what it looks like."

"Holy cow! I wouldn't want to be in his shoes with you guys and the whole damned underworld lookin' for him."

Chambers brushed some doughnut crumbs off his desk and said, "Yup, but so far he's done a real good job of covering his tracks.   We've got nothing but bodies, and the mob guys are getting very nervous."

Six

New Brunswick Hotel—First & Spring Streets, Los Angeles

I sat at the New Brunswick's writing desk with my four-minutes' worth of special crime report in front of me and the telephone handset to my ear. I used the few moments remaining before air time productively by looking over the minute of script I'd added since talking to Poole. The engineer up in San Francisco already had a voice-level on the phone line and the last thirty seconds of KDG's Cocktail Hour—the program of recorded music preceding the news—were coming through the handset.

As the final notes of Ella Fitzgerald's *A-Tisket A-Tasket* faded into the telephone line's static, a tinny sounding Dick Stewart said, "As tonight's Cocktail Hour comes to a close, we remind you that this program is made possible by the Howard Automobile Company, offering the finest in Buick sales and service. Whether you are considering the purchase of a new nineteen-thirty-eight model Buick or need service for a fine Buick you already own, turn to the Howard Automobile Company at the corner of Van Ness and O'Farrell in the City by the Bay. Please join us again tomorrow at five p.m. for another program of recorded music for your cocktail hour enjoyment. Now stay tuned for the news with Parker T. Atkins."

It was all part of a ritual I'd witnessed so many times I could see it in my mind as clearly as if I was there. The engineer flipped a switch that started one of his large transcription turntables spinning and an enthusiastic organ recording of *San Francisco* filled the KDG air waves. Then the engineer turned a knob to fade the music and pointed his finger at Dick through the thick control room glass.

Dick intoned, "You are listening to radio station KDG, at seven-hundred and twenty kilocycles on the dial, serving the greater San Francisco Bay area with the finest in modern broadcast programming."

The organ music came up again for a few more seconds, faded out completely, and Dick got the engineer's finger again. "Ladies and gentlemen, it is six o'clock p.m. in San Francisco, time for The News with Parker T. Atkins, brought to you by the Crocker First National Bank. Now by special remote hook-up, Parker T. Atkins."

That was my cue. Into the handset, I said, "Good evening San Francisco, This is Parker T. Atkins. Here is your news for Tuesday, August Sixteenth."

I paused for effect, and then said, "Tonight I am speaking to you from Los Angeles, where events are unfolding in a legal battle that may have a considerable impact on the entire state. The case concerns a fleet of four ships anchored three miles off the southern California coastline. Each of these ships has been converted from some previous purpose to house a complete gambling casino, as well as restaurants and cocktail lounges.

"As you may know, gambling is against the law in California. The state's jurisdiction over such activities, however, extends only three miles from its shores. Beyond that point jurisdiction belongs to the federal government which has no prohibition against gaming. Thus, the gambling ships are free to operate with impunity. Or are they?

"In the ten years since the first gambling ship appeared off of southern California's coast, repeated attempts have been made by local authorities to rid their shores of what they claim are floating dens of iniquity that lure otherwise God-fearing, honest citizens into immoral and illegal acts.

"One such attempt involved closing down the fleet of water taxis that carry gamblers out to the ships for the modest sum of twenty-five cents. To date, this and all other efforts to rid the coastal waters of gambling ships have met defeat at the hands of California's judges.

"Now, however, a new assault on the owners of the gambling ships has been launched by Los Angeles County District Attorney, Buron Fitts. Yesterday, Fitts argued before a grand jury that the ships are in fact operating illegally within state jurisdiction because they are actually anchored in a body of water he claims is a bay. Under the law, a body of water defined as a bay is considered to be within the state's borders.

"Agreeing that Fitts' argument has merit, the grand jury voted to indict Anthony Cornero Stralla, owner of the *Rex*—the most popular ship in the gambling fleet—on charges of felony bookmaking. Stralla, thirty-eight, is known locally as Tony Cornero. He responded to the charges by agreeing to surrender to sheriff's deputies today and to cease operation aboard the *Rex* at midnight tonight.

"True to his word, Tony Cornero, accompanied by his attorneys, appeared at the County Hall of Justice this morning and surrendered to Sheriff's Captain, George Contreras. Cornero was later released on a bond of five hundred dollars. Speaking to reporters at the time of his arrest, Cornero described the District Attorney's case as 'hogwash' and predicted that he would soon be exonerated of any wrongdoing.

"According to local authorities, Cornero and the other ship owners have a strong financial incentive to see that his prediction of exoneration is fulfilled. One expert estimates that, in spite of operating fair games and paying winners nearly ninety-nine cents of every dollar wagered, Cornero makes a net income of nearly one million dollars annually from operations aboard the *Rex*. Needless to say, the financial losses resulting from a judgment against Cornero in this case would be felt substantially by the gambling ship operators.

"In a few hours your reporter will board the infamous *Rex* on what may be its final night of operation. I will attempt to interview Tony Cornero for his views on the grand jury indictment. You'll hear the results of my visit to the *Rex* tomorrow night. Until then, this is Parker T. Atkins returning you to the KDG studios and wishing you . . . goodnight, San Francisco."

A moment later I heard a click and Charlie's voice said, "Good job, Park."

"Thanks, kiddo. You need me for anything else now?"

There was a pause during which I faintly heard Charlie asking the engineer something. Then she was back in my ear, saying, "No, Park, that's it. Same time tomorrow night?"

"Sure, why not? Save me about the same amount of time out of the newscast. I'll call if there's a change. Now go home and have a good evening."

"Okay, Park. Talk to you tomorrow. Bye."

I said goodbye and looked at my watch as I hung up the phone. The connection had lasted ten minutes and a few seconds. I smiled, imagining the shades of red Kastner's face would turn when he got the bill.

Downstairs, I left the New Brunswick's lobby through the

main entrance on First Street and found a single cab loafing at the curb. I climbed into the yellow and black Checker's wide back seat and said, "Santa Monica Pier, please."

The driver, a curly-headed fellow the size of a small mountain, stepped on the starter and snapped the red flag on his meter down. As we pulled out into the traffic on First, he glanced up at his mirror and said in English heavily laced with an accent that sounded Greek, "You go out to the gambling boats tonight, boss?"

"Yeah, the *Rex*."

The driver nodded. "Maybe your last chance. The cops, they arrested that Tony fellow today. The *Rex*, it is his boat. Maybe they gonna close up all them boats."

"So I heard."

"Be a real shame, they do that. Hurt my business, too. I take many fares to the pier. That's how I know you were going to the boats."

"I wondered how you knew."

"That's how."

We waited for a break in the traffic to make a left turn onto Figueroa. Then a couple of blocks later he swung right on Wilshire Boulevard. Wilshire would take us straight out to Santa Monica. When we stopped for the traffic light at Fairfax, the cabby said, "Escuse me if I talk out of turn, boss, but I think, maybe, somebody is following us."

Looking up at his dark eyes reflected in the rearview mirror, I said, "Oh? What makes you think so?"

"In my mirror I see this gray Chrysler automobile. She is, I think, the same one that was parked near the hotel. I see her behind us on Figueroa, and now in the mirror, I see her again."

I resisted the temptation to turn around and look for a gray Chrysler that might be behind us. Instead, I thought about who might be interested in me and where I was going. Absolutely nobody fit that description.

As the signal turned green and we accelerated across Fairfax, I said, "I can't think of any reason why somebody would be following me. Gray cars aren't that uncommon. Maybe it's a different car."

The driver's eyes flicked up to the mirror again for a moment and he said, "Maybe so, boss." He didn't sound convinced.

Fifteen minutes later we pulled to the curb where the Santa Monica Municipal Pier stretched far out into the Pacific surf—or the surf of Santa Monica Bay, depending on what some judge would soon rule—and I handed the cabby three one dollar bills to cover the amount on his meter plus a fifty-cent tip. The tip was generous, but I felt he deserved a little extra for his diligence with the rearview mirror, even if it was a false alarm.

As he scribbled the receipt I would eventually hand to Bill Kastner along with all my other expenses, I said, "Did you see any more of that gray car?"

He nodded. "The Chrysler, she was behind us all the way out Wilshire, but I did not see her after we turn on Ocean."

I took the receipt and thanked him. He said, "Boss, you are a nice guy, I think. You be careful on them ships."

Seven

Municipal Pier—Foot of Colorado Street, Santa Monica

With an hour of daylight left on a mild summer evening, the rough wooden planks of the Santa Monica Municipal Pier literally vibrated with the giddy vigor of a carnival midway. Garishly-painted horses pranced around a carousel in time to a rousing Sousa march played on a calliope. Kids in damp bathing suits squealed as they darted in and out of the crowds, and the usually refreshing sea breezes were heavy with greasy aromas of onion-smothered hot dogs and burgers hawked by concession stands on both sides of the pier.

Far out to sea, Mother Nature joined in the festivities by painting her ever-present fog bank with the vivid reds and oranges of a reluctantly setting sun. It was all part of the attraction that lures people west in droves from those dull, less endowed states that have names beginning with vowels. I couldn't help wondering if the continent wasn't already tipping in this direction from their added weight.

At the far end of the pier I could still hear the kids and the carousel, but the atmosphere was more business-like. This was where the sport fishing boats and water taxis held forth. There were four of the latter, each with a wooden podium beneath a sign that advertised their destinations. I headed for the one that offered quick, safe and comfortable round-trip service to the gaming ship *Rex*.

A guy in a weathered sea captain's hat behind the podium gave me the once-over as he took my quarter. He told me the taxi was loading at the bottom of the stairs behind him and would be leaving in about ten minutes. I remembered Chambers telling me how the gambling ship operators always seemed to know when cops were paying them a visit, and it made sense that the alarm system began with this fellow and his compatriots. I guessed he had orders to signal an alert of some kind if he spotted anyone who looked like a trouble-maker or a cop. I wondered which he had me figured for, cop or trouble-maker? I'd been both at various times in my life.

The wooden stairway attached to the side of the pier led down to a small floating dock where two hefty, but nicely dressed gents stood watching the steady stream of passengers boarding a sleek little launch of about thirty feet in length. They, too, looked me over as another fellow in a captain's hat ushered me up one of two short sets of steps leading to openings in a canvas cover rigged over the back half of the launch.

The canvas-covered aft cockpit was filled with two rows of wooden benches divided by a central walkway. Up forward there was a small cabin equipped with more seats and the helm. I was disappointed to note the captain of this jaunty little craft steered her, not with a traditional spoked ship's wheel, but with an automobile steering wheel that could've come right off my Ford. So much for nautical tradition.

I plunked myself down in one of the few remaining empty spots on the aft benches and was still reading signs describing the locations and use of such items as fire extinguishers and life vests when the fellow who ushered me aboard strode purposefully to the helm, and after giving a short wave out the window to someone on the dock, nudged a pair of chromium-plated throttle levers. The engines, which until now had been burbling away quietly in the background, rumbled to life as we moved away from the pier. Glancing back over my shoulder I noticed that the two bouncer-types from the dock were also making the voyage. They stood at the back of the cockpit with their arms folded and identical bored expressions on their faces.

The Captain brought us about in a quick U-turn so we were facing into the setting sun and opened the throttles wide. The little launch sprang forward with an impressive display of acceleration that elicited squeals of excitement from a few of the ladies aboard. We were off on a great adventure, and I noted with interest that my fellow adventurers were a fascinating and diverse cross-section of humanity.

The guy next to me, for example, looked like a real sport, dressed in an expensive checked sport coat and a white shirt open at the collar. The woman with him was decked out in what I think is currently referred to as a cocktail dress with a knitted shawl to protect her nearly-naked shoulders from exposure to the elements.

The man across the aisle and two benches forward, on the other hand, was wearing a rumpled suit coat with pants that didn't match. Both were showing their age around the cuffs, and the stubble on his chin said it had been more than twenty-four hours since the fellow made use of a razor. He displayed all the earmarks of a dedicated gambler who hadn't seen a winning hand since his last paycheck.

Further forward I glimpsed a familiar profile. The woman with the prominent nose beneath a stylish wide-brimmed hat was none other than Fanny Brice. Baby Snooks was on her way to play in Uncle Tony's den of iniquity.

We weren't more than fifteen minutes out when the three-hundred-foot hull of the *Rex* began filling the cabin windshield. My first impression was she rode awfully low in the water. Then I realized that was an illusion owing to the fact that the *Rex* carried no superstructure. Her top deck was covered from bow to stern with a long, low structure that resembled nothing more closely than a huge, enclosed dairy shed with a curved roof.

The *Rex's* name was displayed prominently in large black letters painted on her white hull near the bow and even larger letters painted amidships. A red neon sign above the covered boarding platform also blazed with the name *Rex*.

Aside from what seemed like an inordinate number of large life rafts attached to the railing along her main deck, the *Rex* looked rather plain. Then I noticed what very much resembled a war surplus machine gun mounted on the short deck area in her bow. Having such artillery displayed prominently made some sense from Cornero's point of view because it might discourage hijackers, but I thought it might have the same effect on paying customers. Obviously, it did not. There were sounds of great merriment drifting across the narrowing gap between our taxi and the *Rex*.

The skipper brought us smoothly alongside the boarding platform with a series of well-practiced maneuvers and passengers eagerly crowded toward the launch's two exits. I tagged along behind them, but as I reached the top of the stairway leading from the landing platform to the main deck, I found myself flanked by two more of Cornero's stylishly-dressed goons.

The bigger one on my right said, "Excuse us, buddy, but we need you to step over here for a minute."

I didn't argue and found myself ushered into a small cabin

just inside the casino entrance. The door closed behind us and the bigger goon suddenly started a quick frisk of my jacket. I decided it was time to object.

Stepping back and bumping into the other goon behind me, I said, "Hey, what gives?"

The second goon grabbed my arms in a grip I wasn't going to slip out of easily and the first guy nonchalantly continued his pat-down, saying, "Just relax, pal. We don't want no trouble."

"You've sure got an odd way of showing it. How come the frisk?"

He stepped back, apparently satisfied that I wasn't smuggling any howitzers aboard, and said, "It's just routine. You can go."

With that, the guy behind me let go of my arms and I said indignantly, "Hang on a minute, bub. You didn't frisk anybody else. Why pick on me?"

The big guy just glared at me, but the other fellow must've thought I deserved some sort of explanation. He said, "Like he said, it's routine. Whenever some mug comes aboard we haven't seen before or who looks suspicious, we give 'em the once-over."

"And I look suspicious to you?"

The big guy was running out of patience with me. He grumbled, "You look like a trouble-maker to me. Maybe you ought to just climb back on the taxi and get the hell out of here."

I turned to the friendlier of the two and said, "Does Tony approve of you greeting the paying customers this way?"

"Yup. It's just the way he wants it."

"Well, I'd like to hear that from him. Why don't you give him my card and see if he's got a minute to talk to me?"

He took my business card—the one with a KDG logotype on it that said, "Parker T. Atkins, News Director." After looking at the card long enough for a person of average intelligence to read it at least four times, he asked, "You a reporter?"

"Yeah, for a radio station, and I'm here to interview Cornero."

The big goon said, "See? I knew he was a bum. Let's put him back on the launch."

His buddy said, "Naw, we ain't got no rules against reporters. But I don't think Mr. Cornero wants to talk to you."

I said, "Just give Tony my card and let him decide."

He opened the door and said, "Sure, but don't hold your breath."

With that, I was ushered from the little room and the two goons disappeared in opposite directions, leaving me to my own devices. I stepped back out onto the deck, and leaning against the rail, I lit a cigarette. The sun was starting to dip into the fog bank out at sea, making it just dark enough for a few pinpoints of light to stand out against the undulating coastline. They looked a lot further away than three miles.

Eight

Gambling Ship Rex—Three Miles West of Santa Monica

The entrance to the *Rex's* casino was on her main deck a few steps forward of the stairways from the boarding platform. Outside you could clearly hear the enthusiastic chatter of gamblers accompanied by the mechanical clatter of slot machines and strains of Dixieland music provided by a jazz band somewhere in the casino. Inside, the racket was several decibels louder.

The casino ran nearly the entire length of the ship. It was a huge barn of a room that had to be at least two-hundred-fifty feet long by fifty feet in width. Brilliant, almost dazzling, illumination was provided by three long rows of hanging light fixtures. The one-armed bandits were arranged along the outside walls and seemed to go on forever. Down the middle of the room were the faro, roulette, dice, and card tables, each overseen by a stern-faced dealer clad in what seemed to be the *Rex* casino employee uniform of black trousers, a white shirt, and a dark red tie.

At the closest table, bright stacks of silver dollars caught the light and glittered against the green, red and black background of a roulette layout. The dealer—actually, a croupier in this case—said, "All bets down," and gave the big wooden wheel a spin. He flipped a little white ball into the stationary part of the wheel's bowl with a deft motion that caused it to fly around in the direction opposite to the wheel's spin.

There were at least a dozen players around the table and each pair of eyes was riveted hypnotically to the spinning wheel as it gradually slowed and the ball worked its way down toward a blur of red, black and green numbers. Even over the din of the slot machines, you could hear the ball rattle as it hit the spinning part of the wheel and bounced around the thirty-eight numbered grooves in the bottom of the bowl.

After what must have seemed a painfully long time to those around the table, the rattle of the ball slowed and became more distinct. With a few last hops, it settled into a groove and the wheel coasted to a stop. The call of, "Eighteen-red," was met with more groans than cheers as the croupier slid silver back and forth across the table with his long, hooked stick. There were no coins or chips on the red eighteen square, but a few bets on the red, even and second dozen fields were paid off quickly before the croupier announced, "Ladies and gentlemen, place your bets."

The whole process took no more than three minutes. Allowing time for the placement of bets, I guessed the dealer could manage at least ten spins an hour. It looked as if the house had netted around twenty bucks on the spin I'd just watched. If that was an average take, each wheel was worth about two hundred dollars an hour. There were supposed to be six roulette tables aboard the *Rex*, and if my arithmetic wasn't too far off, Tony was raking in twelve hundred bucks an hour off roulette alone. The thought crossed my mind that I might be in the wrong business. Running a casino was certainly more profitable than talking about wars and other mayhem on the radio.

At about the midpoint of the room, the row of slots on the port wall was broken by a long bar. I didn't enquire as to the cost of drinks, but it was a sure bet they were cheap. In addition to drinks served at the bar, several attractive cocktail waitresses in short black skirts and low-cut white blouses with red bowties around their bare necks hustled drinks back and forth between the bar and customers at the tables and slots.

The bar and its waitresses were a reminder that booze is an essential ingredient to a successful casino. Sober customers tend to gamble more cautiously than those whose judgment was slightly impaired by a few shots of an alcoholic libation.

I worked my way toward the bow end of the casino, occasionally stopping to watch a hand of poker or a toss of the dice at a craps table. When I reached the bandstand and could go no further, I turned around and took it all in. From that vantage point, the noise and the crowd—slightly blurred through a haze of cigar and cigarette smoke—blended into an ethereal scene in which it seemed difficult to remain focused on any single object or person.

I knew casinos weren't intended to be viewed the way I was looking at this one. When playing at a table, the busy surroundings had an isolating effect, creating wall of sound and activity that virtually eliminated distractions and kept each player's attention focused on the business at hand. It was all very neatly and profitably done.

I headed back in the direction from which I'd come, intending to go below and take a look at the restaurant. Passing the bar again, I glanced down the row of customers there and was surprised to find one of them staring back at me. As we made eye contact, he quickly looked away, but I was sure the guy had been watching me. I also had the feeling I'd seen him before. He was a little shorter than average and thin, with a pale complexion that, beneath the brilliant lighting, stood out among the tanned sunny southern California faces at the bar.

While I was looking at the guy and trying to remember where I'd seen him before, he glanced back in my direction. When our eyes met a second time, he casually set his nearly full drink down on the bar and wandered off as if he didn't have the slightest interest in me or anyone else in the place. It was a pretty fair performance, and if it wasn't for the fact that I caught him watching me and a nagging feeling I knew the guy, I wouldn't have given him a second thought.

As things turned out, I didn't give him a second thought. This was mostly because of the large Negro fellow wearing a tuxedo made by Omar the tentmaker and who was standing in front of me asking, "You Atkins?"

I looked up at him with a cheerful smile and said, "Yes. Who are you?"

He answered in a deep voice that matched his size and was loaded with authority. "I'm the floor manager. They call me The Deacon. Mister Cornero wants to see you. Follow me."

Without waiting for a response, The Deacon turned and strode purposefully toward a stairway at the aft end of the bar. I briefly wondered what would happen if I didn't follow him, but I wanted to see Tony as much, if not more, than he wanted see me, so I trotted along through the opening in the crowd left in The Deacon's wake.

Tony Cornero's office was on the deck below. The Deacon knocked once and went in without waiting for an answer. He held the door for me as I followed him into a spacious room that was maybe twenty feet deep and at least half the width of the ship. The walls were paneled in some sort of dark wood and the floor was carpeted in a pattern that looked vaguely Persian and expensive.

While the lower deck wasn't as noisy as the casino, some of

the racket leaked down the stairway, but when The Deacon closed the office door behind us, the room became silent as a tomb. Tony liked his peace and quiet.

There were three other people in the room besides The Deacon and me. Cornero sat at a large desk to my right; a swarthy man in a short white waiter's jacket stood unobtrusively next to a built-in bar counter in the far corner of the room; and an attractive dark-haired woman who might have been in her thirties sat in a chair opposite Cornero's desk. Her crimson dress looked expensive, but fit tighter than was fashionable and had a hem-line that rode well above her knees. Nobody in the room paid the slightest attention to my arrival.

The Deacon stopped me just inside the door with a surprisingly gentle hand on my shoulder, and as we stood there, the woman said, "But you have to cash my check."

Cornero looked exasperated, as if the conversation had already lasted much longer than he thought it should have. He said, "No, I don't have to cash your check, Missus Hawley."

"But, I assure you, it's good."

The apparent subject of their conversation was on the desk in front of Cornero. He shoved the check toward her and said, "That's what you said about the last three, all of which bounced higher than a flagpole."

Missus Hawley was beginning to sound a little desperate. "You have my word. That check . . ."

"Quite frankly, Missus Hawley, your word don't mean much around here anymore. In fact, I want you off my boat, and I don't want to see you back until you make good on them other checks. And, if that don't happen soon, I'm gonna have a little talk with that hot-shot hubby of yours."

That idea didn't please Missus Hawley at all. "But you promised you wouldn't . . ."

"That was before you tried to stick me with another bum check. All bets are off now." Cornero looked in my general direction for the first time. "Deacon, show this dame off the boat and tell the guys she doesn't set foot on the *Rex* again until I say so."

Missus Hawley tried to sound indignant, but didn't quite manage it. "You have no right to . . ."

Cornero slammed his fist on the desk hard enough to rattle a heavy glass ashtray. "The hell I don't! Deacon, get this broad outta here. I'm tired of lookin' at her."

The Deacon covered the ten or so feet between where we were

standing and the desk quickly in three easy strides. The woman flinched as if she expected to be struck, but the big Negro simply stood next to her and quietly said, "This way, Missus Hawley."

Nine

Gambling Ship Rex—Three Miles West of Santa Monica

Manny, Cornero's private bartender, carefully set a crystal highball glass of Coke with ice in front of me on a cork coaster so it wouldn't leave a ring on the shiny surface of his boss's desk and Cornero said, "So you're a radio reporter, huh? Okay, I can spare you a few minutes. Whatcha want to know, Atkins?"

Fishing the notebook out of my inside jacket pocket, I came up with a question I thought would get him talking. "Well, for one thing, how'd you get into this racket?"

Cornero exhaled a cloud of blue cigar smoke and said, "Oh, you want the whole works, huh? Okay, anything for the press. I was born on a farm in Piedmont, Italy, fifteen miles from the Swiss border. The Piedmontese, if I do say it myself, are a tough and hardy race of men who till the soil and live to be ninety and up."

Cornero recited the *National Geographic* version of his life story in a way that sounded like someone had written it out for him in proper English and he'd memorized the tale word for word. He told his story with a dramatic flair that also made me think he got a kick out of the recitation.

Cornero continued, "Life taught me my first hard lesson at the age of five. We had three years of bad crops, but in the fourth year the corn grew tall and thick. My father went to market and sold the crop, and then got into a card game and lost all the money. Meantime, I was playing out in the fields and accidentally set the harvested corn on fire. My mother said, 'There's nothing left; we'll all have to go to America.' And we did.

"A few years later we were living near San Francisco. One holiday I went into the city with fifty cents, all the money I had in the world. I saw some kids shooting craps. I have a natural itch to get into any game I see, so I hazarded my four bits and lost it.

"I felt bad. I was miles from home and broke. I walked all the way back and had plenty of time to think it all over. I saw that, by playing the other fellow's game, I was only making a squirrel of myself. So I decided the smart thing was to make the other fellow play my game, and that's what I have been doing ever since."

I looked up and said, "And making a fair-sized bundle in the process."

Cornero smiled. "There is never a shortage of squirrels and California has more of them per square mile than any other place in the world. I don't know why, but I know it's true. Today, on the *Rex*, I am playing to more business than Monte Carlo ever drew."

I must have looked a little skeptical. Slipping back into his normal speech patterns, he said, "You think I'm kiddin'? I ain't. I been to Monte Carlo plenty of times. If you see a hundred people playing at the tables there at any time, that's a big night. Any night in the week you can see at least ten times as many playing with me here on the *Rex*. And the racket is just as airtight."

"Is it? DA Fitts doesn't agree with you."

That raised Tony's dander a little. "Fitts is a pain in the ass! He ain't got no case against me. He's just fishin' for headlines cuz he's worried about gettin' reelected again. Fitts is a screw-up and he knows it. Now the people around here are getting' to know it, too."

"What about his claim that the *Rex* is actually anchored inside Santa Monica Bay?"

"Look, chum, there ain't no such thing as San Monica Bay and we can prove it. Look at the maps and charts. You won't see Santa Monica Bay on any of them. We'll beat this thing without raising a sweat."

"And what happens if you don't?"

He shook his head. "We will. That's all there is to it."

Cornero said it with such assurance that I found myself believing him. I said, "Well, Tony, I think I've got everything I need. Thanks for your time."

"Hey, it was my pleasure. Now you go back and tell the good folks up in Frisco what a great guy I am and how they ought to come down and visit the *Rex*, huh?"

"After the reception I got a little while ago, I'm not sure I can recommend your hospitality."

He looked genuinely hurt. "I'm sorry about that little mix up. We run a tight ship here. We have to for our protection and for our guests."

"But why did your boys pick on me?"

"Atkins, after you've been in this business for a while, you learn to size people up pretty good. My guys had you pegged right off. They could tell you weren't no squirrel coming out here to play. I can see that lookin' at you now. You just don't look like some guy out for a good time. So if you weren't coming out to play and you ain't no vice cop—we know all them on sight—you might be a trouble maker. We have to be sure about guys like you."

We shook hands and I left Tony's office, this time unescorted. His office was just off a long wood-paneled passage way that skirted the *Rex's* four hundred-seat bingo parlor and ended in a large foyer. From there, one could either enter the bingo parlor, have something to eat in a Hollywood reproduction of a French bistro called Le Chantecler, or take a stairway back up to the casino.

The tasty smells coming from the restaurant reminded me it had been a while since lunch and made me look at my watch. I'd promised to call Dandy by ten o'clock. It was a only few minutes past eight, so I gave into temptation and Bill Kastner bought my second meal of the day, a couple of pretty fair pork chops with all the trimmings. The total check with tip was only slightly more than the chicken pot pie I had for lunch. When it came to the incidentals, Tony treated his guests well.

Feeling well-fed and content with the world, I strolled through the casino again on my way to the *Rex's* boarding platform. The place was definitely more crowded than it was earlier, and I encountered even more eager squirrels, as Cornero lovingly referred to them, on my way downstairs to catch the water taxi on which they'd just arrived. The man was right; his racket was air-tight. As long as Tony could keep his doors open, there would be continuous flow of hopeful gamblers willing to bet their shirts they could beat him at his own game.

I had the launch to myself on the way back, and since the air had turned a little chilly, I sat up front in the more protected cabin with the skipper. As we barreled through the fog working its way in toward the coast, I tried to engage him in conversation. My captain made it clear that he wasn't in the mood for idle chit-chat. Maybe he hadn't gotten the word yet that I was one of the good guys.

There was a full boatload of folks waiting on the dock when we got back to Santa Monica, but the rest of the pier was essentially empty, except for an occasional couple hurrying along to catch a water taxi out to the *Rex* or one of the other ships. The carousel and most of the concession stands were already closed for the evening.

Reaching the Colorado Street end of the pier, I waved and whistled at a cab that had just dropped someone off, but the driver didn't see me and drove away empty. Hoping another one might be along soon, I decided to wait it out for a few minutes before hunting down a public telephone and calling a taxi company. Standing next to a darkened hot dog stand, I lit a Camel and gave some thought to heading home. I had plenty of background on the gambling ships in general, and the *Rex* in particular. And I had an interview with Tony Cornero. Since Cornero's arraignment was nearly a week off, there really wasn't much else for me to do in Los Angeles, unless I wanted to interview Buron Fitts. As hungry as he was for headlines, I knew it wouldn't be difficult to arrange, but I couldn't see that talking to the DA would add much to the story.

There are a couple of things you can do when someone jabs a gun in your back and says, "Don't move or I will shoot you," or words to that effect. I can't recall exactly how he phrased it.

Of course, the best thing to do is be smart enough not to get into a situation where that's likely to happen in the first place, but the pistol barrel suddenly pressing against my spine said I'd already missed the opportunity to select that option. There remained two courses of action from which to choose, the safest being to not move, thus reducing the likelihood of being shot. Instinctively, I chose the remaining option, which was attempting to disarm my assailant.

The technique I used is one they taught us when I was a rookie with the LAPD. It's based on the idea that no one but an amateur would forget that the advantage of using a gun over, say, a knife is the assailant doesn't have to get close to his victim, thus avoiding the risks of physical contact. In theory, such an amateur expects you to cooperate and can be taken by surprise with relative ease.

From where he was standing behind me, I sensed the gunman was right-handed. I pivoted quickly to my right and smacked his gun hand with my elbow. He made a surprised sound and I heard something clatter on the wooden pier. So far, so good.

The next step involves subduing your assailant by following through with a left cross to his chin. Unfortunately, this fellow hadn't read the manual and clearly didn't realize he was supposed to stand still and let me slug him. With speed and agility I hadn't expected, he stepped backwards and my fist sailed past him with six inches to spare.

This left me off balance, and before I could recover, he kicked me solidly in the left knee. The pain was instantaneous. It felt like a stick of dynamite had gone off under my knee cap. The way I had pivoted, my weight naturally had to end up on my left leg, which promptly collapsed. I ended up in a heap on the pier, grabbing left my knee as if that would somehow make the pain go away.

My assailant was also occupied. He was frantically looking for the gun I knocked out of his hand. I was about to try taking advantage of the guy's preoccupation with his pistol when a pair of headlights swung onto the pier and caught him square in the face. In spite of the damage he'd done to me, whatever plan he might have had was unraveling like cheap sweater. The guy took off, hotfooting it south on the sidewalk at the end of the pier, but I got a good look at him through the throbbing haze of pain my knee was generating and there was no doubt about it, he was the short, pale-faced man I'd caught watching me from the *Rex's* bar. I also saw that he was a dapper dresser, wearing an expensive, gray three-piece suit. And I still had the distinct feeling I'd seen him somewhere else before.

I became aware of voices; people were heading in my direction. I also noticed something poking me in the right hip. I moved my hand down there, felt around, and came up with a small semi-automatic pistol. I slipped it into my jacket pocket just as man's voice asked, "You okay, buddy?"

Three people were standing there staring at me. The guy who'd spoken wore a Yellow Cab hat. The other two were a man and woman he'd just delivered to the pier.

I got up to my right knee and said, "Yeah, I'll be okay if you can give me a hand to your cab and take me to my hotel."

During the taxi ride I was eventually able to straighten my left leg out and assess the damage. The pain eased up some and it didn't seem as if I would be crippled for life, but I didn't think I was going to enjoy climbing the New Brunswick's stairs. I didn't.

Ten

New Brunswick Hotel—First & Spring Streets, Los Angeles

I hunted down the little bottle of aspirin tablets I'd wisely thrown in my suitcase as an afterthought and swallowed a couple more of the little white pills than the label recommended. After that I hobbled over to hang up my coat. Its lopsided weight reminded me of the pistol I picked up on the pier.

I turned the pocket upside down and dumped the little black semi-automatic onto the writing desk. Sitting to take the strain off my knee, I made sure the safety lever was seated in the slide notch and stuck the New Brunswick's "vacation-to-write-home-about" pencil through the trigger guard so I could take a close look at the pistol without adding any further fingerprints to it. I had no idea who was going to be interested enough to look for prints and the odds of them finding anything useable were pretty slim, but handling the pistol carefully seemed like the right thing to do.

It was a tiny thing, no more than six inches long and gunmetal black in color. The checked rubber grips were also black and adorned with the stylized letters "F" and "N" inside an artistic raised oval. I'd seen the initials before and knew they stood for "Fabrique Nationale-something" in French or whatever language they speak over in Belgium where the gun was manufactured. That it was a foreign pistol didn't mean much in terms of tracking its owner down, though, because FN Brownings have been imported since before the turn of the century and there are literally thousands of them floating around. I've even known American cops who preferred FN Brownings to homegrown Colts or Smith & Wessons, although in larger calibers than the example before me on the writing desk.

Overall, the little pistol was in pretty good shape with the exception of a few minute scratches on the metal part of its grip. It was also well-oiled and clean. The guy took good care of his artillery, even if his choice of pistols seemed better suited to a woman than a tough guy. Of course, he wasn't a very big tough guy. I'm about five-ten and he was at least three or four inches shorter than me. But my throbbing knee was a strong reminder that size isn't everything.

Using my handkerchief, I pressed the release button and let the magazine slip out onto the desk. There were six thirty-two caliber rounds in it. There was also one in the chamber—a clue of sorts.

As with most semi-automatic pistols, you have work the Browning's slide to chamber the first round from the magazine before the thing will fire. Since working the slide takes two hands, it isn't something you leave to the last minute if you anticipate needing to fire the weapon in a hurry.

Both of my hands shook a little as I worked the slide and a shiny little brass cartridge dropped out of the chamber. It had my name on it. They guy was prepared to shoot, and whether he was an amateur or not, I'd come closer to getting my spine blown in two than I wanted to think about. Still using my handkerchief, I pressed the seventh round into the magazine before sliding it back into the Browning's hand grip.

Then I damn near dropped the thing when the telephone rang. It probably wasn't really loud enough to wake the dead, it just sounded that way. Or maybe I was just a little jumpy.

I picked up the receiver, took a deep breath, and said, "Hello," into the mouthpiece.

"Parker, are you okay? I was getting worried."

It was Dandy and her words puzzled me for a moment. I was wondering how she knew about my close call on the pier until she said, "It's almost ten-thirty. You were supposed to call me at ten."

"I'm sorry, Dandy. I went out to one of the gambling ships tonight and ran into a little trouble on the way back." Even though I was trying to sound casual, I knew I'd made a mistake almost before the words were out of my mouth.

"Trouble? What kind of trouble? Parker, are you all right?"

The anxious concern in her voice told me I was right, I should have kept my mouth shut. Since the cat was already out of the bag, I said, "I'm fine. A fellow tried to stick me up, but I scared him off."

"Parker, you're not telling me the whole story. What

happened?"

The problem with Dandy is she knows me too well. I'd thoroughly put my foot in my mouth and didn't have much choice but to tell her more or less what happened. There was a long silence after I finished. When she finally spoke, Dandy simply asked, "When are you coming home?"

It was a good question and I didn't have a good answer. I'd been prepared to head home in the morning, but now there were a whole bunch of questions floating around in my head that needed answers. And, even if my curiosity hadn't been wondering about those answers, my common sense was demanding them. When somebody walks up and sticks a gun in your back it's a good idea to find out why. Sure, it could've been exactly what I told Dandy, a simple stick-up, but that answer didn't ring true.

I said, "I'm not sure yet, Dandy. Maybe on Thursday."

"Well, make it as soon as you can, Parker. I miss you, and now I'm going to be worried sick."

I could imagine the frown on her pretty face. I'd seen it there before and I didn't like it. When Dandy frowned, the sparkle left her big brown eyes and that made me want to go out and slay whichever dragon was responsible for bringing a pall of gloom down on the kingdom. Unfortunately, in this instance, I was the dragon.

"Dandy, there's nothing to be worried about. I'm sure I'll never see that character again." Thinking a change of subject might make things better, I said, "Did you hear the remote broadcast tonight? What did you think?"

"Of course I heard it, silly. I wouldn't have missed it for the world and I think the gambling ships sound terribly exciting. I wish I were there with you so we could break the bank!"

I laughed. "And we'd end up hitching a ride home. Tony Cornero didn't get where he is by letting people break his bank."

I was relieved to hear the sparkle back in Dandy's voice. She said, "Oh, you spoil sport! I bet you didn't even wager a dime tonight."

"Now that's a bet you win. Cornero already had a whole boat-load full of squirrels throwing their money at his tables. He won't miss what's still in my pocket. Besides, I couldn't think of any way to write the losses off to Kastner."

"Yes, that would've taken some fast talking. Will you call me tomorrow night?"

"I will and I'll even be on time."

"You'd better be or I'll give you the dickens!"

By the time we said our goodbyes, the aspirin was starting to do its job. I made a beeline for the bed to get started on a decent night's sleep, but all the questions buzzing around in my brain got in the way.

The gunman was watching me from the *Rex's* bar. That meant the incident on the pier wasn't a random stickup. Was he at the bar watching for a fat pigeon to roll? Not likely. As Tony Cornero so aptly put it, I didn't look like some guy out for a good time, nor was it probable that anyone would mistake me for a high roller with pockets full of cash.

The cabby who took me out to Santa Monica thought a gray Chrysler followed us from the hotel. Was the gunman driving that Chrysler? If so, the guy was on my tail long before he knew I was going to the *Rex*, and the likelihood of a robbery motive went out the window once and for all.

And where had I seen the guy before? I was pretty sure it was since I arrived in LA, and when the same face shows up twice on the first day I'm in a city that's home to more than five million faces, it's more than a coincidence.

All of that logical thinking brought me right back to the jackpot questions of the night. Why the hell did the little jerk stick a gun in my back, and what would have happened if I hadn't taken that gun away from him?

Just after I decided to discuss the matter with Don Chambers in the morning, sleep finally showed up. I didn't expect Chambers to have the answers, but he might offer a suggestion or two. At least it was a plan of sorts, and I always feel better when I have a plan.

Eleven

My second day in the City of Angels dawned to the accompaniment of honking horns, squealing tires, and wrenching metal. I jumped straight out of bed and damned near ended up on the floor when I came down on my newly acquired bum knee. The resulting jolt of pain brought me to full consciousness and then some. Moving gingerly, I made it to my window overlooking First Street.

The scene below me would've warmed the heart of any veteran big city traffic cop. Somehow two sedans, one business coupe, and a Coca Cola delivery truck all managed to find their way into the intersection of First and Olive at the same time. In addition to crunched fenders, broken headlights and large quantities of fizzy brown liquid pouring out of the delivery truck, there were now also several people standing in the midst of the carnage yelling at each other. Welcome to the City of Angels.

By the time I shaved and showered, all that remained of the mishap was a damp sticky spot down the middle of the street. I successfully circumnavigated this obstacle as I jaywalked—or jay-hobbled—to coffee and a Danish at the hash house across First from the Brunswick. The Danish was surprisingly tasty.

A few more aspirin had quieted the pain in my knee down to a mild roar, so I decided to brave the two blocks to Central Headquarters on foot. As long as I took it slow and easy, my knee was reasonably cooperative.

I almost beat Chambers to work. He was just hanging his coat on a hat rack in the corner when I walked in. Don noticed my limp and greeted me with his version of sympathy. "What the hell happened to you?"

"One of your upstanding citizens tried to stick me up on the Santa Monica pier last night. He got upset when I took his gun away from him and he kicked my knee so hard I thought it was broken."

Chambers settled into his chair and said, "Well, if it happened on the pier, he wasn't one of my citizens. That's Santa Monica PD's jurisdiction. Wanna bite of doughnut?"

He held up an old-fashioned that looked hard enough to use as a doorstop, and when I shook my head, he took a big bite out of it. Between chews Chambers said, "So what happened? Somebody mistake you for a tourista with a fat wallet?"

"I think there's more to it than that."

I told him the whole sordid tale. When I was done, Chambers asked, "What did the Santa Monica cops have to say about all this?"

"They didn't have anything to say because I didn't tell 'em about it."

He frowned. "Why the hell not?"

"Mostly because the gunman was long gone and I didn't feel like spending half the night talking to a bored desk sergeant who didn't have anything better to do than harass me because I had the bum luck to get mugged in his town."

He grinned. "Doesn't sound like you have a very high opinion of our Santa Monica brothers in blue."

"Not unless things have changed a whole hell of a lot since the last time I had anything to do with 'em."

Chambers sighed. "Nothin's changed. So what do you want me to do about this? I ain't got no more pull over there than you do."

Using my handkerchief, I lifted the Browning out of my coat pocket and set it on his desk. "The little fellow left his toy gun behind. I thought maybe you could ask your lab guys to give it the once-over."

He looked at the pistol like I just dumped a pile of horse manure on his desk and said, "I guess I could, but I don't know what good it will do. Odds of getting any useable prints off it are next to zero. And, even if they lift a print or two, it'll take a while to see if we can match it up. What makes you so sure this guy was after something besides your money?"

"Well, for one thing, there were quite a few folks around who looked a lot more prosperous than me. If he was just looking for a fat wallet, he'd have gone after one of them. For another thing, he was watching me aboard the *Rex* with a lot more interest than a mugger who was just picking out his target for the evening. Besides that, I'm sure I saw him somewhere else yesterday, I just can't remember where. And, if the cab driver was right, this guy may have even followed me from my hotel to the *Rex*."

"Why would anybody do that? You been stickin' your nose where it ain't welcome again?"

"Not that I know of."

"Then why would this mug be interested in you?"

I shook my head. "That's what I want to know. And another thing, he didn't act anything like your average stick-up artist. He may have been stupid about getting close enough to let me take his pistol away, but he got smart fast and he moved quick, like an athlete. That was no lucky kick. He knew exactly what he was doing."

"You know, Park, if you hadn't been in such a big damned hurry to disarm the guy, you'd probably know what he wanted."

"Yeah, or I'd be on a slab in the morgue. I like my way better."

Chambers threw is hands up in mock defeat. "Okay, okay! I'll send your Browning down to the lab and see what they can tell us. But don't expect much more than that from me. I've got bigger fish to fry right now."

I kidded, "You still frettin' about that parade on Friday?"

"Hell, I wish that's all I had to fret about. A couple of kids found a body up in the Hollywood hills near the sign yesterday afternoon. It turned out to be another one of Nitti's boys."

"Damn! Your mob killer is pickin' 'em off daily now."

"Naw, I don't think he's gotten that ambitious yet. This one had been dead quite a while when they found him—coroner says, maybe, a couple of months. Didn't you see the *Times* this morning? The press has latched onto this thing now. They're calling our guy the 'Mob Avenger'—makin' him out to be a damned hero for bumpin' off mobsters."

"You gotta admit the guy's got guts. Or he's nuts."

"It don't matter which. Either way, we gotta find this character or we're in for big trouble. You headed back to Frisco now?"

"That's San Francisco, and no. I'm gonna stick around at least another day."

He sounded perturbed. "What the hell for? You ain't thinkin' of lookin' for that guy from last night yourself, are ya?"

"I thought I might ask around. Maybe talk to some of Cornero's people. They keep a close eye on their customers. Maybe they know him."

He'd been about to take the last bite of his doughnut. Instead, he tossed it on the desk and shook his head. "Damn it, Park, you never learn, do ya? You were the same way when you were on the force; always going off on your own. Well, you ain't a cop no more and you ain't gonna find this guy all by yourself. If he's really out to get ya, it's more likely he'll find you; only he'll be more careful this time and you're gonna end up dead. Just get on that damned train and go home. I'll let you know if the lab finds out anything about the Browning."

Standing up, I grinned and said, "Thanks for the advice, Don. I'll think about it."

When I was almost out the door he said, "Just watch your butt. And don't go gettin' in Dutch with the Santa Monica PD. They catch you playin' cop in their bailiwick, they'll lock your ass up for sure, and I won't be able to do a damned thing about it."

I stopped in the doorway and said, "Why, Don, I didn't know you cared!"

He glared back at me. "Get your ugly mug the hell out of my office!"

Out in front of Central Headquarters I looked around for a taxi. There were none in sight, so I hiked back up toward the New Brunswick, where I found a cab parked in front of the entrance. As I climbed in, the driver turned around to ask me where I wanted to go and I recognized him as the same hefty, curly-haired Greek who'd taken me to the pier.

He recognized me, too, and said, "Hey, boss, that some bad kind of limp you got there. How you get that?"

I recited a condensed version of my mugged-on-the-pier story and he shook his head. "That's a tough break, boss. You think it maybe had something thing to do with the car was following us last night?"

Shrugging, I said, "It might have."

The cabby looked a little hurt, like he was disappointed I wasn't more impressed with what he obviously considered an event of some importance. He said, "Okay, boss, where you wanna go today?"

"Back to the pier."

His bushy eyebrows went up a little. "Back to scene of crime, huh?"

"Yeah, something like that."

He said, "Okay, boss," and started his engine. It roared to life, then settled into a healthy rumble as he flipped down the flag on his meter with a stubby hand and pulled out into the westbound First Street traffic.

Watching him drive, I noticed some things that escaped my

attention on our first trip together. My initial impression of the cabby was that he needed more exercise and fewer gyros. Looking at him now, though, I realized a lot of what I had mistaken for fat was muscle. He was chubby all right, but he moved with an assurance and economy of motion that would make me think twice about picking a fight with the guy.

I was also feeling a little bad about brushing off his idea that the gray Chrysler belonged to the gunman. If it hadn't been for the cabby's powers of observation, I wouldn't have that particular clue, if it really was a clue.

Trying to let him know I appreciated his interest, I said, "Anybody following us today?"

He looked up to his rearview mirror, not at the street behind us, but at me. I think he was checking to see if I was pulling his leg. He seemed to decide I wasn't and said, "Not that I see, Mister Atkins. If somebody is there, I don't see 'em."

His use of my name took me by surprise. "How do you happen to know who I am?"

We were waiting for the light at Figueroa, and he half-turned so I could see the grin on his face and said, "The husband of my sister is night clerk at New Brunswick. I was curious, so I ask him about you. He say you from up in San Francisco. My name is Nickolopolis. Most people just call me Neeko."

His grin was infectious and I returned it. "Nice to meet you, Neeko."

The light changed and we swung left onto Figueroa. Neeko said, "So you goin' back to that pier and find guy who stick you up?"

"Yeah, that's sort of what I've got in mind."

Neeko nodded. "You gonna have to be careful like crazy."

I said, "That's exactly what I intend to be, careful like crazy.

Twelve

Downtown Los Angeles to Santa Monica Pier Via Taxi

Santa Monica is only about fifteen miles out Wilshire from downtown, but on summer mornings the weather makes that distance seem much greater. The farther west we drove, the colder and gloomier it got. In spite of the gloom, the fog is a welcome phenomenon in these parts because it's one of the features that make the beach so popular during the summer. While LA and the San Fernando Valley were already warming up, the little communities strung along the coast from Malibu to Palos Verdes would be protected from the sun for at least another hour. The morning fog along with the cool ocean breezes makes the beaches a perfect place to escape the summer heat later in the day.

Watching the tiny specks of drizzle accumulating on Neeko's windshield reminded me of the brand of fog we have up in San Francisco, and that made me a little homesick. The Southern Pacific's Coast Daylight I could've caught this morning was in Santa Barbara by now, and here I was in a taxi headed for Santa Monica on what was probably a fool's errand. Chambers was right. I never learn.

Neeko pulled to the yellow curb on Ocean Avenue a few feet from the entrance to the pier. As I handed him the fare, plus another healthy tip, he said, "You want me to wait for you, boss?"

"Better not. I might be a while and I can't afford to pay you for the wait time."

He gave me a short nod and said, "Okay. I stick around anyway. Maybe I pick up a fare back to town. If no, then maybe I still be here when you want to go back. Wednesdays are slow."

Leaning in the curbside back door, I said, "Thanks, Neeko. Maybe I'll see you in a while."

He waved and I closed the door. It was only quarter to ten and, while there were already a few hearty souls with Eskimo blood in their veins out in the surf, the pier wasn't awake yet. The concession stands were still boarded up and the lights were off in the merry-go-round pavilion.

I paused briefly to look around when I came to the spot where I'd been attacked. The guy was wearing a hat—a gray homburg—when I saw him on the *Rex*, but in my last mental picture of him running off into the night, the gunman was bareheaded. He might have lost his hat in the scuffle and I hoped it might still be around with a useful clue in it, like his name. My cursory search turned up no hats or anything else of interest, so I limped on out to the end of the pier.

Of the four water taxi stands that were doing a land office business last night, only one showed signs of life this morning. It was the one offering rides to the *Showboat* and the only activity there was a guy leaning against the counter reading a newspaper. The podium where I'd purchased my round-trip ticket to the *Rex* was unmanned and someone had tacked a hand-painted cardboard sign on it that said, "The *Rex* is temporarily closed for business."

Out to sea, the only thing moving besides endless lines of easy rolling breakers was a small craft making its way through the fog in my general direction. As I stood there feeling my knee ache and trying to come up with another brilliant plan—one that might actually accomplish something—the fellow over at the *Showboat* taxi podium hollered across the pier.

"The *Rex* is closed, but if you're looking for some action, the *Showboat* opens at ten."

I walked over to him so I wouldn't have to yell and said, "I just want to talk to Cornero or one of his boys. Think there might be somebody out on the *Rex*?"

He shrugged. "I wouldn't know, but that's one of their boats coming in. Maybe there's somebody aboard who can tell you."

"Thanks."

"Don't mention it."

I walked back across the pier and stood at the railing to watch the little boat make its way in. Maybe my trip to Santa Monica wouldn't be a total waste after all. When I glanced back over my shoulder, the *Showboat* guy had his face buried in the newspaper again, and that's when I finally figured it out.

Ever since I spotted him at the *Rex's* bar, I'd been trying to remember where I'd seen the gunman before. Now I knew. His face was buried in the *Times* at Clifton's Cafeteria yesterday while I had lunch. The place was virtually empty, and even though I hadn't particularly noticed his face then, I clearly recalled his build and his clothes, including the gray homburg. It all fit.

So the guy had been shadowing me since sometime before I went to Clifton's, which pretty much confirmed my suspicion that robbery wasn't his motive for sticking a gun in my back. Knowing that, however, didn't simplify matters much. In fact, it complicated things even more. I only hit town yesterday morning, and I spent most of the day before lunch with Chambers, which didn't leave many opportunities for me to give someone a reason to dog my trail. Did the guy follow me from San Francisco? Chambers already hinted at that possibility when he asked if I'd been poking my nose where it wasn't welcome. Of course, that was a possibility because it's frequently my job to stick my nose where it isn't welcome, but I usually know when I've stepped on the wrong toes hard enough to get myself into trouble. Nothing like that had happened for months.

The burble of a marine engine jarred me back to the here and now. I looked down and saw the *Rex's* taxi gliding up to their boarding dock. Before the launch stopped, a familiar face appeared and the large body that went with it hopped lithely down on the dock. I recognized The Deacon immediately, even though he was wearing a sport coat instead of his tux. He looked better in the tux, but either way, I was pleased to see him because, if anyone would remember seeing the gunman aboard the *Rex*, he would. I was certain The Deacon didn't miss much.

I met him at the top of the stairs and said, "Hello, Deacon. Remember me?"

Brushing past me, he mumbled, "Yeah, I remember you. You're the radio reporter."

The tone of his voice made it clear that being a radio reporter was somewhere below stealing candy from babies on his list of the world's most honorable endeavors. Undeterred, I caught up with him and said, "A guy tried to stick me up after I left the *Rex* last night. He was also on the *Rex* while I was there. I thought you might know who he was."

Walking at a pace brisk enough to give my knee fits as I tried to keep up, The Deacon said, "What did he look like?"

"He's a little guy with a pale complexion. He was wearing a snappy gray suit and a homburg hat last night. When I spotted him, he was sitting at the casino bar. That was just before you took me down to Cornero's office."

"Yeah, I saw the guy. Figured he was up to something, but I don't know who he is. Never saw him before."

The Deacon was obviously in a hurry to get wherever he was headed and keeping up with him was getting downright painful. So I stopped and said, "Thanks. I appreciate the help."

He just kept going and tossed a "don't mention it" over his shoulder.

I leaned against the pier railing for a moment to give my knee a rest and mentally crossed Cornero's outfit off my list as a source of information. It was a long shot anyway, especially since the gunman was apparently on my trail long before I boarded the *Rex*.

Aside from finally remembering where I'd seen the man before, I knew nothing more now than when I woke up this morning. Worse, I was fresh out of ideas about what to do next. The only thought I had along those lines involved settling my bill at the New Brunswick and catching the Coast Starlight back to San Francisco tonight. Before I could do that, however, I had a remote broadcast to do and time, as they say, was a wastin'.

When I was nearly to the pier entrance, I started looking around for Neeko's cab. My mind was on the quickest way to get the heck out of Santa Monica and that's why it took several seconds for the significance of the hat sitting on the hot dog stand's counter to sink in.

It was the first concession stand on the pier—the one I was standing next to when the gunman showed up. The owner of the hot dog stand was just opening up for the day, and the hat on its counter was a gray homburg. As I approached, the guy working behind the counter looked up and said, "The dogs ain't hot yet . . . just put 'em on."

"I wanted to ask you about the hat."

"Oh, that. I found it behind the stand when I got here. I thought maybe somebody lost it last night. Is it yours?"

Figuring the guy would know the homburg was too small to fit me, I said, "I think it belongs to my friend. We were out here late last night on our way from the *Rex* and he lost his hat somewhere. I guess we were a little drunk, because he didn't notice the hat wasn't on his head until we got back to the hotel."

I turned the hat over to look inside it and the hot dog vendor said, "From out of town, are you?"

"Yes, from San Francisco."

"Frisco's a nice place. Think it's his hat? There ain't no name it. I looked."

It didn't seem like a good time to correct yet another Angelino for calling my adopted hometown Frisco, so I just said, "Yeah, it's a size six-and-an-eighth and he's a little guy, so I bet it's his. How 'bout I take it back to the hotel with me and ask him? If it's not his, I'll bring it back."

"That's jake with me. I was just tryin' to help whoever lost it get his hat back."

I took a dollar bill out of my wallet and handed it to him. "Here's a little something for your trouble. I know my friend will appreciate getting this back."

He took the buck without hesitation and said, "Glad I could help."

Walking away from the stand with my new-found treasure in hand, I heard a car horn gave a short toot and saw Neeko's cab pull up at the pier entrance. I climbed into the back, grateful to be off my knee and pleased as punch about the clue I'd just found. As clues go, the hat probably wasn't worth much, but at least I wasn't leaving Santa Monica completely empty-handed.

Thirteen

Santa Monica Pier to Downtown Los Angeles Via Taxi

While Neeko got us headed back to the New Brunswick, I took a closer look at the hat. The most notable feature was a dark smudge on the brim, which was a shame because it appeared to be a well-made, good quality hat. I guessed the smudge was damage incurred during our scuffle, or the result of spending a night out on the pier.

Otherwise, it was a plain pearl gray homburg with a hatband of darker gray around what seemed to be a slightly taller than normal crown. That fit because a lot of short guys wear hats with higher crowns so they look taller.

Inside, the homburg was lined with white satin, and the lining directly under the crown was emblazoned with a stylized B inside a gold oval. Also printed inside the oval were the words "Azienda del Cappello di Borsalino," whatever the hell that meant. The only other marking inside the hat was the size stamped into the leather sweat band.

I tossed the hat on the seat next to me and stared at it. What I know about high fashion would fit in a thimble with plenty of room left over for a belt and suspenders, but I was pretty sure I was looking at a top-of-the-line imported hat, which with a little luck might offer a clue as to its owner's identity.

"Neeko, is Mullen and Bluett still at Sixth and Broadway?"

"Sure, boss. You wanna go there?"

"Yes. Let's make a slight detour over that way. I won't be long. I just want to see if a salesman in the men's department can tell me something about this hat."

"What so special about the hat?"

"It belongs to the guy who stuck me up on the pier last night."

"And you think maybe it comes from that store?"

"Probably not. This is an expensive imported hat and I doubt if Mullen and Bluett carries anything this swank, but they might know who does."

Neeko nodded and said, "I get you, boss. Maybe there is not so many hats like that one, and if you find out where it comes from, maybe you find who bought it."

I smiled. "Neeko, you catch on quick. Maybe you should be a detective."

He shook his shaggy head and said, "I hear Gangbusters on radio. They too smart for Neeko. I stick to driving cab."

For those who don't know LA, Mullen and Bluett is a downtown clothing store that's been around since the turn of the century. They cater to the sort of men and women who work in offices downtown. Their clothing isn't cheap, but unless things had changed since the last time I bought a pair of slacks there, the store's merchandise didn't include imported items along the lines of the hat on the seat next to me.

In Mullen and Bluett's men's department I found a young man stocking shelves with dress shirts. I showed him the homburg and asked what he could tell me about it.

He immediately looked inside the hat, and after studying what he saw there for a brief moment, he said, "Wow! This is the first Borsalino I've ever seen. This is a very expensive hat!"

"I take it then that you don't sell this brand here."

"Oh, no, sir. We don't sell anything this expensive. A hat of this quality sells for twenty dollars or more. Our customers . . . well, that would be more than most of our customers would want to pay for a hat."

"Do you know of a store in the area that carries hats like this?"

He thought for a moment. "I can't say off hand, but my manager might know. He's in the back having lunch. If you can wait a minute, I'll go back and ask him."

While I fretted about the rate at which Neeko's meter was racking up my cab fare, the kid disappeared into a back room. When he returned a few minutes later, he handed me the hat and said, "My manager says he only knows one store in Los Angeles that imports Borsalino hats. That's Pelletier's in the Crossroads of the World shopping arcade up on Sunset. Do you know where that is?"

I nodded and thanked him for his help. By the time I got back in Neeko's cab, I'd made my decision. This was too good an opportunity to pass up, so damn the meter and full speed ahead.

"Neeko, I need to go to the Crossroads of the World in Hollywood. Can we get there without breaking the bank on your meter?"

Neeko turned around and grinned at me. Then he reached over and flipped the flag up, stopping his meter. "I take you there for nothing if it help you catch a bad guy."

"Thanks, Neeko. It seems the only shop in town that sells this brand of hat is in the Crossroads. With a little luck, we might be able to find out from the store who bought this one."

Neeko gave me a thumbs-up gesture and pulled out into the northeast-bound traffic on Broadway. Twenty minutes later we arrived at 6671 Sunset Boulevard, home of the eighth wonder of the shopping universe.

The Crossroads of the World was under construction when I left LA two years ago, so this was the first time I actually laid eyes on the place. It was something to behold. An outdoor shopping arcade, it was built on property that ran clear through the block between Sunset and Selma. The central building facing Sunset was designed to resemble a modern ocean liner and it is flanked on each side by a row of shops with elaborate old European facades. It's all very swank—the sort of place that would attract customers who could afford twenty bucks for a homburg.

I found Pelletier's Distinguished Men's Clothing in a small shop dressed up with quaint wooden window trim in a diamond pattern and bright blue awnings. I could sense the salesman assessing the balance in my checking account as he stepped forward and said, "Good afternoon, sir. How may I be of service?"

Once again, I held up the homburg and said, "I would like to hear what you can tell me about this hat."

For a moment he stared at the hat, appearing to be torn between wondering what a guy dressed in a ready-made suit was doing in his shop and the opportunity to show off his superior knowledge of distinguished men's clothing. His ego finally got the better of him and he took the hat.

After a cursory inspection, some automatic compulsion set him to brushing at the smudge of the brim with his fingers. When it became apparent the stain was permanent, he said, "What exactly do you wish to know about this hat, sir?"

"Well, for starters, do you sell this brand?"

"Of course, sir. Pelletier's sells only the finest quality men's clothing, and this hat was made by Borsalino of Italy, the fashion leader in stylish men's headwear."

I nodded and asked, "Besides the fact of its fine quality, is there anything unique about this particular hat?"

He gave me his puzzled look again, and then said, "I'm not sure what you are asking, sir. This is the Andrea Bocelli style from Borsalino's Celebrità line. Is that what you mean?"

"Is this a popular style? Do you sell many of this particular hat?"

He was beginning to get suspicious, or annoyed, or both. It was obvious I wasn't of the class that could afford what Pelletier's sells, so I was wasting his valuable time. Displeasure colored his tone as he said, "Sir, many men would enjoy owning a Borsalino hat, but few can afford such luxury. So, no, we do not sell many of them. Now, if you'll excuse me . . ."

I interrupted his dismissal. "Can you tell me if Pelletier's sold this particular hat?"

He frowned. "Yes, I believe we sold this hat. I recognize it both by the style and the size . . ."

I interrupted again, "May I please have the name of the customer who purchased it?"

Now he knew what I was after, and his diminishing cooperation came to a screeching halt. "Pelletier's respects the privacy of our customers. You would know that if you were the sort of gentleman who shops here. Now, please leave our shop."

Several possible approaches that might make him more cooperative occurred to me, but I had at least part of what I came for and Don Chambers had the clout to get the rest. Besides, if I applied too much pressure, it might occur to this guy that he should contact the purchaser of the hat and alert him to the fact that someone had his chapeau and was asking questions.

Heading for the door, I smiled my most appreciative, albeit low-class, smile and said, "Thank you. You've been most helpful."

Fourteen

New Brunswick Hotel—First & Spring Streets, Los Angeles

While Neeko navigated the route back to my hotel, I gave him a brief rundown on what I'd learned at Pelletier's. Since I was riding on his nickel, it seemed only fair to let him in on the progress I was making toward finding the bad guy who assaulted me on the Santa Monica Municipal Pier.

Then I sat back to think about that progress and how best to take my investigation a step further. Mostly, that depended on Don Chambers because I was rapidly running out of time. Tonight's remote broadcast would wrap up my reports on the gambling ships, so I was fresh out of acceptable reasons for being in Los Angeles—at least reasons Bill Kastner would accept. I had no choice but to climb aboard Southern Pacific's northbound San Francisco Lark at nine o'clock tonight, which meant any further progress on finding the guy who stuck a gun in my back on the pier last night would have to be done by long distance. If Don wasn't willing to follow up on what I learned about the homburg at Pelletier's, I was sunk.

That line of thinking left me feeling gloomy. There was a time in my life when I would have just forged ahead without worrying what my boss thought, but that kind of impulsive behavior, along with the booze that encouraged it, was what got me fired from both the LAPD and the *Los Angeles Times*. Now my long-term goals in life held precedence over spur of the moment impulses. Life was decidedly better without the booze, but being a responsible employee wasn't nearly as much fun.

As Neeko pulled up in front of the New Brunswick, I asked if he would still be on duty around seven that evening. He asked, "Why, boss? You gonna need cab?"

"Yeah. I need a lift to the train depot. I'm heading home tonight."

"No kidding? Neeko will miss you. Driving you places is more fun than usual fares. Sure, my friend, I will be here at seven to see you get safe to train station."

"Thanks, Neeko. You've been a big help. I wish I could stay around longer, but my boss wants me back."

"Your boss is spoiled sport! Now we never find bad guy."

"I'm afraid we'll have to leave that job to the police."

"They never find him. Police can't find nothing!"

"Well, I've got a friend on the LAPD. I'm hoping he'll at least give it a try."

Then I used a fair-sized chunk of my rapidly dwindling supply of Bill Kastner's money to pay Neeko and headed into the New Brunswick. On the way to my room I stopped at the front desk to let them know I'd be checking out in a few hours. Then I went upstairs and used the room phone to make a few calls. My first was to the Southern Pacific ticket office. After booking a seat on tonight's northbound Lark, I called Charlie to finalize our plans for my last remote.

Charlie was clearly relieved when I told her I would be arriving tomorrow morning. "Thank goodness! Mister Kastner has been stopping by the office hourly to find out when you're coming back."

"I figured that. There's another story going on down here I'd like to dig into further, but it's a local matter, and I can't think of any way to convince Kastner I need to stay longer. So, home I come."

"What's the other story?"

"It's complicated. I'd better not use up Kastner's long distance time to tell you about it now. I'll give you the details tomorrow."

When it came to reading between the lines of what I said, Charlie was almost as adept as Dandy. Or maybe I'm just not very good at hiding things. Charlie said, "You haven't stirred up some kind of trouble down there, have you?"

"No," I lied, "Everything is fine." Changing the subject, I said, "I'll only need about three minutes to wrap things up on tonight's broadcast."

I could hear the suspicion in her voice when she replied. "Okay, if you say so. You want your three minutes at the end or at the beginning of the broadcast?"

"Let's put it at the end. I'll call in at six-twenty, if you think that will work."

"Six-twenty will do. I'll give engineering the schedule and go over it with Dick Stewart. Anything else?"

Now Charlie sounded miffed at me—probably because she thought I was keeping secrets from her. I said, "Cheer up, kiddo. I'll tell you the whole story tomorrow."

"That's fine, Park. Talk with you at six-twenty. Goodbye."

She hung up before I could say anything further. Oh well, she'd get over it. I just hoped my next call went more smoothly. I gave the desk clerk the *San Francisco Chronicle's* number and told him I wanted to make the call person-to-person to Danielle Harrison.

Hearing Dandy's perky voice on the phone improved my disposition considerably. She said, "Hi, Park! This is an unexpected surprise. I figured you would call tonight."

"That would be difficult, because I'll be on the Lark headed home tonight."

"Oh, that's wonderful! What time do you get in?"

"Tomorrow morning at nine."

"Shall I meet you at the station?"

"If you can get away, that would be great. I expect I'll want to go home and clean up before I go in to KDG. Will that be okay?"

"It will be wonderful, Park. I'm so anxious to see you!"

"The feeling is one-hundred-percent mutual."

She had a more serious tone in her voice when she asked, "What about that trouble you told me about last night? Is everything okay?"

"Yes, everything is fine. I've had no further encounters with gun-toting bad guys."

Dandy took me at my word and sounded perky again. "Okay, darling, I'll see you tomorrow morning. Gosh, I hope you can get some sleep on the train. Knowing how cheap Kastner is, I'll bet you don't even have a Pullman berth."

"You win that bet, too. It's no problem, though. I got a few hours' sleep on the trip south, so I imagine I'll do the same tonight. See you in the morning."

"Okay, darling. Travel safe!"

Placing the receiver back on its cradle, I glanced at my watch and realized why I was feeling a little peckish. It was nearly one-thirty—six hours since I'd wolfed down coffee and a Danish this morning.

Deciding I could probably manage another hour without

passing out from hunger, I dug out my writing pad and put the New Brunswick Hotel's pencil to work on my three minutes' worth of wrap-up on the gambling ships.

At two-thirty I trotted—or more accurately, limped—down the stairs and across the street for a ham sandwich at the same little hash house I visited for breakfast. Another chicken pot pie at Clifton's sounded more appealing, but my level of hunger and Kastner's budget dictated otherwise. Besides, my time in LA was growing shorter every minute, and I wanted to make sure there was time to tell Don what I learned about the hat.

The ham sandwich tasted good, but it didn't fill me up. Promising to treat myself to a decent last dinner at the depot coffee shop, I picked up the gray homburg from where I'd been studying it on the hash house table and set as brisk a pace for Don Chambers' office as I could manage.

Fifteen

Central Police Headquarters–First & Hill Streets, Los Angeles

Don Chambers' office was even more crowded than usual because of the large roll-around blackboard now occupying the narrow space between his desk and the back wall of the office. When I peeked in, Don's chair was swiveled to face the blackboard and he was studying a list of six names with dates and other notes scrawled in white chalk. I recognized the last name on the list. It was Arturo Bellaguisi, and that told me all I needed to know about the subject of Don's concentration.

I rapped softly on the door frame and Don turned around far enough to see me standing in the doorway. "Hello, Park, how's the knee this afternoon?"

"It's still a little sore, but I think I'll live." Then gesturing toward the blackboard, I said, "Is that contraption the latest in the Department's arsenal of crime fighting tools?"

"I guess you could say that. It helps me see how the pieces of a case fit together."

"The Mob Avenger case?"

"Yup. Word came down from the Chief today. All our cases have been handed off to other divisions. Central Division Homicide is on this full time until we nail the guy."

"You getting anywhere with it?'

Don turned his swivel chair around to face me and said, "Not so you'd notice. Have a seat and take the load off that knee." Then he noticed the gray homburg in my hand. "Since when did you start wearin' a hat?"

I tossed the hat on his desk as I dropped into one of the

wooden guest chairs. "It's not mine. It belongs to the guy who assaulted me last night."

Chambers looked surprised. "Oh yeah? How'd you come by that?"

"I went out to the pier this morning to see if I could talk to any of Cornero's boys. They keep close tabs on their clientele, and since the guy was on the *Rex* while I was there, I thought they might know him."

"Any luck?"

"I found Cornero's major domo, the one they call The Deacon. He noticed the gunman at the bar, but doesn't know him. Then, when I was leaving the pier, I spotted the guy's hat sitting right there on the counter of a hot dog stand. He lost it during the scuffle, and the hot dog guy found the hat when he opened up this morning. He left it on his counter in case the owner showed up looking for it. I got there first."

"No kiddin'? You sure it's the same hat the gunman was wearin'?"

"Sure enough to spend some time and cab fare finding out where the hat came from. Turns out that homburg is a genuine Italian import and there's only one shop in town that carries the line—a swank men's store up at Crossroads of the World in Hollywood. I talked to a guy in the shop, and he recognized the hat as one he sold, but he wouldn't give me the buyer's name."

Don grimaced and nodded. "I wouldn't have given you the guy's name either. Geez, Park, didn't you hear what I said this morning about playin' cop?"

"Yeah, I heard you. But nobody else is doing anything about this, so I figure it's up to me."

"Nobody is doing anything about it because you didn't file a complaint with the Santa Monica cops. Listen to me, Park. Even if you find the guy nobody will care because there's no record of the crime." Don sighed an exasperated sigh and added, "If you're done with your gambling ship story, I want you to get your butt on a northbound train and leave the police work to us professionals."

I was tempted to ask Don what made him anymore professional than me, but instead, I said, "That's exactly why I'm here. I've got a reservation on tonight's Lark. I brought the hat in so you can do your job by going up to that men's shop in Hollywood and finding out who bought it."

Don half turned and threw the pencil he was holding across the room hard enough to stick its point in a calendar on the opposite wall. "Damn it, Atkins, the Chief is yelling at me in one ear and the mobs are screaming in my other ear! I've got to find this mob killer or I'll be out walkin' a beat again. I ain't got time to go on wild goose chases for your benefit."

I just sat there a few minutes letting Don's blood pressure settle back down into the normal range. He looked out his office window for the same amount of time, and finally turned back to face me.

"Sorry for yelling at you, Park. I guess this Mob Avenger thing has me pretty riled up. Tell you what, leave me the hat and the name of the shop you think sold it, and when I get this other thing under control, I'll take a ride up to Hollywood and see what I can find out. Remember, though, I'm only agreeing to do that because you and I go back a long way and you saved my bacon a time or two. That jake with you?"

It wasn't what I was hoping for, but it was a far sight better than having Don throw me and the homburg out his office window. "That will be fine, Don. I appreciate it."

"I ain't makin' no promises, but I'll get in touch with you up in Frisco if I come up with anything."

Pushing my luck, I said, "I don't suppose your lab guys have had a chance to look at that Browning pistol yet."

Don glared at me and I braced myself for another outburst, but he just took a deep breath and said, "I haven't heard nothin' yet. I'll let you know on that, too."

I stood up and said, "Then I'll get out of your hair. This piece of paper has the name and address of the men's clothing store that sold the hat."

He took the note and slipped a corner of it under the homburg's hat band. Then he stood up and offered his hand. "Park, I know we haven't had much time to sit around and swap lies about the good old days, but it's been really good to see you again after all this time. Maybe when I get this Avenger mess cleared up, I can take a few days of vacation time and you can show me around Frisco."

I smiled. "That's San Francisco to you, mister, but I'd be happy to give you the Cooke's tour any time. I'll even introduce you to Dandy. I've told her what a swell guy you are. She doesn't think many of my friends are swell, so she'll be happy to meet you."

Don looked puzzled. "Who's Dandy? You got a lady friend up there you ain't told me about?"

Grinning, I said, "Yeah. I don't know what she sees in me, but Dandy's quite a woman. I think you'll like her."

"Imagine that! The eternal bachelor found himself a lady. Listen to a word of advice, Park. Take good care of her, make a lot of money in the radio business, and raise up a bunch of kids while you're still young enough to do it. I let that chance go by. Don't you make the same mistake."

I nodded and we shook hands again. Then I was out on the hot sidewalk limping my way back to the New Brunswick for what figured to be the last time.

I couldn't help thinking about the advice Don gave me. In all the years I've known Chambers that was as personal as our relationship had ever gotten. It surprised me and reminded me of something about Don the people around him tend to forget. He has a soft side under that tough cop act he puts on for the public. He doesn't let it show very often, but every once in a while, like today, I've gotten a peek at it.

Don's comments also told me something about him I never knew. In spite of his success as one of the department's only straight cops, he has a few deep-down regrets about some of the choices he made in his life, or choices he'd let others make for him. I made a mental note to remember his advice.

Sixteen

New Brunswick Hotel—First & Spring Streets, Los Angeles

According to my wristwatch it was six-thirty-three when I dropped the room phone handset back into its cradle. Since leaving Don Chambers' office I'd taken a short nap, packed my suitcase, and wrapped up my last remote broadcast on the gambling ships.

Now I stood in the middle of my room at the New Brunswick Hotel and took one last look around to make sure I wasn't forgetting anything. I noticed the New Brunswick's "vacation to write home about" pencil on the writing desk and dropped it into my pocket, not because I needed another pencil, but because it seemed like a nice souvenir of my first visit to Los Angeles since moving north to San Francisco and beginning a new life. Then I patted my inside coat pocket to be sure I had the return portion of my round-trip train ticket and gave the room a casual salute. "So long, LA."

In the lobby I stopped at the desk and used most of what was left of Bill Kastner's money to settle my account. The night clerk wished me a safe trip home and I headed toward the hotel's First Street entrance.

Through the big plate glass lobby windows I saw Neeko's cab waiting at the curb, but as I neared the double doors, another car pulled up. This one was hard to miss because its arrival was accompanied by a flashing red light and the wail of a siren. The siren was still winding down as the cruiser's curbside passenger door, emblazoned with the Los Angeles Police Department shield, flew open and a young patrolman jumped out.

He came through the New Brunswick Hotel's doors on a dead run. I stepped aside to let him pass and wondered what sort of miscreant warranted such enthusiastic attention. The patrolman glanced at me as he went by, and then stopped so quickly his shoes slid on the tile floor like a Warner Brothers cartoon character. Turning around, he asked, "Are you Parker Atkins?"

During the second that followed several possibilities crossed my mind, but none of them justified lying to the cop, so I said, "I'm Atkins."

The patrolman stepped quickly toward me, put a controlling hand on my shoulder, and said, "You're coming with us, Atkins."

It was too much like the reception I got aboard the *Rex* and I was tired of being strong-armed. Planting my feet firmly, I said, "Whoa, buster! What's the charge?"

The young cop looked surprised, as if I was the first citizen he ever encountered who didn't instantly bow to his authority. He tightened his grip on my shoulder, and trying to maintain an in-charge demeanor, he said sternly, "No charge. We have orders from Homicide Division to pick you up for questioning. Now get moving!"

Still holding my ground, I said, "Is Don Chambers behind this?"

That took a little more wind out of his sails. Bad guys wanted for questioning weren't supposed to be on a first name basis with the homicide boss. He muttered, "Yes, Detective Lieutenant Chambers gave us the order to pick you up."

"That's different. Here, you can take this." I thrust my suitcase at him. "I need to talk to that cabby out in front before we go."

Now thoroughly bewildered, he took my suitcase, and I headed through the lobby doors. The other patrolman was out of the cruiser, and both cops watched me walk up to Neeko's cab.

Neeko rolled down the passenger door window and said, "You got trouble with the cops, boss?"

"Nope. The guy I know in homicide wants to talk to me. It might have something to do with our bad guy, so I'm going with them to Central Division."

"You gonna miss that train, they take too long."

"I might still make it if they drive me to the depot. I just wanted to let you know what was going on and to say thanks again for all your help."

We shook hands through the window, and looking dubious about the whole situation, he said, "Neeko happy to help, but you be careful with them cops, boss. Neeko don't trust no cops."

I nodded in appreciation of his sage advice and walked over to the cruiser. "Okay, gentlemen, let's go see what Don wants."

The patrolman carrying my suitcase opened the curbside back door of the black and white and waited for me to get in. Then, realizing he still had my suitcase, he tossed it in after me. I couldn't help grinning a little as I said, "Thank you very kindly, officer."

We made the short trip to Central Division Headquarters sans lights and siren. They pulled up to a side entrance and I had to wait until the cop opened the car door for me because there was no handle on the inside. With the door open, I climbed out and said, "Thanks again, gentlemen. I can find my way from here." As I strode off, suitcase in hand, the two cops just stood there looking— and probably feeling—a little silly.

Upstairs, I walked straight into Don's office and deliberately dropped my suitcase. He looked up, startled by the resounding thud my suitcase made when it hit the floor. "Why the roust, Don?"

Looking beyond me through his office door, he said, "What the hell did you do with the patrolmen I sent to pick you up?"

"Don't worry, I didn't hurt them. Now, why the roust?

Don grinned. "Sit down, Park. I've got some interesting news."

"And I've got a train to catch, so make this quick."

"I think you'll be canceling that train reservation after you hear what I've got to say."

"Geez, Don. A few hours ago you ordered me out of town, and now you're sending department goons to keep me here. Make up your damned mind!"

Still grinning he said, "Sit down and cool off, Park."

I sat and Don said, "A little while ago the lab guy brought up a report on your Browning pistol. It was a slow afternoon down there and he noticed a coincidence. The slug the coroner dug out of the mob guy they found in the Hollywood Hills was a thirty-two, like your Browning, so just for the hell of it, he fired a test round and compared the slugs. Guess what?"

I didn't need to guess. Don's excitement gave me the answer. "They match."

"They do, which means you have delivered the best and only leads we've got on the Mob Avenger."

"What's more," I added, "I've met him face to face."

"That's a good possibility. Now, do you still want to catch that train?"

I shook my head and said, "Slide your telephone over here. I need to make a couple of calls."

My first call was to Southern Pacific. After canceling my reservation, I placed a long-distance call to Dandy's home. Her mother answered and I said, "Hello from Los Angeles, Missus Harrison. Is Dandy around?"

"Hello, Park. Yes, Dandy is upstairs. Hang on the line and I'll get her to the phone."

A moment later I heard Dandy say, "Park, is that you? Is something wrong?"

"No, nothing's wrong. In fact, something is right down here for change. You remember the trouble I encountered my first night down here?"

She answered hesitantly. "Yes."

"Well, the Los Angeles cops just discovered that the guy's pistol was used in a killing a couple of months ago. Don Chambers called me in to tell me the news and he has some questions for me. It's going to take a while, so I'm not going to make my train tonight."

"I don't know if that's good news or bad news, Park. Either way, it sounds dangerous."

"Trust me, it's good news, especially for Don. He's got a bunch of unsolved homicides down here and this is the first solid lead that's turned up."

Dandy sounded dubious. "Okay, Park, if you say so. Will you be able catch a train tomorrow?"

"I don't know yet. I'll call you as soon as we get this worked out."

"Okay. Just be careful, darling. I need you to come home, preferably in good health."

"Don't worry. Don's going to take good care of me because I can finger his killer for him."

I glanced across the desk and saw Don smiling. He made no effort to hide the fact that he was gleefully listening to my end of the conversation.

Dandy and I said our goodbyes and I slid Don's phone back toward his side of the desk, saying "Can't a guy get any privacy around here?"

"Not while you're making long-distance phone calls on my division budget."

"The cost of a long-distance call is a small price to pay for handing you your Mob Avenger on a silver platter."

"We'll see about that. First, I need a complete description of the guy you encountered on the pier the other night."

"He's a couple of inches shorter than me—say five-six or seven—with a slender build. He has a narrow face with a pale complexion, like he doesn't get much sun. I can't give you an eye color because it was dark when I got close enough to see his eyes, but he has dark eyebrows and what little I saw of his hair gave me the impression of dark brown or black with a receding hairline. He has one of those thin little mustaches and I'd place his age around forty, maybe a little older."

Don was scribbling my description as fast as he could go. I paused a moment to let him catch up, and then said, "He was dressed to the nines in a gray three-piece suit to match the homburg. His shoes were black and well-polished. Like the hat, everything he wore looked custom-made and expensive. Oh, and he had a white handkerchief in the breast pocket of his suit coat. It was folded to show three points—a very Dapper Dan."

Don finally stopped writing and looked over his notes. "Damn! You don't miss much."

"Remembering people used to be part of my job, remember? And I have good reason to remember this particular guy. What's next?"

"The men's shop that sold the hat is closed by now, so we'll have to wait until tomorrow morning to go out to Hollywood, and I have to type up your description of this guy so we can distribute it. Meanwhile, you can go back to your hotel."

"Is the LAPD paying for my room tonight?"

Don was already rolling a piece of paper into the black Remington typewriter on a metal stand next to his desk. He stopped and looked at me. "You broke?"

"Yeah. My boss paid for this trip and I've only got a few bucks left."

Don thought for a moment and said, "Okay, you can bunk on my sofa tonight. If we need you longer, I'll draw a few bucks from the department's emergency fund."

"I hope your offer includes dinner, I'm starving."

Don turned back to his typewriter and said, "I've got bread and baloney at home. We'll make a couple of sandwiches."

While Don hunted and pecked his way through my description of the gunman, my brain started asking questions again. Now that we knew my guy was the Mob Avenger, the questions changed some, like why did the Mob Avenger follow me all over Los Angeles yesterday?

Also, based on what little I knew about him, I guessed he usually didn't waste much time on conversation when he hunted down his targets. Taking time to chit-chat with mobsters he planned to kill gave his victims too much opportunity to turn the tables on him, just as I had done. It was a lot safer to take them by surprise. So if I was a target, why didn't he just shoot me from behind the hot dog stand? It was a perfect set up. The pier was dark and nearly deserted. He could have easily gotten off a couple of shots and disappeared with very little risk.

So clearly I wasn't on the Mob Avenger's list of targets. That brought me right back to the same big question: Why the hell did he stick a gun in my back?

Seventeen

Thursday—August 18, 1938

Don Chambers' Home—1351 Calumet Avenue, Echo Park

First settled around the turn of the century, Echo Park is among the oldest neighborhoods in the city of Los Angeles. Geographically speaking, the Echo Park area is located off Temple, just north of the central downtown area, which makes it an ideal place for Don Chambers to live. His drive to work each morning can't be more than five minutes, including a stop at the donut stop.

Echo Park is an odd mixture of high, middle and low income homes. While Don's little two bedroom bungalow on Calumet Street at the south end of Echo Park is at the lower end of the housing range, there are homes near Echo Park Lake that could fairly be called mansions.

After donning my last clean shirt, I followed the smell of coffee into Chambers' kitchen. He looked up from the *Times* he was reading at the breakfast table long enough to point at a coffee cup on the counter near his scarred and dented metal percolator.

As I poured a cup of hot, black liquid that was only slightly less viscous than old motor oil, I remembered another habit of Don's I'd forgotten since the days I worked for him. He likes his coffee strong—very strong. I diluted my cup's contents with a squirt of water from the tap and sat down at the table.

He laid the *Times* down and said, "Still can't handle real man's coffee, huh?"

"I don't know why you bother to brew it, Don. You might just as well eat the coffee grounds right out of the can with a spoon."

"I might just try that. Here, look at this."

Don turned the *Times* around and pointed to a front page story above the fold. The headline said, "Mob Avenger baffles cops." Below that, a subhead added, "Chief 'Two-Gun' Davis says, 'No comment.'"

I started to read the first paragraph, but Don grabbed his paper back, and waving it in the air, said, "Davis hates that 'two-gun' moniker! I'm surprised my phone isn't ringing off the hook already. Damned *Times*! They printed this just to needle the department, but guess who's gonna catch hell for it?"

"Maybe you should beat Davis to the punch. Call the chief and tell him you have a solid lead."

"Not on your life! If I did that, he'd tell the *Times* he was gonna arrest the Mob Avenger any minute. If your hat turns out to be a blind alley, I'd be back pounding a beat by lunch time."

"I see your point. I guess we better get out to Hollywood and find out how solid the hat lead really is."

It was a few minutes after nine when Chambers pulled his black Ford to the curb in front of the Crossroads of the World shopping arcade. I started to get out, but Don stopped me. "Better let me handle this, Park. You've been in there asking questions already. If you show up again the guy might get stubborn. Then I'd have to go for a warrant, and that might be tough with as little evidence as we've got."

I nodded and lit a Camel while Chambers disappeared into the shopping arcade with the gunman's homburg dangling from his left hand.

I knew Don could be tough when he needed to be, but I was still a little surprised when he returned in less than fifteen minutes. Climbing into the driver's seat, he said, "We're on to something here, but I'm not sure what. The salesman said he's sold three six-and-an-eighth-size hats like this since the style was introduced about a year ago."

"That narrows things down a little."

"Maybe. Two of the hats were purchased by local men, and one of them sort of fits your description of the gunman on the pier. I have his name and address. The third hat was sold to someone from out of town. The salesman doesn't have the guy's name, but thinks he's from your part of the world."

"San Francisco?"

"Yeah. That might rule him out, except the salesman's description of the guy in San Francisco is the best match of the three, so we can't cross him off the list yet."

"All right. Where to now?"

Don thought for a moment, and then said, "The local guy who comes closest to your description owns a Chrysler dealership over on Wilshire, so . . ."

My ears perked up when Don said the word, "Chrysler." I interrupted, saying, "That might be the guy. Remember I told you the cab driver who took me to Santa Monica Tuesday night said he thought we were being followed by a gray Chrysler?"

"Say, that's right. Let's go by and see if we can get a look at . . ." Don consulted his notebook, " . . Mister Kamram Kanasani."

"How we gonna handle this? I can identify the guy, but he knows me, too. If he's our gunman and I show up at his place of business, he's gonna smell a rat."

"I'll drop you off a block or so before we get there, and then I'll go into the dealership with some story that will explain the cop car—like I'm hunting a stolen vehicle. I'll get a look at the guy, and if he fits your description, we'll figure out a way for you to make a positive ID."

It was as good a plan as anything I could come up with, so I said, "Okay, but I'm not holding out much hope for success with this one."

Don frowned at my sudden lack of enthusiasm. "Why not?"

"How many pale-skinned people with Middle Eastern-sounding names do you know?"

Kanasani's Chrysler dealership was in the six-thousand block of Wilshire Boulevard, just west of Fairfax, so Don pulled over and dropped me off in front of the May Company at Wilshire and Fairfax. This time Don kept me cooling my heels a good forty-five minutes.

When he finally came back to pick me up, I could tell from his expression that Kanasani wasn't our guy. Pulling away from the curb, he said, "You'd think a salesman at a fancy men's store would have a better memory for his customers. Kanasani is as big around as he is tall and has a beard, for cryin' out loud."

"That leaves the out-of-town hat customer who might be from San Francisco as our only lead from the homburg. Did the salesman give you anything to go on besides the San Francisco connection?"

"Nope. It was a cash sale, but he did say the guy has been in the store a couple of times over the past several months, so he might be somebody who travels back and forth between LA and San Francisco, which ain't much help."

"Where to now?"

"Central Division to face the music. I bet Chief Davis has

called me at least a dozen times by now.

Eighteen

Central Police Headquarters—First & Hill Streets, Los Angeles

Don was wrong. There were only four telephone messages from LAPD Chief James Davis on his desk when we got to Central Division.

While Don waited on the line for Davis, I filled the time studying the blackboard behind his desk and jotting the information scrawled there into my notebook. Besides what I'd given him, just about everything he had on the Mob Avenger case was summed up in six lines:

12/17/37 – Ivan Glick – Encino (Luciano)
2/16/38 – Johnny "Riz" Rizzo – Downtown (Nitti)
4/18/38 – Bill "Goldy" Goldsong – Laurel Canyon (Luciano)
6/38 (found 8/17/38) – Eddie Conti – Hollywood Hills (Nitti)
8/16/38 – Arturo Bellaguisi – Culver City (Luciano)
8/16/38 – Allan Ponce – Culver City (Just a witness?)

The time pattern struck me right off the bat. Beginning last December, a mobster had been killed every other month just like clockwork. What's more, five of the six were killed on or right after the sixteenth of the month. The actual date of the Hollywood Hills killing wasn't known, but if the coroner's estimate of two months was correct, Conti also fit the pattern.

My concentration on the blackboard was broken by Don saying, "Yes, sir . . . yes, sir . . . yes chief . . . no sir."

His expression filled in the blanks. Chief Davis was reading him the riot act and Don wasn't at all happy about it. I looked at my wristwatch and sighed. It was going on eleven and I hadn't called Charlie to let her know I was still in LA. I, too, was going to get the riot act read to me, and I was pretty sure I wouldn't like it any more than Don. Deciding to face the music, I went downstairs and used a public pay telephone in the lobby to place a long-distance call to KDG.

When I got Charlie on the line, she said, "Park, where in Heaven's name are you? I thought you were coming in this morning."

"I'm still in LA, Charlie. Another story came up and . . ."

"Wait a minute, Park. Mister Kastner just came in and he wants to speak to you."

Kastner's voice came on the line almost immediately, and he asked the same question as Charlie, but he wasn't nearly as polite about it. "Atkins, where the hell are you? You were supposed to be back today!"

Stretching the truth just a little, I said, "A major story broke here last night, and I decided it was worth our while to get the facts before I left LA"

"You decided?" Kastner sounded like he was going to explode. His voice went up another octave as he screamed, "Atkins, you don't make the decisions around here, I do! And in case you've forgotten, we report the news in San Francisco, not Los Angeles!"

"This story will be making the national wire soon, plus it has a San Francisco connection . . ."

"I don't care. Your job is here and I want you in this office tomorrow, or you can damned well look for another job!"

I was sorely tempted to quit on the spot. I had the Mutual offer in my pocket and I didn't need Kastner or his tantrums. Instead, I took a deep breath and said, "Yes, sir. I'll be on tonight's train."

"You'd better be. Here's Miss Blanchard again."

There was a long pause during which I heard the newsroom office door slam four hundred miles away. Then Charlie said, "Park, you still there?"

"Yup."

"You've really upset Kastner this time. I can't recall ever seeing him this angry."

"He'll get over it. As I started to tell you before we were so rudely interrupted, there's a big story breaking down here and I've got an inside track. Have you seen anything on the wire about the Mob Avenger killings down here?"

"Yes. There was an AP story copied from the *LA Times* this

morning. I haven't gotten to it yet, though."

"I figured it would make the wire. That's the story I mentioned to you yesterday. Somebody is killing off mobsters down here on a regular basis—at least five or six, so far. The cops have no leads, except one I gave them. And there's a possibility the killer is from San Francisco. That's why I decided to stay an extra day."

"You said you gave the cops their only lead?"

"Yes. That's how I got the inside track on this thing. Listen, Charlie, can you get Dick to sit in for me again, tonight?"

"Yes, I guess I'll have to. It would have been nice of you to let me know a little sooner, though."

"There wasn't time. I was on my way to the train depot last night when the cops made the connection that got me involved. I've been working with my old boss in the Homicide Division ever since."

"Okay, Park, you're forgiven. Just don't miss that train tonight!"

"I won't. One more thing; put a story about the Mob Avenger killings in tonight's broadcast. Don't mention the San Francisco connection yet. Use the wire copy details and add something about me doing a special crime report about it tomorrow night. That should get Kastner off his high horse."

"If he listens to the broadcast, which he seldom does."

"It doesn't matter. If this thing breaks right, we might even get a national exclusive out of it. I gotta run. See you in the morning."

"Okay, Park. And don't miss that train tonight!'

Before going back up to Chambers' office I dropped some change into the same telephone and told Dandy I would be in on the morning train. That news put a smile in her voice and left me feeling like I'd done at least one thing right this morning.

Don was off the phone when I got back, but he didn't look any happier. I said, "Don't feel too bad. I just caught hell from my boss, too."

"I'm sorry about that. If you want, I'll call your boss and tell him I kept you here as a material witness or something."

"Thanks, Don, but I don't think that will be necessary. I do have to get on that northbound train tonight, though."

Don shrugged. "I figured that. There ain't much more you can do down here, anyway. Who knows? If we get anything more on the hat customer in San Francisco, you might be able to check it out for me."

I nodded. "I'm counting on that. Before I go, though, I've got a couple of thoughts about your blackboard notes there."

"Shoot."

"Have you noticed the date pattern?"

Don turned to look at the blackboard and I could almost see the light bulb go on over his head. "Hey, I see what you're getting at. All of them could have been killed on the same date—the sixteenth of the month. I hadn't pinned it down that tight yet."

"Right. The sixteenth is a special date for the Mob Avenger. Ten will get you twenty that, if he's actually avenging something, whatever it is happened on the sixteenth of the month."

"Yeah, but what month and what year?"

"Unless you've got something else in mind, that's what I'm going to use the rest of my last day in LA to find out."

"How?'

"By visiting the *Times*' morgue and going through some old newspapers. That okay with you?"

"Sure. I have to hold a task force meeting on this thing in an hour, anyway. Chief's orders. Davis is big on meetings."

"One question before I go."

"What's that?"

"Your lab matched the slug from Eddie Conti with the Browning. Were any of the other victims killed with the same gun?"

"Nope. Glick and Rizzo got it with a forty-five. Goldsong was shot at long range with a thirty-thirty rifle and a thirty-eight was used at the Culver City motor court."

"Your Mob Avenger seems to have a large arsenal."

"So? What are you getting at?"

"Have you considered the possibility he might be a cop?"

Don glared at me. "Why? Because he's got guns? Hunters have guns. Gun collectors have guns. Believe it or not, even mob killers have guns." He threw his arms up. "Hell, these days everybody has guns!"

"True enough, but not everybody knows where to find mob goons to shoot with those guns, and a straight cop might have a strong motive for killing gangsters if he was tired of seeing crooked cops and corrupt judges let bad guys off the hook." I could tell Don's blood pressure was on the rise, so I quickly added, "Just a thought. All right if I leave my suitcase with you until tonight? It's still in the trunk of your car."

"Yeah, that's fine. You're coming back here then?"

"I'll be back before five."

Nineteen

Los Angeles Times Building–First & Spring Streets, Los Angeles

The *Los Angeles Times* plant is only a block east of Central Division Headquarters. I knew the route well because my career had followed the same path a little more than four years ago when Don Chambers' predecessor in homicide finally got tired of what he called my "cowboy tactics" and fired me. I was unemployed for about three months—just long enough to iron out the details of a lucrative contract with the *Times* that took me from hotshot homicide cop to hotshot crime reporter.

It wasn't long after arriving at the *Times* that my alcohol consumption took the leap from social drinking to full-blown drunk. A year-and-a-half later the *Times* decided they, too, had little use for Parker T. Atkins.

Hoping I wouldn't run into anyone I knew, I took an elevator up to the *Times* building's fifth floor and presented my business card to the tall, slender woman at the morgue reception desk. She politely informed me that, as a working journalist, I was allowed access to the archive of *Times* back issues stored there, but I would have to find the issues I wanted myself because they were short-handed. She also explained that no back issues could be removed from the room without permission.

The huge, well-lit, and conveniently organized archive into which I was admitted was a far cry from the dank basement in which the *San Francisco Chronicle* kept its back issues. Using signs affixed to the shelves, I found the 1937 editions of the *Times* and began searching for an incident occurring around the sixteenth of the month that might prove to be the Mob Avenger's motivation for killing off citizens of LA's underworld.

The first Mob Avenger killing occurred on December 16, 1937, so I started with the mid-November editions and worked my way backward. By the time I reached May with nothing to show for the effort, I decided to play a hunch. I jumped back to mid-December, 1936—the one-year anniversary of the first killing—and hit pay dirt. It wasn't exactly what I was looking for, but way back on the third page of the Metropolitan section I found an article reporting the murder of one Guido Moretti who was shot to death on the evening of December 16, 1936. His body was found the next morning in Malibu by a man walking on the beach. Moretti was described as a known gangster with a record of convictions for illegal bookmaking.

My search of subsequent issues for follow-up stories resulted in only one additional article published a week after the killing. It reported that Moretti's death was still under investigation by the LAPD, but they had no suspects and no significant leads in the case.

What interested me in Guido's departure from our midst was its similarity to the deaths listed on Don Chambers' blackboard. The timing and circumstances made me wonder if the December 16, 1937 killing of Ivan Glick really was the Mob Avenger's first hit, or did he actually begin killing gangsters a year earlier? How about two years earlier?

I jotted Moretti's details in my notebook and pulled the mid-December, 1935 issues from their shelves. As I did so, a bold front page headline above the fold in the December 17 edition caught my eye. It said, "Thelma Todd found dead in Malibu, foul play is suspected."

I didn't need to read any further because I remembered nearly every word of the article, including the by-line below the head. It said, "By Los Angeles Times Crime Reporter, Parker T. Atkins."

During the last few weeks of 1935 and on into the new year I stuck to Thelma Todd's story like glue. The death of a motion picture celebrity is always big news in this part of the world, but Hot Toddy's star had shone brightly enough for her passing to make front page news in every burg with a newspaper between Hollywood and Todd's hometown of Lawrence, Massachusetts.

Thelma's career as a sassy platinum blonde comedienne began in the silent film era and was still on the rise when she died nearly a decade later. All told, Todd made more than a hundred motion pictures—movies in which she shared the screen with such comedic luminaries as Laurel and Hardy, The Marx Brothers and

Buster Keaton.

The type size of headlines above news articles reporting Todd's death was also increased several points by the weird circumstances surrounding her demise. In truth, those circumstances had more to do with how the LAPD handled the investigation than they did with how Todd met her end. Even with the LA County Coroner missing the time of death by at least twenty-four hours, it was still hard to imagine how LA's finest could botch another celebrity murder investigation as badly as they bungled movie director William Desmond Taylor's strange killing back in 1922.

Admittedly, my view of the case was somewhat clouded by frequent shots from a bottle stashed in the bottom drawer of my desk at the *Times*, but even thus impaired, I had no doubt that Thelma Todd was murdered, and I was even pretty sure I knew who was responsible. Still, unless somebody stumbles across some irrefutable new evidence, it's unlikely that I or anyone else will ever know the whole story of Todd's murder because the LAPD is perfectly happy to live with the coroner's suicide verdict. Case closed.

I was gazing off into space as I thought about Todd when my eyes settled on the morgue's big wall clock. I promised Don I would be back by five and I had less than an hour to keep that promise.

I was scolding myself for getting sidetracked by Thelma Todd when it dawned on me that I might not be sidetracked at all. I came to the *Times* morgue looking for an event occurring on or around the sixteenth of the month that could trigger the Avenger's desire for vengeance and I'd stumbled on a Duesy. Whether or not there was actually a connection between Thelma Todd's murder and the Mob Avenger remained to be seen, but the timing fit perfectly, especially if Guido Moretti turned out to be an unsolved homicide.

In addition, Todd's case had strong ties to the mob. It was a certain fact that Charlie Luciano was involved with Thelma Todd, if only because he was trying to persuade her to let him set up a gambling operation in a second-floor room at her restaurant on the coast road in Malibu. There were even credible witness accounts of a conversation between Luciano and Todd during which he threatened to kill her if he didn't get his way.

My personal conclusions about Thelma Todd's death were that she was gutsy enough to stand her ground against Luciano and he made good on his threat. If those conclusions were right, the mob killing of Thelma Todd could well be the vengeance motive I was seeking.

Of course, it was all speculation at this point. I needed more information and some answers from Don to make any kind of solid connection between Todd's murder and the Mob Avenger.

Twenty

Central Police Headquarters–First & Hill Streets, Los Angeles

Don Chambers was leaning back in his chair staring out the office window when I got there. I gave the doorframe a rap with my knuckles to announce my arrival and he nodded a greeting.

I said, "Was your meeting productive?"

"Not particularly. I told 'em about the Browning and the hat, and I distributed your description of the gunman. I also put a couple of guys to work on tracing the pistol, but I'm not holding my breath on that one. About the only other thing we accomplished was deciding to call Ben Siegel in to see if he has any ideas about why our guy is killing off his and Nitti's boys. All in all, that's not much to show for a three hour meeting."

"Well, cheer up. I found a couple of things that might throw a little more light on the situation."

Don leaned an elbow on his desk and said, "Yeah? Whatcha got?"

"You remember a guy named Guido Moretti?"

He didn't have to think long before answering. "Yeah, I remember Moretti. He went way back with Frank Dragna, and he had a record as long as your arm, partly because he took a couple of falls for Dragna."

I knew Frank Dragna from my days on the force. He and his brother, Tom, took over the LA Mafia about five years ago and he's been making money hand over fist for the family ever since, mostly through gambling and loan sharking. It's even rumored that Frank has a seat on the national council of families, which makes him the only boss west of Chicago with that much clout.

Don continued, "Then, when Luciano sent Siegel out here, Bugsy worked a deal to get Dragna's entire operation working for Luciano. Why?"

"Do you remember what happened to Moretti?"

"Sure. He got bumped off a couple of years ago."

"Did you ever find his killer?"

Don frowned thoughtfully for a moment, and then said, "I don't remember. I know we weren't looking too hard. Is it important?"

"It could be."

Chambers turned to a filing cabinet by the window. "Okay, I'll check my due diligence files."

In LAPD lingo, due diligence files were summaries of unsolved cases. The due diligence part meant detectives were expected to review old unsolved cases at least once a year to determine if any new leads might have turned up since the last time they blew the dust off the files.

After bending over the bottom file drawer for a few minutes, Don sat up and said, "Here it is. Moretti was found shot to death on the beach near Malibu in 1936. Nobody was ever charged with the murder. So what does Moretti have to do with the price of cheese in Denmark?"

"Look at the date he was shot."

He studied the paper in his hand and read, "December sixteen." Suddenly the significance of an unsolved mob killing on December sixteenth sank in. "Damn, another one!"

"I think so."

Don shook his head and walked to the chalkboard, where he squeezed in a new line at the top of the list. It said, "12/16/36 – Guido Moretti – Malibu (Luciano)."

Returning to his chair, Don looked over his shoulder at the list again and said, "Geez, how far back does this thing go?"

"If my hunch is right, Moretti was the first."

"I sure as hell hope so! What's your hunch?"

"I think Moretti was killed on the first anniversary of the event the Mob Avenger is set on avenging."

Don looked at me blankly. "What event?"

"Thelma Todd's murder."

It's damned hard to surprise Don Chambers, but I did it with that bombshell. "What? How the hell does she figure into all this?"

"Thelma Todd was killed in Malibu on December 16, 1935. Exactly a year later one of Luciano's boys shows up dead on the beach practically right in front of the place Todd was killed."

"Whoa! Hold on, there, buckaroo. Thelma Todd wasn't murdered. The coroner's report called it a suicide."

"Come on, Don. You don't believe that any more than I do. Luciano either killed her or had her killed because Todd refused to let him set up shop in her restaurant."

Leaning back in his chair, Don frowned and began rubbing a hand over the day's growth of stubble on his chin. I knew he was doing what any good homicide cop does when something unexpected shows up in a case. He was turning the new puzzle piece around in his mind to see if he could make it fit.

Finally, he said, "Park, I see what you're getting at, but connecting Thelma Todd to mob killings two and a half years later is a long damned reach. For one thing, our killer is going after both Nitti's boys and Luciano's. You might be able to connect Luciano to Todd's death, but Nitti doesn't fit. And another thing, our killer has to have some connection with the mobs. Who else would know the mob boys and where to find them?"

"A cop would." I got Don's glare again, and I knew I was skating on thin ice, but it had to be said.

Chambers got up quickly and started around his desk in my direction. I tensed, figuring I might have pushed him far enough to take a poke at me or throw me out of his office. He didn't do either. Instead, he closed the office door and walked back to his chair.

Then, leaning across his desk, he spoke in a quiet voice that didn't carry beyond the office walls. "Damn it, Park, just because there are a few bad apples in the barrel doesn't mean a crooked cop is behind every crime committed in this town."

Putting my argument as diplomatically as possible, I said, "Don, I know you stand up for the department, but face the facts. Between them, Dragna, Luciano and Nitti own a damned big chunk of the LAPD, plus it's common knowledge that Bugsy is in bed with the DA. We can't rule out the possibility that a straight cop might get angry enough over the situation to take matters into his own hands. And whether Luciano had the fix in with Todd's murder or not, anybody looking at the department's handling of that investigation couldn't help but believe somebody—probably a bunch of somebodies—got paid off."

Don had his thoughtful face on again. He knew I was right, but that didn't make accepting the facts any easier for him. "Okay, Park, suppose for a minute you're right; did the guy who stuck a gun in your back on the Santa Monica pier look or act like any cop you ever met? How many straight cops do you know who can afford to dress in custom suits and imported homburgs?"

"You make a good point there, Don, but look at it the other way around; how many mob goons do you know who would risk doing what the Mob Avenger is doing? And why would they want to? The only reason mobsters kill each other is if there's a war on, and you've ruled that out. Besides, our guy doesn't necessarily have to be a cop; he might just be in cahoots with one."

Leaning forward over the desk again, Don said, "Okay, again assuming you're right, what am I supposed to do about it? You know I walk a thin line around here. If I started rousting cops without hard evidence, my name would be mud and I'd be out of business."

"I'm not suggesting you start rousting cops, but it wouldn't hurt anything to go back through the records and make a list of the cops who were involved in the Todd case. You might find a name or two on the list that would be worth a closer look."

Don leaned back in his chair and sighed. "Maybe. But what about the other stuff? Like, if our guy is avenging Thelma Todd, why is he killing Nitti's boys, too? And what about the timing? The first two killings were a year apart, but now he's going after a new guy every other month."

"He could just be nailing Nitti's boys along with Luciano's as a smoke screen to make it harder for us to connect him with Thelma Todd. Or maybe he figures one mob goon is just as good as another for his purposes" I paused, and then added, "Look, Don, I don't have all the answers yet. All I know is what you taught me years ago; there's no such thing as a coincidence in homicide."

Don grimaced. "I taught you that? Hell, I shoulda kept my big trap shut. When does your train leave?"

"Nine."

"Okay, we've got time to get some dinner before you have to be at the station."

I grinned and asked, "You buyin'?"

"Yeah, cheapskate, I'm buyin'. I guess that's the least I can do for gettin' you in Dutch with your boss up there in Frisco."

Twenty-One

After three days in Los Angeles and my second twelve-hour train ride in less than a week, it felt good to see The City's familiar landmarks rolling past my window as the Southern Pacific's San Francisco Lark approached the SP depot at Third and Townsend. Seeing Dandy waiting for me in the station felt even better. She topped all those good feelings off with the sort of kiss she usually reserved for more private settings.

We zipped across town to my apartment on McAllister in her very snazzy Buick Roadmaster convertible, and as she dropped me off, I got another kiss and a promise of dinner at Fisherman's Grotto after my broadcast. Next came a quick shower, shave and fresh clothes, after which I climbed into my very unsnazzy '34 Ford coupe for the trip to Third and Market, where KDG occupied the fourth floor of the Owl Drug Building.

It was a few minutes after ten when I walked into the tiny office in which Charlene Blanchard and I write KDG's nightly news broadcast. The first thing I noticed was the look of relief on Charlie's face as she said, "Am I ever glad to see you!"

"Gee, I didn't know you missed me so much."

Charlie gave me a look and said, "Who said anything about missing you? I'm just glad you're back so I don't have to give Mister Kastner anymore excuses for you not being in that chair."

I sat in the chair to which she referred and said, "Well, at least somebody around here missed me."

"I'm afraid if Mister Kastner came in this morning and you weren't back, we'd all be missing you . . . permanently. He was in an awful mood yesterday, even after you talked to him on the telephone."

I tried to look appropriately concerned and changed the subject. Did you run a story on the Mob Avenger last night?"

"Yes. I culled the details from the *Times* story the Associated Press copied on the wire. There wasn't much . . . mostly just six known mobsters killed and the police have no leads."

"You can make that seven mobsters killed now."

Charlie's eyes widened. "The Mob Avenger got another one last night?"

"No, but I found another mobster killing back in December of 1936 the police hadn't connected to the current bunch."

"Wow! This really is a big story. How in heaven's name did you get involved in with it?"

"Yeah, it's a whopper, all right, and how I got involved is kind of complicated."

I told her the entire story of my adventures in southern California from Winchell's Motor Court to my research at the *LA Times* morgue. It took a while to tell it all, but the time was well spent because it brought Charlie up to date and gave me an opportunity to reorganize the facts floating around in my head.

She said nothing while I talked, but jotted several notes on one of her ever-present yellow legal pads. When I finished the tale, Charlie said, "I see now why you needed an extra day down there. Do you really think the man from up here who bought the hat is the killer?"

"Unless there's another place that sells Borsalino hats in California, he's a prime candidate."

"What if the killer bought the hat in another part of the country, like on a trip to New York or even Italy? From your description, he sounds like somebody with the wherewithal to travel."

"At this point there are lots of possibilities, but the small hat size limits them somewhat. And since the hat is the only solid lead we've got, I have to follow it until something better turns up."

"So you're going to stick with this Mob Avenger thing?"

"That's my job, and it's also the kind of story that keeps listeners listening and putting their money in Mister Crocker's bank."

Charlie cocked her head and said, "Yes, it's the kind of story people like to hear, but isn't hunting down dangerous criminals what the cops get paid for? I thought our job is reporting the news."

I smiled and said, "Strictly speaking, you're right, but I don't mind giving the cops a hand from time to time."

"You mean like the hand you gave the Sheriff on the Doherty murder last year? That deputy was ready to put you in jail and throw away the key in appreciation for the help you gave them."

"But he changed his tune when we found the killer, didn't he?"

Charlie sighed and said, "Yes, but . . ." She paused briefly, and then continued, "I'm sorry, Park, this kind of thing just scares me to death. I know you used to be a cop and you're fearless, but I'm not. After that Doherty thing last year I was a nervous wreck for weeks. I still have nightmares."

It was my turn to sigh. I did, and then said, "I know, kiddo. You had a rough time of it, and you know I'm sorry for getting you involved, but Dandy's life was at stake. This is a different situation entirely. I promise there won't be any danger this time. I'm just doing some plain, old fashioned detective work."

Charlie still looked dubious, but said, "Okay, Park. I hope you can keep that promise. How much time do you need out of tonight's broadcast?"

"That depends on what else is going on in the world."

Charlie shuffled through the long strips of AP wire service copy on her desk and read off a list of the biggest national and international news items. "Switzerland is up in arms about all the Jewish refugees crossing their border from Germany. Adolph Hitler announced that all Austrians will officially become Germans on January first. FDR signed an executive order extending the Public Works Administration until February. The Navy is commissioning a new destroyer today, the USS Sampson, and a tropical cyclone did some damage in Hawaii last night."

Next she gestured toward the stack of local newspapers on top of her typewriter. "There isn't much going on locally, except the *San Francisco News-Letter* ran a scathing editorial accusing CIO leader Harry Bridges of being a communist and calling for his deportation. There are bound to be some heated responses from Bridges' supporters. That's about it, so you can have as much or as little time as you want."

"Okay, save me three minutes. That will be enough to get the series started. Hopefully, I'll have more to talk about by Monday."

With that, Charlie got to work writing the bulk of the newscast and I rolled a fresh piece of paper into my trusty old Underwood Number Five to begin the first of what I hoped would be an engrossing series of special crime reports on LA's Mob Avenger.

In spite of an interruption when Bill Kastner showed up to tell me what a lousy employee I am, I had my three minutes' worth done by eleven-thirty. After giving the script one last read and marking a couple of changes in red pencil, I put it on Charlie's desk and picked up the telephone. Since I was already in the doghouse with Kastner, another long distance phone call wasn't going to make much difference. I got the number for Hal Roach Studios in Culver City from long distance information, and hoping Ozzie Gallagher still worked there and would remember me, I placed the call.

Like me, Gallagher once carried LAPD tin. Unlike me, Ozzie had the good sense to find a more lucrative job on the outskirts of law enforcement as a studio cop. By the time I left the force, Ozzie Gallagher had risen to the lofty position of Chief of Security for Hal Roach Studios, which is why I hoped he would remember me. We never met when I was on the force, but I called on him frequently while reporting on Thelma Todd's murder for the *Times*. Thelma was under contract with the Roach Studios when she died, and not much went on around the place without Ozzie knowing about it.

After negotiating my way through the studio switchboard, I reached the security office. I identified myself to Gallagher's secretary and asked to speak with him. She told me to hold the line for a minute while she checked to see if Mister Gallagher was available to take my telephone call. A moment later she was back on the line, saying, "Mister Atkins, Mister Gallagher remembers you and wants to know why he should want to talk to you, or words to that effect"

"Tell him he wants to talk to me because I'm really a swell guy and he's missed my charming personality all these years, or words to that effect."

Another brief pause was followed by Ozzie's gravelly voice rumbling down the line. "Atkins, if there's any charm in your personality, I sure never saw any of it. Where the hell are you these days and what the hell do you want from me?"

"'Well, hello and how are you' to you, too, Ozzie."

"Cut the crap, you pain in the butt."

Reminded that Ozzie was never one for niceties, I got down to business. "I'm reporting the news for a radio station up in San Francisco and I want to ask you some questions about Thelma Todd."

"Geez, Atkins, are you still on that kick? Toddy's old news. What the hell could you possibly want to know about her that hasn't already been reported a hundred times?"

"I'm working on a story about a related case and I'm looking for a connection."

"What kind of connection?"

At least I'd peaked his interest. I said, "A connection to a guy in San Francisco."

"Hell, that's more old news. Is your brain so pickled you don't remember the San Francisco angle?"

Puzzled, I ignored his reference to my boozing days and said, "Refresh my memory, old buddy."

He sighed and said, "According to Toddy's actress chum, Ida Lupino, Toddy told her she was seeing some wealthy businessman from San Francisco, but Toddy wouldn't say who he was. Does that ring any bells in what's left of your brain?"

It sure did. I'd forgotten all about the wealthy San Francisco businessman because he was a dead end at the time. Either that or my brain really was too pickled to remember such details. I said, "Thanks for the reminder, Ozzie. I remember that part of the story now. Did you ever find out who he was?"

"Nope. I did a little checking, more out of curiosity than anything else, but that's one secret Toddy took to her grave. You need anything else, 'cuz it's lunch time down here."

"One more question. How do I get in touch with Ida Lupino?"

The pause that followed was long enough to make me wonder if he hung up on me. Finally, Ozzie said, "Why? You uncover something new on Toddy's murder?"

Noting that he used the word "murder," instead of "death," I made a spur of the moment decision to let Gallagher in on what I was up to. I said, "In a roundabout way, yes. You've heard about the Mob Avenger murders down there? Well, I've been working with my old boss at Central Division, Don Chambers, and we made a possible connection between the killer and Thelma Todd."

There was another long period of dead air on the line before Gallagher said, "If what you're telling me is on the level, how come Chambers isn't calling me? He's still a cop, and you ain't."

"Don probably hasn't called you because he hasn't thought of it yet."

"You know, Atkins, you were a pretty fair cop once, and that's the only reason I'm talking to you now. And I think I could put you in touch with Miss Lupino, but I'd have to call in some markers to do it. That's not something I'm willing do unless I'm very damned sure you're sober and what you've got will help prove once and for all how Toddy really died."

Nobody likes to be reminded of their failings, but under the circumstances, his concern about my sobriety was both understandable and reasonable. I swallowed a bunch of pride and said, "Ozzie, I guarantee I'm one hundred percent stone cold sober and have been for more than two years. As for proving Thelma Todd was murdered, I can't guarantee a damned thing. I'm going strictly on a hunch. If that hunch is right, I may be able to find Thelma's mystery man. If I find him, there's a chance he can shed some light on what happened to her. On the other hand, the fact that he has never come forward is a pretty good indication that he doesn't want his name associated publicly with Todd's murder."

A third period of silence added another buck or two to Bill Kastner's long distance tab while Gallagher thought over his decision. When Ozzie's voice came down the line again, it was a little softer in tone. "Okay, Atkins, I'll see what I can do. Where can I reach you later this afternoon?"

I gave him KDG's number and added, "Thanks, Ozzie. I appreciate it."

As I replaced the handset in its cradle, I realized Charlie was still at her desk and she'd heard the entire conversation, at least my end of it. She knew my story, but I still felt embarrassed about having to grovel in front of her. I glanced up and caught her looking at me. I said, "I'm going down to the Owl lunch counter for an egg salad sandwich. You want to join me?"

Surprisingly, Charlie looked almost as if she was about to cry. "No thanks, I brought my lunch from home." Then, after a moment, she added, "You know, Park, if more men had the courage of their convictions you have, this would be a better world."

I went downstairs and ordered my sandwich. As I ate it, I wondered what the hell Charlie meant by her comment about my convictions. It would not surprise me at all if scientists discovered proof that women were creatures from another planet.

Twenty-Two

KDG Radio Studios–730 Market Street, San Francisco

It was around one o'clock when I got back to the office. Charlie was off somewhere, so I had the place to myself for a while. I intended to use the time for some serious thinking about the Mob Avenger and how I was going to find him, except my thoughts along those lines kept getting derailed by Charlie's words: ". . . isn't hunting down dangerous criminals what the cops get paid for? I thought our job is reporting the news."

In other words, finding killers wasn't my job. It had been my job once upon a time, but those days were long past. I think the truth is I miss the challenges of being a homicide cop. I had a real knack for outsmarting bad guys and bringing them to justice, and because I'm good at it, I enjoy doing it. That was the problem.

In moments of brutal self-honesty I could see that, since becoming a journalist, I developed a habit of turning every big crime story that came along into an excuse for playing detective. On a few occasions, as with the Doherty murder last year, my detecting skills paid off in an exclusive story. Most of the time, though, my inherent need to solve crimes resulted in nothing more than frustration.

I was also pretty sure that frustration is part of what got me into trouble with booze in the first place. When playing hunches and failing to follow what I perceived as inane procedures got me fired from the LAPD, I lost my personal identity—I no longer had the power and authority that went with a bright, shiny detective's badge.

I was doing a better job of controlling my behavior these days, but the basic problem was still there—I was still obsessed with the need to solve crimes. If I didn't find a way to accept the fact once and for all that I wasn't a detective any longer, and I was never going to be one again, there was a good chance I would eventually find myself back in the bottle.

I was on the verge of convincing myself to mend my ways when the telephone jarred me back to the here and now. I picked up the handset and was informed by Sally, our switchboard operator, that I had a long-distance call from a Mister Gallagher on the line. She put the call through and I said, "Hello, Ozzie . . ."

"Listen, Atkins, pretty soon you're going to get a call from a gal by the name of Johansson. She's Ida Lupino's personal secretary and she's going to set up an appointment for you to interview Miss Lupino."

"Great, Ozzie! Thanks . . ."

"Forget the thanks because I want something in return. I want anything you get on this Mob Avenger that connects back to Thelma Todd, if there is anything. You got that?"

"I got it, Ozzie. You'll get whatever I get."

"Good, we understand each other. It took a lot of finagling to pull this off, so don't screw it up."

I started to say I wouldn't when I realized I was talking to a dead line. Ozzie Gallagher was indeed a man of few words.

I hung up the telephone and leaned back to contemplate my good fortune, if it was good fortune. Interviewing Ida Lupino about Thelma Todd's mysterious San Francisco businessman was in direct conflict with my newly acquired resolve to stop playing detective, so I promptly heaped a big pile of rationalization on top of that resolve by telling myself that, having come this far, I had to see my Mob Avenger investigation through to its conclusion.

Besides, I never asked the guy to stick a gun in my back on the Santa Monica Pier. I was diligently doing my job as a journalist when the Mob Avenger poked his nose into my business. That was his mistake, not mine.

Conveniently, Charlie chose that moment to show up with another wad of AP wire service copy in her hand, thus ending my personal introspection. I said, "Anything breaking on the wire?"

She dropped the yellow strips of paper on her desk and slid into her chair. "No, nothing important. Most of this is just follow-up on the storm that hit Hawaii last night. I'll plug the new details into tonight's script."

With that, the phone on my desk rang to life again. I picked it up and learned that a Miss Johansson was calling long distance from Los Angeles. Sally put the call through and I said, "Parker Atkins."

A prim and proper sounding female voice replied, "Good afternoon, Mister Atkins. I am Miss Johansson, Miss Ida Lupino's secretary."

"Good afternoon, Miss Johansson. I've been expecting your call."

"I understand you are interested in interviewing Miss Lupino. May I know the subject about which you wish to interview her?"

"Certainly," I lied. "I'm preparing a retrospective broadcast about Thelma Todd's death. Since Miss Lupino was among Miss Todd's closest friends and one of the last people to speak with her, I would like to ask Miss Lupino to refresh our memories about the circumstances of Miss Todd's final days, such as her disposition and frame of mind, that sort of thing."

Hoping I'd taken the right approach, I held my breath for Miss Johansson's reply. She didn't let me down. "I see. I can think of no reason Miss Lupino would object to such an interview. Please meet us at Miss Lupino's bungalow on the Columbia Pictures lot tomorrow at two in the afternoon. I'll let the front gate know to expect you."

Miss Johansson had just thrown me a big fat curve ball. I said, "Ah, Miss Johansson, as you know, I'm located in San Francisco. I was hoping to interview Miss Lupino by telephone."

"I'm afraid that isn't possible, Mister Atkins. Miss Lupino only does interviews in person, face to face, as it were."

Making a choice I hoped my meager finances could afford, I said, "Very well, Miss Johansson. I will be at Miss Lupino's dressing room tomorrow afternoon at two o'clock. Please express my gratitude to Miss Lupino for agreeing to my interview."

Miss Johansson said she would, and that concluded our conversation. When I hung up the receiver, Charlie was staring at me. Knowing full well what her reply would be, I asked, "What's the matter?"

"You're going back to Los Angeles."

"Apparently, I am."

"Well, get a cardboard box and I'll help you clear out your desk. Mister Kastner is going to fire you for sure now."

"Bill Kastner doesn't need to know a thing about this."

"How are you going to get down to LA and back in time to be here Monday morning? The train . . ."

"I'm not going by train. I'll fly down and back."

"Mister Kastner will never approve that kind of expense,

especially in his current mood."

"I'll cross that bridge when I come to it."

Charlie shook her head. "Park, I'm really starting to worry about you. This . . . mission . . . of yours to find the Mob Avenger is really getting out of hand. You can't just fly down to Los Angeles on a whim. It isn't rational."

I grinned at her and said, "Rationality has never been one of my strong traits."

Looking a little frantic, Charlie said, "Park, I'm serious about this!'

"Relax, kiddo. I know what I'm doing." I hoped to hell that was true.

Twenty-Three

I dug up the telephone number for United Airlines' San Francisco ticket office and booked a reservation on their Mainliner Flight 18, departing from San Francisco at seven, Saturday morning. I made it a round-trip reservation, returning on flight 11, leaving LA at four p.m. on Sunday. I didn't think I would need to stay that long, but the kindly reservation lady assured me I could swap the return reservation for any earlier flight with available seats.

The round-trip ticket that would be waiting for me at the United ticket counter was going to cost thirty-four dollars and eleven cents. When I added in the price of a hotel room for Saturday night and a few more bucks for meals, cab fare and incidentals, the total cost of indulging my Ida Lupino hunch came to sixty bucks—roughly equal to a week-and-a-half of my KDG salary.

With that worrisome thought grating on my mind I hiked down Market Street to the Crocker Bank branch at which I keep my meager accounts and withdrew about a third of the savings I managed to squirrel away during the past two years. Walking back to KDG I justified what Charlie called my irrational behavior by convincing myself that Bill Kastner would willingly reimburse my expenses for the trip when his station got credit for ending a crime spree that was getting national attention. I was getting pretty good at the fine art of rationalization.

Back in the office Charlie was making a show of deep concentration as she typed the evening's news script. She clearly didn't want to engage in any further discussions regarding my sanity, which was just dandy with me.

Thinking of dandy things reminded me to call Dandy. My knee was reminding me that it still wasn't ready for hikes up and down Market Street, so I massaged it while I waited for Dandy to answer her telephone. I caught her at her desk on the third floor of the *Chronicle* building. Dandy's cheerful voice raised my spirits considerably.

"Hi, Park. I was just thinking about you!"

Swiveling my chair to face away from Charlie's desk in a small gesture of privacy, I said, "Good. Keep it up!"

"I will! What's up in the exciting world of broadcast journalism? I hope you aren't calling to cancel our dinner plans."

"No, we're still on for the Grotto, but I am going to put a crimp in any weekend plans we might have."

"Oh?"

"I'm flying down to LA tomorrow morning. I have an interview to do for the Mob Avenger story. I hope that's okay with you."

"It's fine with me, Park, because I'm going with you."

It crossed my mind that I was really slipping. I should have anticipated Dandy might relish a weekend jaunt to sunny southern California. For that matter, I would relish a weekend away with Dandy, but my budget was already stretched well beyond its limits. I was about to point that out, but she was way ahead of me.

"Don't worry about the money, Park. I'll pay my own way. That is, I will unless there's another reason you don't want me to come with you."

"Of course not. I'd love your company, but I hate for you to have to . . ."

"Then it's settled. Give me your flight information and I'll make my reservation."

I gave her my flight numbers and seat assignments. Then I said, "Are you sure you want to do this? The round-trip ticket is thirty-four bucks and change."

"I'm sure. I've been very frugal lately—I haven't bought a new outfit in months, so I can afford it. What time are you picking me up for dinner?"

"I should make it to your place by seven."

"Great! I'll be ready. I'm dying for some good seafood!"

I hung up the telephone with mixed emotions. I was excited about the prospects of a weekend out of town with Dandy, but the financial arrangements reminded me of what I considered the biggest reason I still hadn't asked her to marry me.

Dandy had the good sense to pick rich parents, and her salary at the *Chron* was a good deal more than what KDG paid me, so money was seldom the issue for her it was for me. Even though our relative financial circumstances never seemed to bother her, they bothered me . . . a lot. I was the man, and the man is supposed to be the bread winner, but it would be a long time before I could win the kind of bread it would take to pay for the style of living she was used to.

That line of thinking brought the offer from Mutual Broadcasting to mind. The salary they offered would go a long way toward evening things out between us on the money score.

Charlie put an end to yet another of my introspective sessions when she said, "Tonight's script is done. Do you want to read through it before I go home?"

Her intention to go home before the broadcast took me by surprise. Charlie usually stuck around until the last dog was hung, so to speak. I wondered if leaving early had anything to do with our earlier discussions regarding my sanity.

I shook my head and said, "The script will be fine. It always is. I'll look it over before the broadcast."

Charlie began clearing her desk so things would be ready for Monday morning. After a minute or two, she stopped and said, "Park, I'm sorry if it sounded like I was doubting you today. I do believe you know what you're doing. I guess I'm just a nervous Nellie."

"Don't fret about it, kiddo. Sometimes I doubt me, too. Detective work and news reporting are very similar occupations. Whether you're hunting down a killer or a story about a killer, you have to go where the leads take you, and sometimes they take the detective and the reporter down the same road. Closing in on a killer is enough to make anyone nervous."

Charlie was looking at me intently. "And are you closing in on the killer?"

"I don't know. If the fellow who accosted me on the Santa Monica pier and the Mob Avenger really are the same guy, I guess you could say I've met the killer face-to-face. Unfortunately, he didn't leave his calling card, so I still don't know his name or where to find him.

"That's why I want to talk with this actress in LA. Like I told you this morning, I have a hunch the Mob Avenger is avenging Thelma Todd's murder, and Ida Lupino told the police Todd confided in her that she had a new beaux from San Francisco.

Even though Lupino claims Todd wouldn't name the guy, I'm hoping she remembers more details from their conversation that she held back two years ago. It's a long shot, but I need to find out if the puzzle pieces I've got really fit together."

Charlie nodded. "I hope they do. This is a major story."

"Say, you go to the movies. Do you know anything about this Lupino woman?"

"Not much. I saw her in a comedy with Walter Connolly a while back. I can't recall the name of it—something about getting married, I think—but I didn't much care for it. Ida Lupino might be a good dramatic actress, but as a comedienne, she stinks."

I grinned. "I'll be sure to pass along your critique. What does she look like?"

Charlie thought for a moment, and then said, "Well, she's got dark hair and she wore it up and short in that movie. She has kind of a narrow face with high cheek bones and big eyes. She's nice looking, I guess."

"Okay, kiddo. Thanks for the help. Have a good weekend and I'll see you bright and early Monday morning."

"I sure hope so."

After Charlie gathered her things and headed for home, I picked up the phone and made the last call on my list. Don answered on the first ring, saying, "Homicide, Chambers."

"How was the parade this morning?"

"How do you think it was? All I've got to show for a wasted morning is sore feet and horse manure on my shoes. What's up?"

"I've made a connection on the Mob Avenger thing that, at least to some degree, supports my theory about his killings being linked to Thelma Todd's murder."

I could imagine him leaning forward to put his elbows on his desk as he said, "Whatcha got?"

"I started figuring that, if our lead from the guy's hat was legit, there should be other connections in all of this that point to San Francisco, so I called Ozzie Gallagher this morning and . . ."

"Yeah, I know. He called me after I got back from the parade. He wanted to know if you were on the level about working with me on the Mob Avenger case."

"Dare I ask what you told him?"

"I told him you helped us out on the case in an unofficial capacity. Then he asked if you were sober these days. I told him you were."

"Thanks, Don. Gallagher must put a lot of stock in your opinion because he just did me a big favor."

"What favor?"

"While I was talking to him this morning I asked if he could think of any connections between Thelma Todd and San Francisco and he reminded me of a big one I'd forgotten. One of Todd's close friends told an investigating officer Thelma confided in her about a new boyfriend—a wealthy businessman from San Francisco."

"Yeah, I seem to remember something about that. It doesn't do us much good, though. If I have the story straight, the friend said Todd wouldn't tell her who the guy was."

"That's the way I heard the story, too, but there's a possibility the friend wasn't telling everything Todd said about the guy, so I got Ozzie to arrange an interview for me with the friend. She's an actress named Ida Lupino. I'm flying down there tomorrow to meet with her. If she was holding anything back three years ago, she might feel more like talking about it now."

"Maybe." Don sounded doubtful. He added, "So you talked your boss at the radio station into paying for this little junket?"

"Not yet. I'm paying for this trip out of my savings. If I come back with the goods, I think he'll cough up the money to reimburse me."

Don sounded even more doubtful. "I hope this trip doesn't turn out to be a waste of your time and money."

"It might, but I've got to take a shot at it."

"Okay, let me know how it goes."

"Count on it, and I need a favor."

"What kind of favor?"

"Would you have a squad car stop by the New Brunswick hotel and have 'em look for a Checker Cab driven by a big, curly haired Greek guy by the name of Nickolopolis. If he's there, have 'em tell the cabby Park Atkins needs to be picked up at Grand Central Air Terminal in Glendale tomorrow morning at nine o'clock."

"Geez, now you want the Los Angeles Police Department to be your messenger service? Atkins, you're about the nerviest guy I know!"

"Don, if this thing pays off, we'll be a big step closer to finding your Mob Avenger and getting the chief off your back. Delivering a message is a small price to pay for that kind of help."

"Okay, okay. I'll do it, but don't get to expecting this kind of service on a regular basis."

I promised I wouldn't and hung up the receiver. Then I picked up the broadcast script Charlie left on my desk and began going through it.

I paid particular attention to my crime report segment. As crime reports go, it wasn't much—mostly just an introduction to the Mob Avenger case. Writing it, I'd been careful not to say anything about my encounter with the gunman or the two leads resulting from it. If the Mob Avenger really was in San Francisco, it wouldn't pay to let him know we have that much on him at this stage of the game. Hell, for all I knew the Mob Avenger was a regular listener to Parker Atkins Reports the News on KDG. Well, he is a classy guy, after all.

Twenty-Four

Unlike Los Angeles, which sits on flat desert terrain, the ground under San Francisco is either hilly or marshy depending on what part of town you're in. As a result there aren't many suitable locations for airfields in The City. In fact, there's only one airstrip inside the city limits—a little military airport called Crissy Field near the southern anchorage of the new Golden Gate Bridge.

As air travel to The City increased, most airlines serving San Francisco left their passengers across the bay at Oakland's Municipal Airport. Then a year or so ago, when the city fathers decided San Francisco needed a municipal airfield all its own, they chose Mills Field, a private airport a dozen or so miles south of town, and eventually renamed it San Francisco Municipal Airport, even though it's in another county.

At a few minutes after six a.m. on a Saturday morning San Francisco Municipal Airport is fairly quiet, so quiet I found a parking place along the access road no more than fifty feet from the two-story terminal building with a control tower perched on its roof. I lifted our suitcases out of the Ford's trunk and we set off across the oval drive in front of the terminal.

As we got to the entrance a young man in a blue uniform with silver wings on the jacket came out of the terminal and stopped to hold the door for Dandy. He gave her an enthusiastic once over as she passed. He obviously approved.

She was wearing an off-white crepe dress that ended at a point just below her knees. The upper part of the dress was gathered on both sides of a V neckline in a design that might have looked fussy

108

on some women, but draped perfectly over Dandy's trim figure. The color also did nice things for her big brown eyes and soft brown hair, which she'd recently taken to wearing longer in a popular style that fell across her forehead ala Greta Garbo. The adjective to describe Dandy that always came to my mind first was "stunning."

Following Dandy into the terminal, I thanked the fellow for holding the door as I sidled past him with my hands full of suitcases. I don't think he heard me. His mind was elsewhere, probably on Dandy's legs.

Since I'd never flown out of San Francisco before, I relied on Dandy to guide us through the terminal to the airline ticket counters, which were all located at the south end of the terminal waiting room. Three major airlines—Trans World, American and United—were represented there, but United was the only counter that appeared to be doing any business at this early hour. I purchased the tickets, checked our suitcases and made note of the agent's instructions that our flight would be boarding from Gate Two on the east side of the terminal.

As we crossed the lobby toward Gate Two, I noticed a small counter at which passengers could purchase life insurance policies that paid off if the aircraft they were about to board should crash. Most train depots have similar counters for railroad passengers, but what caught my interest was the difference in the price of insuring one's life against an untimely end. Five thousand dollars of life insurance cost airline passengers two dollars, while the same insurance coverage cost train passengers only a quarter.

Insurance companies operate a lot like Tony Cornero runs his gambling ship; making money depended on their ability to calculate odds. The fact that this insurance company figured I was eight times more likely to die in an airplane crash than in a train wreck did nothing for my enthusiasm about our upcoming flight.

Dandy noticed my interest in the flight insurance sign and asked, "Park, this isn't your first airline flight, is it?"

"No. I'm not the seasoned flier you are, but I flew to Phoenix a few years ago on business for the *Times*."

"Oh, okay. I just didn't want you to worry if it was your first flight. These days flying is very safe."

We found Gate Two, and through its large windows I could see our United Airlines Mainliner sitting out on the boarding ramp. It was a sleek, blue and white Douglas DC-3 with one engine on each wing. My flight to Phoenix was aboard an old, boxy-looking Ford Tri-Motor, and it occurred to me that reducing the number of engines that kept these contraptions aloft by one-third hardly seemed like progress.

Aboard the ship with safety belts securely fastened, we heard our pilot start the engines, and at precisely seven a.m., we rolled away from the terminal. A few minutes later we were climbing through clouds that streaked droplets of water on our windows.

Somewhat relieved that our trusty craft made it that far, I turned to Dandy in the window seat next to me and said, "You know, there's a subject we need to discuss."

Dandy smiled. "I know, Park. I figured you would get around to discussing the Mutual job offer when you felt the time was right. Have you made a decision?"

"Not yet. This is a decision we need to discuss because it affects both of us."

"Well, it sounds to me as if their offer would be a big step up for you."

"It's a big step, alright, but is it really a step in the right direction? We've talked about getting married when I'm making enough money to support a family and Mutual is offering me nearly three times what I earn at KDG. It comes to more than sixty-one hundred dollars a year, which ought to be enough to raise a family."

"I should think so!"

"The only problem is we would have to move to Chicago."

"A move to Chicago isn't out of the question, is it?"

"I'm not sure. What about your career? You've got a pretty good deal going at the *Chronicle* . . ."

"San Francisco isn't the only large city in America with newspapers. In fact, there are a couple of pretty good newspapers in Chicago. Besides, I'm getting tired of the society beat. It was a natural for me when I was fresh out of college, but now I want to write real news."

We hit an air bump and the plane felt like it was going to drop out of the sky. I instinctively grabbed the armrest between us, and then felt silly when the ship smoothed out.

Dandy put her hand on mine in a reassuring gesture and said, "Our careers aren't the only issues here. You mentioned raising a family, and if we're going to have kids, we can't wait too much longer. I'm not getting any younger, you know. How do you feel about that?"

At twenty-six, Dandy was a long way from spinsterhood, but she was closing in on the age at which having children became riskier. I said, "I guess how I feel about it depends on how you feel about it."

Dandy gave me the sly look she inherited from her mother and said, "Parker T. Atkins, you're evading my question. Do you want kids or not?"

She said it loudly enough to make a middle-aged woman in the seat in front of her turn around and glare at me. I was trapped. If I didn't give her a straight answer, she'd have the whole damned plane mad at me.

Quietly, I said, "Yes, Dandy, I want kids, but unless medical science has achieved a breakthrough I haven't heard about, it still takes two people to conceive a child, so as I said, how I feel about the subject also depends on how you feel about it."

Dandy gave me a small victory smile and said, "I want kids, too, Park. I want them enough that I will gladly set my career aside to have them. Does that answer your question?"

"It does, but we're right back at the beginning of the circle again. We can't raise a family on my KDG salary, so as things stand right now, we have to move to Chicago to have kids. Do we really want to do that after spending our entire lives on the west coast?"

Dandy gave my hand a squeeze. "Park, I can get used to any place so long as you're there. Moving across the country and setting up housekeeping in a brand new place might even be fun, but I'm getting a definite impression you aren't too strong on the idea. Have you ever been to Chicago?"

"Yes, I took a train back there in twenty-nine to visit mom. That was right after I made Detective Sergeant and was reassigned to Homicide Division. Mom moved back to Illinois to live with her sister after dad died in '24, so I hadn't seen her in a while. She actually lives in Hedgewisch, which is in the southeast corner of Chicago. Anyway, I spent a few days there seeing the sights and, honestly, I didn't like the place. It seemed old and dirty compared to Los Angeles. In spite of enjoying the time with mom, I couldn't wait to get on a westbound train."

She nodded and said, "So you think living in Chicago wouldn't work out well for us?"

"I'm just saying it would be a hell of a change."

Dandy looked thoughtful for several minutes, and then she leaned close so as not to be overheard by the woman in the next row and said, "Park, I don't know if I would like living in Chicago or not, but I do know taking the Mutual job would mean we could move on with our lives together. I want that more than a career or anything else. Sometimes, though, I wonder if you feel the same way, or if you'd be happier leaving things as they are. I don't want to make you go against your instincts, but we can't continue with things the way they are much longer. If you don't really want to get married and start a family, you need to tell me soon so I have a chance to make some decisions of my own."

Dandy didn't say what those decisions might be, but the possibilities gave me a sinking feeling in the pit of my stomach. That started me wondering if I was shying away from the Mutual job because I feared the responsibilities that went with being a husband and father. The saddest part was I really didn't know the answer to that question.

Still leaning close to my ear, Dandy added, "Park, I know you love me and want the best for me. I feel that in my heart just from the way you look at me. And please don't take what I just said as an ultimatum or a question you have to answer right this minute. Just please make it soon, darling."

With that, she gave me a kiss on the cheek and the discussion was over. At least it was over for the moment. Monday was the deadline by which I'd promised to let the Mutual Broadcasting System know whether or not I would be joining their ranks. I was rapidly running out of shillyshallying time.

Twenty-Five

Grand Central Air Terminal—Glendale

Grand Central Air Terminal is situated eight or nine miles north of downtown Los Angeles in the San Fernando Valley community of Glendale. The terminal, itself, is one of those buildings that could only have been created in southern California—a picture postcard of Spanish and deco architecture surrounded by palm trees and set against a stunning backdrop of the Verdugo Mountains. It's a fitting preview of the excitement to come for air travelers arriving in Los Angeles for the first time.

After a short wait while the plane's baggage compartment was unloaded, I found our suitcases in the pile on the cart, and we headed through the terminal and out the main entrance to the airport's circular drive. I was wondering if Don succeeded in getting my message to Neeko when I spotted him standing next to his yellow and black cab at the end of the taxi line. He waved and we headed in his direction.

Neeko shook my hand enthusiastically, saying, "Is good to see you again, boss. Neeko think he won't see you no more when the cops take you away last time."

"It's good to see you, too, Neeko. I had to come back so we can catch our bad guy. Oh, I want you to meet Dandy Harrison. Dandy, this gentleman is Neeko Nickolopolis, the best cab driver in all of Los Angeles."

Neeko bowed slightly from the waist and Dandy surprised both of us by saying something in a language I assumed was Greek. I couldn't be sure, though, because all foreign languages are Greek to me.

Suddenly Neeko was grinning from ear to ear and jabbering back in whatever language they were speaking. Their short conversation ended with Neeko giving Dandy a hug, during which she winked at me over his shoulder.

When the hugging was over, Neeko deposited our suitcases in the trunk of his cab and asked, "Where we going today, boss?"

"We have several places to go. How much will you charge me to rent your cab for the whole day?"

He made a face like he was deep in thought for a moment, and then grinning, he said, "If it just for you, Neeko charge ten dollars, but with pretty lady along, we make deal for only five dollars. Okay, boss?"

"You've got yourself a deal."

With that, we all climbed into the cab and Neeko said, "Where to first, boss?"

"Do you know Thelma Todd's old Sidewalk Café on the coast road?"

"Sure, boss, but that place all closed up now, nobody there no more."

"I know, Neeko. I just want to get another look at the building to refresh my memory."

Neeko's expression in the rearview mirror told me my reason for going to an old, closed up restaurant didn't make much sense to him, but he put the cab in gear without a word and we headed out of the airport.

Looking at Dandy in the seat next to me, I said, "Where in heaven's name did you learn to speak Greek, if that was Greek you were talking with Neeko?"

"It was Greek, all right. A wonderful old Greek woman worked for my parents when I was a little girl. She taught me enough words and phrases to hold up my end of a simple conversation. Then, during the summer after I graduated from high school, father took me along on a business trip to the Greek Isles and I learned more of the language there. It's a beautiful part of the world and the people are the nicest you could ever meet."

"Dandy, you are a constant source of amazement to me."

She grinned. "And don't you forget it."

It took the better part of an hour for Neeko to navigate across Los Angeles to the Roosevelt Highway, better known locally as the coast road. Once there, he swung north and a few minutes later we pulled into the empty parking lot of a three-story building shaped like a backwards L and tucked back against a steep hillside on the east side of the highway. Up until a few years ago this place bustled with activity as Thelma Todd's Sidewalk Café. Now the Spanish-style building with its tile roof and arches looked empty and gloomy in the morning fog.

With Neeko and Dandy in tow, I got out and walked to the arched entry at the inside corner of the L. To our left, the long leg of the L was two-stories and ran north, parallel to the highway. The first floor façade featured seven equally-spaced arches, each providing an opening for a door or window. Above the arches, windows with spectacular views of the beach across the highway lined the second floor, which once housed the restaurant's main dining room.

To our right, the short leg of the L was a continuation of the same façade, except there was only room for two arches. I remembered buying a pack of cigarettes in a drugstore that occupied the first floor on this side of the L. Like Thelma's restaurant, the drugstore was long gone. The second floor area above the drugstore housed the apartments used by Thelma Todd and her business partner.

Directly above the building's main entrance in the corner of the L was a large, cupola-shaped third floor area that Todd and her partner planned to make into a steakhouse addition to their restaurant. It was this spot Charlie Luciano was eyeing as the perfect place for a gambling operation.

Standing there, letting my memories from the time I spent in this building covering Todd's death for the *Times* come back to life, I heard Dandy ask, "What is this place, Park?"

"This was once the hottest night spot on the coast, Thelma Todd's Sidewalk Café. It's also where Todd was found dead almost three years ago."

Neeko nodded in agreement with my answer as Dandy said, "She was killed in her restaurant?"

"Nobody knows for sure where she was killed. Her body was found in the garage of that house." I pointed to a multi-story residence climbing the hillside above the restaurant. "Todd's business partner and lover, Roland West, owned the house and his wife lived there at the time. Todd and West lived in adjoining apartments on the second floor at this end of the café."

"That sounds like a cozy arrangement."

"It was, except West was the jealous type. The Saturday night before Todd was killed she was going to a party in Hollywood, leaving West stuck here to run the restaurant. West got upset and told Thelma he would lock her out of the building if she wasn't home by two a.m."

"Charming fellow. Did she make it back by his deadline?"

"No. Thelma didn't leave the party until around three Sunday morning. That was the last time she was seen alive by any reliable witnesses, although she was reportedly seen by several people in Hollywood on Sunday. One witness even claimed to have talked with her on the telephone Sunday afternoon. Regardless of whether or not any of that's true, Todd's maid found Thelma in the garage of that house up there Monday morning. Todd was in her car still dressed for the Saturday night party and deader than a doornail."

"Wow! That story has all the makings of a great mystery novel."

"You haven't heard the half of it. Things went from bad to worse when the LAPD and the county medical examiner showed up. They managed to mess things up to the point where almost none of the case's evidence was reliable."

"Was your former boss part of all that?"

"No. If he'd been there the case would have been handled differently. The chief of police assigned a special elite homicide squad to work on the case, ostensibly because it involved a celebrity and he wanted the investigation to look good for the press. Or, if you believe some people who were around back then, the chief used a hand-picked team for the investigation because he and the DA wanted to control the outcome of the investigation."

Tilting her head slightly to one side, Dandy asked, "Are you one of those people?"

I nodded. "It's hard for me to accept that the department, the district attorney, and the county coroner could foul up an investigation as bad as they did without working at it."

"Why would they do that?"

"Because the fix was in. It's fairly common knowledge that Charlie Luciano and his boy, Bugsy Siegel, own the district attorney down here. The guy's name is Buron Fitts—the same guy who's trying to close down the gambling ships—and he's in his third term as DA. It doesn't seem to matter how badly he fouls things up or how many scandals he's connected to, the people keep electing him."

Sounding very much like the trained reporter she is, Dandy asked, "You said the county coroner made mistakes in Thelma's case?"

"Yeah, some big ones. First off, the medical examiner initially set the time of death at two a.m. Sunday morning. That meant Todd was dead for more than thirty hours when she was found, but rigor mortis usually sets in about twelve hours after death, and she was just starting to stiffen up when the cops got here Monday morning a little before noon. The ME's time of death also contradicts several reliable witnesses who testified that Todd was still at the Trocadero at two a.m. Sunday morning.

"Ultimately the time of death was revised twice and ended up at six p.m. Sunday evening. The coroner's office also issued a final ruling that Todd's death was accidental, disregarding strong evidence to the contrary. About the only piece of irrefutable information to come out of the coroner's office was that the cause of death was carbon monoxide poisoning."

Dandy looked puzzled. "How did she get carbon monoxide poisoning?"

"The official explanation was that Todd found herself locked out of the restaurant, so she climbed back up the hill to the garage and sat in her Packard touring car with engine running to stay warm. When she was found, the garage door was closed, which allowed the garage to fill with exhaust fumes from her car."

Neeko chimed in to add, "Exhaust smoke is bad to breathe. It make you very sick, maybe even dead."

Dandy nodded her understanding of Neeko's comment and said, "You would think she'd have known better."

"Yes you would, but the autopsy showed more than enough alcohol in her blood to qualify her as drunk at the time of death. The conclusion was she was too drunk to realize the danger.

"Even if you buy that, though, there are other holes in the theory, like the shoes she was wearing. The soles looked brand new despite her supposedly hiking first down, and then up a 270-some step concrete stairway on her way from and back to the garage after discovering she couldn't get into the restaurant. And she didn't take her shoes off for that hike because her stockings showed no wear either.

"The long and short of it is DA Fitts convinced the Grand Jury to return a verdict of accidental death. When the verdict came down Toddy's body was released and immediately cremated, putting the kibosh on any possibility of reexamining the only real evidence in the case. End of story."

Dandy shook her head. "Amazing."

"Isn't it? Okay, I've seen all I need to see here. Let's move on before time gets away from us."

Neeko asked, "Where to next, boss?"

"To Hollywood; the Trocadero nightclub."

Neeko got his cab headed back in the direction we'd come

from without comment. I was pretty sure, however, that he was wondering why I wanted to go to a Hollywood nightclub at eleven o'clock in the morning.

Twenty-Six

Café Trocadero—8610 Sunset Boulevard

Traffic got heavier the closer we got to Hollywood, and while Neeko skillfully bobbed and weaved his way through and around lines of drivers who drove as if they had no idea where they were going, I gave Dandy the lowdown on the Café Trocadero, or the Troc, as it is commonly called by Hollywood highbrows.

"The Trocadero was opened by a guy named Billy Wilkerson back in thirty-four."

Dandy interrupted my dissertation. "Is that the same Wilkerson who publishes the *Hollywood Reporter*?"

I nodded. "They are one and the same. I think Wilkerson figured out it was easier to get celebrities coming to him than chasing them all over town to gather the latest gossip for his paper, so he built the Troc to be the classiest joint in town."

"I see. And why are we interested in this place?"

"Because it is the last place Thelma Todd was seen alive by enough people to make it a sure bet she was actually there. Toddy's pal, Ida Lupino along with Lupino's father, Sidney, threw that party Saturday night and Thelma was the guest of honor."

"Okay, I get that, but what are you accomplishing by visiting Thelma's café and this supper club?"

That was a good question and I gave Dandy an honest answer. "When I covered Todd's murder for the *Times* I was under the influence a good part of the time. I have the facts of the case down pat, but my memories of the people and places need to be in clearer focus if I'm going to make good use of my interview with this Lupino woman. Returning to the scene—or scenes—of the crime is sort of clearing out the cobwebs in my head."

Dandy nodded without comment and Neeko pulled his cab into the Café Trocadero's parking lot on the north side of what is locally referred to as the "Sunset Strip." I leaned forward to look at the place through Neeko's windshield and my heart sank. Apparently the Troc underwent a major remodeling sometime during the past couple of years.

When I last saw the place it had character with large ornate windows looking out on the street, awnings over the sidewalk, and a stylish gabled roof topped by dormer windows and a nifty cupola. Now it was just a big, white cube of a building with a few pieces of deco art painted on the walls and a modern neon sign spelling out "Café Trocadero."

I leaned back in my seat and sighed, causing Dandy to ask, "What's the matter?"

"They remodeled the place. It doesn't look anything like it did when I last saw it. Coming here was a waste of time."

Neeko piped up from the front seat, "Yeah, boss, they have big fire here last year. They build it again, but everything different."

"I see that, Neeko."

"You get out to look?"

I glanced at my wristwatch and said, "No, I don't think so. I'm not going to accomplish much by looking at this version of the Troc. Besides, we're due at Columbia in a little over an hour. We should probably get ourselves some lunch so my stomach doesn't start growling in the middle of the interview. Let's jump up to Hollywood Boulevard and grab a bite at the Pig 'N Whistle."

Neeko worked more of his steering wheel magic and a few minutes later we pulled to the curb a few doors from the Pig 'N Whistle restaurant, which thankfully looked just like it did the last time I saw it.

Neeko said, "Neeko wait for you here. Have good lunch."

Feeling flusher than the thickness of my wallet warranted, I said, "No you don't, Neeko. You're part of this team and you're having lunch with us. Park this thing and let's go eat."

I saw Neeko looking at me in the rearview mirror. With a big smile on his face he said, "Okay! Thanks, boss."

By one-thirty we were rolling east along Sunset Boulevard again approaching Gower Street—an area that was considerably less affluent than the other parts of Hollywood we'd been through. This detail did not escape Dandy's notice. She said, "This must be the low-rent part of town."

"Yup. We are in what's generally known as Gower Gulch or

Poverty Row, take your pick."

"Where did those names come from?"

"Well, the Columbia Drugstore up here at the corner of Sunset and Gower is where cowboys from local ranches hang out in hope of getting studio work as extras and sometimes as stuntmen. When a studio like Columbia or Republic is filming a western they send someone over here to round up a few cowhands to ride around in front of the cameras and look like . . . well, like cowhands. That's how Sunset and Gower became known as Gower Gulch."

"What about Poverty Row?"

"That goes back fifteen or so years when the picture business was just getting started around here. Movie making seemed to a lot of guys like a good way to make a fast buck, so just about everyone who could buy or rent a motion picture camera came to Hollywood and started up a movie studio. Most of them were operating on the cheap and they settled in this part of town because building rents were lower, hence the name Poverty Row."

Dandy gave this some thought, and then said, "I thought Columbia was a big studio. How did they end up in Poverty Row?"

"Columbia is one of the few little studios that made a success of it. Over the years they got bigger and bigger, buying out the smaller companies and expanding. Now they take up two or three city blocks south of Sunset on Gower."

With that, Neeko took a right onto Gower and a hodge-podge of large and small structures appeared on our left. A warehouse-style building that was half a block long bore a gigantic sign announcing we had arrived at Columbia Pictures. Columbia's main entrance was further down the block, and as Neeko turned into it, a big guy in an overstuffed guard's uniform lumbered out of his shack.

The guard walked up to Neeko's window and said in a brusque tone, "State your business."

I rolled down the driver-side rear window and said, "Parker Atkins to see Ida Lupino."

The guy bent over a little to see who was talking, and then consulted his clipboard. I could see his lips moving as his eyes slowly followed his finger down a list of names. Finally he said, "Okay, you're on the list. Drive straight ahead and turn left at the second street you come to. Miss Lupino's bungalow will be the third one on your right. Don't go anywhere else on the lot."

With that he turned, making a beeline for the comfort of his shack and Neeko pulled forward to creep through the heavy lunchtime pedestrian traffic clogging Columbia Pictures' main artery. I could tell from Dandy's expression she was getting a kick out of the odd population just outside the cab's windows. From technicians in overalls to important looking guys in suits to actors costumed as everything from cowboys to Roman gladiators, she was seeing a living cross-section of the movie business, and the scene clearly fascinated her.

At one point we came upon a guy in a shaggy gorilla suit riding a bicycle. She pointed him out and said, "Now there's something you don't see every day."

The only reply I could think of was, "Thank God."

The foot traffic thinned out after we made our left turn. This was the studio's high-rent district—the realm of those whose elite star status earned them the luxury of a private bungalow in which to relax between sessions in front of the camera. While lesser actors settled for trailer accommodations scattered around the lot, stars of Ida Lupino's stature spent their off time in small, but pleasant little cottages, complete with tiny flower beds and shade trees. A tidy little sign affixed to the third bungalow on our right read, "Miss Lupino."

As Neeko pulled up behind a bright yellow four-door Packard convertible with tall white-sidewall tires and gleaming nickel trim, I turned to Dandy and said, "I wish you could come in with me, but my sense of the situation is that I'd better fly this one solo."

Dandy smiled and said, "I understand, Park. I don't mind waiting for you. Neeko is good company and we have plenty of entertainment outside the windows to keep us occupied. Good luck with your interview."

Promising not to be any longer than necessary, I got out of Neeko's cab and walked toward the little white bungalow with pale blue trim. Stepping up onto a small concrete porch, I gave the door a couple of light raps with my knuckles.

Twenty-Seven

Ida Lupino's Cottage—Columbia Pictures Lot, Hollywood

The short, round brunette who answered my knock on Ida Lupino's bungalow door stared up at me through ornately framed glasses with lenses so thick they made her eyes appear enormous." Yes?"

"Good afternoon. I'm Parker Atkins."

Recognition dawned after only a moment's hesitation and the woman said, "Oh, yes, Mister Atkins. I'm Janet Johansson, we spoke on the telephone. Miss Lupino is expecting you. Please come in."

She held the door open wide and I stepped past her into a small sitting room, thus increasing the room's occupancy to a total of four. Miss Johansson closed the door and introduced me to the attractive dark-haired woman sitting comfortably at one end of a couch upholstered in a blue and gray floral print. Her dressing gown perfectly matched the blue in the couch.

"Mister Atkins, please meet Miss Lupino. Ida, this is Parker Atkins, the radio reporter from San Francisco I told you about."

Ida Lupino was easily one of the most striking women I've ever met, which made me think I ought to go to the movies more often. Under medium-length dark brown hair done in soft curls, her narrow features were balanced with high cheekbones, a smallish mouth with full lips, and a pair of dark sparkling eyes below carefully arched eyebrows. She had an expressive face and it was expressing a warm welcome with a smile that looked sincere as she said, "Hello, Parker. Please have a seat, won't you?"

She gestured toward an overstuffed chair facing the couch and

I sat in it. As I did so, the fourth person in the room, a muscular, Italian-looking fellow standing quietly in the corner followed my every movement with alert eyes. Since we hadn't been introduced, I guessed he was hired help—judging by his inexpensive black suit, perhaps a bodyguard or chauffer, or both. He definitely wasn't a butler. Butlers don't come with the muscles this guy had.

I said, "Thank you for seeing me on such short notice, Miss Lupino. I appreciate you making time for me."

Wearing an expression that said she appreciated my appreciation, Miss Lupino said, "That's quite all right, Parker. I understand you are doing a story on Thelma. Is that correct?"

Her face underwent a subtle change as she spoke. When she finished the question, her expression was one of curiosity with more than a modicum of suspicion mixed around the edges. It told me I needed to tread carefully if I was going to get the cooperation I was hoping for. Initially, I planned to stick with my original story that I was doing a retrospective report on Thelma Todd, and then try to subtly sneak the subject of Todd's San Francisco boyfriend into the conversation, but I tossed that plan out the window. Ida Lupino struck me with the strong impression of being a no nonsense type of gal—one who wouldn't take kindly to being duped. I decided to lay my cards on the table right off the bat and take my chances on her reaction.

I said, "Essentially, but there's a little more to it than that. You see, I was a reporter for the *Los Angeles Times* when Miss Todd died and I covered her story in detail then, so I'm familiar with the circumstances." I paused and took a breath.

Then, throwing all caution to the wind, I said, "At the time I had some doubts about the official cause of her death, and now some things are happening down here that may be tied in and give me even more reason to doubt the coroner's suicide verdict."

I watched Ida Lupino's face intently as I spoke and saw her eyebrows rise when I mentioned my doubts about Todd committing suicide. As her eyebrows were going up, she was also staring intently into my eyes. When I finished, our eyes remained locked for several seconds before she blinked and shifted her gaze. Now her head was cocked slightly to one side and she stroked her chin with a well-manicured thumb. She was making up her mind about something.

Finally, Ida Lupino said, "I see." Then she turned to the brunette, who was propped up on the opposite arm of the sofa, and said, "Janet, now would be a good time for you to take a break." Then, turning toward the quiet gorilla in the corner, she said, "Giorgio, you can go, as well." Glancing at me, she added with a twinkle, "I don't think Parker has any evil intentions."

The brunette started to protest, but Giorgio simply nodded and walked toward the door. Miss Lupino sent Miss Johansson a glance that sent her scurrying after Giorgio without another word.

We both watched them leave, and when the bungalow door closed, Miss Lupino looked me in the eye again and said, "Parker, I pride myself on being a good judge of character, and I sense that you are on the level, despite not being entirely forthcoming when you made this appointment. I see now, though, that you may have had a good reason for caution then. So pray tell me what 'things' are happening down here that may be connected to poor Thelma's murder."

With confidence bolstered by her words, I began my story. "While I was down here last week gathering material on another story, I learned about what the newspapers are calling the Mob Avenger case. Are you familiar with it?"

Miss Lupino's eyes never left mine as she answered, "Somewhat. I've seen a few of the *Times* articles. I don't know all the details, but it seems to me that anyone bent on ridding us of vermin, albeit illegally, is doing a public service. The city ought to award him a medal."

I smiled. "I imagine many Angelinos agree with you on that score; however, the cops see it differently. Anyway, to make a long story short, I was curious about the case, so I asked a homicide detective friend of mine for the details. That's when I stumbled on a coincidence the police missed."

Ida Lupino leaned slightly forward, apparently intent on every word I spoke. She said, "And what is the coincidence?"

"According to the police timeline, the five murders they knew about occurred every two months since February of this year, and always on or about the sixteenth of the month."

If I hadn't already figured it out, Miss Lupino's immediate response to that tidbit left no doubt in my mind that she was a sharp cookie. She said, "On the same day of the month as Thel's death."

"Exactly. What's more, with a little research, I turned up an earlier mob killing the police hadn't connected to the most recent deaths. That one took place on December 16 in 1936—the one year anniversary of Miss Todd's death. The second murder occurred exactly one year later. On top of that, the first victim was found on the beach across the highway from Miss Todd's café. There is also a seventh victim, but the police think he just happened to be in the wrong place when the Mob Avenger killed his most recent victim."

Ida Lupino's forehead was slightly furrowed in a thoughtful frown as she said, "So what you are telling me is that someone is out there killing Charlie Luciano's men in revenge for him killing Thelma. The killer isn't the Mob Avenger, at all, he's the Thelma Todd Avenger. Is that right?"

"That's my hunch. There is, however, a flaw in that theory. Only four of the six mobsters killed were associated with Luciano. The other two were Frank Nitti's boys."

Miss Lupino leaned back on the couch, apparently digesting the information. Then she leaned forward again and said, "Maybe the killer is mixing things up to keep the police from making a connection with Thelma."

That she came to the same possibility I reached about the Luciano-Nitti issue again reminded me I was dealing with one very savvy woman. I nodded and said, "Or the killer doesn't know which mob members belong to which mob. We don't know how he's identifying his victims, so that might also account for the discrepancy."

Ida Lupino's eyes were glued to mine again as she said, "Your discoveries are very interesting, Parker, but how does any of this provide the proof necessary to change the coroner's official findings and charge Charles Luciano with Thelma's murder?"

"If the killer has made a connection between Miss Todd's death and Charlie Luciano, it means he knows something we don't know—possibly he even has some kind of evidence that points to that connection."

"But if that's the case, wouldn't it be more logical for him to take his evidence to the police rather than going on a two-year murder spree?"

"Not if he believes, as I do, that DA Fitts is in Charlie Lucifer's pocket. Walking through the door to police headquarters with evidence that Luciano killed Thelma Todd, and in turn, that Fitts rigged the investigation of her murder wouldn't just be counterproductive, it could be suicidal. So, if I can identify the Avenger before the cops do, I could make whatever he knows public. That would blow the lid off of the cover-up and leave Fitts in a heck of a jam. Helping me find the Avenger before the police do is where you come into all this."

Certainly Miss Lupino was way ahead of me and knew where our conversation was going, but she gave nothing away in her reply. "How on earth do you think I can help you find this killer?"

"While I was down here last week I spent quite a bit of time with my friend the homicide detective, and on our way to look at something related to the story I was covering, he had to make a side trip to the scene of the most recent Avenger killing. That's how I became interested in the case. Then, later the same day, I was assaulted by a gunman on the Santa Monica pier for no apparent reason. In the scuffle, the gunman lost his hat. That hat turned out to be an expensive Italian import I traced to a Hollywood men's store. From the store we learned that the man who purchased the hat lives in San Francisco.

"When I connected all of the dots, I came to the conclusion that this man's interest in me stemmed from my visiting the scene of his last murder, making me an unknown element in the Avenger investigation. And that points to the San Francisco connection in Miss Todd's death."

"You mean her mysterious beau from San Francisco." It wasn't a question. Miss Lupino was still a jump ahead of me, and she still wasn't letting on that she knew where all this was going.

"Yes. I'm hoping you may have some additional information about him you didn't give to the police—maybe something you remembered since the investigation."

Now we were down to the meat of the matter. If I'd played my hand right, I'd given her enough good reasons to overcome any objections she might have to helping me find the Avenger. If not, I'd just wasted a lot of time and money on a wild goose chase.

While I waited, she gave the appearance of being deep in thought about my request. It's possible she actually was deliberating the matter, but my feeling that she'd been a step or two ahead of me throughout our conversation made me wonder. Ida Lupino was, after all, an actress and presumably capable of emoting with the best of them.

Finally she ended my apprehension by saying, "Okay, Parker, I will try to help you. What, specifically, do you want to know?"

With relief I hoped didn't show too much, I said, "Everything you can remember Miss Todd saying about the fellow in San Francisco. What he did for a living, how she met him, what he looked like . . . anything might help."

Without hesitation, she said, "Honestly, Thel really was very secretive about the fellow. That was unlike her. The main points I remember are that he lived in San Francisco, he was a successful business man, and she thought she'd finally found the right man for her."

"Did Miss Todd say how she met the guy?"

"I can't recall anything specific, but I have a vague memory of her saying something about meeting him at a party, I also have the feeling he spent a lot of time in Los Angeles—maybe on business. I'm not sure."

"Of course you never actually met him or saw him."

"No," she said thoughtfully, "but I almost caught them together once."

"Oh?"

"Yes. It was a weekday afternoon and I was in Santa Monica for some reason or other. I remembered Thel saying Roland was going to be away somewhere on business all week. You remember Roland West? He was her business partner in the restaurant."

"I remember him."

"Well, I never cared much for Mister West, so knowing he wouldn't be around made me think it would be a good time to visit Thel, so I drove up the coast to the café. When I arrived there were two cars in the front parking lot and one of them was Thel's new Packard, so I was pretty sure I'd find her home.

"I went up to Thel's apartment above the drugstore and knocked on the door. It took her a while to answer, and when she did, she only opened the door far enough to see who knocked. When Thel saw it was me, she came out of the apartment and closed the door behind her, saying something about she didn't have time for a visit because she was getting ready for a business meeting. Then she ushered me downstairs in what seemed like a rush. She even went out to my car with me. Thel was friendly, but it was obvious I'd picked the wrong time to call.

"When I opened the car door to get in, I noticed my Kodak on the seat and I asked Thel to pose for a photograph with her snazzy new car. She said okay, but to make it quick because she was running late.

"After I snapped the picture, she hurried back into the café and I drove home. That night Thel called me and apologized for, as she put it, giving me the bum's rush. She admitted the real reason she couldn't visit was that she was entertaining her friend from San Francisco and they only had a little time before he needed to leave. I told her I understood and that was the end of that."

I mulled her story over in my mind and came up with a long shot. I said, "You said there were two cars in the lot when you got to the café that day. Is there any chance the second car showed up in the picture you made of Miss Todd with her Packard?"

"Why yes, I believe it did. The cars were parked next to each other with Thel's Packard on the left. I took the picture from that side and slightly from the rear, so the other car must be in the shot. Also, the top was down on Thel's car which would have made the other car even more noticeable. Why?"

"I'll explain in a minute. Did you notice what kind of car it was?"

Miss Lupino thought for a moment, and then said, "I'm really not very good about automobiles. All I remember is that it was a big pale gray sedan. It looked new and expensive."

"Do you still have that photo?"

"I'm sure I do. It should be in one of my photo albums at home. Now, please tell me why the picture is so important."

"We believe the Avenger drives a gray Chrysler. If he and Miss Todd's mysterious man from San Francisco are the same person, you may have inadvertently taken a snapshot of his car. If the license plate is in the photo, it could lead me right to him. Is it possible I could see the picture today before I have to fly back to San Francisco?"

"I see no reason why not. I have one more scene to shoot at three, but it's a reaction close-up, so I ought to be home by four-thirty. Can you come to my apartment about then?"

I told her I could and Miss Lupino said she would write down the address for me. We both stood, and she left the room. I was still standing next to the chair when she returned with a small calling card. On one side elaborate script spelled out, "Ida Lupino." On the other side neatly hand-printed letters provided an address on North Rossmore Avenue in Hancock Park.

Slipping the card into my jacket pocket, I thanked Miss Lupino and was about to say I would see her at four-thirty when she interrupted me, asking, "Is that your cab out there?"

I turned and looked out the window behind the chair I'd occupied. "Yes, that's how I got here from the airport."

"Who is that cute girl in the cab?"

"That's my fiancée. She . . ."

"Please bring her with you to my apartment. I would love to meet the sort of woman who is attracted to a cagey fellow like you."

I think I may have blushed a little as I said I would bring Dandy with me and Miss Lupino ushered me out the front door of her bungalow. As I climbed into the cab Dandy asked, "So how was your meeting with the famous Miss Ida Lupino?"

"It was productive."

"More to the point, what's she like?"

"You can find out for yourself. We are going to her apartment later and she specifically requested that I bring you along."

Dandy smiled her coy smile and said, "Really?"

Twenty-Eight

Melrose-Hollywood Hotel—5100 Melrose Boulevard, Hancock Park

Leaving the Columbia lot, Neeko asked, "Where to next, Boss?"

That was a good question. I couldn't think of anywhere else I needed to go, but it was only two-thirty, which meant we had about two hours to kill. I said, "Our next meeting with Ida Lupino isn't until four-thirty, so it looks like we won't be flying home tonight. I guess we should find a place to stay. Her apartment is in Hancock Park. Neeko, you know of a decent place to stay in that area that isn't too expensive?"

Neeko gave the matter a few second's thought and said, "I think maybe the Melrose-Hollywood Hotel is good."

"Expensive?"

"Not so much, maybe ten dollar for night. Is closest hotel I know to Hancock Park. We go there?"

Ten bucks was nearly twice what I paid at the New Brunswick on my last visit, but Dandy was with me this time, so it seemed like a little higher class place was in order. I did the mental arithmetic and decided I could afford the extra tariff for one night. I said, "Okay, Neeko, the Melrose-Hollywood it is."

Neeko took a left out of the studio lot onto Gower, and three blocks later he took another left onto Santa Monica Boulevard. A long concrete wall on our right marked the northern boundary of Hollywood Memorial Cemetery, the final resting place of just about everybody who was anybody in Hollywood's sordid past.

The cemetery grounds took up five of the seven blocks to Wilton Place, where Neeko turned right and headed south.

Between Santa Monica Boulevard and Melrose we were in a quiet, respectable residential neighborhood with plenty of vacant lots waiting to accommodate the continuous flow of newcomers to paradise.

A left turn put us in the 5100 block of Melrose with the Melrose-Hollywood Hotel on our right. In fact, the Melrose-Hollywood took up the entire block with a long three-story brick and white edifice decorated to the hilt with gewgaws and gargoyles.

As Neeko pulled into a parking space near the hotel's entrance, Dandy said, "Will you look at that! It looks like something right out of classical French literature."

Staring at the hotel's gaudy red entrance doors, complete with gold filigree trim, I muttered, "If you say so."

Dandy grinned at me and said, "Oh come on, Park. Be a sport. This will be fun!"

I said, "Uh-huh"

While I opened the door on Dandy's side of the cab, Neeko opened the trunk and set our bags on the sidewalk. Then he said, "Neeko wait here, make sure you get room. Then be back four-fifteen for drive to Hancock Park. Not far."

I thanked him and in we went through the bright red doors. Inside, the Melrose-Hollywood was just as gaudy as it was on the outside. The walls were covered in flocked maroon wallpaper surrounded by broad white trim moldings. A white fireplace filled the wall opposite the entrance, and overhead gilt chandeliers hung from a white ceiling decorated in what looked like gold relief. The word "ostentatious" comes to mind, but doesn't begin to describe the scene.

Hoping Neeko was right about the cost of lodging in this shrine to opulence, I stepped up to the desk and asked about a room for the night. The young man behind the counter said a room with private bath was available on the second floor for nine dollars. I said we'd take it and signed us into the registration book as Mister and Missus Parker Atkins of San Francisco.

After completing the registration process I stuck my head out of the hotel's front entrance and gave Neeko a thumbs up signal. Then Dandy and I hiked up a flight of stairs, giving my bum knee more punishment it didn't need, and down a long hall to see what wonders our home away from home offered. It wasn't quite as bad as I expected.

Dandy was delighted with room 217. She wandered around the room pointing out such amenities as the French Provincial furnishings, a large gilt-framed wall mirror, a fully tiled bath, and sheer pink curtains tied back with wide maroon ribbons on each side of the windows. Even the bed was a sight to behold, with a large ornate headboard and matching night stands. Dandy flopped on said bed and pronounced it comfortable while I stowed our bags in the small closet adjacent to the bathroom.

I sat at a small writing desk to make a few notes in my book from my Lupino interview. After that, Dandy insisted I tell her all about Ida Lupino, which I did. And after that, I joined her on the bed for a short nap to give my knee a rest. It had already been a very long day.

At four-fifteen on the dot Dandy and I went out through the Melrose-Hollywood's red and gilt doors to find Neeko's cab at the curb. We climbed in and I leaned forward to show Neeko the address on the back of Ida Lupino's calling card. He took a look and said, "Sure, Boss. We be there in no time."

I slid back in the seat, helped by Neeko's rapid acceleration from the curb as he took advantage of a lull in the traffic to make a quick U-turn. Outside our windows the small businesses that populated this section of Melrose rolled by—mostly small retail shops and light manufacturing businesses interspersed with the occasional storefront eatery or filling station.

Further along Melrose, the scenery grew more prosperous in the form of larger retail shops, fancier restaurants, and RKO Radio Pictures with their giant world globe symbol over the studio entrance. This part of town was familiar territory to me because my first assignment after making Detective Sergeant was with the Hollywood Division. Based on that experience, I was fairly certain I knew what we'd find at 570 North Rossmore Avenue, although I didn't actually recognize the address.

A few minutes later, when Neeko swung left onto Rossmore, I knew my guess about our destination was right. There was only one apartment building in this part of town that catered to movie people of Ida Lupino's means, the Ravenswood Apartments.

The Ravenswood is a large, seven-story Deco-Moderne building with a sidewalk awning over double glass entry doors. After promising Neeko he wouldn't have too long a wait, we went through the glass doors into a starkly streamline decor and stopped in front of two elevators, their doors finished in a bronze deco motif.

In traveling from the Melrose-Hollywood Hotel to the Ravenswood Apartments, we had gone from the sublime to the ridiculous. Or maybe it was the other way around. I wasn't sure which.

I pressed the "up" button between the elevator doors and Dandy said, "Very chic. I take it this is home to the rich and famous of Hollywood."

"Some of them. There are several swank apartment buildings and garden courts in town, but most of them are north of Hollywood Boulevard. Hancock Park is more for those who prefer a quieter lifestyle."

The self-service elevator dinged at us and I held the door open for Dandy. Following her into the mirrored box, I pressed button number five and up we went. On the fifth floor a tastefully lettered sign told us apartments 506 through 512 could be found to the right. A glance at my wristwatch told me we were right on time.

I was about to knock on the door marked "511" when I noticed a small doorbell button set in the wall next to the doorframe. First class all the way at the Ravenswood.

After only a moment's wait, the door was opened by a mature woman of Mexican heritage. Her costume told us she was Miss Lupino's maid. After determining that we were invited guests, the woman ushered us into the living room. Mees Lupeeno would join us in a meenute.

The living room had an open, airy feeling and was simply decorated in the Deco-Moderne style, with just a few paintings and decorative vases adding touches of color to mostly black and white furnishings. The place had an unembellished, no nonsense look that appealed to me. Apparently Dandy found it appealing as well. Quietly, she observed, "Miss Lupino has excellent taste in interior decorators."

While Dandy took a seat on the couch, I wandered over to one of the large multi-pane windows for a look at what sort of view the rich were having this season. The apartment was on the west side of the building, so it overlooked the leafy-green residential area of Hancock Park. In the distance were Beverly Hills and Bel Air against a backdrop of the Santa Monica Mountains—not at all a bad view.

As I turned to comment on the scenery, Ida Lupino entered the room. She was again wearing a dressing gown—this one in a dove gray material with a slight sheen to it. She said, "Good afternoon, Parker." Then turning to Dandy, she added, "And whom do we have here?"

Before I could make the introductions, Dandy said, "Hello Miss Lupino. I'm Danielle Harrison, better known to my friends as Dandy."

Ida Lupino offered her hand and said, "Then please call me Ida. I'm so pleased to meet you."

They shook hands in the dainty way women do such things, and I noticed Dandy remained comfortably seated on the couch throughout the exchange. Her demeanor was friendly with no indication of being thrilled to meet a motion picture star. That figured because Dandy is much more at home in the company of the rich and famous than I am.

Still facing Dandy, Miss Lupino said, "May I offer you a cocktail?"

"Thank you, Ida. If it isn't too much trouble, I would enjoy a dry vodka martini."

Then turning to me, Miss Lupino said, "And what will you have, Parker?"

"Just ginger ale on the rocks, please."

Ida Lupino gave me what might have been a knowing look in response to my request for a nonalcoholic beverage and issued instructions to her maid, who magically appeared when the word "cocktail" was uttered.

Ida joined Dandy on the couch and I said, "Miss Lupino, I want to thank you again for being so generous with your time. I'm sure you have more important things to do."

"You are entirely welcome, Parker. As for having more important things to do, I can't think of anything more important than finding poor Thel's murderer. Speaking of which, I believe you will find the picture you want to see in that photo album on the coffee table."

Picking up the maroon leather-bound album, I retired to a chair near the windows and began turning pages. As I looked through the collection of well-known faces Ida Lupino had captured with her Kodak, she and Dandy chatted about the differences between living in San Francisco and Los Angeles.

About a third of the way into the photo album I found what I was looking for. In the small black and white image Thelma Todd was standing with one foot on the running board of her Packard and grinning a typical snapshot grin. I was pleased to see that Miss Lupino made the same mistake most people make when using a Kodak.

Seen through a Kodak viewfinder, things appear closer than they really are. As a result, most snapshots included much more of the scene than one expected. The Thelma Todd photo was wide enough to encompass most of the car parked next to her Packard.

Interrupting the stimulating conversation taking place on the couch, I asked, "Miss Lupino, by chance do you have a magnifying glass?"

"I believe I do. I'll get it for you."

A moment later she returned to the living room with a good-sized lens encased in a brass ring with a turned wooden handle. Holding the photo album up to the light from the windows, I focused on the car next to Todd's Packard. I easily identified the second car's distinctive shape as that of a Chrysler Airflow, although the model year was in question. I remembered that the Airflow was introduced in 1934 because its sleek aerodynamic shape created quite a stir in automobile circles. The problem was the basic design of the Airflow remained essentially unchanged for several years and I wasn't familiar enough with Chryslers to recognize the subtle trim pieces or features that would tie down the model year.

Neither could I say for sure that the Chrysler in the black and white photo was gray. It appeared light enough, however, to support Miss Lupino's recollection of the car's color.

Next I focused in on the Chrysler's license plate. It was mounted above the left tail light and was surprisingly clear. Until 1935 California issued new license plates every year, alternating annually between yellow numbers on black backgrounds and black numbers on yellow, but for several years beginning with 1935 all plates were yellow on black. Since the Chrysler's plate showed up in the photo as light numbers against a black background, and since Miss Lupino described Thelma Todd's Packard as new, and since the photo was taken before Thelma Todd died in December of thirty-five, it was a pretty safe bet the Airflow was a 1935 model.

Finally, I squinted at the numbers on the plate. California license numbers consist of three groups of two numbers, with the exception that the second character in the first group is a letter rather than a numeral. The style of the characters on license plates is designed to be read from a distance, but expecting to pick them out from a small Kodak print is asking a lot. However, after staring at the plate for several minutes, I was fairly sure the first two characters were a six and an H, and the last two appeared to be two and four.

I set the photo album and magnifying glass in my lap and took out my notebook to jot down the details I'd picked out from the photo. As I wrote, Ida Lupino said, "Parker, you look just like Sherlock Holmes over there with that magnifying glass. Are you learning anything useful from the picture?"

"Yes, I am. I've identified the car as a Chrysler and I have four of the six numbers on the license plate. May I borrow this photo? I promise I'll send it back to you in good condition."

"Of course. You have my address. Just drop it in the mail when you're through with it."

I thanked Miss Lupino, and shortly thereafter, we said our goodbyes. During the elevator ride to the first floor, I said to Dandy, "You and Miss Lupino seemed to be hitting it off pretty well."

"She's lovely, Park. Sometimes celebrities put on airs, but I don't think there's a phony bone in Ida's body. She's as real as can be."

"She's also an actress. Don't forget that."

"Oh, Park. You are such a cynic. Take my word for it. Ida Lupino is a hundred percent real."

Back in Neeko's cab, I looked at my wristwatch. It was a few minutes past five, and I felt pretty good about what I'd accomplished since arriving in LA about eight hours ago. Ida Lupino had proven cooperative, and as a result of her cooperation, there was a fair chance we could now identify the Mob Avenger— not at all bad for a day's work. My only remaining chore for the day was to call Don Chambers with the new information I had so he could check it out with the Department of Motor Vehicles in Sacramento.

"Where to now, Boss?"

"I think we can call it a day, Neeko. Let's head for the barn."

"Okay, Boss."

Back at the Melrose-Hollywood I thanked Neeko again for all the time he'd devoted to us and asked if he could give us a ride back to Grand Central Air Terminal in the morning. He asked what time and I deferred to Dandy who produced a United Airlines timetable from her purse and informed us there was a flight to San Francisco leaving at ten-fifteen. Neeko said he would pick us up at eight-thirty.

In the hotel lobby, I gave Dandy our room key and slid into a public phone booth. Figuring it was unlikely Don would be at Central Division this late on a Saturday, I tried his home phone first. I figured correctly. Don answered on the second ring.

"Don, it's Park."

Sounding like he was chewing something—probably a baloney sandwich—Don said, "I was wondering if I was going to hear from you today. You get anything useful out of that actress dame?"

"Maybe."

"What did she tell you?"

"It's not so much what she told me; it's what she showed me."

"Okay, what the hell did she show you?"

"A photograph of the Mob Avenger's car with part of its license plate."

I recounted my interview with Ida Lupino and described the photo to him. When I finished, he said, "Sounds like you could have something there. Give me the partial plate number and I'll teletype it to DMV. We might get a name and address back by Monday."

I gave him the license numbers I had, along with a description of the Chrysler. Then he said, "You heading back to Frisco now?"

"In the morning. You come up with anything new?"

"Not a thing. I've had officers canvassing the neighborhoods around the crime scenes again and we've gone back over the autopsy reports. I even called Ben Siegel to see if he could tell us anything. It all adds up to zero."

"Chief Davis still lookin' over your shoulder?"

"What do you think?"

"Well, maybe you'll have something to tell him on Monday."

"I sure hope so." After a pause he added, "Thanks for the tip, Park. I'll call you as soon as I get word back from DMV. You be in your office on Monday?"

"I expect so."

"Okay, have a good flight home."

I climbed the stairs to room 217 and found that, while I was calling Chambers, Dandy used the room phone to change our United Airlines reservations to the ten-fifteen flight.

Deciding food was the next order of business, we walked across Melrose and enjoyed a pretty decent spaghetti dinner at a mom and pop Italian joint with red and white checkered tablecloths and candles stuck in wine bottles coated with candle drippings. After dinner we came back to the room and ended the day on an extremely pleasant note.

Twenty-Nine

When I managed to drag myself up out of a restless sleep Monday morning, there were two gremlins staring me in the face. One was impatience over having to wait for the DMV information on the partial license plate number from Ida Lupino's snapshot.

The other gremlin thumbing his nose at me was my indecision about the Mutual Broadcasting System job offer. This was the day I'd promised to call Jack Carpenter—Mutual's National News Director—in Chicago with my answer, and I still didn't know what that answer was.

The Mutual offer was the main topic of discussion between Dandy and I during our flight home the day before, and the discussion continued right up until the time I dropped Dandy off at her parents' home. After all the talk, Dandy's thoughts on the subject were still the same as they'd been from the beginning.

She had no qualms about up and moving to Chicago, but insisted the final decision had to be mine. It seemed clear to me, however, that she was in favor of me taking the job because it meant we could be married and get busy raising kids. The truth of the matter was that accepting the Mutual job was the only way that was going to happen in the foreseeable future.

While shaving, I took a good look at the guy in the mirror and it finally dawned on me that my indecision was a decision in itself. Regardless of Dandy's feelings on the subject, if I couldn't get committed to the idea of moving to Chicago, I really didn't want the job.

It wasn't necessarily a rational decision, but over the years, I'd learned to pay attention to my gut instincts. Back in my LAPD days those instincts had more than once gotten me out of jams that might have otherwise been fatal. Of course, my hunches weren't always right, but their batting average was pretty damned good.

Suddenly I felt like a ton of weight was gone from my shoulders. Yes, Dandy would be disappointed, and yes, I was throwing away an opportunity to make the big time right away, but none of that outweighed the feeling we would be miserable in Chicago. There had to be a better way to move in the direction I thought I wanted to go.

When I arrived at the KDG news closet a few minutes before eight, Charlie was already knee-deep in her morning chore of mining news nuggets from the AP wire service that were worthy of inclusion in my nightly broadcast. She looked up from the long yellow sheets torn off the wire service teletype, and clearly relieved that I was back from LA, said, "Good morning, Park. How was your trip?"

"Productive, I think. Hopefully, we'll know for sure before the end of the day."

I spent the next ten minutes giving Charlie a rundown on what I'd learned from Ida Lupino. Then Charlie asked a question on another subject.

"Park, isn't today the day you're supposed to tell Mutual whether or not you want the job they offered you? I don't mean to stick my nose in where it doesn't belong, but can you tell me what you decided?"

Somewhere in the back of my mind I knew Charlie was another reason behind my gut feeling Chicago wasn't for me. She's very, very good at what she does and we work well together. I was pretty certain there wasn't another Charlene Blanchard in the Windy City.

Sliding into the chair behind my desk, I said, "Yeah, I can tell you. I decided to stay right here at good old KDG for the time being."

Charlie looked surprised. "You're turning the job down? Why? It's the opportunity of a lifetime!"

"Maybe, but it's not the right opportunity for my lifetime. We can talk about all the reasons later, but that's my decision."

"What does Dandy think about your decision?"

My face must have given me away, because Charlie quickly said, "You haven't told her yet, have you? Oh, Park, she's going to be so disappointed."

I sighed. "I know she will, but I can't help it. I just don't want to move to Chicago."

Charlie studied my face for another moment, and then said, "I guess you know I have mixed feelings about this. On the one hand, I'm happy you're staying here and we can continue working together, but on the other hand, it makes me sad that you're disappointing Dandy and passing up a great opportunity."

I was aware that Charlie and Dandy had developed a close friendship over the past year or so, but I was a little surprised to discover they were close enough for Dandy to share so many of her feelings about our relationship. Apparently she had, though, because otherwise Charlie wouldn't have been so sure of Dandy's disappointment over my decision not to take the Mutual job. For some reason I was a little irked about that.

I said, "I know, Charlie. Now, we'd better get back to work."

Charlie looked a little hurt by my dismissal, but she said nothing and returned to her AP wire copy. I turned to my trusty Remington Model Five with the intention of writing the next installment of my special crime report on the Mob Avenger and accomplished nothing. My concentration was shot and it was going to stay shot until I made a couple of phone calls. So about nine I got up and headed down to the Owl Drug Store on the first floor.

After a sales clerk converted a couple of paper bills into a stack of coins, I closed myself into one of their payphone booths. I poked a nickel into the slot and dialed Dandy's number at the *Chronicle*. She was her usual perky self, but I had a bad feeling that was about to change.

"Good morning, Dandy Harrison."

"Hi, Dandy. It's Park."

"Hello, darling. How are you this morning?"

"I guess I'm okay. I'm just about to call Mutual, but I wanted to call you first and tell you what I decided about their job offer."

"Okay, I'm all ears."

"Dandy, I just don't think either one of us would be happy in Chicago, so I've decided not to take the job."

After a long pause, Dandy said, "I see."

"A better job is bound to turn up here in The City before long. I think that would work out a lot better."

"Park, you aren't concerned about your ability to do the job, are you? You're very good at what you do and I'm sure you could handle it."

Her question was valid given the self-esteem issues I've had in the past. I'd even asked myself the same question a few times. I said, "No, Dandy. I'm sure I could do the job. I just don't want us to wake up one morning two thousand miles away wishing to hell we'd never left San Francisco."

I heard her sigh before saying, "Okay, Park. I said you should do what you think is best, but I was really hoping the Mutual job would be a new start for us."

"I know, Dandy. I was hoping the same thing. I just can't get past the feeling that it is the wrong thing to do."

"I understand, Park."

Trying to perk her up again, I said, "Are you free for lunch? Maybe we . . ."

"I can't today. There's a Children's Welfare luncheon I need to cover. Maybe tomorrow."

I could tell from the tone of her voice that Dandy wasn't happy with me. I expected that, but I was hoping for something else. I said, "Okay, Dandy. I'll let you get back to work. Call you tonight?"

"That would be fine, Park. Goodbye."

I sat back in the phone booth and sighed. Now I was in Dutch with both of the women in my life. I could handle Charlie being unhappy with me, but Dandy was different. I expected her to be upset, but her reaction was worse than I anticipated. Convincing Dandy I made the right decision was going to take some doing, assuming I really was making the right choice.

Jack Carpenter was much more understanding. He appreciated my reluctance to move and promised to give me a call if a position opened up at one of Mutual's California affiliates.

Back upstairs, I returned to my typewriter and renewed my efforts to write Monday night's edition of my crime report on the Mob Avenger. I got a little further this time, but I still wasn't cooking on all four burners.

Part of the problem was that I really didn't have anything new to tell my listeners. It would be foolish at this point to spill the beans about my Thelma Todd theory and the San Francisco connection from Ida Lupino. If I reported those details and we were on the right track, my broadcast might tip off the Mob Avenger that we were on his trail. If we were on the wrong track, I would end up with egg all over my face. So my crime report became a summary of the bits and pieces Don gave me about how he was pursuing the case. It wasn't much, but it was all I had.

Around noon, Charlie announced that she was going out for lunch and asked if I wanted her to bring something back for me.

The way my stomach felt, I wasn't much in the mood for lunch, so I said no thanks.

Then Charlie looked me in the eye and said, "Dandy's upset, isn't she?"

I wondered how Charlie knew I already talked to Dandy, but I gave her a straight answer. "Yes."

Charlie just nodded knowingly, picked up her purse, and headed out the door. Relieved that the discussion ended there, I opened my notebook and began reviewing my Ida Lupino interview notes. That was when the phone rang. I picked it up and said, "Atkins."

A tinny version of Don Chamber's voice said, "Good, you're there. I was afraid you might be out to lunch."

"There are those who think that's my normal state. You hear from DMV?"

"Yeah, the teletype just came in. We asked 'em to put a rush on it and for once they did."

I picked up a pencil and prepared to jot down whatever Don had from the DMV. "What did they come up with?"

"They found eleven Chryslers that matched your partial plate. Of those, I pulled out four registered to owners with addresses in or near San Francisco. All four are either white or light gray. You want me to read 'em off?"

"Shoot."

"Okay, number one is Jonathon W. Barker, 78 Buena Vista Avenue in Mill Valley. Next we have Martha DiCasito, 18896 Brickell Way in Castro Valley. That's in your neck of the woods, isn't it?"

I was busy writing, so I nodded my reply. Of course, he couldn't see me, so there was silence on the line for a moment until I said, "Ah, yeah. Castro Valley is just across the bay, south of Oakland."

"Number three is Abraham Feingold at eleven-twelve Vancouver Avenue in Burlingame, and the last one is Elmer C. Wilkes at 593 Eighth Avenue in Frisco. Got that?"

I quickly finished jotting the last address and said, "Got it. What now?"

Don paused for a moment, and then said, "Well, I'm going to send these names off to central records in Sacramento to see if they set off any alarms, but that could take several days. I was kind of hoping you might do a little unofficial sniffing around for me . . . maybe take a drive by those addresses and see if anything looks interesting."

"Sure. That's what I planned to do anyway. It's nice to have your official approval."

"Hey, I said 'unofficial' sniffing around. Remember, Park, you ain't got a badge in your pocket anymore. Just take a look from a safe distance and see what you can see. That's all."

"Sure, Don. I'll have a look-see and let you know what I find. Anything else new with the case?"

"Not a blessed thing."

"Okay, Don. I'll be in touch."

"Thanks, Park. And remember, don't be a cowboy on this."

"I won't. Bye, Don."

I read through the list Don gave me and shook my head. The guy on the Santa Monica pier was a sharp dresser. With the possible exception of the Chrysler owner in Mill Valley, the addresses on the list weren't those of people who could afford imported Italian hats. It seemed more likely my guy lived in a higher class neighborhood.

Then it dawned on me that just because I couldn't afford to buy a new car every couple of years didn't mean there weren't people who could and did. The photo Ida Lupino took was three years old. It was possible, even likely, the car in that photo was no longer registered to its original owner. Maybe Mister Avenger traded the car in the photo for a newer model. Finding the name of previous owners from DMV would take more time, but I had a hunch I knew where I could get the information a whole lot faster.

Charlie had a glum expression on her face when I passed her leaving the office. Her expression didn't change when I said I was going out and I'd be back in plenty of time for my broadcast.

Thirty

The only Chrysler dealership in The City, McAlister Chrysler-Plymouth, took up half of the twelve-hundred block on Van Ness Avenue in the middle of San Francisco's "automobile row." The building housing McAlister's showrooms, service shop and offices was less ornate than most of the dealerships along Van Ness—a white three-story cube with large windows overlooking the intersection of Van Ness Avenue and Post Street. Huge stylized white letters spread across the full front of the building left no doubt as to its occupant: "JAMES W. McALISTER INC." Apparently you can't be humble in the car biz.

I pulled to the curb and headed for the used car department. I know the way because McAlister's was where I purchased my four-year-old Ford coupe about two years ago. The salesman I dealt with then was a friendly fellow named Jim Carney and I was hoping he still worked at McAlister's. He does. A voice off to my left said, "Mister Atkins! Hello! You ready to trade that Ford of yours for something newer?"

I was face-to-face with a large fellow who had a receding hairline and a broad smile on his face. I shook the big hand he offered and said, "No, Jim, the old gal still has plenty of life in her."

"You sure? I've got a really great deal on a spiffy 'thirty-seven P-Four Deluxe—a pretty blue one with low miles and good tires. It would be perfect for you."

"No thanks, Jim, but I could use a great deal on some information."

145

Jim looked a little puzzled, but ever the trooper, he said, "Sure. What kind of information do you need?"

I handed him Ida Lupino's snapshot and said, "Ever seen this car before—the one behind the Packard?"

He studied the photo for a moment and said, "Hey, that's Thelma Todd, the actress who died, isn't it? Sure looks like her."

"Yeah, that's Thelma Todd. The photo was taken outside her restaurant down in Malibu. What about the car?"

Still looking at the picture, he said, "Well, it's a 'thirty-five Airflow sedan. I can't tell much else, like the color or anything."

"It's light gray. I was hoping you might be able to tell from the license tag if you sold it here as a used car—maybe as a trade-in from someone who bought a new Chrysler."

He peered closely at the picture. "I can't really make out the plate number."

"The first two characters are six-H and the last two are twenty-four. That help?"

"Well, I could check it against our sales records, but that will take a few minutes. What's this all about?"

"I'm chasing down leads on a story for my news broadcast. The person I'm looking for lives in The City and drives a new Chrysler, but I think he owned the car in that photo before he bought the Chrysler he has now. Since you guys are the only Chrysler dealership in town, I thought he might have bought his new car here and left this one in trade."

He nodded. "Okay, Mister Atkins, I'll take a look." He hollered over to a salesman on the other side of the showroom, "Mike, I'll be off the floor for a few minutes. It's all yours."

Jim was gone about fifteen minutes, which I killed by imagining myself cruising along the coast on the Great Highway behind the wheel of a gleaming maroon nineteen-thirty-six model Chrysler Deluxe Eight convertible sedan, complete with an enclosed spare tire carrier on the driver-side front fender and a hundred-fifty horsepower eight-cylinder engine under the long, sleek hood.

I was enjoying the fantasy immensely until a neatly printed card on the windshield informed me that my dream could become a reality for only nine-hundred-and-fifty dollars—a sum nearly equal to half of my annual KDG salary. Oh well, easy come, easy go.

Jim's broad smile returned with him. "You were right, Mister Atkins. We took the car in your picture as a trade for a 'thirty-eight model just a few months ago. I remember this car now. It was in beautiful condition and we got it in at a good price, so the guy who bought it got a great deal." He looked at a slip of paper in his hand and added, "The name of the guy who bought it is Elmer Wilkes."

I glanced at my list of Chrysler owners from the DMV and knew I was on the right track. Elmer Wilkes was the sole Chrysler owner on the list who lived in San Francisco. Now it was time for the jackpot question. "Do you have the name of the man who traded it in?"

"Sure do. I figured that was what you wanted to know." He consulted his slip of paper again and said, "He's got quite a moniker, Arden Kendall, Junior."

I jotted the name in my notebook. "Got an address?"

"Mister Kendall lives at 338 Sea Cliff Avenue."

As I added the address to my notebook, Jim stepped closer and said quietly, "I'm glad I could find the information for you, Mister Atkins, but I hope you won't tell anyone where you got it. We're not supposed to give out information about our clients, but you being a customer and in the news business, I wanted to help you out."

I finished writing and said, "Mum's the word, Jim." I held the notebook up and added, "This will be just between you and me. Okay?"

"Thanks, Mister Atkins."

"Just out of curiosity, what did this Kendall buy when he traded in the old car?"

Without having to consult his notes, Jim said, "He drove out in a brand new 'thirty-eight Custom Imperial Eight Coupe. I sure remember that car. It was a beauty—one of the most expensive cars we've ever sold—a real sporty luxury model with plush seats and loads of shiny chromium plating. And with a 110 horsepower under the hood that little number can really fly!"

I already knew the answer to my next question, but I asked it anyway. "Color?"

"Phantom Gray with Pearl Gray interior trim."

I had to wonder about Mister Kendall's passion for gray. It seemed he dressed to match his cars, or vice-versa. Maybe he thought gray was so neutral it made him invisible.

Leaving the showroom, I sat in my aging Ford a few minutes going over what I just learned. If I had this thing figured right, the name and address of the most wanted man in the state were now scrawled on a page in my notebook. The address fit the man on the Santa Monica pier perfectly.

Sea Cliff was the hands-down winner for the snootiest neighborhood prize in a city that prides itself on snooty neighborhoods. Sea Cliff's name comes from its location high on a bluff overlooking the entrance to San Francisco Bay west of the Golden Gate bridge. It's relatively small as neighborhoods go, with, maybe, a hundred homes, but those homes are like nothing else in The City. Most of them easily qualify as mansions, and they have spectacular views of the ocean, the bridge, and the Marin Headlands across the Golden Gate.

If, as I was now almost certain, Arden Kendall, Junior was the Mob Avenger, I was getting closer to putting the noose around his neck, but first I had to make sure the resident of 338 Sea Cliff Avenue was the same dapper little jerk who poked a gun into my back. If he was, the pistol he left behind tied him to at least one of the mob killings and I had him.

Getting a look at the guy, however, was going to be tricky. I couldn't very well go up and knock on his door. I might be able to stake out his house and get a peek at him coming or going, but people who can afford to live in Sea Cliff and drive big luxury automobiles value their privacy, so somebody was bound to notice my definitely non-luxury Ford parked where it had no right to be.

My best move at this point was to do some background research on Mister Arden Kendall, Junior. Learning whatever there was to know about him might even provide me with more options for getting a look at the guy. In the meantime, I figured it wouldn't hurt to drive by and take a gander at his digs.

I pulled away from the curb and continued north on Van Ness. Five blocks later I turned left onto California Street and followed it all the way out to Twenty-Fifth Avenue, where I turned right. A block later, a left turn onto El Camino Del Mar led me to Sea Cliff Avenue and the twin stone pillars with their bronze plaques announcing to all who passed they were entering the little piece of coastal paradise known far and wide as Sea Cliff.

Not more than two minutes later I was looking at what might very well be the abode of the Mob Avenger. It was the last house on my right before Sea Cliff Avenue dead-ended half a block later.

Perched on a cliff above China Beach, the Kendall residence was a two-story affair reminiscent of a Mediterranean villa, or reminiscent of what I thought a Mediterranean villa might look like. It had an Italian tile roof with multiple chimneys growing out of the tiles. There were also wrought iron balconies, arched windows and other decorative doodads peeking out from behind a beige concrete wall with a sturdy iron gate and a lots of shrubbery.

At the far right of the property two parallel strips of concrete driveway met the street at a sharp angle and led off to a garage somewhere behind the house.

I learned all that in one slow pass. This was not the time to stop and gawk. It was clear, however, that I was right in my assumption that staking out Kendall's home would be difficult. The narrowness of Sea Cliff Avenue and the plethora of windows in the surrounding mansions pretty much eliminated any possibility of finding a spot from which I could watch the house without somebody calling the cops to roust me for loitering. In Sea Cliff they even roust seagulls for loitering.

I made a U-turn at the end of the street and took another quick look at Kendall's mansion as I passed it in the opposite direction. There were no visible signs of life, but that didn't mean anything. I didn't really expect to see the Mob Avenger out mowing his lawn.

When I got back to my office a little after three, Charlie was nowhere to be found. What I did find was my Monday night broadcast script placed carefully in the middle of my desk. On top of the script was a note from Charlie saying she left early to see a friend who needed her help, or words to that effect. The note struck me as strange because this was the second time in two days she'd left early. My script was done, however, and I certainly couldn't begrudge Charlie a couple of hours off for personal reasons.

I had plenty of time before my six o'clock broadcast, and I decided to use some of it finding out what there was to know about Arden Kendall, Junior. When it came to the rich and/or famous, my number one source was Dandy. Being The City's most-read society columnist, she knew the stories on everyone who was anyone in San Francisco.

Hoping Dandy had recovered some from her disappointment over my decision to turn down the Mutual job, I picked up the phone and dialed her office number. After several rings a voice I recognized as belonging to her assistant, Susie, said, "Miss Harrison's Desk."

"Hi Susie. This is Park Atkins. Is Dandy around?"

After a brief pause, she said, "No, Mister Atkins, she finished tomorrow's column and left early. I don't think she was feeling well."

That wasn't what I wanted to hear. I had a bad feeling I knew what was ailing Dandy—in a word, me. I said, "Okay, thanks Susie," and hung up the phone.

I now had a pretty good idea which friend Charlie left early to see. If I was right, Dandy was taking my decision to turn the Mutual job down a lot harder than I ever imagined. From somewhere in my brain an inner voice said, "Now you've done it, Atkins. You tossed away the job opportunity of a lifetime and the girl you love all in one shot. Nice work, jerk!"

Not wanting to hear any more of that kind of talk, I picked up the phone again and called Bobby Neumann down in the *Chronicle's* basement morgue. At least he was around to answer his phone. "*Chron* Morgue, Neumann."

"Hey Bobby, Park Atkins."

"What the hell do you want now, Atkins?"

"What makes you think I want anything, Bobby?"

"Because you always want something. You never call me for any other reason. What is it this time?"

Not feeling up to the witty comeback he was expecting, I said, "What do you know about a guy named Arden Kendall, Junior?"

"Not much. I know a little about Kendall, Senior, though."

"Okay, what do you know about Kendall, Senior?"

"He was a big shot in the ship building business . . . had a big facility out at Hunter's Point—a company called Kendall Marine Constructors, or something like that."

"You say he 'was' a big shot? He's dead?"

"Yeah, he died maybe four or five years ago. Junior took over the business for a while, but I think he sold it a year or so later. That help you any?"

"At this point anything helps. Any chance you might have a photo of Junior?"

"Maybe. I'm sure we ran pictures of his father, but I can't say for sure about Junior. I'd have to pull the clips."

"Could you do that for me?"

"This ain't the public library, Atkins. What's in it for me?"

"My everlasting gratitude and an exclusive for your crime reporters to run the morning after I break the story on my broadcast."

"You can keep the everlasting gratitude. What the hell are you working on?"

"I don't want to say until I nail this down for sure, but it's a major murder case and I'm damned close to solving it."

"Something like the Dougherty deal a year ago, huh?"

"Bigger. This one goes all the way to Los Angeles and back again."

I heard Bobby sigh before he said, "Okay, Atkins. You hit a

homerun on the Dougherty case, so I'm giving you the benefit of the doubt on this one. I'll pull whatever we've run on the Kendalls and have the clips for you sometime tomorrow."

"Thanks, Bobby. Any chance you could have those clippings for me today?"

"That's pushin' it. I've only got an hour and some change 'till quitting time."

"I hate to ask it, Bobby, but this thing is moving fast and I need to keep up with it. It would be a big help if you could find whatever you've got and leave it for me with the night guard at the front entrance so I can pick it up tonight after my broadcast."

"Geez, Atkins, I suppose you want the clips gift-wrapped and tied up with a pretty bow, too?" After a pause, during which I kept my mouth shut, he said, "Okay, I'll pull what clips I can find before quitting time and leave 'em at the front door, but you'd better be right about this, or we're kaput."

I was planning to call Don Chambers next, but I decided to wait until I saw what Bobby found for me. Instead I put in a long-distance call to Ozzie Gallagher at Hal Roach Studios. I owed him for the lead he'd given me and for setting up the Ida Lupino interview. Now was as good a time as any to repay that debt."

When his secretary put me through, Gallagher's gravelly voice said, "Hello, pain in the ass. What do you want now?"

His tone was nearly identical to Bobby Neumann's, and it occurred to me that my reputation as a crime-busting news reporter was in serious need of an overhaul.

"I've got something for you this time, Ozzie."

"Yeah? What's that?"

"The name of Thelma Todd's mysterious San Francisco boyfriend."

His response was loaded with skepticism. "Is that so? Okay, Mister Detective, what's his name?"

"Arden Kendall, Junior."

"How'd you come up with that gem?"

I explained the trail I'd followed from Ida Lupino's snapshot of Thelma Todd to the Chrysler dealership in San Francisco. When I finished, his tone was a little more respectful. "Sounds like you might have something there. And what's more, I'm pretty sure I've heard that name before?"

"Oh? In what context?"

"Well, don't quote me on this, but back in 'thirty-three RKO was in receivership and in bad need of new money. They hustled several new investors, and if my memory is right, this Arden

Kendall, Junior was one of them. It's the sort of name you don't hear often, so I think it might be the same guy."

"Could that be where Thelma Todd met him?"

Ozzie was quiet for a minute, and then said, "You know, it might be. Roach loaned Thelma out to several studios during that period and RKO was one of them. She made a loony thing called *Hips, Hips, Hooray* with Bert Wheeler for them in 'thirty-four, so the timing is right."

That was an important connection because it added credence Ida Lupino's impression that the Chrysler in her snapshot belonged to Todd's San Francisco boyfriend. It was another piece of the puzzle that slipped nicely into place. I said as much out loud, and Ozzie said, "So you think this Kendall guy has been killing off mobsters down here to avenge Thelma's murder?"

I wasn't surprised that Ozzie came to that conclusion. He was a sharp guy. "It's sure looking that way, but please keep all this under your hat for a while longer. If I'm on the right track here, I don't want to spook the guy before we can nail him."

"I can keep a secret. Nobody will hear it from me until the guy is locked up tight."

"Thanks, Ozzie. I'll let you get back to work now."

"Okay. And, Atkins, thanks for keeping me on the inside of this thing."

It was the first time I could remember Ozzie Gallagher ever thanking me for anything. Maybe I had risen above "pain in the ass" status in his book. I said, "You're welcome, Ozzie. Talk with you again soon."

I spent what was left of the afternoon reviewing Charlie's script and making a few annotations in the margins. Then, at quarter to six, I headed down the hall to my news booth in the studio.

Thirty-One

KDG Radio Studios–730 Market Street, San Francisco

My regular listeners might have detected slightly less enthusiasm than usual in my Monday night broadcast. Given the success I'd had tracking down Arden Kendall, Junior, I should have been enthusiastic as hell, but the knot in my stomach over Dandy's reaction to my decision against accepting the Mutual job put a big damper my mood.

So, before my closing theme ended, I was back at my desk dialing Dandy's home number. My hope that she was expecting my call and would answer the phone was shattered when Samantha Harrison's voice interrupted the third ring.

"Hello, Missus Harrison, this is Park. Is Dandy home?"

"Hello, Parker. Yes, Danielle is home, but I'm not sure she is up to talking right now."

With concern, I asked, "Is she okay?"

"Physically, she is fine. Her emotional state, however, is a different matter."

I sighed and said, "I guess she's pretty upset because I turned down the job offer in Chicago."

After a short pause, Samantha Harrison said, "Parker, I have always been frank with you in the past, and I shall be the same now. Danielle's expectations were probably set too high with regard to your job offer and what it meant to for your mutual future. She was certain you would take the job and you two would be off to Chicago and a new life together. I am not certain why she was so sure of that outcome, but whatever the reason, her dream for the future evaporated with your decision and Danielle is not able to see beyond that yet."

"Missus Harrison, I'm sorry . . ."

"Parker, stop that this instant! You have done nothing that requires an apology. In the year or so I have known you, I have come to respect your judgment, so I am confident you have good reasons for the decision you made. So, unless you led Danielle to believe you were going to accept the job, she brought this on herself."

"I tried very hard not to do that, Missus Harrison. She knew I was up in the air about what to do."

"That is as I suspected."

After a moment of silence, I said, "Missus Harrison, what should I do? I don't want to lose Dandy. She means everything to me."

"Not quite everything, Parker. I have no doubt that you sincerely love my daughter, but there are other factors in life you must naturally consider, both for your sake and for Danielle's. My opinion of you would not be as high if that were not the case.

"As for what you should do, the only suggestion I can offer is to give Danielle some time. I cannot say with any certainty how all this will turn out, but I know that Danielle is not seeing things clearly at the moment. Perhaps a few days' time will improve her vision."

"I guess, if she won't talk to me, I don't have any choice but to give her some time."

"Parker, I did not say she wouldn't talk with you. I said I wasn't sure if she was up to talking with you. I can try to put her on the line, but I sincerely doubt there is anything you could say tonight that would improve the situation. Shall I ask her if she would like to speak with you?"

"No, what you've said makes sense. Would you please just tell her that I called and . . ."

"And that you love her? Yes, Parker I will pass your feelings on to Danielle. I will also tell her you are concerned and anxious to set things right between you."

"Thank you, Missus Harrison."

"You are welcome, Parker, and as long as I am sticking my nose into your affairs, May I make one more suggestion?"

"Yes, please do."

"When you and Danielle do speak, the two of you must establish some reasonable expectations for the future. She desperately needs assurance that her relationship with you is going somewhere she can accept. I am afraid that, without such assurance, Danielle will find it difficult—perhaps, impossible—to continue your relationship. Does that suggestion make sense to you?"

"Yes, it makes very good sense. Again, thank you for your council."

"You are entirely welcome, Parker. Goodbye for now."

Feeling only slightly lower than a snake's belly, I rode the elevator down four floors and walked to my car. Really, the problem was simple to understand. Dandy wanted a commitment, and so far, I'd been content to let fate guide our path. What should have been obvious all along was finally clear to me. If I wanted to spend my life with Dandy, I needed to promise her a not too distant future that included marriage and children. The difficult part was deciding how—or even, if—I could realistically make such a promise. Doing so meant I had to honestly answer one question: Are marriage and children what I really want? Before today, I wouldn't have hesitated to answer that question in the affirmative. Now that push was coming to shove, however, I was no longer so positive of my answer.

Bobby Neumann was as good as his word. I picked up the manila envelope that bore my name from the *Chronicle's* night guard and headed for home. There, I put the remains of this morning's coffee over a burner and sat at the table to see what Bobby found for me.

The envelope contained four articles, neatly clipped together in chronological order. According to Bobby's notation, the first article was from the Sunday, April 10, 1932 edition's business section. Under the headline, "Hunter's Point shipyard celebrates tenth anniversary," the article described the launch of the steam freighter, Adriatic Sea, in conjunction with the ten-year anniversary celebration of Kendall Marine Constructors.

The second item was an obit dated February 21, 1934. It announced the passing of Arden Gordon Kendall, age 56, who resided in the Pacific Heights region of San Francisco. According to medical authorities, Kendall died of heart failure on February 19. He was survived by his son, Arden Kendall, Junior.

Immediately upon seeing the third article, I knew we had our man. The clipping was dated July 12, 1934 and the headline read, "Violence narrowly averted at shipyard." The article reported how San Francisco police officers were called out to prevent a riot when non-union workers hired by Kendall Marine Constructors in defiance of a general strike attempted to cross picket lines.

It wasn't the article, but a photo accompanying it that made me certain Arden Kendall, Junior was the guy we were looking for. Even without the aid of a magnifying glass I could clearly identify the man I encountered on the Santa Monica pier standing just inside the shipyard gate with his arms folded in a defiant posture. It was him, right down to the homburg cocked at a jaunty angle.

The final article was dated June 29, 1935 and announced the sale of Kendall Marine Constructors to a Seattle firm for the sum of twelve million dollars. Typically such articles were run with a photo of the old and new owners staring at the camera in the midst of a posed handshake sealing the deal. The fact that no such image accompanied this story made me suspect that Arden Kendall, Junior disliked and avoided publicity in all matters, not just when it came to his romance with Thelma Todd.

I got up from the table, poured a mug of stale coffee, and contemplated the case I was building against Kendall in terms of the traditional legal elements needed for a conviction; means, motive and opportunity. Because of the news photo, there was no longer any need to visually confirm Kendall as the gunman I encountered in Santa Monica, and a test slug from the gun he left behind on the pier connected him directly to the murder of Nitti henchman, Eddie Conti. That took care of the means for at least one of the Mob Avenger murders.

I also established a reasonable motive of revenge by identifying Kendall as Thelma Todd's mystery lover through Ida Lupino's account of her visit to the restaurant and the snapshot that included Kendall's car she took there.

All that remained was to establish that Kendall had the opportunity to kill Conti, which simply meant it had to be proven he was in Los Angeles last June 16. That would be easier to do once Kendall was arrested for the murder, which it seemed I could give Chambers reasonable cause to do. It was time to call Don.

Thirty-Two

Parker Atkins' Apartment—1284 McAllister St., San Francisco

With what I felt certain was the beginning of a resolution to the LAPD's Mob Avenger case, I picked up the telephone in my kitchen and dialed O for operator. Then I waited through the series of clicks and buzzes required for the long distance operator to connect me to Don Chambers' home number.

A slightly distorted voice said, "Hello." As seemed to be the routine lately, it sounded as if I had again interrupted Don in the middle of a sandwich.

I said, "Baloney or peanut butter?"

"If you must know, baloney. What's going on, Park?"

"Nothin' much, except that I've got your Mob Avenger's name and address."

"Oh, you do, do ya?"

"Yeah, I do. His name is Arden Kendall, Junior and he lives at 338 Sea Cliff Avenue in San Francisco."

"Wait a minute. Where the hell did you come up with that name? It isn't on the DMV list."

"That's because nobody on that list seemed right to me. Then I realized that, being a well-to-do sort of fellow, our Avenger probably traded his old car in for a new one since Ida Lupino made that picture of Thelma Todd. With that idea in mind, I checked with the Chrysler dealer in San Francisco and hit the jackpot. That's where I got Arden Kendall's name and address."

"That's pretty good detective work, but what have we got as evidence that this Kendall is our guy?"

"A visual identification. Once I knew the guy's name, and

figuring he might be a prominent enough citizen to have made the newspapers at some point, I asked a pal at the *San Francisco Chronicle* to check the morgue for articles with photos of our man. He came up with an article about the Kendall family business—a ship building concern—that included a clear photo of Arden Kendall, Junior. From that picture I can say without a doubt he's the same fellow who accosted me on the pier in Santa Monica, which is where we got the pistol that killed Eddie Conti. Only thing we need is proof that Kendall was in LA when Conti was hit. With that you've got means, motive and opportunity all ready for the DA to prosecute."

After a momentary pause while he digested what I'd just told him, Don said, "Damn! I guess you have found the Mob Avenger after all, or at least a damned good suspect. Give me his name and address again."

I repeated the information and Don said, "Okay, Park, I'll take it from here. Thanks."

"Whoa! Hold the phone, Don. I want to be in on this. What are you planning to do?"

"I'm going to see if I can get a judge to issue an arrest warrant for Kendall tonight, and then, after I notify San Francisco PD that I'll be arresting the guy in their bailiwick, I'm going to hop a train to Frisco tomorrow morning and put the cuffs on Arden Kendal, Junior. You can tag along if you want. I guess I owe you that much."

"I sure as hell guess you do! I'll pick you up at the station."

I broke the long distance connection to LA and swallowed more stale coffee. That's when I saw the potential flaw in Chambers' plan of action. We know Kendall spends a fair amount of time in Los Angeles, and if he was there now, Don was going to make an eight-hundred-mile roundtrip for nothing.

Don said he was going after an arrest warrant tonight, which meant he'd catch the Coast Daylight at 8:15 tomorrow morning to come up here. If there was a way to find out Kendall's whereabouts without tipping him off that we were on to him, it had to be done tonight.

I had an idea I thought might work, but it hinged on Kendall being listed in the San Francisco telephone directory. That wasn't likely, but I pulled the directory down from its perch atop the refrigerator to make sure. Resisting the temptation to check the A listings for "Avenger, Mob," I flipped through the Ks.

Son of a gun! There was an A. Kendall listed at the right address. This might work after all. I dialed the number in the book, crossed my fingers, and waited for an answer. It wasn't quite nine, so my timing was close.

After several rings, I was about to give up when a voice fringed with the hint of a European accent of some sort said, "Kendall residence."

I'd only heard Kendall say a few words out on the Santa Monica pier, but I remembered his voice being higher pitched without an accent. This wasn't him.

In my best hardworking servant of the people voice, I said, "Good evening, sir. My name is Clark and I'm with Pacific Gas and Electric Company. We're contacting residents of Sea Cliff because we suspect there may be a gas leakage in the pipeline under Sea Cliff Avenue. In order to determine where the leak is, we may need to dig up the street and we are warning residents so as not to inconvenience them unexpectedly."

Sounding slightly bored with the conversation, the voice asked, "And when is it you expect to do this digging up of the street?"

"If it's necessary, we will probably begin digging tomorrow."

After a pause that lasted at least ten seconds, the voice said, "That will not be an inconvenience. The owner of the house is away for several days."

"Wonderful. Thank you for your help. Goodnight."

I broke the connection and called Chambers again. When Don answered, I said, "Cancel your train reservation for tomorrow. Kendall isn't in San Francisco, at least he's not at his residence."

"Oh yeah? How do you know that?"

"He's listed in the directory, so I called his number and talked to someone at the house—probably Kendall's valet or butler. I told him I was with the gas and electric company and we were warning residents we might have to dig up the street he lives on to find a gas leak. The guy said it wasn't a problem because the owner of the house was out of town for several days."

"I gotta admit you've got nerve, Atkins. Slick trick, though."

"I thought you'd approve, especially since I learned it from you."

"Well, at least you were payin' attention some of the time. Too bad you didn't find out where Kendall went."

Sarcastically, I said, "Yeah, that's just the sort of question an employee of a utility company would ask. Hell, Don, I was lucky to get as much as I did."

"Hey, don't get your nose all out of joint. You just saved me a lot of time and money, only now we've got to find Kendall all over again. I'll call DMV in the morning and get the license plate number of his new car so we can get an APB out. What year and model Chrysler is Kendall driving now?"

"It's a '38 Chrysler Imperial Eight Coupe. The color is Phantom Gray."

"Got it. With some luck we'll get a hit on it in the next few days."

"I hope so. There's no way in hell my boss will let me take another trip down there so soon after the last trip. Will you give me a call when you have something so I can plug it into the crime report I'm doing on this guy?"

"Sure, Park. I'll keep you informed on everything we get, and I'll do it before the local news people get a hold of it. Fair enough?"

"Fair enough, Don. Thanks and good luck."

I felt a little twinge of sadness when I dropped the telephone handset back in its cradle. Don was where the action was going to be and I was stuck four-hundred miles away with nothing more to do but wait for him to tell me what was going on. I wanted to be in on it so badly I momentarily considered telling Kastner to drop dead and driving down to LA.

Of course, going down there would be irresponsible. Besides that, I didn't have the money for another trip and, as Chambers kept reminding me, I wasn't a cop anymore. On that happy note I turned in for the night.

Thirty-Three

Tuesday—August 23, 1938

KDG Radio Studios—730 Market Street, San Francisco

After another fitful night's sleep I woke up feeling irritated with the whole damned world, and by the time I got to the news closet at KDG, I was ready to take a poke at the first person who looked sideways at me. Unfortunately, the first person who looked sideways at me was Charlie, and since I have a hard and fast rule about not hitting women, I'd have to wait until somebody else showed up before I could do any poke taking.

That didn't mean Charlie wasn't deserving of a poke. It annoyed me no end that my assistant knew all about my love life, and worse, she was clearly on Dandy's side. That was disloyal. Charlie didn't have to be on my side, she just needed to keep her damned nose out of my business.

Charlie greeted me cordially when I came in and I mumbled something in reply. I don't even remember what I said. I remember her smart aleck reply though. "My, aren't we in a fine mood today."

"No we are not."

A worried expression crossed her face. "I see. Is it anything you'd like to talk about?"

"Yes. I'd like to talk about work. That's what we're here for. I won't know until this afternoon if I'll have a crime report for tonight or not, so put together the script without one and we'll cut from the bottom if I've got anything to report."

She made no reply and got busy going through wire copy. I rolled a fresh sheet of paper into my typewriter just to be doing something and went to work typing the Mob Avenger's victim list

I'd copied into my notebook from Don's blackboard. Maybe a nice clean copy would make things clearer.

I'd just about reached the end of the list when Bill Kastner walked in with a cheery, "Good morning, Park . . . Charlene. What's going on in the world today?"

Why the hell was everyone so damned cheerful this morning? I kept typing and Charlie said, "Just more of the same, I'm afraid."

Kastner stood there for a moment, apparently waiting for me to say something, and when I didn't, he walked to my desk and looked over my shoulder at what I was typing. "What's that?"

Glowering, I said, "It's a list of the Mob Avenger's murder victims."

"Why are you still fooling around with that story? It's in LA. In case you've forgotten, you report the news in San Francisco."

"Bill, there is a strong San Francisco connection to this story. It isn't apparent yet, but it will be. Besides, this fellow is the most wanted person in the state. That makes him news."

"Not here it doesn't. Now stop playing cop and concentrate on what's going on in San Francisco."

I was getting hotter under the collar with every word he said. I ripped my list from the typewriter and tossed it in the wastebasket.

"Kastner, you hired me to do a job and I'm doing it. In fact, I'm doing it damned well. You see that plaque on the wall there? That's the National Print and Broadcast Journalism Association's 1937 award for the most outstanding local radio news reporting in the whole damned country. You see whose name is on it? My peers know the journalism business pretty well and they say I'm doing a good job, so maybe you ought to butt out and let me do what I do best."

Kastner turned a vivid shade of crimson and began sputtering like a flivver on its last legs. "Who the hell do you think you're talking to, Atkins?"

Before I could think up a snappy comeback, Kastner dropped the last straw. "Atkins, are you drinking again?"

I slammed my fist on the desk and jumped out of my chair. Kastner took a defensive step backward and I said, "No, Kastner, I'm not drinking again, but if I work for you any longer I'm damned likely to start. I'm giving you my two week notice here and now, so you'd better tell Chef LeBlanc to whip up some new recipes, because his is the only revenue producing programming you have left. Now get the hell out of here and leave me alone."

At that point Kastner finally showed some good sense. He got the hell out of there.

I flopped back into my chair and fished my freshly typed Mob Avenger victim list out of the wastebasket. I was smoothing the page out on my desk when soft sniffling sounds reminded me that Charlie was in the office and had witnessed my confrontation with the boss. I looked over at her and she was staring at me with tears in her eyes.

I muttered, "Sorry you had to see that."

She stood up and I figured she was heading for the lady's room, but she wasn't. Charlie surprised me by kneeling next to my chair and taking my right hand in both of hers. "My God, Park. What's gotten into you?"

"Kastner."

"No, you don't usually let Mister Kastner get to you like that. There has to be something more to it. Is it Dandy?"

"I don't know. She probably has something to do with it."

"Park, you are one of the only two real friends I have in the whole world. You're also my hero and my teacher. Please let me help you through whatever's going on."

"Charlie, you've already got your hands full being Dandy's pal. I'll work this . . ."

"Is that part of this, too? Are you upset with me because I've been trying to help Dandy understand what's going on?"

"Yeah, I suppose . . ."

Charlie threw her arms around my neck. "Oh, Park. I love both of you. What I try to do for Dandy is for you, too. I want you both to be happy, and the only way that will happen is if you get back together and stay together. You know that."

She stood up and I nodded. I was a little choked up myself when I said, "Okay, kiddo. I'm sorry I was so hard on you. You didn't deserve any of it. Let's get tonight's broadcast together, and then take a long lunch somewhere more pleasant."

Charlie managed a weak smile despite the wetness in her eyes. "Okay, boss. You've got a deal."

At half past eleven my phone rang. Don Chambers was calling to tell me he had Arden Kendall, Junior's current California license plate number. I jotted it in my notebook as he read it off: 6G 41 29.

Trying to muster enthusiasm I didn't really feel, I said, "That's great, Don. You got an all-points out on it yet?"

"It's going out to Central Division cars as we speak. The outlying divisions will all have it in a few hours. The information is going out top priority as per Chief Davis' orders. I'm hoping for a quick pick up."

"I hope you get your wish. Thanks for the information."

Even though a lot of years had passed since we worked together on a regular basis, Chambers still knew me too damned well. He said, "What's going on, Park? You don't sound right."

"Everything's okay, Don. I'm just having a rough day here."

"All right, buddy. I hope your day gets better. Talk with you soon."

As I hung up, Charlie asked, "Was that the call you were waiting for?"

I leaned back and tossed my pencil on the desk. "That was one of them. Don Chambers got the Mob Avenger's automobile license number from the Department of Motor Vehicles, and since we think Kendall is in LA now, Don's putting out an All-Points Bulletin for the guy's car.

"I won't put that in a crime report, though, because we don't want Kendall to know we're that close to nabbing him. If Don calls back with a hit on the APB, then we'll have something to report."

"I see. Well, depending on what else comes through on the wire this afternoon, I think tonight's script is as ready as it's going to be."

"Good. Let's get out of here."

On the way out, I told Sally we would be gone a while. A few minutes later when I asked Charlie what kind of food she wanted for lunch and she said she wasn't very hungry so she'd be happy with whatever I picked.

I wasn't in the mood to eat much either, but I wanted a quiet, peaceful atmosphere, so we walked two blocks west on Market to Ellis and turned to the right. That brought us to John's Grill.

Thirty-Four

John's Grill—63 Ellis Street, San Francisco

None of the regulars at John Konstin's grill, whose ranks I enthusiastically joined on those rare occasions when I felt flush, seems to remember a time when the joint wasn't sitting there on Ellis in its narrow three-story storefront. A notice on the front cover of the menu says, "Established in 1908," and since nobody seems interested in arguing the point, we take John's word for the founding date.

John specializes in preparing fresh seafood of all kinds according to his unique recipes that bring out flavors most of San Francisco's fish joints only dream about. The menu also includes chowders, salads, and if you must, steaks.

Inside, John's main dining room is welcoming and tranquil with dark oak paneling, cozy tables, and walls lined with San Francisco photographs that might go all the way back to when Sir Francis Drake sailed through the Golden Gate, if he actually ever did that. It was just the kind of place I needed.

Once we were seated, Charlie said, "Park, John's is pretty steep and you are about to be unemployed. Are you sure you can afford this lunch?"

I was looking around the room to see if I recognized anyone in the lunch crowd. Not seeing anyone I knew, I said. "Don't worry, we won't have to spend the afternoon washing dishes in the kitchen."

Looking dubious, Charlie said, "Okay, Park, if you say so."

I lit a Camel and leaned back in my chair. I was thinking how good a shot of quality bourbon on the rocks would taste right then.

Thoughts like that were becoming fewer and farther between the longer I was sober, but I still had them from time to time—usually when I found the other things I had to think about unpleasant.

We placed our orders, a small Shrimp Louie for each of us and a cup of chowder for me, and when our waiter went off to deliver our choices to the kitchen, Charlie cleared her throat as if she was about to say something important.

That was as far as she got, though, so I said, "Say what's on your mind, kiddo. I'm through flying off the handle today."

She still looked a little nervous, as if she wasn't sure I was really under control again. Finally Charlie said, "Well . . . I'm not suggesting this, but I was just wondering, if you apologized to Kastner, if he might consider forgetting about your resignation."

"In a few days when the ramifications of my leaving fully sink in, he might, but that's not something I'm willing to do. I wasn't kidding when I said he was going to drive me to drink if I stayed there any longer. I've put up with Kastner's lack of trust and little insinuations for a long time because I had no choice. Now that I have a few accomplishments on which to build a resume' I think I'll be able to find another job."

"There's no doubt that you have the talent and skills to work at a top-rated station, but I wouldn't use Kastner as a reference." After a pause, she added, "Is it too late to call Mutual back and tell them you've reconsidered?"

Shaking my head, I said, "That train has left the station, and telling them that would be a lie. I haven't changed my mind about working in Chicago."

At that point our waiter showed up with our lunches. They looked good and I knew they would taste good, but my appetite was still eluding me.

Charlie took a taste of her salad and pronounced John's Louie dressing delicious. Then, with deep concern on her face, she said, "If KDG and Chicago are no longer options, what you going to do, Park?"

"I'm not sure yet, Charlie. I need to give it a little thought. Plus, I still have Dandy on my mind. Of course, when she hears I'm leaving KDG, it will be like adding insult to injury for her. I doubt she'll ever speak to me again once she learns that piece of news."

Charlie shook her head. "Park, I think you've got Dandy all wrong."

I stared across the table at Charlie for a moment, and then decided it might be beneficial to hear her take on the situation.

"How so?"

"Dandy hasn't stopped loving you. She isn't even mad at you. Dandy is just very disappointed, which she fully realizes is her own doing."

"I don't know about that, Charlie. Dandy . . ."

"Park, she told me as much last night. She said she set herself up for a disappointment by pinning her hopes on a dream rather than looking at the situation rationally. I honestly believe Dandy feels worse about the pressure she put on you than she does about not moving to Chicago."

I found myself shaking my head again. "She doesn't need to feel bad about that. I gave her the right to tell me what she thought and I knew exactly what she wanted. I'd do anything to make her happy, but I think any happiness either of us got out moving to Chicago would be short-lived."

"You need to tell that to Dandy, Park, not to me."

"Her mother said almost the same thing to me last night on the telephone, but I'm not sure I can tell Dandy how I feel."

Charlie looked puzzled. "For heaven's sake, why not?"

"Well, for one thing I don't think she wants to hear from me right now, and for another . . ."

"That's baloney, Park. I'll bet you anything that if you called her right now, she'd be very pleased. I'll even give you the nickel to find out if I'm right."

Again I shook my head. "That might have been true last night, but now that I'm about to be unemployed, I'm pretty sure she'll want to wash her hands of me once and for all. There's no future in hanging around with Parker T. Atkins."

"That's not true and you know it. You'll have a new and better job before you know it."

"I sure hope you're right about that. And, by the way, wherever I go, there will be a place for you, too. I owe you that, and even if I didn't, I'm not sure I could do the job without your help."

She smiled at that. "It's nice of you to say so, but unless Kastner gives me the boot, I've still got a paycheck for the moment. Now, stop changing the subject. I told you Dandy would be very happy to hear from you. If you don't want to call her, would you consider a compromise?"

"What sort of compromise?"

"What would you think about me calling Dandy this afternoon and telling her what's going on? If, as I suspect, she wants to talk with you, I'll set up a meeting between you two tonight after your

broadcast. That way you keep your pride intact and still find out . .
."

"It's not a matter of pride, Charlie. I . . ."

"Yes it is, Park. You're a man who's had his whole world collapse around him in a matter of two days. All you have left is your talent and your self-respect—what I'm calling pride. If you don't see that, you're just fooling yourself."

I'd worked up enough enthusiasm to swallow a spoonful of chowder. It tasted pretty good, so I had another. All the while I was thinking about Charlie's pride comment. She was right, of course, and maybe I was selling Dandy short.

"Okay, Charlie, if you're up to it, I'll go along with your compromise. I'm just not getting my hopes up."

"All right, Park, you've got yourself a deal. I'll call Dandy from one of the payphones in the drugstore when we get back."

Since there didn't seem like there was much more to say, we both dug into our lunches. My mommy would be proud of me. I ate all my soup and most of my salad before paying our lunch bill of three dollars and heading back to KDG.

As we walked back on Market, Charlie said, "Thanks for lunch, Park. It was very good."

"And thank you for the straight talk. I don't know if we resolved anything or not, but I'm feeling a lot more human now."

Charlie laughed. "That's probably more due to eating lunch than anything I did, but I'm glad to hear you're feeling a little better about things."

Back at the Owl Drugstore I went on up to the fourth floor, leaving Charlie to make her telephone call to Dandy. I even found myself somewhat hopeful that Charlie's interpretation of the situation might be right.

Thirty-Five

KDG Radio Studios–730 Market Street, San Francisco

I stopped at the reception desk on my way into the station and asked Sally if I had any calls. She said there were no calls. Then, on a whim, I asked her if Kastner was in. I didn't want to see the guy and I wanted to know how likely it was I might run into him.

"No, Parker. He left around eleven and said he didn't know when he'd be back."

Sally looked as if she had something more to say, but she didn't say it. By now word that I'd quit had probably made the rounds all the way to the front desk, so maybe she was going to say something about it and decided it would be better keep her thoughts to herself on that subject. Smart girl.

I stopped by the news wire room—the only room at KDG that was smaller than our office—and tore AP's latest news updates from the teletype. I was back in the office looking through the wire service printout when Charlie walked in with a big grin on her kisser.

I looked up from the wire copy and said, "From that grin, I gather you have some good news."

She dropped her handbag in the filing cabinet drawer where she keeps it and said, "I sure do, Park. Just as I expected, Dandy wants very much to see you and to work your problems out. I said you'd pick her up for a late dinner around seven. That okay?"

Feeling almost lightheaded with relief, I said, "That's fine, Charlie. Is Dandy at work today?"

"Yes. I figured I'd call her office first and that's where I got her."

"Did you break the news about my run-in with Kastner and leaving KDG?"

"Yes, and that upset her, but not for the reason you might think. Dandy said you must have been at the end of your rope to do a thing like that, and she's very worried about you—not about you finding another job, but about your emotional state. She cares about you, Park, just like I do. Dandy is one hundred percent behind you and so am I."

"Thanks, kiddo, and thanks for calling Dandy. I guess I really misread her."

Nodding, Charlie said, "You did, but in your mental state that's no wonder. I hope you will be honest tonight and tell her how you really feel about things. I told her the same thing." Then Charlie got a little grin on her face and added, "In fact, I told her if she didn't start really communicating with you she was going to lose you to a certain assistant who works in the same closet with you."

I was somewhat taken aback by that comment. I thought she was kidding, but there was something odd in her expression I'd seen there before. I can only describe it as a look of longing. I don't mean she was longing for me—she just wanted somebody in her life who cared and brought some romance with him.

When I looked up, Charlie was blushing. "I'm sorry, Park. I shouldn't have told you that."

"Don't worry about it, kiddo. I know what you were getting at." At least I hoped I knew what she was getting at. If there was more to it, things could get complicated. Don't get me wrong, Charlie is a wonderful woman and if I wasn't already devoted to Dandy, I could do a lot worse than Charlie, but that was a complication I didn't need at the moment.

The afternoon dragged by at a snail's pace, but that was just because I was anxious to see Dandy. When it was finally time to walk down the corridor to the studio news booth, Charlie said, "Good luck, Park. Do you want me to stick around?"

"No, kiddo, go on and get out of here. We'll compare notes in the morning."

"Okay, Park. See you tomorrow. And don't worry. Everything is going to turn out all right with Dandy; you'll see."

In the last few seconds before the big control room clock's minute hand pointed straight up at the 12, indicating six o' clock on the button, Dick Stewart and I went through our usual routine of switching places in the booth, and on my cue from the engineer, I delivered the news all of San Francisco was waiting for. Well . . .

the news at least a few folks in San Francisco were waiting for. After bringing sports fans up to date on how their Pacific Coast League Seals were doing in the league standings and telling weather fans what to expect on Wednesday, I delivered my usual tagline: "That's your news for Tuesday, August Twenty-Third. This is Parker T. Atkins. Goodnight, San Francisco."

As always, Charlie had timed the script out perfectly, and at precisely 6:29 p.m. by the control room clock, the engineer rolled our recorded closing theme song, San Francisco. I was out of the booth and heading for my office before the song got to the part about not letting any strangers wait outside your door. In our office, I filed the night's script, rolled down my sleeves, and slipped into my sport coat. I straightened my tie on the way out the office door and a few minutes later I was walking east on Market in the direction of my car.

That morning I'd found an unusually convenient parking spot at the east end of the 700 block—the block of Market in which KDG is located. I was within about ten feet of my Ford when what started out as a lousy day did what I thought was impossible. It got even lousier.

Market Street's crowded business traffic was done for the day and the broad avenue was almost eerily quiet, so the two gunshots echoed loudly between the tall buildings. The shots came in quick succession, one right after the other—pop . . . pop. I have no idea where the first slug went, but the second ricocheted off the Ford's radiator frame and smacked me just above my right ear.

I hit the sidewalk like a ton of bricks and lay there in a state of semi-awareness as two Phantom Gray Chrysler Imperial Coupes sped away on Market. Well, maybe there was only one Chrysler. My vision wasn't too reliable at that moment. A moment later everything kind of faded to black.

Thirty-Six

Wednesday—August 24, 1938

Saint Mary's Hospital—450 Stanyan Street, San Francisco

When the lights came on again, my surroundings had changed considerably, although they looked vaguely familiar. Also, the light that came on was daylight coming through a window. A large white-faced clock on the wall said it was a few minutes after seven. Those were clues. From them I deduced I'd lost at least one night of my life, maybe more.

Then a voice that was also vaguely familiar said, "Good morning, Mister Atkins."

I looked in the direction from which the voice came and saw a young man with a stethoscope draped over the shoulder of his white doctor coat. I knew him. "Hello, Doctor Phalen. From your presence here, should I assume I've landed in Saint Mary's Hospital again?"

He smiled a friendly smile. "You should, and the fact that you remember me is a very good sign. It means your concussion is probably minor."

"Well, don't take this personally, Doc, but we've really got to stop meeting like this."

Phalen laughed. "I'm also pleased to see your sense of humor is still intact. You're right, though, the last time we met was just 14 months ago—according to your records here, that was in June of '37. However, I'm happy to report you're in much better condition this time than you were the last time you came to visit. How are you feeling?"

I took stock and decided my only serious complaint was some throbbing on the right side of head. I told Phalen and he said, "I'm not surprised. The throbbing will be there for a while, but we should be able keep it at a minimum with acetylsalicylic acid." He grinned at the expression on my face and added, "That's aspirin to you."

"Thanks for the translation, Doc."

"Can you tell me what caused your injury?"

"Don't you know?"

Looking at some sort of paperwork on the clipboard in his hand, he said, "All I know is what it says here: You were brought into Emergency at 7:35 last night. You were unconscious with a small scalp laceration along with a significant contusion and a large lump, both caused by a blow the right side of your head just above your ear."

By this time my thinking was getting clearer and I was pretty sure I didn't want the good doctor to know exactly what happened to me. If he knew I'd been shot, he'd have to involve the cops, and I didn't need them lousing up my efforts to find the Mob Avenger. I said, "Could we just say I accidently bumped my head and let it go at that for now?"

Doctor Phelan studied my face for what seemed a long time, and then he very deliberately removed the cap of his fountain pen and wrote something on his form. Aloud, he read, "Patient states he accidently bumped his head, sustaining injuries described above."

After returning the cap to his fountain pen and hanging the clipboard on a hook at the foot of my bed, he said, "You have a couple of visitors outside who've been here almost since you were brought in last night. I remember Miss Harrison from your last stay with us. She has a Miss Blanchard with her. Would you like to see them now?"

I had no idea how Dandy and Charlie even knew where I was, but it didn't matter. Suddenly I felt a whole lot better . . . on top of the world, even. I said, "Most definitely, but first, tell me when can I leave these delightful accommodations. I feel fine. I'm ready to go right now."

Again Phalen stared at me for several moments before answering. "I'd prefer that you stick around until tomorrow morning for observation, but I have no authority to make you stay against your will, so I guess when you leave is mostly up to you, Mister Atkins. Your clothes are hanging in that small closet next to the hall door. Your valuables can be picked up at the business office in the lobby when you make arrangements to settle your bill."

On that note he walked out of the room. No more than ten seconds later the door opened again and Dandy peeked in through the opening. I said, "Hi, Honey. Come on in."

She literally ran to my bedside. "Oh, Park, I've been so worried about you. Are you okay?"

Sitting up, I set off another round of head throbbing and put my arms around her. "I'm doing pretty well, especially now that you're here."

"What on earth happened to you, Darling? I was worried when you didn't show up for our dinner date at seven last night, and then I got a telephone call from the police because they found an emergency card with my name and telephone number on it in your wallet. They wanted to know if I knew you. I said I did and they asked if I knew who you would want notified if you were in the hospital. I said I was your fiancée and you had no family nearby. I hope that was all right."

"It was exactly right. That's why the card was in my wallet. Did the cops say anything else?"

"Yes, the policeman told me they'd found you unconscious with a head wound on Market Street and that you'd been brought to Saint Mary's. I called Charlie and she came straight over to meet me here. You were still in the emergency ward when we got here.

"That nice Doctor Phelan remembered me from when you were here before and said you were still unconscious, but your injuries didn't seem too severe. He told me he preferred to let you regain consciousness on your own rather than waking you up. He also said we'd have a better idea of how badly you were really hurt when you came around. Charlie and I have been waiting for you to wake up ever since.

"Just now Doctor Phelan said you were awake and anxious to see us. Charlie said I should go in first and see if you were up to having two visitors now."

I'd been watching her eyes as Dandy spoke. They were a little red around the edges, but she seemed sincerely happy to find that I was still among the living. When she finished explaining things, I simply said, "Dandy, I love you."

That started the tears flowing. "Oh, I love you, too, Park. I love you more than I could ever tell you. I'm sorry I behaved so badly when you told me we weren't going to Chicago. I was being selfish."

"It's okay, Dandy. Charlie helped me see what was going on. I understand and I don't blame you one bit for being disappointed.

Charlie also convinced me we could work things out, despite the fact that I'm going to be unemployed in two weeks. Do you think she's right about that?"

"Park, I know with all my heart she's right. We have to. Otherwise we're both going to be miserable for the rest of our lives."

We hugged again and she gave me a kiss that raised my pulse several notches. When the kiss ended, she said, "Oh, gosh. I almost forgot about Charlie. Should I tell her to come in before you tell me what in heaven's name happened? That would save you from having to tell the story twice, assuming you want to tell the story at all. She was just as worried about you as I was."

"Yes, please tell Charlie to come in. The more the merrier. Besides, she needs to hear what happened because we have to get moving on some things."

Dandy gave me a look and I knew she was wondering what things we had to get moving on, but she didn't ask. She just stuck her head out into the hall and a moment later Charlie came in. We hugged and Charlie said, "Thank goodness you're okay! You gave us quite a scare."

"I know, kiddo. I gave myself quite a scare, too."

Charlie said, "What happened? How did you end up with that lump on your head?"

"This is strictly between the three of us for now, but simply put, I was shot."

Almost in unison they said, "Shot!?"

"Yeah. The shots—there were two of them—came from the south side of Market Street just as I was about to get into my car last night. One of the shots ricocheted off my car and hit me. It was a fluke, but that's what happens when people play with guns."

Dandy asked, "Who was shooting at you? Do you know?"

"Yup, I know. I saw him drive away. I was shot by the guy Don Chambers and I have been trying to find . . . the Mob Avenger. I thought he was in LA, but obviously I was wrong about that little detail."

Dandy said, "You mean the same fellow who attacked you on that pier while you were down there?"

"They are one in the same, and quite frankly, I'm getting a little tired of his obnoxious behavior."

"What are you going to do?"

"Charlie and I are going to put him in the slammer once and for all. You up to that, Charlie?"

Looking a little unsure, she said, "If that's what it takes to keep you alive, I guess so."

"Good, kiddo. Your part is easy. Go to the station and find Don Chambers' office number in my telephone file. Call him, explain who you are, and tell him what happened last night. If I know Don, he'll be on the next train north. Okay?"

"I have it, but you aren't coming in today, are you?"

"Darn tootin' I am! I'll be in as soon as I can get checked out of here. I'll go home and get cleaned up, and then I'll be in. That is assuming you'll give me a lift, Dandy. Oh, and leave me at least five minutes for a crime report in tonight's script. I'm going to roast this little jerk in the hot seat tonight!"

Charlie and Dandy exchanged looks, and after giving me a kiss on the cheek, Charlie headed out the door. As I swung my legs over the side of the bed, preparing to get up, Dandy said, "Are you sure you should go in today? Wouldn't it be better to take the day off for some rest?"

"Honey, if I was going to take the day off for any reason it would be to spend it with you. The problem is, every minute we delay gives the Mob Avenger more time to do whatever he plans to do. Besides, in a couple of weeks I'll have plenty of time to rest."

I stood, throbbed, and wobbled for a moment. Then as Dandy rushed over to steady me, I found my balance. Dandy took my arm. "Take it slow, Park. I need you in one piece."

Putting my hands on her shoulders, I said, "Honey, you've been very patient with me and I've been dragging my feet. Well, the foot dragging is over. As soon as I nail this guy so we don't have to worry about your husband getting shot again, we're going to sit down and work this out. Can you be patient just a few more days?"

Dandy kissed me again. "Park, I can be patient for as long as it takes, just so I know you want us to be together soon."

I got my clothes out of the little closet and Dandy started out of the room so I could change. I said, "You don't need to leave. It's a little late for us to be worrying about modesty."

She giggled. "I guess you're right."

In the lobby Dandy and I headed for a door marked "Business Office." Inside, I gave the woman at the desk my name and she looked up the account they'd opened for me. She said my bill came to $108.26 and asked how I would like to pay it.

I told her to send a copy of the bill to my home address and I'd send payment in about a week when I got my next paycheck. She jotted that down on an invoice and had me sign it. That chore completed, she removed a large manila envelope from a file drawer and handed it to me.

"Here are the things you had with you when you arrived. Please check the envelope and make sure everything is there."

I took inventory as I transferred my keys, billfold and other items to my pockets. Then I thanked the woman and a few minutes later we were eastbound on Fulton Street in Dandy's bright yellow Buick convertible.

When we got to my place, Dandy stationed herself at my front window and kept her eyes open for gray Chryslers while I took a quick shower, shaved, and packed an overnight bag. If Kendall knew who I was and where I worked, I had to assume he also knew where I lived. The bag gave me options.

Finally, I took my Colt Detective Special revolver down from the cabinet over the kitchen sink and slipped into its shoulder holster. After dropping a handful of spare .38 caliber rounds and a small aspirin bottle into my jacket pocket, I locked up and we headed downstairs.

Thirty-Seven

KDG Radio Studios–730 Market Street, San Francisco

As she dropped me off in front of the Owl Drug Building, Dandy and I made arrangements to meet after my broadcast that evening. Then Dandy headed for the *Chronicle* plant over on Mission Street and I took a short walk up Market Street to where my Ford was still parked at the east end of the 700 block.

I immediately spotted the point where Kendall's second slug chipped paint off the radiator frame on its way to whacking me on the noggin. That just confirmed what I remembered of the incident from last night. What interested me more, though, was across the street. I wanted to know exactly where Kendall was when he shot at me.

My recollection was that his Chrysler came from the west when he drove off. That meant he must have walked from a parking place further west on Market to the point opposite my car where he did the shooting. That would have put him in front of 703 Market—the Spreckels Building—a dome-topped skyscraper that dominates The City's skyline.

Looking up at the 15-story monster, I realized why Kendall parked his car further down Market. The Spreckels Building was originally built before the turn of the century and although it withstood the '06 earthquake with relatively minor damage, it was in need of refurbishment. That refurbishment was underway and, as a result, the curb in front of the building was now a temporary no-parking zone to keep the area clear for the contractor to move equipment in and out of the job site.

Also, a wooden cover had been erected over the sidewalk to

protect pedestrians from falling debris, and that structure offered lots of convenient concealment for someone standing on the south side of Market. I was pretty sure Kendall must have been lurking in the shadows over there while waiting for me to finish my broadcast and leave the studio.

When the traffic gave me a break, I trotted across Market, setting off a round of throbbing in my head. I vowed there would be no more trotting for a while.

Walking along the section of covered sidewalk where I figured Kendall stood when he fired his shots, I studied the edges where the concrete met the two-by-fours on which the temporary sidewalk cover rested. I didn't spot anything useful in the accumulated debris there, but when I turned around to walk back, I noticed something shiny on the street side of the two-by-fours. I reached out into the traffic lane and picked up what looked like a shell casing. It had been run over and flattened some, but there was no mistaking it as a shell casing—most likely a .32 caliber shell casing.

Dropping the small smashed brass tube into my jacket pocket, I re-crossed Market and headed for the office. I didn't know whether the shell casing would yield any evidence, but at the least it was proof someone had fired a semiautomatic pistol over there. I knew it had been a semi-automatic because revolvers don't eject spent shell casings.

After taking the elevator up out of consideration for my head and still slightly sore knee, I walked into KDG's reception area. Of course Sally noticed the wad of gauze, cotton, and adhesive tape stuck to the right side of my head, but she didn't comment. Sally did say Mister Kastner would like to see me if I came in today and had a free moment.

I wondered if Kastner had actually phrased his request in the words she used. It was not the way he usually worded his requests—not by a long shot.

Walking into our news closet, I said, "Good morning again, kiddo. What's new?"

Charlie stood up and gave me a brief hug and a quick kiss on the cheek. "That's for being alive. As for what's new, I called Detective Lieutenant Chambers as you asked, and you were right. He said he would arrive in San Francisco on the Sunset Limited at 8:10 tomorrow morning. Lieutenant Chambers also said to tell you he expected you to be at the station to pick him up and buy his breakfast."

I grinned. "That's Don, all right. Anything else doing?"

Glancing toward the office door, Charlie said, "Well, sort of. Mister Kastner came in a while ago."

"What did he want?"

Frowning, Charlie said, "It's a little complicated. I don't know if Dandy told you, but I called Mister Kastner at home last night after we got to the hospital. We still didn't know how badly you were hurt and I thought it would be good to let him know you probably wouldn't be in for a few days. Under the circumstances, I didn't want him getting the wrong idea."

"What did he say about that?"

"Just that he was sorry to hear you were laid up. He did ask what happened, and I couldn't tell him much because we didn't know you'd been shot at that point. All I could say was that the police found you passed out on Market Street near here. Then he asked me to keep him informed on how you were doing. That was it.

"Then, when I got here this morning, I was going to call his office to tell Mister Kastner you planned to come in after all, but he showed up in here before I had a chance to call. I brought him up to date on your condition and said you intended to come in today."

"Did you tell him I'd been shot?"

Charlie nodded. "I hope that was okay. I asked him to please not repeat that part until you broke the story tonight." She looked thoughtful for a few seconds before adding, "You know, it was strange. He almost looked relieved when I told him you'd been shot."

I smiled. "That's because up until you told him different, he figured I'd passed out drunk on Market Street."

Looking shocked, Charlie said, "You think so? That's horrible. I don't know how you've put up with that man as long as you have!"

Figuring Charlie's question was rhetorical and didn't require a reply, I said, "When I came in a few minutes ago, Sally said Kastner wanted to see me. Any idea what that's about?"

"No. Maybe he wants to apologize and ask you to reconsider leaving the station."

I couldn't help laughing. "Kastner? Apologize? That'll be the day. He probably just wants to tell me he's docking my pay for coming in late this morning." Then, changing the subject, I said, "Charlie, go ahead and work on tonight's script. I'll go see Kastner, and then I'll get going on the crime report. Okay?"

"Okay, Park. No matter what he wants to see you about, try

not to let Mister Kastner upset you. Oh, and before you go, how's Dandy?"

"She's feeling better. I am, too. We talked things out some and decided we have to be together no matter what it takes. We're going to talk about that more after my broadcast tonight."

"Good, Park. I'm really happy to hear you two are back on the same wavelength."

"Me, too."

As I turned to go, Charlie stopped me again. "Ah, Park, it might be a good idea to button your jacket. If Kastner sees that gun you're wearing, he's liable to dive out the window thinking you're going to shoot him."

I smiled at Charlie's humor, and recalled a time not long ago when seeing my shoulder holster terrified her. "Okay, kiddo. I'll button up."

Kastner's office is on the south side of the building overlooking Market Street. His secretary announced my arrival through an intercom gizmo and a tinny voice told her to send me in.

As I came through the doorway, Kastner hurried around his desk and offered his hand. "Park, thanks for stopping by. I'm pleased to see you on your feet. Are you feeling all right?"

Shaking Kastner's hand, I said, "Yes. I've got some throbbing in my head, but the doctor said that was to be expected and told me to take aspirin until it goes away."

Kastner ushered me into a chair in front of his desk and said, "Park, I asked you to come in for a talk this morning because I've been thinking about our conversation yesterday and I've come around to your way of seeing things about this Mob Avenger story.

"Charlene explained more of the story to me and I can see why you've been so anxious to pursue it. I just wanted to tell you that and to apologize for getting a little hot under the collar and saying some things I wish I hadn't said yesterday."

I nodded and said, "Apology accepted. Now, unless you have something else on your mind, I have a crime report to write."

Kastner was standing behind his desk and staring down at the busy street below. After a few seconds, he turned around and said, "Yes, there are one or two other things on my mind. For one, I wanted you to know I called Saint Mary's and told them to send me the bill for your hospital care. From Charlene's description of last night's incident, it seems what happened to you was more or less in the line of duty and that makes your medical bill the station's responsibility. That okay with you?"

"That's kind of you, Bill. Thank you."

"You're welcome, Park. The other thing I wanted to mention is a request." Kastner stopped for a deep breath before saying, "Park, I would appreciate it if you would reconsider your decision to leave us. I know I'm not always easy to get along with, but that's partly because I believe pushing my employees helps them achieve new heights that benefit them as well as the station. Do you follow what I'm getting at?"

"I think so. The thing is, there's a big difference between pushing employees for motivational reasons and harassing them about their past to keep them in line.

"I've been on a long, hard road for the past two years and I'm proud of my success. That's my motivation to keep going. Your snide remarks and implied accusations haven't made my trip along that road any easier. So, yes, I'll give my resignation further thought, but at this point I don't see any reason to continue with things here as they've been."

I stood and offered Kastner another handshake. He accepted it without saying anything and I made my way back to KDG's news closet. Kastner surprised me with his apology and decision to pay my hospital bill, but I had a feeling none of that would have happened if I hadn't given him my resignation yesterday.

No, Kastner was still playing at being an executive and proving he wasn't very good at the game. To be good at that game you have to know and appreciate people. He didn't and probably never would.

Thirty-Eight

KDG Radio Studios—730 Market Street, San Francisco

Returning to the news closet, I found Charlie literally knee-deep in AP wire service copy. She looked up expectantly and I said, "Well, kiddo, you were right about why Kastner wanted to see me. It was the first time I've ever heard that man apologize to anyone for anything."

She looked as surprised as I was. "Really?"

"Really. He also told me he called Saint Mary's and told them to send my hospital bill to him. He said my getting shot at was in the line of duty and my medical bills should be paid by KDG."

In disbelief, Charlie said, "Park, I'm shocked!"

"I was too at first. Then he dropped the other shoe."

"What other shoe?"

"He wants me to reconsider my resignation. That's what the apology and paying my hospital bill were leading up to. Kastner is about as subtle as a bull in a china shop."

"What did you tell him?"

"I said I'd think about but not to get his hopes up, or words to that effect."

"Gee, you're really pushing the limit. Are you thinking of holding out for a raise or something?"

Shaking my head, I said, "No. I mean, a raise would be nice, but this isn't about money. I'm just sick and tired of the way he treats us, and I'm through putting up with his . . . nonsense."

I thought Charlie looked a little disappointed, but she nodded her understanding of my reasoning. I said, "Anyway, let's get our broadcast together, so if anything breaks before tonight, we'll be ready to deal with it."

Sitting at my trusty Underwood, I banged out a Special Crime Report that led listeners through the case from my recognition of a pattern in the killings that pointed to Thelma Todd's death, to my interview with Ida Lupino, to a simplified description of the process I used to track down Thelma Todd's mysterious beaux from San Francisco. From there I reported my theory that the Mob Avenger was avenging Todd's death, which he apparently believed was caused by the Lucky Luciano mob. In all that, however, I never mentioned Kendall by name. I simply referred to him as a "prominent San Francisco resident."

I was rereading the script a final time when Charlie said, "It's just about lunch time, Park. Would you like me to bring you a sandwich or something from downstairs when I go out?"

That was when it dawned on me I hadn't eaten anything since Charlie and I went to John's Café the day before. I fished around in my pocket for a dollar and said, "Yes, I'm actually kind of hungry. Would you mind bringing me an egg salad sandwich from the Owl lunch counter?"

"I wouldn't mind at all."

"Where are we with tonight's script? I've got the crime report ready to go."

Charlie gestured to a yellow legal pad on her desk. "I've got all the pieces together for the rest of the script. I'll check the wire once more after lunch, and then I'll plug your report in and type the script."

"Good. While you do that, I'm going to try and figure out where we go with the case from here. My guess is Kendall has gone underground by now. The trick will be figuring out where he's hiding."

"Okay, Park. Good luck with that. I'll see you in an hour or so."

As Charlie walked out of the office, I sat back in my ancient wooden desk chair and tried to get into Arden Kendall, Junior's head. Where the hell would he figure was a safe place to go?

The problem was, with Kendall's money, he could go just about any place he wanted. We needed to enlarge the dragnet and plug more of the holes he could slip through. For that, I picked up the telephone and put in another long-distance call to Don Chambers. Don answered on the first ring.

"Chambers, homicide."

"Hi, Don, Park here. Thought I'd check to see what's going on at your end."

"I'm glad you called. It saves me a call to Frisco. I have a couple of pieces of news. First, though, how are you? Your assistant said you got shot but weren't hurt seriously."

"She told it to you straight, Don. Aside from a pretty nasty headache, I'm doing okay. What's your news?"

"First off, when I told Chief Davis about your run-in with our suspect last night, he decided to extend our APB state-wide. The information went out on our teletype network about an hour ago. He's also talking to the feds about this thing, although I doubt they'll have much interest at this point. What do you plan to do on your broadcast tonight?"

"My plan is to break the story wide open up here. I've written a script that tells the whole sordid tale except Kendall's name. If the wire service picks the story up, it ought to put even more pressure on Kendall. My assistant will put the story out on our AP wire just before my broadcast, so it might make some morning papers."

"You mention the Ida Lupino connection?"

"Yeah. That gives the story a Hollywood connection . . . a little glamor."

"Yeah," Don said in a skeptical tone, "I guess we need glamour to get anybody's attention these days. I've talked to my counterpart up there in Frisco—a guy named Bailey—and he's already got an APB out and he's offered us whatever help we need up there. He's also got people watching the train depot and the airport. We might get lucky, but this guy Kendall is a sharp operator. It's going to take more than a chance sighting to nail him."

"Agreed. In fact, that might even be an understatement."

We confirmed that I would pick Don up at ten past eight the next morning and ended the conversation. After sitting there for a few minutes trying to sort out my thoughts, I went over and swiped one of the yellow legal pads Charlie kept stashed in the bottom drawer of a filing cabinet. I needed to write some thoughts down before I lost them in the jumble of questions my brain was trying to juggle.

I began a list of questions, the answers to which would shed some light on the whereabouts of Arden Kendall, Junior. The list went like this:

1. *How did Kendall learn who I was and where to find me?*
2. *Why did Kendall shoot at me?*
3. *Was Kendall trying to kill me last night or just scare me?*

4. Does Kendall have someone spotting his victims for him?

5. If Kendall is working with someone, who? A cop?

6. Does Kendall own property here besides his Sea Cliff house?

When I got right down to it, all I really had were six questions. There seemed to be a lot more before I wrote them down. That there were only six didn't make things any easier, though, because I had no answers for any of them.

Setting my list of questions aside, I re-read the articles Bobby Newman at the *Chronicle* dug up for me. I was hoping there might be a connection in one of them that would be helpful. If there was, I didn't see it.

Charlie returned a few minutes after one. After setting an egg salad sandwich wrapped in wax paper on my desk, she asked, "Anything new?"

"A couple of things. I checked in with Chambers and he said his boss is making their All-Points Bulletin state-wide and Don is in touch with SFPD Homicide. They're keeping an eye on the train depot and the airport for Kendall. That turns up the heat some, but Kendall still has a lot of options. We need more information to narrow down the possibilities. I've been looking for that information, but I haven't found anything useful so far."

"Okay. I'll get busy wrapping up tonight's script."

I spent most of the afternoon doing the same sorts of things I'd been doing—going up blind allies and backing out of them. Charlie was being more a lot productive. Around four she said, "Here's tonight's script."

"Good. Would you please summarize the facts in the crime report segment and send them to AP via the wire service just before the broadcast?"

"Will do."

"Put both our names on the byline for the AP summary. And please make two extra copies. Send one copy over to Bobby Neumann with a note for him to pass the information on to the *Chron's* crime reporters. You can send that over by messenger as soon as it's ready. Leave the third copy on my desk. I'll take it with me in the morning so Don Chambers will know what we said on the broadcast."

"Got it, and thanks for the byline." Then, after a moment's pause, Charlie said, "Park?"

"Yeah, kiddo?"

"You're gonna think I'm being a worry wart again, but have

you given any thought as to how you're going to leave here safely tonight after the broadcast?"

"A little. Why? You have a suggestion, like landing one of those autogiros on the roof?"

"Well, nothing quite that exotic, but I don't think this Kendall has any interest in me. How would it be if I walked up the block and brought your car back to our building's front entrance so you won't have to be out on the street so long?"

I gave her idea some thought, and then said, "Actually, that's a good idea, and when I come out, I can take you home so you don't have to ride the streetcar. Thanks for the suggestion, kiddo."

In truth I wasn't too concerned about Kendall trying the same gambit two nights running. He would know I'd be on my guard and might even set a trap for him. I was going along with her suggestion mostly to put Charlie's mind at ease and make her feel like she contributed something useful to the cause.

"Park?"

"Yeah, kiddo?"

"Where are you meeting Dandy tonight, or is that a secret?"

"It's not a secret where you're concerned. Since Kendall seems to know who I am and where I work, it's a pretty safe bet he also knows where I live, so I'm staying in an auto court out on Mission tonight. Dandy's going to meet me at a coffee shop out that way after I call her and let her know the coast is clear."

Thirty-Nine

KDG Radio Studios—730 Market Street, San Francisco

When I returned to our office from the news booth, Charlie was ready to go. She had her coat on and her purse was on her desk.

As she filed the night's script away, Charlie said, "Good job, Park. You put a lot of drama into it. I bet your listeners were right on the edges of their seats as they listened."

"Thanks, kiddo. I'm pleased with it, but I'd be even more pleased if I knew Arden Kendall, Junior was tuned in tonight."

"I bet he was. I know I would be listening if I were in his shoes right now. By the way, I sent the crime report summary out on the wire service and sent a copy over to the *Chron* morgue as you asked. The other copy is there on your desk."

Grabbing the copy of the crime report summary off my desk, I folded the eight-and-a-half by eleven sheets in half vertically and slipped them into my inside jacket pocket. Then I grabbed my coat off the rack and said, "Okay, kiddo, let's do this. You sure you're up to it?"

With determination in her voice, Charlie said, "I'm positive."

Downstairs, I waited just inside the entrance while Charlie walked out and headed east on Market. While I didn't really expect any trouble, I was still a little apprehensive during the time she was out of sight.

I felt a lot better when my Ford pulled up in the loading zone just beyond the Owl drugstore's entrance doors. Charlie slid over to the passenger side of the seat, I climbed in, and off we went. I'd taken Charlie home a few times before for various reasons, so I knew the route.

We continued down Market to the end of the block and turned right on Grant Avenue. Two blocks later I turned left on Post and continued out past Union Square to the block between Jones and Leavenworth, where I pulled to the curb across Post Street from the Warrington Apartments.

The Warrington is a six-story brick building that looks to be about 25-years old. It's in the Tenderloin district and Charlie swears it's the nicest apartment building downtown. She considers herself very lucky to find an apartment in the building she could afford.

As she climbed down out of my car, I thanked Charlie for helping me make a safe getaway. She said, "I'm glad I could help. Would you like me to call Dandy and tell her you just dropped me off and you're on your way to that auto court on Mission?"

"Thanks, Charlie. I would appreciate that. I called her a little before the broadcast, but it would probably make her a little less nervous if you let her know what's going on."

"Will do, Park."

"Oh, and don't forget I'm picking Don Chambers up at the depot a few minutes after eight tomorrow morning, so I'll be a little late getting in. If we stop for breakfast, it might be close to ten by the time we get to KDG."

"I hadn't forgotten, Park. I'll be there at the usual time, so I can let anyone who asks know you'll be a little late."

"Thanks, kiddo. Have a good night."

"You, too, Park."

I waited until she gave me a wave from inside the building lobby before I pulled across the traffic on Post and turned left turn on Leavenworth. From there I continued south to Mission Street, where I turned left. I kept my eyes on my mirrors and the traffic ahead for Kendall's car, but saw no sign of it. I didn't really figure I would see him back there. Kendall had no reason I could think of to kill me, so I was working on the theory that last night's attack was simply intended to scare me off the story, and the bullet that hit me was a chance incident. By now he had other fish to fry, specifically, keeping out of sight. Still, a little extra caution, like staying somewhere other than my apartment, didn't hurt anything except my bank balance.

The Mission Auto Court had been my temporary home when I arrived in San Francisco a little over two years ago, and I'd stayed there once since then on another occasion when it was prudent to avoid my apartment. As a result, the night clerk and I were old pals. He welcomed me like long-lost kin and checked me into my usual accommodations, bungalow number one, the unit closest to Mission Street in the southeast corner of the complex. Because of its proximity to the highway, it was noisier than most of the units, which also made it cheaper than most of the other rooms.

The Mission Auto Court had more than a hundred units laid out in a rectangle with bungalows around the perimeter of the property and more apartments arranged in a cluster inside the perimeter. The bungalow facades were done appropriately in the Spanish Mission style with arched doorways and window openings, red tile roofs, and attached garages. Inside the apartments and bungalows were spacious with inexpensive but comfortable furnishings.

Since my bag was still in Dandy's Buick, I just let myself in, looked the bungalow over, washed up, and took a drive around the rest of the complex to make sure there were no gray Chryslers hanging about. There weren't, so I turned north on Mission and drove five blocks to the Mission Café on the southwest corner of Mission and Hillcrest.

The café occupied the ground floor corner section of a three-story Streamline Moderne building that took up a full block in what served as the business district of Daly City, one of San Francisco's many suburbs. I'd eaten at the Mission Café often while living at the Mission Auto Court. The food was nothing fancy, but the place was clean and the help was friendly, which is a lot more than could be said for most of the eateries in the vicinity.

I parked off the main drag on Hillcrest and got a table for two at a window facing Mission Street where I could keep an eye on the traffic. After ordering a cup of coffee, I walked to the back of the restaurant and used their public telephone to call Dandy. She was waiting for my call and answered on the first ring.

"Hello, Park. Where are you?"

"I'm at the coffee shop in Daly City I mentioned to you this morning."

"Good. Charlie called a while ago and told me you were on your way south from her place. Shall I come down there?"

"I think it's safe. I checked into the auto court and saw nothing out of order there. In fact, I haven't seen hide nor hair of Kendall since last night."

"All right, Park, I'm on my way."

"Okay. I'll be inside the café. Do you remember where it is?"

"Yes, I wrote the location down. See you soon."

I returned to my table and took a swallow of the coffee my

waitress had delivered while I was on the telephone. Then, for the first time in 24 hours I leaned back and relaxed. I'd done all I could toward putting the Mob Avenger behind bars until Don Chambers got here in the morning. I deserved a break.

It was almost eight-thirty when I spotted Dandy's Buick. She parked close to the corner on Mission and walked briskly into the café. I waved to catch her attention and she slid into the chair opposite me. Dandy was wearing a dark blue skirt and a pale blue sweater, and she was a sight for sore eyes. I told her so.

"Thank you, Darling. I've been rather anxious to see you, too. How is your head?"

I shrugged in a casual manner. "It's okay. I've get a little throbbing up there when my pulse gets elevated and I've got a few sore muscles, but nothing too bothersome."

Dandy smiled. "Translation: It hurts like hell, but I'm tough; I can take it."

Chuckling, I said, "It's not that bad. Really."

"Okay, Darling, if you say so." She picked up the menu our waitress left when I first came in and asked, "What's good to eat here? I'm starving!"

"It's been a while, but if I remember right the pot roast was good—lots of vegetables and a thick gravy."

Setting the menu down, she said, "Okay, decision made. Pot roast it is."

Our waitress—Helen according to the embroidery on her apron—must have been paying attention because she came right over to take our orders the minute Dandy set her menu down. I ordered two pot roast dinners, coffee for Dandy, and a refill for me.

Dandy reached across the table and took my hand. "How did your day go, Park? Anything new?"

"Well, there was one interesting turn of events." I told her about my meeting with Bill Kastner, his apology, and him paying my hospital bill.

When I finished the story, Dandy's glare was intense. "That louse! Kastner finally figured out he's losing the best thing that ever happened to his lousy little radio station and he's trying to make you feel indebted to him so you'll stay."

"That's about the way I see it."

"What did you tell him, Park?"

"I said I would think about it, but not to hold his breath."

I studied Dandy's face for some clue to her feelings on the subject as she said, "It will teach him a lesson if you turned him down." Then she suddenly sat up straight and reached for her handbag. "I almost forgot. Bobby Neumann sent an envelope up to my office for you. I guess he figured I'd be seeing you before morning and you'd get it faster if he sent it with me. Here."

I opened the envelope and pulled out three clippings and a note. The hastily scrawled note said, "I found a few more items on your man, Kendall. Maybe they'll be useful. And don't forget you owe us a story!"

Dandy asked, "I bet you have Bobby doing your research for you again, don't you?"

"Yeah, but the *Chron* has been well compensated. Charlie sent everything that went into my crime report tonight over to Bobby just before we went on the air. Hopefully one of your crime reporters will be pleased to get it."

"I'm sure he will. Now I see why Bobby cooperates with you."

I took a quick look through the clippings. The first one, dated July 10, 1936, announced the Moore Dry Dock Company—the firm that purchased Kendall Marine Constructors—would be hiring more than one hundred workers for a large project in August. The second article, published in January, 1937, reported the donation of a large and valuable collection of maritime books to the San Francisco Public Library by the estate of Arden Gordon Kendall.

The headline on the final article, which was dated February, 14, 1937, read, "A-K Holdings, Incorporated wins county court battle over permits." Someone had circled "A-K Holdings" in the headline and written "Arden Kendall, Jr." above them.

As I slipped the clippings back into their envelope, Dandy asked, "Anything useful?"

"Not that I can see, but I didn't read them very carefully. I'll go over the articles more thoroughly later."

After we finished our pot roast we lingered over coffee for a while, and then reluctantly left the Mission Café. I got my overnight bag out of Dandy's car where it had been since we left my apartment that morning and we kissed goodnight. I said, "Thanks for coming down here, honey. I know we didn't resolve anything about our future together, but just being together for a while is a step in the right direction. I expect to wrap up this Mob Avenger thing in a few days, and then we can make some decisions about how we're going to get on with our lives."

Dandy put her head on my chest. "I'm looking forward to that, Park. I understand your need to see your Avenger story through, but I'll be happy when we can make those decisions you mentioned. In the meantime, please take care of yourself and stay in close touch, okay?"

"I will. Don Chambers is arriving by train tomorrow morning, so I'll be late getting into the office. I don't know what we'll be up to after that, but I'll let you know."

I watched Dandy drive away and make a U-turn at the end of the next block to head back to her folks' home in Pacific Heights. Then I tossed my bag into the Ford and drove back to the Mission Auto Court. It had been a long day and I was ready for some sleep.

Forty

The Southern Pacific Railroad terminal at Third and Townsend was built more than two decades ago as a temporary facility to handle the influx of tourists attending San Francisco's Panama Pacific Exposition of 1915. The depot still in regular use today, serving thousands of commuters who ride twenty, thirty, or more miles each way between their jobs in The City and their homes down the peninsula. Good old SP got their money's worth and then some on that deal.

From the outside, the depot was designed—like practically every other municipal or commercial building in the state—to look like an early California mission. The entrance doors set in three large side-by-side arches with a bell tower standing at each end of the entrance. Between the bell towers and above the entrance is another, broader arch with a pair of mission bells set in it over the words "SOUTHERN PACIFIC."

Extending off to the left of the main building is a long narrow wing that houses the gates used by arriving and departing passengers. Its facade is made up of nine more smaller arched windows and another set of double doors. The entire depot is topped with a red Spanish tile roof.

Inside the main building, the waiting room is two stories high, but the floor space is relatively small compared to that of depots in other major metropolitan cities like Los Angeles. Large windows fill the arches above the entrance doors and two rows of six chandeliers, each with eight frosted globes, add considerably to the light from the windows. The ticket counters are stretched out

194

along the wall opposite the entrance doors. Most of the interior floor space is occupied by long wooden benches while the usual newsstands and other traveler services are stuffed into the waiting room's corners.

I arrived a little before eight because Don's train, an extension of the SP's New Orleans to Los Angeles Sunset Limited, was due in at eight-ten. Between the commuters and the folks who'd shown up to meet the train from LA, the waiting room was full almost to capacity. I asked a Red Cap where the Limited would unload and he directed me to the Track One gate in the long wing of the building.

I elbowed my way through the crowd and found a place to stand alongside the Track One doors through which passengers arrived and departed. The big white-faced clock above the waiting room door said it was eight-oh-five. Five minutes later, almost to the second, one of those deep authoritative train depot voices came over a loudspeaker above my head: "Announcing the arrival of Southern Pacific's Sunset Limited from Los Angeles and points east on Track One."

A few minutes later a mob of passengers began streaming through the doors. Don Chambers was among the first half-dozen of these folks. He spotted me right away and shifted the overnight bag he was carrying to his left side so we could shake hands.

"Good to see you, Park. How's your head today?"

"Better, thanks."

Don grinned. "I figured it would be. You're about most hard-headed guy I know."

Politely smiling at his humor, I pointed to a pair of exit doors on the opposite side of the crowded room and said, "Go that way."

There was a parking area outside the exit doors and my Ford was parked a half dozen spots away. We climbed in and I turned right on Townsend, following it east for a couple of blocks to the point where it turns north and becomes The Embarcadero. From there we drove four or five blocks further to Pier 40, where I pulled to the curb in front of a little joint called the Java House.

Don looked out his window and frowned at the tiny twenty-by-thirty shack just beyond the sidewalk. "I thought we were going to breakfast. What the hell is this?"

"This, my friend, is the home of the best coffee and breakfast in town."

"Come on, you gotta be kiddin' me."

"Don, I might kid you about a lot of things, but never about something as close to your heart as food. Nobody knows more about good breakfasts than the longshoremen who work up and down The Embarcadero. You can ask any of them and they'll tell you the Java House is the place to go for breakfast. It isn't fancy, but the food can't be beat."

Don looked at me like he was still trying to decide if I was pulling his leg. Finally, he said, "Okay, Park. If you say so."

Inside, about a quarter of the joint was taken up by the kitchen, which was open to the dining area. Smells coming from the sizzling grill were already making my mouth water.

The rest of the place was filled to overflowing with eight tables and a counter with seats along the wall on the bay side of the shack. That wall was mostly windows, providing great views of the water, ships, and the mountains across the bay.

Ordering at the Java House is simply a matter of walking up the counter, picking something from a crude hand-lettered cardboard menu thumbtacked to a post, and pouring yourself a cup of coffee from a big blue speckled enameled iron pitcher on the counter.

The items on the menu included two eggs with or without bacon, ham or sausage; a couple different omelets; and pancakes with or without eggs or meat. Toast and home-fried potatoes were served with most of the menu items except the pancakes.

Don picked pancakes with sausages and I told the mustachioed fellow behind the counter I'd have eggs sunny-side-up with ham. After pouring our coffees, I led Don over to a table by the windows that a trio of hefty longshoremen had just vacated.

While we waited for our breakfasts, Don asked, "You got anything new since we talked?"

"Nope. How 'bout you?"

"Only that, by now, just about every cop in the state is looking for Kendall, and none of them have found him yet."

"I'm guessing he's gone underground, leaving us the job of figuring where the hell he's hiding. Also, I have a few questions to answer that are still bothering me."

"What questions?"

"Well, for one thing, why the hell did Kendall shoot at me the other night?"

Don frowned. "That's no mystery. We've been squeezing him pretty hard and somehow he figured you were doing a lot of the squeezing. He wanted you off his trail before you got any closer."

"That's what I figured, but the puzzling part is whether or not he intended to hit me when he fired those shots. We know from past history Kendall usually hits what he shoots at, but the slug that whacked me in the head was a fluke. It ricocheted off my car. I've come to the conclusion it was just a scare job that went wrong."

"That would be my take on it. You can ask Kendall when we find him."

Reaching into my jacket's right side pocket, I pulled out the partially smashed brass shell casing I found on Market Street. "Before I forget, here's a casing I found where Kendall had to be standing when he took those shots at me."

Don examined it and came to the same conclusions at which I had arrived. "Looks like .32 caliber, and if you found it on the ground, it's probably from an automatic. A good lab might be able to come up with the make and model pistol from the mark left by the firing pin or something. You want me to keep it and give it to our lab when I get back?"

"That's what I had in mind."

He dropped the casing into his coat pocket and said, "Okay. What other questions are puzzling you?"

"Here's a good one: how does he know who I am and where to find me? My theory is he staked out that motor court in Culver City to see who showed up and saw me there with you. That's when he started following me, probably to find out who the hell the new guy was, but how did he get my identity and my connection with San Francisco?

Our breakfasts arrived, and by the way Don dug into his pancakes, he must have been starving. I gave my eggs and ham a try. The eggs were cooked perfectly and everything else was just as good as it always is at the Java House.

After getting a couple of forkfuls of pancake in him, Don took a shot at answering my question. "He could have asked the right people the right questions and got lucky, maybe even at that hotel where you were stayin', the New Brunswick. We know the guy is resourceful enough to track down relatively unknown mobsters on both sides of the fence."

"All right, here's another question for you. How's he finding those mobsters? Is he just getting lucky, as you put it, or does Kendall have someone helping him by fingering his victims? And who is the guy with the European accent who answered Kendall's telephone the other night, and how does he fit into all of this, if he does?"

Between bites of pancake and sausage, Don said, "Those are all good questions, and there's a lot more about Kendall we don't know, but right now all I want to do is find him and get Chief

Davis off my butt. What worries me is Kendall could be three thousand miles from here by now, in which case we might never find him."

"He could have taken off, but I don't think so. Even after my broadcast last night I think he'll stick close to see what we're doing. He's so damned confident, I wouldn't be surprised if he's already picked his next victim.

Talking about my broadcast, I remembered something else I'd intended to give Don. I pulled four sheets of paper out of my inside coat pocket and handed them to him.

"What's this?"

"A summary of the crime report I did on my broadcast last night. I thought you might want to read it. I don't know if Kendall heard it, but if he did, he has to be sweating a little more now."

Chambers held the pages in his left hand and read them while the fork in his right hand kept working on his pancakes. When Don set the summary down, he said, "I don't know, Park. If he heard this, he could be headed for parts unknown in a hurry. I'm not so sure your theory about Kendall's confidence is right."

"I guess we'll find out soon enough. He's cocky and committed. I don't believe he'll be scared off by anything short of a bullet, and even that might not do it."

Don sighed. "You could be right. It just goes against a cop's grain to tip his hand with this much information."

"That's why freedom of the press was invented."

Don gave me a glare and went back to finishing his breakfast. When we were both done, I paid our breakfast tab with two dollar bills, and on the way out to my car, I said, "Any place special you want to go, or shall I just head for my office so we can find out what's going on this morning?"

"I should probably let that San Francisco homicide cop I talked to the other day know I've arrived, but I can do that by telephone from your place. I can't think of anything else, other than wandering around town trying to figure out where the hell Kendall is."

"Okay, let's go to KDG. You can see what a real live radio station looks like."

Don's "Oh, swell" was dripping with sarcasm.

Forty-One

KDG Radio Studios–730 Market Street, San Francisco

I held the door open for Don and followed him into our news closet. Charlie was hard at work on the night's script when I interrupted her to introduce Don.

Charlie said she was pleased to meet Detective Lieutenant Chambers and Don said he was pleased to meet the brains of the outfit. In preparation for Don's visit, Charlie had moved a third chair into the office, which filled the room to capacity.

Don made himself comfortable and dialed my desk telephone to call his contact at SFPD while I hung my jacket on the coat rack. He immediately noticed my shoulder holster and made a face at me. I'm sure the face he made was meant to show his disapproval of me, as he would have put it, playing cop.

To Charlie, I said, "What's going on in the world, kiddo?"

Consulting the notes on her legal pad, Charlie said, "Well, according to the *New England Journal of Medicine* there is a problem with congenital syphilis in Boston, the *Chicago Daily Tribune* reports that more than 23,000 crimes and 125 murders have occurred there since the first of the year, and the Japanese shot down a Chinese passenger plane flown by an American pilot. Fourteen people were killed and US officials are expressing the usual diplomatic outrage. That's the lead story for tonight unless something bigger comes along."

"Okay. Let's hit that Chinese passenger plane hard. Hitler's antics in Europe have been getting all the international headlines. We need to remind people there's a war going on in China, too."

Charlie made a couple of notes on her pad, and then asked,

"What about a crime report?"

I gave her question a moment of thought and came up with what I thought was a pretty good idea. Turning to Don, I said, "How would you feel about letting me ask you some questions on the air tonight?"

"What kind of questions?"

"Oh, just lightweight stuff, like how people in LA are reacting to the Mob Avenger and how the LAPD is involving law enforcement agencies throughout the state in a manhunt for the guy. I won't put you on the spot and we'll record it ahead of time so you won't have to worry about doing it live on the air."

Don thought for a few moments before saying, "I guess it would be okay. Just don't ask me anything that will get me in Dutch with the boss."

"Don't worry, I'm on your side, remember?" Turning to Charlie, I said, "Ask engineering to set up a recording session whenever they can fit it in today. Tell 'em we want to use it on the broadcast tonight."

"Got it. I'll do that now so we'll make sure to get it in."

Charlie headed for the studio and I leaned back in my chair. "Don, anything new from SFPD?"

"Not so far. They're doing everything Bailey said they'd do, but there's been no sign of Kendall."

"Okay, how do you want to proceed today?"

"I was kind of hoping you'd have some ideas about that."

"Well, I was thinking we ought to drive out to Kendall's house in Sea Cliff. Now that you have a warrant for his arrest we can legitimately knock on his door to make sure he isn't sitting around at home laughing at us spinning our wheels."

"That makes sense. I'll set it up with Bailey. He should be there, too."

As Don reached for my telephone again, Charlie returned. "Chet said he could set up a recording session right now if you're ready. That gives him plenty of time to do whatever editing is needed."

"Thanks, kiddo." Looking at my wristwatch, I said, "It's a little past ten. Don, why don't you ask Bailey to meet us at Kendall's house about eleven-thirty? That gives us an hour to do the recording and time to drive out to Sea Cliff."

Picking up the telephone handset, Don said, "Okay. I'll find out if he's available then."

Charlie headed out the door again, saying, "I'll tell Chet to get set up."

Bailey agreed to meet us as requested and I escorted Don to the studio. Rather than trying to squeeze two of us into the announce booth where I do the news, engineering set up a bidirectional RCA ribbon microphone on a table in the large studio. Don and I sat on opposite sides of the table with the mike between us. A third chair was provided for Charlie so she could take notes during the interview.

Don and I spent a few minutes discussing the questions I would ask him, and then, knowing the mike was live and they could hear me in the engineer's booth, I said, "Okay, Chet, we're ready when you are."

Chet answered me via the squawk box. "All right, Park. Slide the mike about six inches closer to your guest, and then ask him the first question so I can set the gain."

We did as requested and after about thirty seconds, Chet squawked, "Okay, Park. I've got the levels. I'll roll the wire, and give you the finger when we're rolling."

"Okay, Chet. Let her rip."

Don seemed quite at home during the interview, answering my questions succinctly and intelligently. After listening to the playback, Don said he wanted to redo one of his answers, and that was it. We easily had five minutes of useable interview, which is exactly what I needed.

Leaving Charlie behind to give Chet my editing instructions, Don and I made our way back to the office. As we walked, I said, "That was pretty smooth, Don. You've done this sort of thing before, haven't you?"

Don grinned at me. "You ain't the only guy who knows how to talk on the radio. There's nothin' to it. All ya gotta do is keep your mind on what you're saying."

I laughed. "Yup, that's all there is to it."

We had a few minutes to kill before leaving for Sea Cliff, so I stopped at the coffee pot in the hall and grabbed us two cups. Back in the office, Don said, "Park, you need to show these people how to make a decent cup of coffee. This stuff is like warm brown water."

"Yeah, by your standards it is. If we made our coffee like you do, this whole place would be flying higher than a kite!"

Charlie showed up then, saying, "Chet says, 'Good job'. You made his job a piece of cake. He's already editing the interview onto a transcription disk."

"He can thank Detective Chambers for that. Don handled the interview like an old pro. If I didn't know how much he likes being a cop, I'd think he was after my job."

Don laughed and Charlie said, "Maybe we should tell Kastner. He might want to talk with Detective Chambers in two weeks."

I said, "Not on your life, kiddo. Don's a friend. I wouldn't do that to him."

Looking puzzled, Don asked, "You wouldn't do what to me?"

"Well, it seems my days at KDG are numbered. I gave my two week notice the other day. I assume the boss is looking for a replacement."

Don still looked a little puzzled. "You didn't tell me you'd found a new job. Congratulations!"

"Save the congratulations, Don. I don't have a new job yet. So far all I've done is quit this one."

Chambers shook his head. "Same old Park Atkins, jumping out of the airplane without a parachute. I figured you knew better than that by now."

I started to reply, but Charlie beat me to the punch. In a heated tone, she said, "Mister Chambers, you shouldn't be so darn quick to judge. Park is doing the right thing. Our boss is a real jerk and he's treated Park terribly. Mister Kastner even apologized to Park the other day for his rude behavior."

Don was clearly taken aback by Charlie's outburst. A little sheepishly, he said, "I apologize, too, Miss Blanchard. I spoke out of turn."

Later, as we drove to Sea Cliff, Don said, "Geez, Park. That gal in your office is a little hellcat! She got downright hostile when she defended you. Remind me not to cross swords with her again!"

I didn't reply. I didn't have to. The point had been made. I just smiled.

Forty-Two

Arden Kendall, Jr. Residence—338 Sea Cliff Avenue, San Francisco

I drove a block west of the studio on Market, turned right on Kearny, and made an immediate left on Geary. That got us heading west through the downtown area toward a mostly residential area out near the coast known as "The Avenues." I turned right on 30th Avenue and followed it north until it ended at El Camino Del Mar in Sea Cliff. El Camino Del Mar ran into Sea Cliff Avenue at point nearly in front of Kendall's place. The whole trip, about five-and-a-half miles, took 30 minutes.

Don told me the SFPD homicide detective told him to go past Kendall's residence and park above China Beach a block further on. Bailey said he would meet us there.

Since there were no SFPD cruisers, marked or otherwise, to be seen, I turned around, pulled to the curb, and lit a Camel. Chambers mooched one and a light. When he got it going, Don said, "This is quite a place out here. It's kind of a miniature Palos Verdes."

"Yup. And these houses are some of the most expensive in San Francisco. A few of the houses out here date back to the 1910s, but most of them, especially the big mansions, were built during the past five years."

Don said, "I don't suppose there's much crime out here."

"None. At least none involving riff-raff or that you're going to read about in the newspapers. The SFPD handles this neighborhood with kid gloves. I'm surprised your guy Bailey even agreed to come out here."

"Sort of like Beverley Hills, huh? Those who aren't white and

203

filthy rich need not apply."

"You've got the idea."

"Where's that beach Bailey mentioned . . . China Beach?"

"It's at the bottom of the bluff down that trail over there. You get a great view of the new Golden Gate Bridge from the west down there."

"From the west? You mean we're on the ocean side of the Golden Gate here?"

"We are." Pointing east, I said, "The Army Presidio is just on the other side of Sea Cliff. The Army has a huge amount of land out here and it forms a point to the north. The southern anchorage of the bridge is out on the end of that point."

"I'm having trouble getting oriented. I'll have to find myself a map."

"I've got one at the station you can have." Then I saw what I'd been watching for. "Here comes your SFPD homicide guy. He'll be in that black Chevrolet sedan and it looks like he brought along a couple of patrolmen in a black and white."

I can't explain the phenomenon, but I've observed that most experienced homicide detectives look as if they were stamped out with the same cookie cutter. Detective Sergeant Bailey of the SFPD Homicide Division was wearing civilian clothes, and except for being an inch or so shorter than Detective Lieutenant Don Chambers of the LAPD Homicide Division, the two men could have been twins. Like Chambers, Bailey had the beginnings of a paunch, wore a wrinkled suit that looked to be a size too large, and combed his thinning hair in way that made it obvious he was trying to hide a bald spot.

Chambers and Bailey shook hands and Don said, "Bailey, this is Park Atkins. He's a news reporter here in San Francisco who's been helping us out with this case."

Bailey didn't offer his hand. He just glared at me and said, "Yeah, I know him. We've talked on the phone a couple of times."

I couldn't remember anything I'd done to make Bailey mad at me, so I assumed his manner was the one he reserved for all news reporters. I nodded my recognition and that was that.

Turning his attention back to Don, Bailey said, "Listen, Chambers, it's not that I mind helping out a fellow officer, but I gotta know how sure you are that Arden Kendall is the guy you're after. If you have any doubts, now's the time to tell me. I could lose my pension over this if you're wrong."

Don handed Bailey an official-looking form from his inside coat pocket. "I've got enough solid evidence on him to convince a

Superior Court Judge we needed a warrant to bring the guy in."

Bailey unfolded the warrant and read it carefully. When he was through, he said, "Okay, this makes it official, but we gotta do this legal like. That means we're polite and courteous, and no rough stuff. Got that?"

"Okay, Sergeant, it's your show. We'll just follow along quietly."

Bailey glared at me again and said, "Atkins, if you weren't with Lieutenant Chambers, I'd run your butt out of here. I heard what you reported last night and you're about as far out on a limb as you can get. If you report anything that isn't the gospel truth about what happens here, and I'll come down on you so hard you'll think City Hall landed on you. You understand what I'm sayin'?"

What I now understood was Bailey's attitude toward me. He'd heard my Special Crime Report last night and even though I didn't name any names or make any accusations aimed at the SFPD, he could see his pension sprouting wings and flying off to points unknown if I made him look bad to his superiors or the taxpayers in a crime story that was going nationwide.

I just looked him in the eye without saying anything. He glared at me for another moment or two, and then turned away and said, "Okay, here's how we'll do this. Patrolman Winters, you go down the China Beach trail a ways to where you can keep an eye on the back of the house. McCloskey, you come with Lieutenant Chambers and me. We'll leave the cars here and walk back to Kendall's place so as not to make a big fuss out of this. Atkins, you can come as far as the sidewalk in front of the house, but that's as far as you go. Don't set foot on Kendall's property. Got it?"

Again I looked him in the eye without saying anything, and then we all headed off in our assigned directions. Kendall had a four-foot concrete block wall in front of his house with a gate opposite his front door. Bailey opened the gate, and as he, Don and the patrol officer went up the walk, I waited at the gate and watched.

When the little procession reached the heavy dark oak front door, Bailey reached up and gave the black wrought iron doorknocker a rap that was so gentle it was if he was hoping nobody would hear it. The door remained closed, and after 30 seconds or so, Bailey gave the knocker a firmer rap. Another 30 seconds went by and there was still no response.

Looking relieved, Bailey turned to Don and I heard him say, "Nobody home. Let's go."

Back where we'd left the cars, Bailey sent officer McCloskey to fetch Winters. To Don, he said, "Well, that's that. If Kendall really is your man, a guy as smart as he is wouldn't be hanging around his house waiting for us to come calling. You got any other ideas?"

Chambers shook his head. "No, Bailey, we've done what we came out here to do. I'll have to look elsewhere now. It might be a good idea, though, if you sent a patrol car by a couple of times later in the day to see if any signs of life show up at the house."

Bailey nodded, implying he would follow Don's idea, although I was pretty sure he had no intention of taking another chance of offending the taxpaying citizens of Sea Cliff. "All right, Chambers, I'll be in the office or they'll know where to find me if you need help serving the warrant at another location."

On that note, Bailey climbed into his Chevrolet, his patrolmen climbed into their cruiser and they all took off, leaving Don and me standing next to my Ford. Don looked at me and said, "Well, if that's how the SFPD goes after murderers, I have some new respect for our outfit. The LAPD might be corrupt through and through like some people seem to think, but when we go after someone, we usually make an honest effort to get 'em. Bailey was shaking in his boots the whole time we were here."

"I'm not taking his side, Don, but you can't blame him for using caution when dealing with high-jingo suspects."

Don glowered. "You call that 'caution'? Hell, I wouldn't be at all surprised if fearless Detective Sergeant Bailey called ahead to warn 'em we were coming."

I glanced at my wristwatch, and seeing that it was almost twelve-thirty, I said, "Actually, Don, Bailey was right about figuring a smart guy like Kendall wouldn't be sitting around at his known address waiting for us to show up. I just thought it would be a good idea to cover the obvious before we looked further."

Don glowered some more. "I guess."

"Come on, it's lunch time. Let's go find something to eat and figure out our next move."

Forty-Three

Fisherman's Wharf—2800 Block of Taylor Street, San Francisco

From Sea Cliff I took Thirtieth Avenue south to California Street, where I turned left to circumnavigate the Presidio and cross over to Taylor Street. There, I turned north and drove us up a mile and a half to San Francisco's most famous attraction.

Fisherman's Wharf, according to a plaque I stopped to read on my first visit to the wharf, dates back to the 1880s. That's when Italian immigrant fishermen began operating their tiny fleet from a small inlet of the bay in The City's North Beach area. Other Italian immigrants set up wholesale outlets to sell the fish their countrymen brought in, including the much sought after local delicacy, Dungeness crab.

From that point it was only natural that other Italian businessmen would establish restaurants along the wharf where seafood lovers could enjoy meals of freshly caught seafood from tables overlooking the picturesque fishing fleet. Over time the restaurants gained world-wide fame and the prices went up proportionately.

A few entrepreneurs, however, came up with a way of serving seafood to local folks who were hard pressed to afford the prices charged by the highbrow tourist restaurants. They simply set up sidewalk kitchens where they sold crab, chowder, and other seafood creations over their counters at a fraction of what they charged in their restaurants. It was to one of these establishments I planned to take Don Chambers for lunch.

I pulled into a parking spot next to the sidewalk running alongside the wharf, and as we got out of the car, I stopped to inhale a lungful of ozone straight off the bay. Along with the ozone came all manner of fresh seafood smells that promised a great lunch.

Overhead, the sky was that deep shade of blue that only skies can be, providing a backdrop that made the bright white seagulls spiraling overhead seem even brighter and whiter. A lazy breeze fluttered gay red, white and green streamers hanging from the buildings along the wharf, giving the whole scene a Funiculì, Funiculà atmosphere. Fisherman's Wharf was a perfect place to be on a perfect San Francisco day.

Don was taking it all in, too. "So this is the famous Fisherman's Wharf, huh? Looks like a street out of an Italian travelogue."

I said, "And it tastes like it, too."

Don was eyeing the menu attached to a board outside Alioto's Waterside Café. "Holy cow! They must serve this stuff on solid gold plates. These prices are a little steep for a cop's salary."

"For a reporter's salary, too, but step over here and get an education in seafood economics."

He followed me a few feet to the counter of Alioto's sidewalk crab stand, where I pointed to a sign offering crab cocktails for 50-cents and clam chowder served in a carved out bowl of San Francisco sourdough bread for 75-cents. I ordered two of each and said to Don, "It's the same fresh seafood they serve inside at ten times the price."

The Italian fellow behind the counter handed over our chowder and cocktails, and I said, "Come on, Don, now comes the best part."

We walked around the corner to the end of Fisherman's Grotto, the last restaurant on the wharf, and came face to face with the fishing fleet and a half-dozen wooden picnic tables. We settled ourselves at one of the tables closest to the water and dug into our lunches.

Don was clearly enjoying his lunch, but he did take a second out between bites to say, "I gotta hand it to ya, Park. You really know how to live. This is great!"

"Not being a rich guy like Kendall, high living just takes a little more ingenuity, that's all."

"Well, then, thanks for sharing your ingenuity with me." Don paused for a moment for another bite of crab cocktail, and then added, "Speaking of Kendall, you have any idea where to look next?"

"Not yet. I asked Charlie to call the county recorder's office and get them looking for any other property he may own in San Francisco. I'll give her a call after we're through with our lunch and see if she's heard anything."

Don nodded and we both went back to our lunches. When we were done, I pulled the pack of Camels out of my pocket and offered Don one. When I went to put the pack back in my shirt pocket I felt the envelope I'd slipped in my inside coat packet at dinner last night. I pulled it out and removed the three clippings Dandy brought me from Bobby Neumann.

Since I'd only glanced at the articles when Dandy gave them to me, I spent a few minutes reading them to see if they revealed anything of value. I was looking at the last one—the one with the headline that read, "A-K Holdings, Incorporated wins county court battle over permits," when I struck gold. Accordingly, I said, "Eureka!"

Don turned from looking out over the fishing fleet and said, "Whatcha got?"

I held up the clippings. "These are from the *San Francisco Chronicle's* morgue. The guy who runs the place sometimes helps me research stories. The other day I asked him to find what he could on Arden Kendal, Junior. It was a photo in one of the articles he found that gave me the positive ID on Kendall.

"Well, yesterday, he gave me three additional clippings he'd found, and I was just taking a look at them. The third clipping he found has a gem hidden in it. Apparently Kendal owns a holding company called A-K Holdings, Incorporated, and last year they sued the County of San Mateo—that's the next county south of San Francisco—because the county wouldn't issue building permits for a couple of lots on which A-K Holdings wanted to build houses. The county wanted to incorporate the lots into a park on San Bruno Mountain.

"To make a long story short, A-K Holdings won the suit and got their permits. The article describes the property as the 1000 block of San Bruno Avenue in Brisbane. That's where we look next."

"All right, that sounds good. Where is this Brisbane place?"

"Not far. It shouldn't take us more than half an hour to get there after I call the office."

Don picked up the debris from our lunches and dumped it into a trash can. "Okay, let's get to it! Oh, and thanks for lunch."

I ducked into a public telephone booth in the Fisherman's Grotto's lobby and placed a call to Charlie. When I got her on the line, I said, "Hi, kiddo. Anything cooking there?"

"Hi, Park. No, there's nothing going on here and I haven't heard anything from the County Recorder's office about property owned by Arden Kendall, Junior."

"All right. I'm guessing that query is going to come up empty. Would you please call them again and ask 'em to check for property in the name of A-K Holdings, Incorporated? That may get some results."

"Will do. What are you up to?"

"We just had lunch at the wharf and we're about to head down to Brisbane. I have a lead on property in San Mateo County owned by that A-K Holdings outfit. We're going to see what's there."

"Okay. I've got the stories ready to plug into tonight's script, but I need to know how much time you want to devote to the crime report."

"Just figure on three to four minutes of the interview with Don. I'll make sure I'm back there in time to write up an intro and closing to the crime report segment."

"Okay, Park. Good luck."

Forty-Four

Intersection of Bayshore Blvd. & San Bruno Ave., Brisbane

Leaving Fisherman's Wharf, we started south on Taylor and zigzagged our way through downtown until we connected to Bayshore Boulevard below Army Street in the produce district. From there it was a straight shot down to Brisbane where the south end of San Bruno Avenue meets Bayshore. Bayshore Boulevard is also US Highway 101 Bypass in these parts.

I pulled over onto the shoulder a hundred yards or so before we got to San Bruno Avenue and stopped. According to my wristwatch it was 1:45 p.m. Getting to Brisbane had taken about 40 minutes.

We were on the eastern fringes of the town, which were bordered by the bay. Most of the terrain around us to the east was wet and swampy.

To the west was Brisbane proper—mostly tiny inexpensive wood-frame houses, small businesses, and a few acres being farmed. Needless to say, Brisbane is not a prosperous area. In fact, I'd bet the only people in town making money are the land subdividers selling miniscule lots at a hundred bucks a crack to blue collar workers who toil in The City, but can't afford to live there.

The exceptions to this dismal scene were in the lush hills south of town. This was prime real estate at the foot of San Bruno Mountain. These properties offered great views of the bay and roomy lots shaded by large oak trees—country living for those who worked in The City and could afford to live any damned place they wanted. Somewhere in those hills was the property owned by A-K

Holdings.

From where I'd parked, the high-priced property was off to our right. I pointed in that direction and said, "Don, that's San Bruno Mountain over there. San Bruno Avenue turns off the highway to the right just up ahead here and winds its way through those hills. If I'm guessing right, the property owned by Kendal's company is just a short way up that road. What's your pleasure?"

Chambers gave my question a few moments of thought. "Well, we need to take a look at what's up there, but Kendall apparently knows your car and what you look like. Also, if you're right about him picking up your trail when we were in Culver City, he also knows who I am. If he spots this car or us going by his front window, it'll tip our hand for sure."

"True. We might be able to get above San Bruno Avenue on another street further up the hillside and look down on the property, but with all those trees, I doubt we'd see much. Of course, this all assumes Kendall is actually occupying one of the houses he planned to build up there."

Nodding, Don said, "That's what we're here to find out. What would you say to coming back after dark when we won't be so visible?"

"I'd say that's the only safe way to do this. I suppose a few hours won't make that much difference one way or another. All right, let's head back to the barn so I can get my script together for tonight's broadcast. I finish it at six-thirty."

As I restarted the car, Don said, "I've also got to find a place to stay tonight."

"That's no problem. Last night I stayed at an auto court southwest of town so I wouldn't get any surprises at my apartment. I have the room reserved for tonight, too. It's got two beds, if you don't mind bunking together, we can save the great city of Los Angeles a few bucks."

"Sounds good to me as long as there's a decent breakfast place nearby."

Chuckling, I said, "Don't worry, there is. It's not the Java House, but the food ain't bad and the place is convenient."

It was around two-thirty when we got back to KDG. While Don used a public telephone down in the Owl Drugstore to check in with his office, I went up to the fourth floor and checked in with Charlie.

"Hi, Park. You have any luck finding Kendall's property in Brisbane?"

"Yes and no. We know where it is, but there's no way we

could get a look at it without being conspicuous, so we decided to save that job until it gets dark. We'll take another trip down there after my broadcast. You have any luck with the County Recorder's office?"

"Actually, I did. I don't know if it will help, but they came up with something almost immediately when I gave them that A-K Holdings name. A-K owns a warehouse out in the Hunter's Point area by the shipyards. I wrote the address down and put it in the corner of your desk blotter."

"Good work, kiddo."

I picked up the note and was reading it when Chambers walked in. "Hi, Don. Charlie here has come up with another possible location for Kendall. His holding company has a warehouse near the shipyard he owned. We can swing by and take a look on our way back to Brisbane."

"I'm glad to hear some good news. I just got read the riot act by Chief Davis."

"What's his nose out of joint about?"

"Oh, Davis is just under a lot pressure from the press and he wants an arrest pronto."

"Hell, you haven't been up here a full day yet."

Don shook his head in frustration. "I think he expected Kendall to meet me at the railroad station and turn himself in." Then he turned to Charlie and said, "Young woman, would you please explain something to me?"

"Sure, if I can."

Smiling, Don said, "What I want to know is how a cute young thing like you got saddled with a nickname like Charlie. Whoever gave it to you must need glasses."

Charlie blushed a little and said softly, "Thank you, Detective Chambers. That's very kind of you to say."

I was dumbfounded. This was a new side of Don. I'd never seen him being charming before. I figured he was making up for his blunder before we went out to Kendall's place.

Since Charlie was obviously uncomfortable, I said, "Don, stop flirting with my assistant and let's get to work."

Don mumbled, "Spoilsport."

I handed him a San Francisco street map from my desk drawer and suggested he learn his way around while Charlie and I wrapped up my broadcast. She had the script all ready to assemble, and since I didn't have anything new for the crime report, I just wrote an introduction to my interview with Don and we were done. I did, however, pencil in a line at the end of the report saying, "Information that is helping police pin down the whereabouts of the Mob Avenger is coming in almost hourly." It wasn't quite accurate, but I wanted to keep the pressure on Kendall. Guys under pressure are more likely to make mistakes.

Next, I called Dandy at the *Chron* and brought her up to date on what Don and I'd been doing all day. She said the only part of it that sounded like any fun was lunch at the Wharf. I told her she was absolutely right and that, if time permitted, I would call her that evening after Don and I checked out Kendall's property in Brisbane. Throughout the call she seemed cheerful, but a little distracted.

A few minutes before six the entire KDG news staff plus Detective Chambers trekked down the hall to the studio for my broadcast. Charlie and Don went into the engineers' booth so they could watch the proceedings while Dick Stewart and I played our nightly game of musical chairs in the announcers' booth.

Despite not having a whole lot of news or a particularly revealing Special Crime Report, the broadcast went well and I felt pleased when I finally said, "That's your news for Thursday, August Twenty-Fifth. This is Parker T. Atkins. Goodnight, San Francisco."

Back in the news closet we filed the night's script and headed out. After walking Charlie to the streetcar stop, Don and I set out to find Kendall. Getting into my Ford, my eye was again drawn to the dent and shiny spot of bare metal where Kendall's slug had taken a wrong turn toward my head. Instinctively, I checked my shoulder holster to be sure my Colt Detective Special was where it belonged.

Don noticed and said, "That looks like the same rig you had when you were with the department."

"Yup, but it doesn't get much use these days. Tonight it's more for moral support than anything else."

I expected Chambers to remind me that I wasn't a cop anymore, but he didn't. Don just said, "Yeah, an ounce of prevention and all that."

Forty-Five

Hunters Point Shipyard—Bayview District, San Francisco

Hunters Point Shipyard sits in an area southeast of downtown usually referred to as the Bayview District. This part of town is mostly tidal wetlands and has been the home of shipbuilding in San Francisco since the 1800s. More recently, though, the Bayview District has become better known as one of the highest crime areas in San Francisco.

Aside from the actual dry docks and ship-building facilities, some of the useable space at Hunters Point is taken up with warehouses and small companies supporting the ship-building industry with materials, parts and tools. The rest of the area is cheap housing—mostly Public Works Administration projects—for blue-collar laborers who work on the ships being built at the shipyard.

Needless to say the Bayview District is not a popular place for late-night strolls. Even with an armed police detective in my passenger seat and a revolver in my shoulder holster, I'll admit to feeling a little nervous while we looked for Arden Kendall, Junior's warehouse at the southwest corner of Griffith and Quesada streets.

When we arrived at our destination, we found about what I expected, a large boarded-up concrete building that gave every indication of being deserted. We drove around the block looking for signs that someone was there or had been there recently, but found nothing.

Don summed up the situation pretty well. "This definitely isn't the sort of neighborhood where a guy with Kendall's money is likely to hang out, no matter how desperate he is to stay out of

215

sight."

"Agreed. Let's get out of here and down to Brisbane before some hoodlum steals the wheels off the car while we're driving down the street."

Since we were only a hoot and a holler from Brisbane, the rest of the trip only took about fifteen minutes. When we reached the point where San Bruno Avenue intersects Bayshore Boulevard, I turned right and drove slowly up the hill. According to the addresses on the first few residences we came to, we were in the 1100 block.

There were no street lights along this relatively uninhabited section of San Bruno Avenue, which made navigation a little tricky. In addition, the blocks were long. We did a lot of twisting and turning before coming to a cross street and the 1000 block.

The first and only residences we encountered there were located to our left on the west side of the street at a point where San Bruno Avenue curved sharply to the right. The vacant lot opposite the houses was thick with eucalyptus trees, but through the spaces between their narrow trunks we could make out the lights of The City to the north and those of Oakland and Hayward across the bay. The two houses we'd come to see were built on a hillside a little above street level, which gave them even more spectacular views.

Don was looking for house numbers as we got closer and he found them. "The first house there is 1002 and the second is 1000."

"Any signs of life?"

"No, they're both dark, except for a porch light above the front door of the second house."

I slowed to a crawl for a better look. The two houses were right next to each other and surrounded by eucalyptus and pine. Further up the hillside we could see a couple of lights from houses fronting on another street. The question was, which of the two houses in front of us might be occupied by Arden Kendall, Junior, if he actually occupied either of them?

We were almost past the second house when a band of light appeared along the bottom of its lift-up garage door. Not wanting to get caught lollygagging in front of Kendall's property, I stepped on the gas. At the same time Don turned so he could see out the rear window as we accelerated up the hill.

"Slow down, Park. Let's see who's going out for an evening drive."

I slowed, and then stopped just before the next curve. "I hope to hell he goes down the hill instead of in our direction."

Almost a minute passed before Don said, "Turn around! It's a light colored coupe and it's heading down the hill."

After as quick a Y-turn as I could manage on the narrow road, I doused the lights so whoever was in front of us wouldn't see us following him and drove back down the hill as fast as I dared in the dark. When the tail lights ahead of us disappeared around the bend near the bottom of the hill I gave it the gas again. In a few seconds the car ahead would have to turn left or right onto Bayshore Boulevard. If we weren't there to see which way he went, we'd lose the guy, whoever he was.

Rounding the bend on two wheels, we saw tail lights turning right on Bayshore Boulevard, and because there was a streetlight at the intersection, we also saw the car clearly enough to identify it. I said, "That, sir, is a Chrysler Imperial Eight Coupe in the fashionable hue of Phantom Gray."

"Damn, maybe we're finally getting a break!"

Approaching Bayshore Boulevard I switched on my headlights and said, "Maybe. Keep him in sight while I get us heading the same direction."

"Got him."

I made the turn and pushed the foot-feed to the floorboard. We closed the gap quickly, which meant Kendall wasn't in any hurry. If he'd known we were following him, we'd be hard pressed to keep up with him in my Ford.

I was beginning to think Don might be right about us finally getting a break when he said, "Okay, we've got the Mob Avenger in our sights, what are we gonna do about it?"

As I slowed down to match the Chrysler's speed about a quarter mile behind it, I said, "That's up to you, Mister Detective Lieutenant, but having him in our sights and having him in cuffs are two different things."

"True. You think we can stay behind him long enough to see where he's headed?"

"I think so, as long as he sticks to well-traveled roads and doesn't spot us following him. If he sees us, we're done . . ."

"Watch it! He's turning!"

The now familiar Chrysler tail lights swung abruptly to the right. As I slowed to make the turn, I saw a street sign out of the corner of my eye. We were now heading west on Hillside Boulevard, which wasn't at all to my liking. Hillside is a rural road skirting the southern edge of San Bruno Mountain. We were in the hinterlands again on a road that did a lot of twisting and turning. Worse, there was no other traffic on the road.

Dropping back, I switched the headlights off again and focused all my attention on the side of the road to keep from driving us into a ditch. Up ahead the Chrysler's tail lights kept disappearing and reappearing as Hillside wound its way through one curve after another. Thanks to Don's sharp eyes, though, we got another break.

"He's turning again, Park . . . left in about a quarter of a mile."

Hoping we weren't close enough for Kendall to notice, I switched my headlights on again and sped up. A few seconds later Don said, "The turn should be just about here."

I spotted the road and swung left. I didn't catch the name of the street, but it didn't matter. The new route was heading into a populated area with houses, businesses and an occasional streetlight. I could also see a major thoroughfare up ahead. It was US 101, or El Camino Real as it's known hereabouts.

When Kendall's Chrysler stopped at the intersection, I slowed way down so as not to end up on his back bumper. I was just about to pull over and stop when Kendall got a break in the traffic and made his turn. Don said, "He turned left onto that highway."

"Got it."

I made my own break in the traffic and squealed the tires as we turned south onto El Camino. "You still have him, Don?"

"Yeah. He's up there about half a mile."

"Good. I'll close up the distance some."

The City of San Bruno, through which we were passing, had grown up along El Camino and was a substantial suburb of San Francisco. As such, there were a fair number of business on both sides of the road—mostly one- and two-story wood-frame retail outlets purveying everything from appliances to real estate. Streetlights illuminated a maze of overhead wires going every which way, some of them over the streetcar tracks running down the center of the road. Yes, indeed, San Bruno was doing quite well for itself.

We were passing one of San Bruno's major attractions, a popular horseracing track called Tanforan, when Don announced that Kendall was making yet another turn. This time he turned west onto Sneath Lane.

Sneath Lane is a long, fairly straight avenue through a quiet residential district, so I lagged back again in case Kendall was watching his rearview mirror. I also tried to remember where the hell Sneath Lane ended up. If my memory was right, it dead-ended at a north-south road appropriately named Skyline

Boulevard. The name was appropriate because Skyline runs along the crest of the low hills separating the Pacific Ocean coastal communities from the rest of the San Francisco Peninsula.

Less than five minutes had passed before Don said, "Looks like we're coming to a T-intersection...yeah, we are, and Kendall turned left."

As we approached the same intersection a sign planted on the right shoulder said "Skyline Boulevard" with arrows pointing in both directions. For a guy who didn't know he was being followed, Kendall was sure taking a roundabout route. Maybe he was just a naturally cautious sort of fellow.

A fairly well traveled thoroughfare, Skyline has gradual curves, but it goes up and down over hill and dale so the Chrysler's tail lights occasionally disappeared from sight. There were few cross streets, though, so I wasn't too worried about losing Kendall.

Skyline's route takes it through a dense forest of redwood and fir trees, although at night the trees were little more than tall dark shapes closing in on both sides of the road, They created the impression of driving through a long tunnel. Our surroundings reminded me of Dandy talking about a tradition according to which her dad drives the family up here every year to cut down their annual Christmas tree.

Besides keeping an eye on Kendall, Don was also taking in what he could see of the scenery. Finally his curiosity got the best of him. He said, "Where the devil are we?"

I explained Skyline Boulevard and gave him my best tour guide description of the natural wonders through which we were passing. I ended my dissertation by saying, "Except for crossing the Golden Gate Bridge, spots along this road are the only places on the peninsula where you can see both the Pacific Ocean and San Francisco Bay from the same location."

In a tone soggy with sarcasm, Don said, "That's just swell, Atkins, but I don't think the Mob Avenger is out here in the sticks on a sightseeing trip. You got any idea where the hell he's going?"

That question had been on my mind since we began following Kendall and a hunch had taken shape in my mind. I said, "Well, there are still several possibilities, but one of those possibilities is he's heading for a coastal community—maybe Half Moon Bay—with a protected harbor large enough to accommodate an ocean-going vessel.

"If we've put enough pressure on him, he might be feeling the need for a vacation and, with his maritime background, it may have occurred to Kendall that a cruise down the coast to Mexico or up to Canada would be a good way to get lost for a while without taking public transportation."

Don seemed to mull that idea over for a while. Finally, he said, "Makes sense, but if that's what he's planning, we have to nail him before he gets on a boat. After that, catching him will be damned tough. How far is this Moon Bay place?"

"Half Moon Bay? Not far, maybe 30 minutes from here. It's a small town made up largely of Portuguese fishermen, and a good-sized fishing boat could make the trip to Mexico in calm seas without much difficulty."

About nine-fifteen we began catching glimpses of a good-sized body of water in a shallow valley to our right. I pointed it out to Don, saying, "That's Crystal Springs Reservoir down there. It's San Francisco's primary water supply."

Apparently not impressed, Don said, "Goody, let's stop and pee in it."

"Hey, part of that water came all the way over here from the Hetch Hetchy Valley in Yosemite. It's some of the purist water in the state."

"Big deal."

"It's a big deal to us for one important reason. The shortest route to the coast from here is Half Moon Bay Road, which heads west across that reservoir in another mile or two. If Kendall takes it, we'll have a much clearer idea where he's headed."

Forty-Six

Crystal Springs Reservoir—Skyline Blvd, San Mateo County

The dim light from the Ford's dashboard showed me the hands on my wristwatch, which were pointing at nine-twenty when Don announced, "Looks like you might be right about that Moon Bay being Kendall's destination. He's slowing up, maybe to make a turn."

A moment later the Chrysler's tail lights disappeared for a few seconds. When they reappeared, they were heading west. At almost the same time an Automobile Association directional sign showed up alongside the road with an arrow pointing to the right. The words said, "Half Moon Bay – 7 Miles."

I made the turn and stepped down on the gas to close up the distance between us and Kendall. We were now on Half Moon Bay Road, a narrow winding two lane thoroughfare passing through the same sort of dense forest we'd seen on Skyline. It certainly wasn't an ideal road for following someone if you wanted to remain unseen. On the other hand, there are no cross-roads that go anywhere worth going, so I still wasn't worried about losing the Chrysler. We had seven miles to cover before that became a concern again.

Explaining this to Don, I said, "Well, that cinches it. Kendall is heading to the coast. Whether or not Half Moon Bay is his ultimate destination remains to be seen, but there aren't any places to turn off between here and there."

By nine-thirty we were starting to see signs of civilization again—a few small houses and roadside produce stands that were boarded up for the night. The produce stands were indicative of

Half Moon Bay's other industry besides fishing. The coastal soil lends itself to growing produce—mostly onions, garlic, artichokes, lettuce, carrots, and the like. I've actually heard of folks living on the peninsula making the trek all the way over here just to buy fresh vegetables. Not being a big fan of vegetables, though, I have no first-hand knowledge of that.

Alerting Don, I said, "Shortly this road dead-ends at California Route One and Kendall will make a turn north or south toward his destination. I'm going to close up on him a little so we don't miss his turn."

As I picked up our pace, Don's apprehension and impatience were both showing as he said, "Good. I'm tired of all this wandering around. Let's nail this son-of-a-gun."

We topped a small rise about a quarter mile from Route One just in time to see the Chrysler turn north. Now I was so sure of Kendall's destination I'd have bet money on it. He was headed for Pillar Point harbor.

"Don, a few miles up the road there's a little inlet called Pillar Point. It's a protected harbor, and that's where most of the local fishing boats tie up. I'm ninety-nine percent sure that's where Kendall is headed."

"Ya think so? How come you know so much about this place?"

"I used to come down here on a regular basis for Saturday night poker games with some of the fishermen."

Don chuckled. "I should've figured it was something like that."

"Getting back to Kendall, there's something else you should know."

"What's that?"

"We're in a completely different law enforcement district here. This is San Mateo County. Now, I've worked with a deputy from the county sheriff's department down here and he's pretty sharp. If you think some back-up would be helpful, I can try to get a telephone message through to him."

Don said, "We may not have time to wait for anyone to get out here, but it might be a good idea to let him know we're in his bailiwick if there's a telephone around when Kendall lights somewhere. I mean if there's time. Otherwise, we'll just have to take Kendall ourselves."

I experienced a flash of deja vu when Don said that. Suddenly we were moving cautiously through a dark alley in East LA stalking a suspect—something we'd done often when I was on the force. Pursuing Kendall wasn't exactly fun, but I felt a tingle of excitement at being part of that team again.

"Okay, Don. It's your call. Do you have Kendall in sight up there?"

"Yup, I've got him. If you're right about his destination, I guess he'll be making that turn soon."

"Should be."

During the next few minutes we passed the beach communities of Miramar and El Granada, and then I saw the lights of Princeton-by-the-Sea, the tiny community built around Pillar Point harbor. I said, "Those lights up ahead on the left are the little village at Pillar Point. Kendall ought to be making a left turn . . ."

"There he goes."

Feeling a little smug for having figured out Kendall's destination, I slowed and prepared to follow him out to the harbor at a reasonable distance. After making the turn I switched off the lights and rolled slowly along the gravel road that leads to the harbor.

Pillar Point, itself, is the tip of a hook-shaped piece of land that runs west, and then curves back around to the southeast, creating an inlet about a mile wide on its open side. Moonlight reflected off ripples that slowly moved through the harbor past a dozen or so commercial fishing boats and a two-masted yawl that looked to be at least fifty or sixty feet in length. It caught my attention because I wasn't used to seeing yachts in the Pillar Point harbor, particularly yachts that large.

Pillar Point was quiet. The only sound we heard was the crunch of our tires on the gravel road as we passed a small fish market and general store, and then curved from west to southwest.

Up ahead a scattering of weathered wooden shacks lined our route and Kendall was slowing to a crawl. I stopped to see where he was headed before we got any closer. The big barn-like doors on one of the larger buildings, a shed about the size of a large garage, stood open and Kendall drove through them. He shut off his lights and seemed to be sitting there in the dark waiting for someone or something.

I said, "That looks like a good place to stash a car while on an ocean voyage."

"Sure does. I wonder what he's waiting for."

"If we're on the right track, he's probably waiting for someone from the boat he'll be boarding. I'm going to pull up alongside that next shack so we won't be so visible."

"All right. This might be a good time to take him. What do you think?"

As I pulled up next to a deserted shack on our right and shut off the engine, I said, "I'd feel more comfortable knowing who he's waiting for. I'd hate for us to get caught in our own trap."

"Fair enough. Did you notice that fish shop we passed when we drove in?"

"Yeah, and I also noticed it has a telephone. Want me to make a call while you keep an eye on Kendall?"

"As long as we've got the time, it wouldn't hurt."

"Okay. Be right back."

Moving as quietly as I could, I slipped out the driver-side door and trotted fifty or so yards back up the road to the fish market. Stepping into the telephone booth, I dialed for an operator. When she came on the line, I said, "This is a police emergency. I need the San Mateo County Sheriff's headquarters."

She simply said, "Yes, sir."

That was followed by a couple of clicks and a single ring sound. "San Mateo County Sheriff. Deputy Collins speaking."

"Deputy Collins, my name is Parker Atkins and I need to get an emergency message to Deputy Will Framm."

"He's in the next room. Stand by while I get him."

I heard wooden chair legs scrape a floor and Collins' voice saying, "Sergeant Framm, I have an emergency call for you."

Ten seconds after that, Framm's voice said, "This is Sergeant Framm."

"Will, this is Park Atkins."

"Hi, Park. What kind of trouble have you gotten yourself into this time?"

It was meant to be a joke, but my sense of humor was out of order at the moment. "Will, I'm out at Pillar Point with a Los Angeles Police Department Homicide Lieutenant. He has a fugitive warrant to serve on a suspect we think is about to leave the country by boat. I wanted to let you know what was going on and ask for some back-up if that's possible."

"I take this suspect is armed and dangerous?"

"He is."

"I'm on my way, but it'll take me 30 minutes to get there."

"That may get you here too late, but do the best you can."

Returning the telephone receiver to its hook, I took a quick look at my watch. It was a few minutes short of ten o'clock.

As I headed back to my car, I noticed the passenger door was open. I looked around for Don, but he was nowhere to be seen. I also noticed that the barn doors on the shed where Kendall parked his car were closed.

Whoever Kendall was waiting for must have showed up and Don was forced to follow. The question was, where did he follow them to? The water seemed like the best bet, so I started jogging toward the beach to my left.

That's when I heard Don shout, "Freeze, Kendall! Police! Get your hands over your heads, both of you."

Don's voice seemed to be coming from the last shack on my left, about a hundred feet ahead. I turned on the speed, and as I did, two gunshots shattered the quiet of the peaceful little harbor. A flock of sleeping seagulls on the beach to my left took to the air squawking to beat the band.

At the shed, I peeked around the corner toward the beach. In an instant the situation became abundantly clear. Don was on the ground next to the shack behind a wooden crate of some kind, his thirty-eight pointed toward the water. At the water's edge about 150 feet away were three beached rowboats. At that moment another shot popped and I saw a muzzle flash from the vicinity of the middle rowboat. A small puff of sand erupted two feet from where I was standing.

Diving for the ground, I said, "I'm right behind you, Don." As I worked my Colt Detective Special out of its holster, I asked, "How many?"

Keeping his eyes on the beach, he said, "There are two of 'em behind that middle skiff. They were about to take it out into the bay when I identified myself. Your pal in the Homburg, turned and fired without any hesitation. I don't know if the second guy is armed or not."

Sizing things up, I suggested the only plan I could think of. "There's no cover between us and them, but if you can keep 'em occupied, I might be able to work my way around to flank them from the other side of this shed."

"That's as good a plan as any. Your sheriff buddy coming?"

"Yeah, but he's still at least twenty minutes away."

"Somebody's gonna be dead by then. Let's make sure it's one of them. Go."

I slithered back to the road side of the shed and ran around to the side opposite Don's position. The only cover I could see on the beach were two sizeable chunks of driftwood near where the seagulls had been snoozing. The driftwood would have to do for cover. I slipped the Colt back into its holster and getting into a crouch, I took off running for all I was worth.

I hadn't made more than twenty-five feet when another shot and muzzle flash came from behind the rowboat. Don fired once to draw their attention back to him while I dug into the sand on my belly. I didn't see where the slug went, but now I knew something I didn't know before. There were at least two guns behind the cover of the boat, and the second one was a large caliber piece, maybe a forty-four or a forty-five.

I got moving again, this time on my stomach, inching along through the sand. It was slow going, but the two men behind the boat apparently couldn't see me. The large caliber pistol fired again, but the slug went well behind my position toward where they last saw me.

Don was conserving his ammo. He fired again, but just once. That made me think he might only have the rounds in his revolver or maybe six spares in his pocket. I was a little better prepared because I had six rounds in my Colt and the handful I dropped into my jacket pocket when I took the pistol from its hiding place in my kitchen. Still, I hadn't anticipated a damned shootout.

Another four or five minutes on my belly brought me to the first log of driftwood. I hunkered down behind it and risked a look. My position was better than I expected. If I could make it to the next piece of driftwood—ten feet away—it looked like I might have a clear shot at the first one of them who raised his head to fire at me or Don.

Rather than exposing my position by climbing over the driftwood, I crawled around the closest end and went back to inching my way through the sand. Things had gotten very quiet. Then Don yelled, "All right, you guys, you're surrounded. Toss out your guns and stand up. Otherwise both of you will have to be carried off this beach."

If I hadn't known Don as well as I did, I might not have noticed the strain in his voice. It sounded to me as if he was in pain. Had one of Kendall's shots hit him?

With that thought on my mind, I picked up my speed through the sand as much as I could. If Don was hurt, I might not be able to count on him to keep their attention much longer.

When I finally got into the position I wanted, I pulled my Colt out again and braced it on top of the driftwood. I carefully aimed at where I expected one or the other of the men would appear and waited.

It seemed like forever, but one of them finally stuck his head up over the gunnel of the rowboat and aimed his pistol at Don. At least, that's what I figured he was doing because there wasn't enough light to see more than a silhouette. I swung my sights slightly to the right and squeezed the trigger.

Instead of ducking down, the dark shape pitched backward. I'd hit one of them with an improbable shot at a range of nearly a hundred feet. A second later a voice I didn't recognize came from behind the rowboat.

"All right, mate, I give up. Here's my gun."

Something dark flew from behind the rowboat. When Don didn't say anything, I did. "Okay, mister, stand up and get your hands over your head. You'd be smart to do exactly as I say because I won't need much of an excuse to blow your damned head off!"

I was talking with a lot more confidence than I was feeling, and I was actually a little surprised when the guy followed my instructions to the letter. I shouted, "Now walk around this side of the dingy and keep coming."

Again the fellow did exactly as he was told. With him standing up, I got a better look. He was a good head taller than Kendall and hefty—not a guy I'd want to meet in a dark alley. When he was ten feet beyond where he'd thrown his gun, I shouted, "Now stop and get face down on the sand."

Figuring it was safe to stand up at that point, I walked toward the rowboat and looked for Kendall. I could see a dark shape lying on its back. The incoming tide was lapping at his head and a homburg hat on the sand. Since he didn't appear to offer much of a threat, I picked up the second guy's revolver—a long-barreled British Webley Mark VI. The damned thing was heavy as hell. Making sure the hammer was down so I wouldn't shoot myself, I shoved the little cannon into the waistband of my slacks.

All this time I was wondering about Don. I hadn't heard a sound out of him and that convinced me he was hurt. Well, first things first.

I walked within five feet of the fellow on the sand and said, "Okay, pal, on your hands and knees and crawl toward that shack over there."

As he got to his hands and knees, it finally dawned on me that I'd made a critical mistake that could prove fatal. There had been TWO pistols behind that rowboat!

The guy quickly rolled onto his back and I saw the barrel of Kendall's little semi-automatic poking out of his right hand. I jumped left and fired at the same moment he did. I felt something tug at the right side of my coat and my would-be killer's right arm flopped onto the sand, dropping the pistol. I'd put my slug straight into his chest.

That's when I heard Will Framm's voice say, "Guess I'm a little late for the party."

Feeling very relieved, I said, "Yeah, just a little, but I'm still damned glad to see you."

Leaning down to pick up Kendall's Browning from the sand, Will said, "This your suspect?"

"No, this is the guy who was going to take him out to a boat. Our suspect is back there behind that middle skiff. I've already picked up the other gun. Would you mind checking on them. I think the LAPD detective was hit during the shooting. He's over by that shack and I want to check on him."

"Go ahead. I'll take care of anything that needs doing here."

On slightly wobbly knees, I ran to Don. He was face down behind the crate he'd been using for cover, and when I rolled him over, the sand under him was soaked with an alarming amount of blood. There was so much blood I couldn't tell where he'd been hit. I checked for a pulse and found one—a weak one, but he was alive.

I looked back at the beach and saw Will dragging Kendall across the sand. I shouted, "We're gonna need an ambulance, fast!"

Will shouted back, "Run over to that fish market. There's a payphone you can use. Have the operator connect you to Purisima Ambulance Service. They're in Half Moon Bay. Tell 'em to send two. This guy is still with us. The one you shot on the beach is gone."

As I turned to run for the telephone, a mental picture flashed in my mind. The yawl that had been anchored in the harbor was in a different place. It was heading out to sea—this time the ship was deserting the sinking rats.

Forty-Seven

While Deputy Will Framm gave a last look to the homicide report we'd spent the past hour writing, I leaned back in the old wooden chair Mills Hospital provided for my comfort. The chair groaned and creaked. The chair and I were kindred spirits.

Will, the creaky chair and I were in a room that said "Staff Lounge" on the door. Mill's Hospital had kindly donated the space to our use while we sorted out the Pillar Point shootout.

Before joining Will for the paperwork, I'd paced a waiting room floor like an expectant father while the doctors worked on Don Chambers and Arden Kendall, Junior. I didn't really care much one way or another what happened to Kendall. At worst, his death would be an inconvenience because it would leave some unanswered questions.

Don was an entirely different matter. We'd known each other a long time and were friends. He'd been around during the lowest and highest points of my life thus far, and I hoped that relationship would continue for a lot of years to come.

Don made it. He'd taken a shot below the ribs on his right side. The slug nicked an artery and he'd come close to dying from loss of blood, but the Mills doctors pulled him through. Don would be laid up for a while, but he would live to eat a lot more donuts and baloney sandwiches.

Kendall made it, too. My lucky shot out on the beach at Pillar Point had tumbled after entering his body and it did a thorough job of tearing up his insides, but he would live long enough to be convicted of multiple murders and take a seat in California's gas chamber.

Will said, "It looks like we've got all the I's dotted and T's crossed in this homicide report. Anything else you want to add?"

I'd already given that question some thought, and aside from my personal feelings about killing the sailor, I was confident we'd included all the salient details. "No, Will. I'm pretty sure we've covered it all. You think I'll have any problems getting cleared of the shootings?"

"You've got nothing to worry about on that score. You were a duly deputized officer of the Los Angeles Police Department performing your duty—at least that's the way I put it here. Besides, you acted in self-defense. If Detective Lieutenant Chambers agrees with this report, you're home free. I don't think you'll even need to show up at the inquest."

Standing, I said, "That's good news. If you're through with me for now, I'd like to check on Don again, and then go home for some sleep."

"Sure. I know where to find you if I need to." Then something about my jacket caught his eye. Will said, "Wait a minute, Park. Come over here."

I walked around the table and Will grabbed the right side of my jacket. He promptly stuck his finger through a hole in the fabric about where my hip would normally be. "Damn! You came a lot closer to being in here as a patient than I thought."

Remembering the tug I'd felt on my jacket as I dodged away from the sailor's aim, I said, "Yeah, I guess I did. I wonder if the LAPD will cover the cost of a jacket damaged in the line of duty."

Will chuckled. "I wouldn't count on that, Park."

Then we walked down the corridor to Don's room. Well, Will walked. I sort of stumbled along after him because I suddenly had a case of wobbly knees caused by the realization of how close I'd come to buying the farm because of a stupid mistake the greenest rookie wouldn't have made. The hole in my jacket, however, did a lot to alleviate the guilt I'd been feeling about killing the sailor.

As we walked by the room Kendall now occupied I took note of the sheriff's deputy standing in front of the door. Will said, "We're taking no chances. Now that you caught this guy, I don't want him disappearing on my watch. By the way, the county will have some charges to bring against Kendall, but LA has first dibs. We need to make arrangements with them to take him into custody when he can be moved. You want me to put in a call to the LAPD or do you want to have them call me?"

After a moment of thought, I replied, "I think I better initiate the process. This whole thing is kind of complex and it will take some explaining. If you don't mind, I'll call Chief Davis in LA later this morning and brief him on how things stand. Then his people can call you to make whatever arrangements need to be made."

"I don't mind at all, Park, but we need to get together for lunch sometime soon so you can tell me the whole story of how you tracked this guy down. I imagine it's a hell of a tale."

"It is, Will. In fact, it's going to take me some time to sort it all out for my broadcast tonight. The Mob Avenger, as the papers call Kendall, is a smart cookie. He planned his murders well and did a good job of covering his tracks. On top of that, he came damned close to getting out of the country sight unseen. If Don and I hadn't been there at the right moment to see him leave his hideout tonight, he'd be long gone by now.

"Plus, there are still a lot of bits and pieces about this case we don't know, but no matter how noble his motives, the guy is a cold-blooded killer. The sad thing is, if they send him to the gas chamber, it will be an unpopular verdict with the people of Los Angeles. They look at this guy as some sort of hero."

"I can see how that would be. Some good might come of it, though. This might just motivate the cops down there to straighten out their act."

"It might, but that will be a tall order. The corruption goes all the way from beat cops to the DA's office, and if the state moves in to investigate the situation, a lot of heads will roll."

We didn't spend much time in Don's room. He was still out and would be for a while, but he was breathing and looking a hell of a lot better than he had out by that shack on Pillar Point. I left a message with his nurse to the effect that I would be back around mid-morning for a visit.

Out in the hospital parking lot Will and I shook hands and I said, "Will, I can't thank you enough for coming to our rescue out there."

With an aw-shucks tone in his voice, he said, "I didn't do much, Park. If I'd had more advance notice, I could've been a lot more help."

"That couldn't be avoided, Will. We followed Kendall all the way from Brisbane without any idea where he was going until he finally led us to Pillar Point. Believe me, if I could have gotten you involved earlier, I would have."

"I understand. That's how it often goes in our business. Until we learn how to read minds, all we can do is try to be in the right place at the right time. Now go get yourself some sleep. You've earned it."

"Thanks, Will. I'll see you later."

Traffic on El Camino Real was almost nonexistent at two o'clock in the morning, so I made the trip to my temporary home at the Mission Auto Court in less than thirty minutes. I was dog-tired at the hospital, but after cleaning up and flopping on the bed, I was wide awake. I guess that was sort of a delayed reaction to the evening's events. As I lay there, I heard Will Framm's voice saying, "That's how it often goes in our business."

Our business? Was I in his business? I certainly had been a few hours ago, and I recalled the tingle of excitement I felt being on the hunt with Don again. Was I just a cop at heart? That was a possibility, but at the moment, I was a radio news reporter. On the other hand, in eleven days I wouldn't be anything. The sixth of September was to be my last day at KDG, and that date was approaching rapidly.

Given the feelings I'd experienced during the past day or two, maybe the solution to my unemployment problem was returning to a job in law enforcement. No, that wasn't possible. Given my record with the LAPD and subsequent drinking, no law enforcement agency was going to have any interest in adding Parker T. Atkins to their payroll. And even if I had a spotless resume', there was Dandy to think of.

We'd patched things up when she came to see me at Saint Mary's Hospital, and over dinner that night we agreed to discuss our future together as soon as the Mob Avenger was behind bars, which he now more or less was. The thing is, Dandy thought of me as a journalist, not a cop, and I was pretty sure in her mind journalists occupied a much higher position in the overall scheme of things than cops. Lots of cops had kids and wives, but not wives like Dandy. No, the door to a career in law enforcement was closed to me. The real trouble was, I didn't know if that was a good thing or a bad thing.

Forty-Eight

KDG Radio Studios–730 Market Street, San Francisco

I walked into our news closet at KDG and received a warm welcome from Charlie. "Gosh, Park, you look like hell. What did you do all night instead of sleeping?"

Sliding into my chair, I stifled a yawn and said, "Not much. Oh yeah, we caught the Mob Avenger, but besides that, not much."

Charlie's head popped up from the yellow strips of AP wire service copy on her desk. "You caught him!? Tell me!"

I gave her the Reader's Digest condensed version of the night's events, promising to fill in the missing parts as they occurred to me. When I finished the tale, Charlie said, "Wow! I'm sorry to hear Detective Chambers was hurt. He's a nice guy."

"He is," I agreed. "And despite appearances sometimes, he's also a good friend."

Grinning, she said, "I'll bet Sergeant Framm was thrilled to hear from you again."

"Actually, he didn't seem to mind, even though we dumped a load of paperwork on him. Will's a good cop and I was damned glad to see him when he finally got out to Pillar Point."

"Does Dandy know what you were up to last night?"

I nodded. "Yes. I called her a little while ago from home."

Charlie's expression changed to concern. "What did she say? I mean, if you don't mind telling me."

"No reason not to. Sometimes I think you know more about Dandy and me than I do."

She looked embarrassed. "I'm sorry, Park, I don't mean to . . ."

"It's okay, kiddo. I know you ask because you care. Dandy reacted about the way you'd expect. She was upset, but relieved Mob Avenger thing is all over now. We're gonna have dinner after the broadcast tonight."

I was watching Charlie's face and I could tell she wanted to know more, but didn't want me to think she was sticking her nose where it didn't belong again. There wasn't much more I could have told her anyway. Whatever the future held for Dandy and me was still very much up in the air.

Changing the subject, I said, "I gotta call the LAPD and let 'em know what happened last night."

"They should be pleased."

"You'd think so, but with those guys, you never know."

Charlie returned to her wire service copy, asking, "How much time for your Crime Report tonight?"

"Unless you've got a lot of hot news there, try to leave me eight or nine minutes. I need to recap the story and wrap things up."

"Okay, Park. Oh, and congratulations on last night. I'm proud of you!"

On that note I slid the phone on my desk closer and picked up the receiver. When I got the long distance operator on the line, I told her I wanted to make a person-to-person call to Los Angeles Police Chief James Davis. When she asked who was calling, I said, "Please tell them it's Parker Atkins calling on behalf of Detective Don Chambers."

Apparently getting the chief of the LAPD on the phone is a complex affair. It took most of 15 minutes before I heard the man say, "Davis."

"Good morning, Chief Davis. This is Parker Atkins. You don't know me, but . . ."

"I know who you are, Atkins. Where the hell is Chambers? I haven't heard a word out of him since yesterday afternoon!"

"You'll be hearing from him soon, but at the moment he's in a hospital up near San Francisco recovering from a gunshot wound."

That didn't faze Davis in the least. "How the hell did he get himself shot?"

"Don was shot last night during the apprehension of suspect Arden Kendall, Junior."

That got the chief's attention. "What? Chambers finally got him?"

"Yes, we finally got him. The suspect was also wounded during the arrest. Kendall is in the same hospital as Don. My reason for calling is to put you in touch with Sergeant Will Framm of the San Mateo County Sheriff's office so you can arrange to have Kendall transported down there when he can be moved."

"Yeah, okay. Now tell me what the hell happened up there. Where'd Chambers find Kendall?"

By this time Davis' attitude had thoroughly ticked me off. He wanted to know what happened so he could tell the press what a hero he was for single-handedly leading the department to the capture of the Mob Avenger. Davis never once asked about Don's condition.

"Davis, I'm tired of talking to you. Call the San Mateo Sheriff's office and talk to Will Framm. He can read the homicide report to you."

I heard him shouting something about who the hell got killed as I dropped the receiver back into its cradle. I glanced up at Charlie and she looked absolutely shocked. I said, "What's the matter with you?"

"Did you just hang up on the most powerful cop in California?"

"If that's what Davis is, the answer is yes. He's also the most crooked cop in the state and he ticked me off. He doesn't give a damn what happened to his detective, who will not receive a lick of credit for collaring the most wanted killer in the state. Davis is nothing but a pile of . . . garbage."

"Holy cow! Remind me not to tick you off!"

Smiling, I said, "That's a good thing to keep in mind."

"I guess so!"

I looked at my wristwatch and said, "It's nine. I'm going down to San Mateo. I want to see how Don's doing. I'll make it quick so I can get back and finish tonight's script."

It was a few minutes before ten when I parked my car in the Mills Hospital parking lot. Up on the second floor it was obvious Will had increased his security. Besides the deputy in front of Kendall's room, there were deputies at each end of the hall. The one I passed at the head of the stairs stopped me. "You're Atkins, aren't you?"

"Yeah, that's me."

"Sergeant Framm said to tell you he heard from the LA Police Department and everything is under control."

"Good. Thanks for the message. How's your prisoner doing?"

He shook his head. "All I know is the doctors and nurses in this place are in and out of his room about every ten minutes. I know that because we have to check every single one of them in and out."

I thanked him and walked on down to Don's room. I opened the door quietly so as not to disturb him if he was sleeping. He wasn't.

"Get your butt in here, Atkins. This place is already driving me nuts. They won't tell me a damned thing about what happened last night."

"That's probably because they don't know what happened out there. In fact, you, me and Kendall are the only ones who know firsthand what went on out at Pillar Point."

"Yeah, I heard Kendall's in bad shape, but still breathing. My boss told me that piece of news. He also mentioned you. In his words, 'That SOB hung up on me!'"

"I'm surprised he noticed."

"Geez, Park, I have to work with that guy. He said if you show up in LA, he's gonna toss you in his slammer and throw away the key."

Grinning, I said, "That's gratitude for you."

"Well, he did change his tune a little when I gave you credit for finding Kendall and nailing him. I also pointed out that you saved my life and put a happy ending on a really screwed up situation."

"I'm sure I'll be receiving a formal apology and a letter expressing his undying gratitude. Heck, maybe he'll even give me a commendation."

Don's sense of humor was returning. He smiled. "Don't push your luck, Park. I'm sure Davis never apologized to anyone in his life. As for gratitude, you'll have to be satisfied with mine. Thanks. You haven't forgotten how to be a good cop."

"You're welcome, Don, but I have to admit I made a rookie mistake out there that almost got me killed. I'm not too proud of that."

"I don't know what the hell you're talking about, but you're still here, aren't you?"

"Mostly. Listen, Don, I have to get back to the studio and write up my script for tonight's broadcast. I'll stop by again after that. Anything I can get for you?"

"Only if you happen to go by a bakery that makes good donuts."

I laughed. "I'll see what I can do, but if the nurses find out, it's on your head."

With a broad grin, he said, "That's one rap I'll gladly take."

Forty-Nine

KDG Radio Studios–730 Market Street, San Francisco

Even stopping to pick up a small bag of donuts and other assorted delicacies at an Italian bakery up on Stockton Street, I made it back to the office about eleven-fifteen. Charlie was nowhere to be seen, but that was fine with me. I had a script to write. After rolling a fresh sheet of paper into my Underwood, I began typing the words I'd strung together in my head on the way back from Mills Hospital.

By one o'clock I had a little over nine minutes of Special Crime Report on the capture of the Mob Avenger. I smiled as I gave the script a final read-through. I'd captured the excitement of the "Shootout at Pillar Point" and I'd given credit where it was due, especially for Don. I also stuck in a pretty sharp jab at a crooked LA cop named James Davis—not anything he could sue me for, just enough to remind him he should never underestimate the power of the press, or in this case, the power of the airwaves.

I penciled in a date at the top of the first page and was placing the script on Charlie's desk when she walked in. She didn't look happy. I said, "This is tonight's Crime Report. It's a little over nine minutes."

She stowed her handbag in the filing cabinet drawer where she keeps it and sat wearily at her desk. All she said was, "Thanks, Park."

"You're welcome, kiddo. Now tell me what's got you down in the dumps."

Charlie frowned. "I had a long talk with Kastner before lunch and I didn't much care for what he had to say."

Trying to give her spirits a boost, I said, "That's to be expected. In two years I've never had a conversation with Kastner during which I much cared for what he had to say."

"I know, but this was especially bad. He called me in to tell me how the news department is going to run after you leave."

"Don't tell me . . . he's hired Edward R. Murrow to take my place."

Shaking her head in a dejected manner, Charlie said, "No, he told me I will run the department and Dick Stewart will read the news."

"I see, and I assume he's giving you a big fat raise to compensate you for the added responsibility."

"Ha! That'll be the day. But that's not the worst of it."

"Oh?"

Charlie looked as if she was on the verge of tears. "He said some terrible things about you . . . called you ungrateful and a lush. I hate that man!"

Leaning back in my chair, I said, "I'm sorry he upset you, but just remember that old saying, 'Sticks and stones may break my bones, but words . . .'"

"Oh, baloney! If I could afford to quit, I'd have done it right there and then just like you did. William Kastner is unappreciative and downright mean. You are the only good thing that ever happened to his lousy little radio station and he knows it."

I walked over and put a comforting hand on her shoulder. "We're going to figure out a way to fix this situation. In the meantime, we need to keep doing the best job we know how to do. That's the way to show Kastner what a jerk he is."

Charlie looked up at me and a single tear rolled down each cheek. "How are we going to fix it, Park? You don't even know what you're going to do yet, and I'm behaving like a spoiled brat."

"Come on, kiddo, we're a team. I didn't earn that National Journalism Association award on the wall over there all by myself. It's as much yours as it is mine."

I hesitated a moment, and then made a decision about my future and a promise I hoped I could keep. "Charlie, where I go, you go. True, I don't know how or where yet, but as far as I'm concerned, that's how it's going to be."

She jumped up and threw her arms around my neck. Sobbing, Charlie said, "Oh, Park. I want more than anything for it to turn out that way, but . . ."

Hugging her back, I said, "No 'buts' about it. Even if I have to stay at KDG, we're sticking together. Got that?"

I felt her head nod against my chest. "Thank you, Park, but I'll understand if we can't work that out right away. Whatever happens, you're not staying here. I won't let you!"

"You won't, huh?"

She looked up at me with damp eyes and the start of a smile on her lips. "I know that sounds silly, but I mean it."

Planting a brotherly kiss on her forehead, I said, "I know you do, kiddo. Now let's get to work at the job we do best."

Charlie stepped back and looked at me with an expression I couldn't read. "Okay, boss."

While she started assembling the night's final script, I put in a call to the San Mateo Sheriff's headquarters. Since Will worked all night, I didn't expect him to be there, so I planned to leave him a message. I was surprised to find he was in his office.

"Don't you ever go home, Will?"

"My wife keeps asking me the same question. By the way, I heard from Chief Davis, himself, this morning."

"So one of the deputies at the hospital told me. He said you have everything worked out with the department down there."

"As far as Arden Kendall is concerned, that's true. You, on the other hand, are a different matter."

"Oh? Didn't he like the part about me acting as a sworn officer of the LAPD?"

"Actually, he didn't have any problem with that."

"Then what's Davis griping about?"

"Apparently he doesn't appreciate your charming manner the way those who know and love you do. Davis was upset because you got, to use his word, 'testy' with him on the phone this morning. Did you actually hang up on him?"

I chuckled. "That must of really gotten his goat. He grumbled at Don Chambers about it, too. All I can say is listen to my Special Crime Report tonight. Too bad he won't hear it. I outdid my usual witty repartee."

"Oh, swell. I'm telling you, Park, you'd better be careful. Davis carries a lot of weight, even up here."

"Not for long, Will. Chief Davis is up for reelection in a few months and the Hearst newspaper down there, *The Examiner*, is doing everything they can to see that anybody but Davis gets the job. Even a crooked cop can't win against odds like those."

"I didn't know that."

"Well, now you do and you can stop worrying about what Davis thinks. I just called to see if you needed me for anything."

"No, except for that lunch you promised me when you're going to tell me the story behind the story of how you caught Kendall.'"

"I haven't forgotten, Will, and I'm likely to have a lot of time on my hands for such things in a few days. I've quit my job at KDG."

"No kiddin'?"

"Yeah, the sixth of next month is my last day."

"I take it you got a better deal?"

"Not yet. I just got sick and tired of the deal I had."

"Well, I hope it works out for you. If not, I've got a spare room I can loan you."

I laughed. "Thanks, Will. I might have to take you up on that."

The rest of the day went according to plan. Charlie sent a transcript of my Crime Report to Bobby Neumann by messenger so the *Chron's* crime reporters would have the final story. She also teletyped a copy to AP for distribution as they saw fit.

We were wrapping things up after the broadcast when the phone on my desk rang. Charlie answered the call and it was Bea, KDG's night switchboard operator. Bea called to tell us the phones were ringing off the hook with listeners calling to congratulate us on the Special Crime Report.

Charlie looked a little awed when she told me the news. "Nothing like this ever happened before!"

"Well, kiddo, that just goes to show you, if we do our job, people notice."

Looking like she was about to jump for joy, Charlie said, "I guess it does. This is so exciting!"

Giving her a wink, I said, "Always leave 'em wanting more. If we can keep the level of excitement up, we're not going to have much trouble solving the problem we discussed earlier."

Charlie gave me another impromptu hug. "I'm sorry I was so upset. Kastner just got to me."

"I know, kiddo. There was a time when he got to me, too."

We went down to my car and I gave Charlie a lift home because it was more or less on my way to Dandy's folks' place. Then Dandy and I headed off for dinner at a quaint little joint on Bayshore Boulevard called The Old Clam House. I was reminded of the place when Don and I passed it on our first trip to Brisbane. It's nothing fancy, but in a town known for great seafood, the Clam House is second only to John's Grill.

Unfortunately dinner didn't turn out to be the joyful celebration I was hoping for. Dandy was cheerful, but she seemed distracted again. If I didn't know her as well as I do, I might not have noticed, but I got the idea something heavy was weighing on her mind.

While we ate I filled in some of the details I'd left out when I told Dandy about our capture of Arden Kendall, Junior. When I finished, she said, "Park, I listened to your broadcast tonight, and even though I knew how it all ended, you had me on the edge of my seat! You are a darn good newscaster."

"Thanks. I guess a few people agree with you at the moment. Before Charlie and I left the station Bea called to tell us the switchboard was jammed with calls from listeners who were praising the Special Crime Report."

Smiling, Dandy said, "That doesn't surprise me in the least."

"Well, it was a good thing for Charlie. She had an unpleasant conversation with Kastner before lunch and he upset her."

I told Dandy about Charlie's reaction to Kastner and how I tried to raise her spirts. After that, Dandy was quiet for a few minutes.

Finally, she said, "Park, you did the right thing, but I'll admit to feeling a little jealous of Charlie sometimes. You two are really close. In fact, she as much told me if I didn't patch things up with you, she would gladly take my place. She said it in a kidding way, but I don't know if you realize how she feels about you. It's more than just a working relationship for her."

Nodding, I said, "I know, Dandy, and that worries me sometimes. Charlie would never intentionally come between us, but I occasionally get the feeling she wishes . . . well, that things were different."

Looking thoughtful, Dandy said, "You know, Park, thinking about you and Charlene objectively . . . I mean if I had to pick out a woman for you besides myself, she'd be a great choice. Charlie is pretty, smart, witty, and you two think a lot alike. Besides all that, she'd do anything for you."

"I don't know how true that last part is, but I already have a woman picked out for me, and you are she."

Dandy smiled and reached across the table to take my hand. She didn't say anything, though. Maybe she didn't feel she needed to, or maybe she was telling me something else entirely.

After dinner we drove down to San Mateo and paid a brief call on Don to deliver his contraband donuts. I should say "I" paid a brief call on Don. Dandy claimed she was tired and waited in the car. That gave me more reason to think thoughts I didn't enjoy thinking. Dandy has more energy than anyone I know. She's never tired.

Fifty

Saturday—August 27, 1938—11:00 A.M.
Mid-Span—Golden Gate Bridge, San Francisco

It was one of those San Francisco days that remind me what a wise decision I'd made two years ago when I moved from LA to The City. The morning fog burned off just after sun-up and the Pacific Ocean was wafting whispers of ozone-filled breeze—the sort that raises your spirits with just one whiff.

Since Dandy was tied up for most of the day at some ritzy wedding reception in Sausalito, I went into the office to wrap up some chores the search for Arden Kendall, Junior had pushed to a back burner. Chores done, I figured it was a shame to waste such a beautiful day being diligent, so I drove to the view point at the southern anchorage of the Golden Gate Bridge and set out for a walk across the span. It was a must-do activity for all true San Franciscans, and I'd never done it.

The hike across the bridge and back is about three-miles, and by the time I'd reached the middle of the span on the northbound leg of my trip, I was feeling quite chipper. There was a lot of scenery to see and I was determined not to miss any of it. The dark blue of the bay was dotted with the shimmering white sails of little boats riding the breeze and the buildings of San Francisco's skyline glittered in the dazzling sun like fairytale castles in an enchanted land.

All might not be perfect in the world, but standing there watching a freighter headed outbound against a backdrop like that made whatever problems the world might be experiencing seem distant and indistinct. It was a great day to be alive.

I knew that completing some of the chores I'd done at the

office was also adding to my enjoyment of the day. For one, I'd mailed Ida Lupino's photograph of Thelma Todd back to her with a letter describing how the photograph and other information she provided led to the capture of the Mob Avenger, something that quite likely would not have happened without her involvement. I thanked Miss Lupino for her help. Meeting her had been a joy and I told her so.

Another overdue chore was a letter to Neeko Nickolopolis, the LA cabby who'd run me all over town with his meter off much of the time. I told him we caught the "bad guy" and thanked him for all of his help, especially for spotting the gray Chrysler following us out to the pier. I also folded a crisp new twenty dollar bill into the letter and addressed the envelope to his attention at the New Brunswick Hotel as Neeko had instructed me to do should I ever need to get in touch with him.

Finally, I put in a long-distance call to Ozzie Gallagher at Roach Studios. Knowing Ozzie's dedication, I was pretty sure he'd be there, even on a Saturday. He answered my call, saying, "Geez, Atkins, people are gonna start talking if you don't stop calling me all the time."

"I promise this will be the last time you hear from me. I figured you'd want to know we nailed Arden Kendall, Junior for the Mob Avenger shootings. We caught him trying to slip out of the country. It will be covered in the local news down there, but I wanted you to hear it straight from the horse's mouth, especially since I'm sure we never would have made all the necessary connections without your help."

There was a grin in his voice when he asked, "Ah, which end of the horse was that?"

"The end that will bite you in the butt if you don't watch out."

"Oh. Well, in that case, congratulations. I'm glad I was able to help." He paused a moment, and then added, "Look, Park, I'm sorry if I was hard on you when you first called me. I didn't realize you'd . . . well, that you'd sobered yourself up. Congratulations on that, too."

While some recovering drunks might not like being reminded of the past, I didn't mind that much. Comments like Ozzie's made me realize how far I'd come and gave me motivation to continue the journey I'd begun.

By one o'clock I'd finished hoofing my way across the bridge and back and I was feeling more than a little hungry. I've heard fresh sea air will do that to you, so I stopped off at Fisherman's Wharf and ate more chowder and another shrimp cocktail from

Alioto's sidewalk crab stand. The fishing boats were just returning from their daily trips out beyond the Farallon Islands and, in addition to lunch, I got a practical lesson in the art of unloading nets full of live crabs.

Being at the wharf again reminded me of the lunch Don and I shared there and that got me moving toward my next two stops. The first was the nearby Italian bakery in North Beach for more donuts. My second stop was Mills Hospital to deliver the donuts and see how Don was fairing.

He, too, was in a brighter than usual mood. Don was sitting in a chair next to his bed and, after stashing the small bag containing two glazed donuts and a couple of tasty looking cannoli in his nightstand, he gave me a hearty handshake and asked how things were going.

"I'm doing fine, Don, but more important, how are you?"

"Well, I had a long visit from one of my doctors earlier. He told me they were tired of me taking up valuable space in their hospital so they're going to toss me out on my butt Monday."

"That's swell news, Don! Find out what time they're going to cut you loose and I'll pick you up. Depending on the timing, we might be able to get you on Southern Pacific's Lark Monday night. It leaves about quarter to seven in the evening and gets to L.A. the next morning."

"Geez, Atkins, are you that anxious to get rid of me?"

I wasn't sure if he was kidding me or not. "Hell no, Don. I'd be pleased if you stayed longer. I just figured you'd want to get home and catch up on stuff at headquarters."

Grinning, Don said, "I do. I was just ribbin' you, Park. I've seen enough of your fair city for one trip. I'd like to come back sometime and take the tour that doesn't include getting shot."

"Just name the date, Don, and I'll give you the Cooke's deluxe tour. Say, did you hear my broadcast last night?"

"Yeah. I got 'em to bring in a table radio so I could hear it. Nice job, and thanks for the kind words you said about me. I'm glad they don't play your program down home, though. If the guys in the department heard you makin' me out to be a hero, the jokes would last 'til Christmas. And speaking of your program, any leads on a new job yet?"

Smiling, I said, "Oh, sure. They're lined up around the block with offers."

Don nodded his understanding, and then said, "Ever give any thought to going back into police work?"

"I thought about it, but with my background . . . well, you

know."

"Yeah, I know. It'll take a while to live all that down. Too bad. You were a good cop, and you just proved you still are."

"Thanks, Don. It was like the old days working with you again and I have to admit I felt pretty darn good about it."

Don is far from the sentimental type, so his response took me by surprise. "Me, too. To be honest, I've missed working with you. I'd partner with the new and improved Park Atkins in a heartbeat, but I can see that ain't in the cards. Still, let me know if there's anything I can do to help with the job situation. If nothing else, you can always bunk on my sofa 'til you get back on your feet."

It felt good to hear Don say that, and moreover, it was the second time in two days I'd been offered a place to bunk until I got back on my feet. The surprising thing was, I didn't feel I was off my feet. In fact, I don't remember feeling as good as I did in quite a while.

"Thank you, Don. I might take you up on that, but only if you let me make the morning coffee."

"Hell no!"

Grinning at his vehemence, I said, "I see how it is. Listen, Don, I've got some errands to run so I should shove off, but before I go, any word on when Kendall can be moved?"

"I asked the doctor that when he was here earlier. He checked and the word is it'll be about a week. The best part is he's not my problem anymore. Chief Davis is making the arrangements. All I have to do is get the paperwork ready for when they finally get him into a cell at headquarters."

I told Don I'd be back to see him on Sunday and to let me know if he needed anything besides more donuts. He said he would and I headed out of his room.

On my way down the hall I noticed something new had been added in the way of security. A uniformed LAPD patrolman was standing by the stairs chatting with one of the sheriff's deputies. Obviously, Davis was taking no chances on losing Arden Kendall, Junior. Good for him.

Fifty-One

Sunday didn't turn out as expected. Dandy and I originally planned on taking a picnic lunch out to Golden Gate Park, but she called early to ask for a raincheck because she wasn't feeling well. Faced with another day of free time, I spent part of it at my kitchen table with a legal pad writing summaries of previous Special Crime Reports we could use to keep the excitement level up on the broadcast. They weren't really news, but I plugged a lot of drama into rehashing a few of our more thrilling reports from the past. If there was ever a time when we needed to stimulate our listeners, this was it.

I also took another drive down to San Mateo to see Don. A Mills paper-pusher had paid him a visit and reported they would have his release papers ready so he could leave around two Monday afternoon. I told him I'd be there to pick him up and take him to catch the Monday night Lark for Los Angeles.

Monday morning I arrived at our news closet bright and early with a sheaf of yellow legal tablet pages containing crime report rehashes in my hand. As usual, Charlie was already there. She was also looking about as low as I'd ever seen her, even lower than she had after her meeting with Kastner.

Hanging my jacket on the coat rack, I said, "Good morning, kiddo. You ready for another exciting week in the radio news biz?"

Charlie seemed a little taken aback by my cheerful greeting. After several seconds, she shrugged and said, "I guess I'd better be because this is our final week in the radio news biz together. Your last day is a week from tomorrow."

I held up the crime reports and said, "Here are a few stories I wrote yesterday. They run four to five minutes each and rehash some of our more interesting crime reports. I figure they'll help keep the intensity level of our broadcasts up . . . you know, keep things exciting. I'll type 'em up so you can plug them into our scripts over the next few days."

She sat there staring at the stack of yellow pages for a moment, and then just said, "Okay, Park."

I plunked myself down in my desk chair and swiveled left to face her. "Why all the gloom, kiddo? Aren't you feeling well?"

"I'm okay, Park. I had kind of a rough weekend, and . . . don't worry, I'll be okay."

I studied Charlie's face for a moment. It was clear she was miserable about something, and it was equally clear she didn't want to talk about it. "Okay, kiddo. I'm here if you need me."

In a quiet voice Charlie said, "Thanks, Park."

She returned to her AP Wire Service stories and I went to work typing my crime reports. About half an hour later Charlie got up and left without a word—more unusual behavior.

Shortly after that the telephone on my desk rang and startled me out of my contemplative state. "News Department, Atkins."

The voice on the other end sounded as if the caller was speaking from a public place like an airport or a railroad depot. "Hello, Park, this is Jack Carpenter with Mutual. How are you this morning?"

Jack was the last person I expected to be hearing from and it took me a second to shift mental gears. "Hello, Jack. Ah . . . what can I do for you?"

"You can give me an hour or two of your time this morning, if you're available."

"Sure. You in town?"

"Yes, I'm out at your municipal airport. I've got another flight to catch early this afternoon, but I got myself routed through San Francisco so we could have a talk. I take it you didn't get the telephone message I left for you on Friday."

Grabbing the stack of "While You Were Out" slips in my inbox, I frantically thumbed through all the listener calls from Friday night until I found Jack's message.

"Ah, no, Jack, I just found it. Things have been jumping here. We had a major story break Thursday night."

"Then I'm glad I caught you in this morning. Can you make it down here in an hour or so?"

"Yes. I'd be glad to see you. Want to give me a clue about

what's on your mind?"

A few seconds of relative silence came down the line before Jack said, "It's kind of complicated. I'd rather wait until we're face to face. Let's just say I think you'll be happy with what I have to say."

His mysterious reply left me curious and a little hopeful that something promising was in the wind. I said, "Okay, Jack. I'll get out of here and see you in an hour or so. Where will you be?"

"There's a coffee shop here off the main waiting area. That's where I'll be."

"All right. See you there."

I was just slipping into my jacket when Charlie returned to the closet. Her eyes were a little pink, as if she'd been crying. Seeing her gave me an idea.

"Charlie, grab your bag and come with me. We've got some urgent business to take care of."

She was startled, but she got her purse out of the filing cabinet and grabbed her coat as she followed me out the door. As we past the reception desk I told Sally we'd be back sometime after lunch.

Riding down in the elevator, Charlie said, "Where in heaven's name are we going, Park. I've got a broadcast to assemble."

"We'll do that when we get back. This is more important at the moment."

"What's more important?"

"Meeting Jack Carpenter."

"The fellow from the Mutual network?"

"Yup. He called Friday to say he was coming out to talk with me, but the message got lost among all the listener calls that came in Friday night. He's waiting for us right now at the airport."

Out on the sidewalk, Charlie said, "You mean he's waiting for you. Why am I going along?"

"What do I keep telling you about all this, kiddo?"

She was silent for a few paces, and then said in a small voice, "That we're in this together?"

Opening the car door for her, I said, "Bingo!"

Charlie was quiet as we zigzagged our way across town to Bayshore Boulevard. Finally, she said, "I sure hope he has some good news for you."

"You mean good news for us."

"Well, yes, but . . ."

In as stern a voice as I could come up with, I said, "kiddo, either spit out what's got you so down or cheer up. Enough with the gloomy disposition, already."

After a few seconds, I heard her sob, and when I looked over, Charlie's hands were covering her face. "Oh, God, Park. It's awful."

"What's awful?"

"It's Dandy, Park. I promised to let her tell you, but I can't. I saw her yesterday and we had a long talk."

Based on Dandy's behavior over the weekend, I had a pretty good idea what was coming. "She told you she wants to call it quits with me, didn't she?"

That jolted Charlie out of her crying jag. Quietly she said, "How did you know that if you haven't talked to her?"

"I don't need a house to fall on me to know what's going on. Dandy's been showing me all the signs, but she hasn't worked up the nerve to actually tell me yet."

Charlie was looking at me with a startled expression. "Aren't you upset?"

"Of course, I'm upset. I love Dandy, but I've already resigned myself to the idea it won't work. My turning down the Chicago job and the shootout at Pillar Point the other night were the last straws. Oh, I think she tried her best to move on, but she can't."

"I'm sorry, Park, I really am. I know you love Dandy and . . ."

Interrupting, I said, "I bet I know something else she told you."

Still staring at me, she said, "What, Park?"

"Dandy told you that you and I are perfect for each other and hinted that you should take her place in my life, didn't she?"

More sobbing came from the passenger seat. Finally, Charlie calmed down enough to say, "Yes, Park. I tried my best to convince her there is nothing between us besides work, but I couldn't make her believe me."

Giving her what I hoped was a reassuring smile, I said, "That's because she's right, and you know it."

"Park! I would never come between you and . . ."

"You didn't. What's gone on between Dandy and me has nothing to do with you, so get that idea out of your head. If at some point you want to talk about you and me, we can do that, but in the meantime, you have done nothing you need to feel guilty about. Now, dry your eyes. We're almost to the airport and I want Jack to be as impressed with you as I am."

Glancing at Charlie, I saw her clamp her jaw shut and dig into her bag for a tissue. Surprisingly, my feelings at that moment were quite clear. I now had it semi-officially that Dandy and I were done. It would have been quite a different matter if I wasn't expecting it, but I was. Sure, I would miss Dandy and spend some time feeling sorry for myself. That was to be expected. All in all, though, I was feeling something like relief knowing how things stood. Thinking back, it was always a mystery to me what Dandy ever saw in Parker Atkins. She'd finally asked herself the same question.

Fifty-Two

San Francisco Municipal Airport—Bayshore Blvd., San Bruno

San Francisco Municipal Airport's waiting area is a narrow north to south rectangle with two long upholstered benches centered end to end down the center. The coffee shop is at the north end of the waiting area next to a grand staircase leading up to an open mezzanine.

As terminals go, it isn't particularly large or impressive. Even little Glendale's Grand Central Air Terminal made our airport look puny by comparison.

Being there again reminded me of my last visit. Dandy and I were at San Francisco Municipal Airport catching a flight to Los Angeles, where we met with Ida Lupino. That was only ten days ago, but all of the life that happened in between made it seem like ages ago.

We caught an early morning flight that day and the terminal had been mostly empty. Today there were more passengers milling about, but you could hardly say San Francisco's dinky municipal airport was bustling with activity. Surely a city that could build the Golden Gate Bridge could do better by its air travelers.

As we approached the coffee shop, Charlie stopped me. "Park, I just don't feel right about barging in uninvited to your meeting. Would it be okay with you if I waited out here and, if you think it's the right thing to do, you can call me in?"

"Okay, kiddo. We'll do it your way. I'll come get you as soon as the time is right."

Charlie seated herself on the padded bench at the north end of the waiting area and I strolled into the coffee shop. Since it was between breakfast and lunch hour, the little eatery was mostly empty, so I spotted Jack immediately. He was sitting at a table next to a window overlooking the runways on the east side of the terminal. On the other hand, Jack would have been easy to find even if the coffee shop was full.

He's a large man with broad shoulders and a muscular physique. I guessed he might have played football in school. He looked the type.

Jack spotted me about the same time I saw him and he stood to greet me. Offering his hand, he said, "Hello, Park. It's good to see you again."

As I sat opposite him at the table, he said, "Sounds like you've been a busy guy. What was the big story you broke Friday?"

"You probably didn't hear anything about it back in Chicago, but we had a guy down in Los Angeles who was killing known mobsters."

"Are you talking about the Mob Avenger?"

"Yes. I guess you did hear about him in Chicago."

Jack grinned. "You bet we did. AP picked up your stories and we ran them on our hourly network news broadcasts up through the weekend. They were well written with a lot of drama—the kind of stories that make listeners perk up their ears. I take it you were in on the arrest?"

"Yeah, an LA homicide detective came up when I tracked our suspect to San Francisco. We caught up with the Avenger Thursday night out on the coast. It was touch and go for a while, but we took him into custody. At the moment he's in a hospital not far from here. The LAPD is waiting for him to recover from a gunshot wound so they can take him down to Los Angeles for the trial."

Jack leaned back in his chair and shook his head in what I took to be minor amazement. "Wow! That's one of the qualities I like most about you, Park. I appreciate a newsman who isn't chained to his desk, the kind of guy who follows the story no matter where it takes him or what dangers he might encounter. In fact, that's why I'm here today."

"Oh?"

"Yes. I was disappointed when you turned down the position we offered you in Chicago. I know you had your reasons, but I suspect you were a little disappointed, too."

I just nodded and said nothing. Jack continued, "You were on my mind for several days afterward, and that led me to a brilliant idea that benefits both you and Mutual. Want to hear my idea?"

Using a lot of restraint to keep from sounding too eager, I said, "Sure, I'm all ears."

"Well, as you know, our network puts a lot of emphasis on news. You might say we're building Mutual on a foundation of quality dramatic programing and accurate, timely news reports. Reporting news the way we want to do it requires a professional team of topflight journalists. That's not a problem in the midwest and east. We have experienced stringers all over those parts of the country, but the west coast is a different situation.

"Out here you've got a lot of wide open spaces between population centers, and the journalists available to us in those cities, like San Francisco and Los Angeles, are young guys with lots of enthusiasm, but not much practical experience. My idea is to hire an experienced journalist to be our west coast news director.

"I'm not talking about the humdrum, day-to-day news. The wire services are full of that stuff. What we need is somebody who can get us scoops on the big stories, especially crime stories. In other words, very much the same sort of thing you've been doing with your Special Crime Reports."

I was surprised. "You know about our crime reports?"

"You bet I do. I've listened to recordings of them made by our San Francisco affiliate at my request. They're exactly the kind of reporting we want at the core of our network news broadcasts, and you are the logical choice for making that happen. You've got the journalistic skills, a dramatic delivery style, a police background, and a natural instinct that puts you in the right place at the right time to get the news firsthand, just as you did with the Mob Avenger the other night.

"Also, our experts tell us the hostilities in Europe and China are very likely to put the US in the middle of two wars. Having a sharp newsman on the west coast will be an absolute necessity if that happens." Jack paused a moment, and then added, So, there's my idea. What do you think of it?"

Trying to conceal my excitement at the prospect of becoming Mutual's West Coast News Director, I hoped I sounded nonchalant as I said, "So far I like it. Tell me the details."

Jack smiled broadly. "I knew you were going to like the idea. As for the details, you would have a choice of making your headquarters at our San Francisco affiliate, KFRC, or at our Los Angeles station, KHJ. You might even want to have an office in both places so you'd always be close to a typewriter and production facilities. Plus, we have fifteen other affiliates in

California and coverage in Portland, Seattle, Reno, Salt Lake, and Denver. That would be your beat.

"Now, I'm authorized to offer you a two year contract starting at nine-hundred a month for the first year with an automatic increase of a hundred a month at the end of the first year. Also, Mutual will cover all of your work-related travel expenses and you'll be provided with an automobile . . . from Don Lee Cadillac, of course. How does that sound?"

It took all the self-control I had left to remain calmly seated in my chair as I listened to Jack's offer. Nine-hundred a month was more than five times what Kastner was paying me, to say nothing of travel expenses and a car. I was tempted to pinch myself to make sure I wasn't dreaming. Still, there was one more issue that needed resolving.

"Jack, all that sounds good, but there's one other expense we need to discuss."

"Oh? What's that, Park."

"You're asking me to cover a lot of territory, and I can handle it, but I want an assistant, someone who will serve as my editor, researcher, and who will take care of the paperwork. It has to be someone I can really count on in the sort of life and death situations in which I could find myself if I did the job the way you want it done."

Jack appeared to be giving what I said some thought. Finally, he said, "It goes without saying that you would need some help, but I was figuring on you getting it from the staff people at our affiliates. I can see your point, though, and the need for consistency you wouldn't get from affiliate staff. Would I be right if I guessed you have someone in mind for the, call it, Assistant West Coast News Director?"

"You would. I've got a topnotch assistant at KDG. We've worked together for two years, and in that time we've developed a working relationship that gets the job done smoothly and efficiently."

Jack smiled at my enthusiasm. "You must really be sold on this guy. How much do you think he'd want in the way of salary?"

I grinned at him. "First of all, he's a she, and second, how much have you got?"

Jack laughed his hearty laugh again. "I think we could come up with an adequate salary proposal, but first, what are the chances of me meeting this wonder woman while I'm here?"

"They're damned good. She happens to be out there in the terminal at this very moment."

Now Jack was laughing his head off. "Talk about cagey! Atkins, you knew what was coming all along, didn't you? Well, what are you waiting for? Bring her on!"

Without another word, I walked to the coffee shop entrance and gave Charlie a "come on in" gesture. She got up, smoothed out her skirt a little, and headed toward me. I ushered her to our table and said, "Charlene, this is Jack Carpenter, News Director for the Mutual Broadcast System. Jack, meet Miss Charlene Blanchard, Assistant News Director at KDG."

Jack stood and shook hands with Charlie, saying, "Well, now, Miss Blanchard. I can see why Park puts so much stock in you. Even if you had no other skills, you are obviously a charmer."

Charlie smiled. "I could say the same about you, Mister Carpenter."

Jack laughed again. He seemed to be enjoying our meeting immensely. We all sat and he said, "All right, Miss Blanchard, here's what's going on." Jack spent the next five minutes describing the job he offered me without going into the financial details. He finished with, "And, so it seems, Park here will take the job if I agree to hire you as his assistant. What do you think of that idea?"

"I think Park is perfectly capable of doing the job you've offered him, and if he says he needs me, I'd be very interested in continuing our working relationship."

Jack glanced at me, paused a moment, and then said, "Okay, how does a two-year contract starting at five-hundred per month with an automatic increase of fifty dollars a month at the end of the first year sound? Of course, all of your travel expenses and the like will be covered by Mutual."

Charlie looked at me questioningly. I nodded once and Charlie said, "All right, Mister Carpenter, if Park accepts your offer, so do I."

Jack turned to look at me. "Parker?"

I stuck out my hand and said, "Jack, you've got yourself a west coast news team."

He looked quite pleased as we shook hands on the deal. "When can you start?"

"I'd say we can report for duty a week from Wednesday. That soon enough?"

"Perfect. I have a contract here for you, Park. I'll call back to Chicago and have my secretary get one in the mail to Charlene. What's your address, Miss Blanchard?"

Charlie wrote her home address on the back of one of my

business cards and handed it to Jack, saying, "Thank you very much, Mister Carpenter. We won't let you down."

Jack laughed yet again. "Miss Blanchard, with you around to keep Parker on the straight and narrow, I don't doubt that for a minute."

Five minutes later Charlie and I were sitting in my car staring at each other in something like disbelief. This was proving to be an emotional day for her. Once again there were tears forming in her eyes. "You did it, Park. You did exactly what you said you would do. Thank you, thank you!"

"I'm not going to say 'I told you so,' kiddo, but I told you so."

"And at more than three times what Kastner is paying me! I can't believe this is really happening."

I took her hand and gave it a squeeze. "My mom used to say, 'Good things happen to good people who work hard.' I think she was right."

Charlie squeezed my hand back and with tears starting to make tracks down her cheeks again, she leaned over intending to give me a kiss on the cheek. I reached up and gently redirected her aim so the kiss landed on my lips. We stayed like that for several seconds, and then she suddenly backed away as if she just realized what was happening.

"Oh, Park. I didn't mean for that to happen. I . . ."

"I meant for it to happen. And I wouldn't be at all disappointed if it began happening frequently in the not too distant future."

"But Dandy . . . I feel like I'm cheating on her or . . ."

"Dandy already made her choice. Now it's our time to make some choices—not today or even in a week, but when we do make them, let's make the right ones."

The tears stopped and Charlie was smiling at me with something I'd call joy in her eyes. "Amen to that, boss!"

Fifty-Three

KDG Radio Studios–730 Market Street, San Francisco

It was already eleven-thirty by the time Charlie and I returned from meeting with Jack Carpenter. She got right back to assembling the night's broadcast while I finished typing the crime report rehashes for her to insert into scripts.

When I dropped the crime report scripts on her desk, Charlie stopped what she was doing and said, "You know, there is one bad thing about both us leaving KDG at the same time."

"Bad thing? Oh, you mean telling Kastner he's losing you, too?"

"Yes, and I'm only giving him a week's notice. He's going to have a fit."

"Good. It couldn't happen to a more deserving fellow."

"That might be, but I'm the one who will be on the receiving end of his fit."

Grinning, I said, "I'd be happy to go along for the show. He might even give me cause to knock his stupid block off."

A half-smile crossed Charlie's face. "I'd enjoy seeing that, but I have to stand up like a big girl and face the music. It's really a small price to pay."

Looking up at the electric clock on our wall, Charlie said, "Maybe I'll do it when you go to take Detective Chambers to the depot. You'll have to leave about one-fifteen?"

"Yes, that sounds about right, but I'll probably bring him back here to kill some time. His train doesn't leave until six-forty-five. On the other hand, I don't want to take a chance on driving him over there after the broadcast. That would be cutting it much too close."

"If you bring him back here, I could take him over to the depot in your car while you're on the air."

"Would you mind doing that? I'd appreciate it and I know Don would."

"I wouldn't mind at all."

"Thanks. Then after the broadcast we can go out for a low budget celebration dinner. How does that sound?"

Grinning, Charlie said, "It sounds swell to me! I'd settle for a hotdog with mustard."

"I think we can manage the hotdog, but mustard might be pushing it."

Looking convincingly insulted, she said, "Say, what kind of a cheap date do you think I am?"

"All right, all right. You get mustard, but absolutely no relish. In the meantime, I'll run downstairs and get a couple of sandwiches to hold us over. Lunch hour is upon us."

"Okay. Tuna salad for me please."

"You've got it. Be right back."

Later, driving down to pick Don up at Mills Hospital, my mind wandered back over what had already been an eventful day. Actually, "life-changing" was a better choice of words than "eventful." In a few hours I'd lost a fiancée and gained an incredible job opportunity.

It still surprised me a little that I wasn't more upset about the first of those two events. I decided part of it was because I'd felt it coming so I was already resigned to the possibility. Another part of it was the feeling that Dandy was being exactly what she thought I was being about moving to Chicago. She was being selfish.

Packing up and moving two thousand miles was not something to be taken lightly, but she seemed to be of the opinion that love conquers all. It doesn't, a fact she was proving by deserting what she perceived as a sinking ship.

Walking into Mills Hospital, I concluded there were no answers to be found by going over and over it all in my mind. The answers would come in time.

I found Don waiting for me in the lobby. He was sitting in a wheelchair with a stern looking nurse standing behind him. I said, "Hi, Don. You already to roll?"

"I'm not going to roll anywhere. I'll walk to your car just as soon as this . . . kindly nurse sees me out of her damned hospital."

The woman behind him said quietly, "And that can't happen

too soon for me."

Outside on the walkway, Don stopped the wheelchair and stood up on legs that seemed a little wobbly. Once he was vertical and walking toward my car, though, he was steadier. The nurse watched his progress for a moment and then returned herself and the wheelchair to the hospital.

Don saw her leave and muttered, "Old battleax."

I couldn't help laughing. "Don! They aren't going to welcome you back if you behave like that."

"Good! And the next time I get shot, kindly take me to a hospital run by human beings instead of female gorillas."

"I'll try to remember that."

As we drove out of the parking lot, Don said, "Say, Park, do you still have my suitcase?"

"Sure, it's in the trunk, right where you left it Friday morning. Why?"

"Your Sergeant Framm returned my service revolver yesterday and I want to stash it away in my bag. Also, a change into some fresh clothes would probably do me a world of good."

"All right. We'll make a stop at my place. You can even take a bath and clean up if you have a mind to."

"Thanks, Park. I would appreciate that."

"You're welcome. By the way, it looks like I won't have to bunk on your sofa, after all."

"Oh? You found a job?"

"It would be more accurate to say a job found me. This morning the Mutual Broadcasting System offered me the lofty position of West Coast News Director. I'll be making a salary that verges on obscene and I'll be working mostly out of San Francisco and Los Angeles."

With the hint of a smile in his voice, Don said, "Oh, hell! That means I'm gonna have you in my hair even more than before."

"No, Don, it means you'll have a highly placed friend in the news business who understands the problems cops face."

"In that case, congratulations. I can't think of anyone who deserves a break like this more than you do. Good luck with it."

"Thanks, Don. Your blessing means a lot to me."

"Well, for what it's worth, you've got it. What does your intended think of all this?"

"I'm afraid my intended is now my unintended, but that has nothing to do with the job. She decided I'm hopeless and she's calling it quits."

"You don't seem too upset over the situation."

"I am, Don, but I saw it coming so I had a little time to adjust."

In a thoughtful tone, Don said, "I guess that's good. You know what I'd do if I were you, Park?"

"What?"

"I'd be making time with that spunky little assistant of yours. She's cute as a bug's ear and I suspect she wouldn't hesitate to give you a good swift kick when you need one, which in my experience is frequently."

"Thank you, Don. I might just take that advice."

Don looked at me suspiciously. "Think nothing of it, Park."

I called the station from my place to tell Charlie we were making a brief stop for Don to clean up and change. She told me the evening's script was all ready to go and to take my time.

It was close to four o'clock when we arrived at KDG. As the elevator door opened on the ground floor, Bill Kastner walked out. I could tell at a glance he wasn't happy. Staring me in the eye, he said, "You . . . you ungrateful jerk! I ought to punch you in the nose!"

Returning his glare, I said, "Go ahead, Kastner, give it a try if you think you can handle the consequences."

Kastner just walked away. Riding up in the elevator, Don said, "What the hell was that all about?"

"That was my soon-to-be former boss. I forgot to mention that Charlie is going to Mutual with me. She must have just given Kastner that piece of good news. His entire news staff will be out the door next Tuesday."

Don nodded. "I see. So you aren't really an ungrateful jerk then?"

"Not on that score, anyway."

"Oh, good. I'm glad we got that sorted out."

In the news closet Charlie stood up to welcome Don. "Hello again, Detective Chambers."

"And hello to you, Miss Blanchard. I'd come over there and give you a hug, but I'm afraid Park might slug me. He seems to be in that frame of mind this afternoon."

Charlie looked at me with a questioning expression and I said, "Oh, we ran into Kastner coming out of the elevator. He called me a jerk and threatened to punch me in the nose. When I suggested he give it a try, he lost interest in the idea. I figured you gave him the good news that you're leaving, too."

Charlie smiled. "You figured right, but don't worry, Detective Chambers, Park only slugs the most deserving of his acquaintances. I sincerely doubt if you are in that category."

Don was enjoying himself. "I might be if I tried to make time with his girl."

"Well, yes," Charlie said, "you might be. Ah, just what makes you think I'm his girl?"

"Detective intuition. If I was in his shoes, you'd sure as heck be my girl."

Thinking Don was treading on ice that was still a little thin, I said, "Okay, you two, behave yourselves. I've got a radio show to do in two hours. I have to go over the script so I don't sound like Porky Pig when I read it on the air."

Charlie and Don left the station about quarter to six and I made for the studio to enlighten San Franciscans about their latest news, weather and sports. By six-thirty-five I was back in the news closet. Charlie arrived a few minutes later.

She asked, "Did everything go all right?"

"Just like clockwork. You get Don off to catch his train?"

"I sure did. I like him, but he did raise one question in my mind."

"Oh? What question is that?"

Standing about as close to me as one human being can stand to another, Charlie looked up into my eyes and asked, "Am I really your girl?"

I put my hands on her shoulders. "Being the democratic fellow that I am, I think your question is one we should put to a vote. All in favor of Charlene Blanchard being my girl so signify by saying aye. Aye."

Leaning her face so close to mine that our lips were nearly touching, Charlie said, "Very definitely, aye."

I took Charlie home to the Warrington after dinner and got back to my apartment around nine-thirty. The telephone was ringing when I walked in. I was fairly certain I knew who was calling and I considered not answering the telephone. Then I decided it was better to get the settled once and for all, so I took a deep breath and picked up the handset.

"Hello."

"Hello, Park. This is Dandy."

"Hello, Dandy. Feeling better today?"

After a short pause she said, "Yes, Park. I'm fine."

The rest of the conversation isn't worth repeating. The gist of it was that Dandy had come to the realization she couldn't cope with me taking risks that might leave her a widow, and since she didn't expect me to change, she felt she had to end our relationship.

Well, that seemed as good a reason as any she could have come up with, so I wished her all the best and said goodbye. I hung up hoping she'd expected me to give her an argument.

Fifty-Four

Tuesday—September 6, 1938

KDG Radio Studios—730 Market Street, San Francisco

Our final days at KDG flew by quickly. A farewell party was planned for lunchtime on our last day, but besides that, the most notable events of the week were Bill Kastner's absence from the station and a telephone call I received Tuesday morning from Jack Carpenter.

"Good morning, Parker. I'm just calling to congratulate you and Charlene on your last day at KDG and to welcome you to the Mutual Broadcasting System."

"Thanks, Jack. Charlie . . . ah . . . Charlene and I stopped by KFRC last Friday to introduce ourselves and we received a warm reception. They seem like nice folks."

"They are, and my impression is they are excited about you joining our ranks. You may not know it, but you've developed quite a reputation on the west coast, which is remarkable for a guy on a radio station with a signal that barely makes it out into the street in front of the studio."

"Oh, come on, Jack. It's not that bad. I've had people tell me they can hear us clear over in Oakland. That's at least ten miles!"

Jack chuckled. "I stand corrected. Speaking of that one-watt-wonder you've been working for, I just saw an interesting piece of news in the monthly announcements from the Federal Communications Commission. It seems the Holy Cross Evangelical Church has applied for a license to operate KDG beginning on January First, 1939. It appears Kastner has sold out to the holy-rollers, or at least he's trying to."

The thought that another rat was deserting yet another

sinking ship crossed my mind as I said, "How 'bout that? I guess that means some of the staff around here will be looking for work around Christmas time."

"If the FCC approves the change-over, that's a strong possibility."

"Well, if it does, keep in mind we've got some pretty good people around here, especially the engineering guys and an announcer named Dick Stewart. If any openings come up in the Mutual System, you could do a lot worse."

"I'll keep that in mind. You might also put a few bugs in some ears at that end so they'll have a head start getting their job applications out."

"I plan to do just that, Jack."

"Good. Also, give me a call in a few days when you're set up at KFRC and ready to go to work. We need to get a system of communications working so I know what you're up to. I don't plan to look over your shoulder, Parker, but until we get things rolling, you and I need to stay in touch. That okay with you?"

"I was thinking the same thing, Jack. I'll be in touch soon. And thanks for the call."

I knew Charlie realized who was on the line from listening to my end of the conversation. She sounded a little nervous after I hung up. "Is everything okay, Park?"

"Everything's fine, kiddo. Jack just called to congratulate us on joining Mutual and to pass along a piece of news about KDG."

After hearing the news about KDG's proposed change of ownership, Charlie said, "I heard you putting in a good word for Dick and the engineers. That was nice of you."

"We also need to pass the word around today so folks have some idea of what might be coming. The deal isn't done yet, but some advance warning might make a lot of difference, especially before the holidays."

Charlie stood up and walked over to lean a hip against my desk. "Do you plan a farewell to your listeners for tonight?"

"Yeah. I owe 'em a lot and I want them to know I appreciate their loyalty. I was just going to type something up, maybe three minutes' worth if there's room."

"For that you can have all the time you want." After pausing for a long moment, Charlie put on the expression she reserves for serious topics of discussion and said, "Park, I met Dandy for dinner last night. I hope you don't mind."

"I don't mind at all, kiddo. You and Dandy have gotten pretty close, and I can see no reason you shouldn't continue being friends."

"I'm glad you feel that way." Then, frowning, she added, "I'll admit I felt a little awkward telling her about you getting the Mutual job. I told her I was going over there, too. I hope it was all right for me to tell her all that."

"It doesn't matter to me. San Francisco's news community is pretty tight, so she'd have found out about me getting the job sooner or later. I suspect, however, that what was making you feel awkward had more to do with you and me."

She nodded slowly. "Yes, to be completely honest, I was nervous about that more than anything else. I didn't want her thinking I stole you away from her or something. It also crossed my mind that she might change how she feels about things when she heard about your new job."

"For the last time, you didn't steal me away from her. In fact, you went out of your way not to. Dandy opened the door for us to get together. She even encouraged it. If she has any problems with our relationship, they are her own doing."

Still looking serious, Charlie said, "Well, the subject didn't come up and I tried my best not to give her any clues, but I don't think I was fooling her. She knows darn well how I feel about you."

"Then don't worry about it. We've got plenty to occupy our minds for the near future."

She glanced at the door, and then leaned over to give me a kiss on the cheek, quickly saying, "Don't worry, I won't be doing that at KFRC, at least not right away."

I gave her a grin. "Don't make promises I won't let you keep."

Our party was scheduled for eleven-thirty. The staff took over the main studio and the gals laid on a lunch spread that looked and tasted terrific. There was no caviar or champagne, but that was fine with me. I'm not big on fish eggs.

As lunch wound down, Dick Stewart stood and proposed a toast to a successful future with Mutual for Charlie and me. Then I stood and thanked everyone, saying, "Up until two years and four months ago, I'd never sat before a microphone in my life. That I've been able to pull this job off says a lot more about all of you than it does about me. Your patience and support saved my life. Without it, I'm afraid I would have failed miserably."

That brought on a chorus of comments like, "That's not true," and "Baloney!"

I held up my hands and said, "Then I fooled you folks, too! Really, though, taking on this job was one of the scariest things

I've ever done and I honestly couldn't have done it without you. So, thank you, thank you, and thank you!"

Dick stood again and said, "On behalf of everyone here, Park, you're welcome. It's been a real pleasure working with you." With a big smile, he added, "And now, I think we should hear a few words from the real brains of KDG's news department, Charlene Blanchard."

With some encouragement, Charlie stood and looked around the studio for a few seconds. Finally, she found the words she wanted, "Thank you for saying those nice things, Dick, but let's not be so formal. I'm still Charlie to all of you and proud of it. I've never worked with so many good friends before and I want you to know I'll miss each and every one of you."

One of the engineers shouted, "Even Bill Kastner?"

Charlie laughed. "In a way, yes, even Mister Kastner." She made a show of looking around to be sure Kastner wasn't in the room, and added, "He taught me how *not* to do a lot of things!"

The room burst into laughter, and when it quieted down again, Charlie said, "There's one other person I want to thank, . . . my boss. Parker became my mentor and a good friend during the past two years. And while he's scared the heck out of me more than once going after hot stories his way, I understand that's the only way he knows how to report the news—by doing whatever it takes to get the facts."

That resulted in a brief round of applause, and I got a laugh out of the group by moving my hand to hide the bandage I was still wearing over my ear where Arden Kendall's slug got me.

Charlie said, "As you all know, Park arranged for me to continue as his assistant in his new job as West Coast News Director for the Mutual Broadcasting System. In doing that, Park honored me beyond what I can express in any words. The only thing that would make my new job better would be if all of you could be there with us." With tears in her eyes, Charlie added, "Thank you all so very much."

The rest of the day passed with staff members dropping by to say personal farewells and offer good wishes. Then, at quarter to six, Charlie and I walked down the hall to the studio, where Dick Stewart and I played our last game of musical chairs in the announce booth. Twenty-nine minutes later, I paused for a poignant moment, then said, "And that's your news for Tuesday, September Sixth. This is Parker T. Atkins. Goodnight and farewell, San Francisco."

Fifty-Five

I awoke Wednesday with a mixture of emotions floating around in my head, the strongest of which was a warm sensation resulting from waking up next to Charlie. We didn't plan to spend the night together, it just sort of happened.

After the broadcast Charlie seemed at loose ends. As we prepared to leave the news closet for the last time, she had tears in her eyes. To be honest, I was feeling a little misty. too. A lot had happened in the past twenty-eight months, much of it centering on the tiny room Bill Kastner allocated for his "news department."

I deliberately left the National Print and Broadcast Journalism Association achievement plaque on the wall until we were ready to walk out the door. Thus, my last official act at KDG consisted of taking the award down and handing it to Charlie.

Charlie took the plaque and ran her fingers over the engraved words. "Why are you giving this to me?"

"You are now the official custodian of our first achievement award. There will be more, but none will ever mean as much to us as this one."

She dabbed at her eyes with a handkerchief and said, "Okay, I'll take care of it until we have a new wall to hang it on."

"Thanks, kiddo."

Since neither of us was particularly hungry after our big farewell lunches, we decided to skip dinner, but it was clear we weren't ready to say goodnight either. Rather than going someplace public and noisy, I suggested we go to my apartment, noting that when and if we did get hungry, there was a good late night deli a block away. Charlie accepted the invitation without hesitation. The next morning we were still there.

The other feelings floating in and out of my mind had to do with the new adventure we faced. I'd thought about the Mutual job and how I would approach it, but nothing about the job seemed quite real until I opened my eyes that morning. In that instant I became the West Coast News Director for the Mutual Broadcasting System. If someone had predicted that eventuality when I first moved to San Francisco, I'd have laughed at them. Now the time had come and accepting the responsibilities of the job was no laughing matter.

Charlie woke up about the same time I did and slid over to rest her head on my shoulder. "Good morning, Mister West Coast News Director."

"Good morning, kiddo. I trust you slept well."

Leaning over to kiss me, she said, "Never better, but now we have to get moving."

"What's the hurry?"

Sitting up, she modestly covered herself with part of the bedsheet and said, "In case you've forgotten, this is your apartment. I don't have anything to wear here except for what I had on yesterday. We need to stop at my place so I can shower and change. It's like the first day of school each year when I was a little girl. I want to make a good impression on our first day at the new job."

I nodded, kissed her, and said, "All right, if you insist. Would you please put on a pot of coffee while I get myself presentable for the teacher?"

"Why don't you wait until we get to my place. You'll have time for coffee while I get dressed. Okay?"

I muttered, "Slave driver," and stumbled off to the bathroom.

By seven we were at Charlie's apartment and I was sitting in her living room drinking coffee from a filched Santa Fe Railroad dining car cup while she got ready for her first day at school. Looking around the room, I studied Charlie's taste in décor.

Her furniture, while certainly classier than the secondhand store stuff at my place, was relatively plain and simple. The sofa and a Morris chair were upholstered in bright, cheery shades of blue that neither complimented nor fought with the maroon and brown area rug covering most of the hardwood floor.

A golden oak coffee table that matched the sofa, chair, and two small end tables filled a spot in front of the couch. The only other piece of furniture in the room was the Zenith console radio

I'd given her last Christmas so Charlie would have a good radio on which she could listen to the fruits of our labors. Dandy helped me pick the radio out and I spent more than I could afford on it, but when Charlie saw it, she was as excited as . . . well, as a kid at Christmas.

The living room walls were a neutral shade of apartment beige and it was on those walls that Charlie made the high-ceiling room her own. She framed and mounted six colorful *Vogue* magazine covers featuring art deco illustrations from the 1920s. They fit well with the apartment's style and wall-sconce lighting fixtures. There was also a life-size ceramic face sculpture humorously depicting a surprised-looking woman in a fedora hat and an exaggerated bow under her chin. Very chic.

When Charlie arrived in the living room she was also very chic in a classy fitted blazer over a skirt and blouse outfit in shades of blue and gray. She would definitely make a good first impression at KFRC, and I told her so.

Our new workplace was on the top floor of the Don Lee Cadillac dealership at the intersection of Van Ness and O'Farrell, in the heart of San Francisco's automobile row. The early-1920s vintage building is four-stories with Corinthian columns and an adequate assortment of gewgaws appropriate to a luxury car showroom, including a colorful Cadillac crest over the arched entrance.

The connection between KFRC and Cadillac dates back to when Don Lee was still with us—he died in '34—and owned a chain of radio stations throughout California. Since he also owned the Cadillac franchise for the west coast, he used good real estate sense by locating his radio stations in his dealerships whenever possible. The Don Lee Network became affiliated with the Mutual Broadcast System in 1936, about the same time I arrived in San Francisco.

After an elevator ride to the fourth floor, we were greeted warmly by the station's office manager, a bubbling blonde, blue-eyed woman in her late twenties named Irene Boles. She escorted us to a spacious room on the south side of the building overlooking O'Farrell Street.

Compared to our old KDG news closet, our new digs were positively opulent. The room was outfitted with a pair of large stylish desks, a neat row of filing cabinets, four padded leather guest chairs, and all the latest modern office devices, including intercoms.

As we looked over our new home away from home, Irene

explained, "We moved two desks in here because we understood you wanted to share one office. If you change your mind, there is an additional office available next door to this one."

I couldn't help laughing. "Irene, in light of where we just came from, if you gave us more space, we'd have to leave trails of bread crumbs to keep from getting lost. This will fit our needs quite well."

Charlie asked, "Where are your wire service teletypes?"

"They're in our news room across the hall. I was told to tell you we have both Associated Press and United Press International wire services. Did I get that right, Miss Blanchard?"

Charlie smiled, "Right as rain, and please call me Charlie or Charlene."

"Oh, okay. We have a Charlene on the staff, so I'll call you Charlie, which by the way, is a really cute nickname."

Turning in my direction, Irene said, "Mister Atkins, our GM, Ed Levi, told me to ask if you would please stop by his office when you get settled in so you can go over the procedures and such you'll want us to follow. Also, I've loaded that cabinet behind the second desk with paper, pencils, and the other office supplies you'll need. If you want anything else, just let me know and we'll get it for you."

Charlie said, "I like to work with lined yellow legal pads, so a big stack of those would be nice."

"All right, I'll call the office supply store and order them. The store is just two blocks down on O'Farrell, so the pads will be here by noon. Oh, and before I forget, we've already taken a telephone message for you this morning."

Irene handed Charlie one of those preprinted "While You Were Out" message forms. Charlie read it and said, "It's from Don Chambers. He's letting us know that Arden Kendall is being transported to LA today."

I nodded. "Good riddance to bad rubbish," was all I could think of to say.

On that note Irene left us to our own devices and we just stood there in the middle of our gigantic office grinning at each other for a while. Then we set about making ourselves at home. Sitting at my snazzy new desk, I inspected the typewriter I requested. It was a spanking new Royal KHM 12, and it made my old Underwood look like an antique. Yes, sir, we were definitely several rungs up the ladder from where we'd been. I still kept pinching myself to be sure I wasn't dreaming.

A little before ten Charlie announced she was going to explore

KFRC. I, on the other hand, set off to find Ed Levi, KFRC's General Manager. We agreed to meet back at the office at lunch time.

Ed, it turned out, had the office in the southwest corner of the building. "Hello, Parker, welcome to KFRC and the Mutual System. How's your office? Do you have everything you need?"

"Thanks, Ed. The office is perfect, and I think we have everything we'll need and then some."

We spent the next half-hour discussing the nuts and bolts of our new relationship. Since, technically, we were running separate, independent operations, the procedures and arrangements we discussed had mostly to do with the cooperative use of the facilities, which didn't seem to present any problems.

Upon completing our discussion, Ed handed me a business card from the Cadillac dealership on the ground floor. "This is the fellow you need to see down in the showroom to pick up your company car. He's expecting you, so just introduce yourself and he'll get you all set up."

The gentleman in the showroom was, indeed, expecting me. He had instructions to supply me with a fast, comfortable road car because it was expected my responsibilities would include a lot of driving, especially between San Francisco and Los Angeles. To meet this need, he provided a shiny new cream colored 1939 Cadillac LaSalle Opera Coupe. It was equipped with folding jump seats in the rear to accommodate a total of three passengers in addition to the driver. It also had a radio, heater, clock, and a 125 horsepower V-8 engine that would run circles around most other cars on the road.

Charlie and I gave the coupe a trial run around town, ending up at Original McCarthy's in the Mission District for lunch. There, we ate some terrific corned beef and cabbage in celebration of our good fortune. We also agreed that, since she had no car, Charlie would inherit my Ford, which she appreciated because it meant no more streetcars.

I was still pinching myself.

Fifty-Six

Monday—October 31, 1938—9:00 A.M.

Los Angeles County Hall of Records—320 West Temple St.

Don Chambers sat with Charlie and me on a wooden bench in the hallway outside the California Superior Court Criminal Division waiting for the day's proceedings to begin. It was a noisy place, with the voices of reporters, attorneys, and spectators ricocheting around the granite walls and off the high ceiling.

We were all there for the same reason: To hear the jury's verdicts on the seven felony murder counts for which Arden Kendall, Junior had just been tried.

Kendall's trial started at the beginning of October, with LA County District Attorney Buron Fitts prosecuting the cases personally and at least half a dozen assistant DAs backing him up. The prominent and highly successful New York criminal attorney, William Foster, pled the cases for the defense. Because both the UPI and AP wire services covered the daily proceedings in great detail, Jack Carpenter and I had seen no reason for me to be in the courtroom for the bulk of the trial.

The reading of the verdicts, however, was another matter entirely. I wanted to see Kendall's face personally and report his reaction when the judge handed down his death sentence.

Don Chambers called us Friday to say the jury would probably be delivering its decisions after the weekend break, so Charlie and I packed up and raced down US 101 to be on hand for the big moment. When we met him outside the courtroom, Don was in high spirits. For one thing, he'd received a department commendation for Kendall's arrest, and for another, he had it on good authority that despite Kendall's semi-hero status as the Mob

Avenger, the jury was going to throw the book at him because DA Fitts had successfully tried the case on the strong premise that no citizen has the right to take the law into his own hands.

It was ten minutes after nine when a pair of bailiffs opened the tall, ornate entrance doors to the courtroom and we joined the crowd rushing in to get seats. Fortunately, Don had some pull and reserved seats for us in the first row behind the defense attorneys' table. It took a good fifteen minutes to get everyone seated, after which two more bailiffs escorted the defendant, followed by his lawyers, into the courtroom.

Kendall was resplendent in a medium gray three-piece suit. His face was passive and devoid of emotion until he arrived at the defense table. That was when he noticed me. We made eye contact and his expression became a sneer. He paused and his hands balled into fists. If the bailiffs hadn't forcibly seated him, I think Kendall might have come over the railing with intent to kill. I felt Charlie shift nervously in the seat next to mine.

Don leaned over and whispered, "That's the first emotion I've seen out of Kendall since the trial started. If I didn't know better, I'd think Mister Arden Kendall, Junior doesn't much like you, Park."

I glanced at Don and gave him a grin as the clerk of the court said in a loud voice, "Hear ye, hear ye, the Superior Court of California in and for the County of Los Angeles is now in session, the Honorable William H. Waste, presiding. All rise."

We all rose and I noticed Kendall look back over his shoulder in my direction. His sneer had turned into a glare, but it was no less menacing. I gave him a kindly smile.

Judge Waste entered the courtroom through a door behind the bench. He was a slender man with thick glasses, receding hair, and prominent ears who wore his black robes with dignity. Waste was actually California's Chief Justice, but because the LA County Superior Court Judge had prior commitments, Waste was trying the case and making some politically valuable national headlines.

The judge seated himself at the bench, tapped his gavel once, and in a clear voice said, "Be seated." Then, to the court clerk he said, "Bring in the jury."

With that, a side door opened admitting twelve men, good and true, to take their seats in the jury box. Judge Waste studied the jury for a few moments, shuffled some papers around, and said, "All right, I understand the jury has completed its deliberation, so let's get on with the verdicts."

The court clerk spoke next. "Will the jury please rise. Will the defendant also please rise and face the jury. Mister Foreman, has your jury agreed upon your verdicts?"

The foreman, a tall, dapper young man whose suit appeared to be every bit as expensive as Kendall's said, "Yes we have."

The clerk said, "What say you, Mister Foreman, as to complaint number one, wherein the defendant is charged with the murder in the first degree of Guido Moretti. Is he guilty or not guilty?"

The foreman consulted a piece of paper in his hand and said in a clear voice, "Not guilty."

A murmur of surprise passed through the courtroom and the judge banged his gavel. "Order!"

The Moretti verdict didn't surprise me. He was the first victim and there was very little in the way of evidence pointing to Kendall or anyone else. I glanced at Don. His expression was impassive.

The clerk said, "What say you, Mister Foreman, as to complaint number two, wherein the defendant is charged with the murder in the first degree of Ivan Glick. Is he guilty or not guilty?"

"Guilty."

I thought I heard a collective sigh of relief rising from the prosecutor's table. The first guilty verdict was followed by five more, one for each of the remaining names I'd copied from Chamber's blackboard more than two months ago. Now Don looked much happier. Each guilty verdict confirmed that Detective Lieutenant Don Chambers and his homicide squad had done their jobs diligently, albeit with a little help.

Each guilty verdict also seemed to deflate Kendall a little, like an inflatable swimming pool toy with a leak. I don't know what his attorneys told him to expect, but that he was now a convicted murderer six times over caused his dapper persona and supreme confidence to evaporate.

After the verdict was heard for the murder of Allan Ponce in the dingy Culver City hotel room where the Mob Avenger case began for me, the court clerk said, "Members of the jury, hearken to your verdicts as the court will record them. You, upon your oath, do say that the defendant is guilty of murder in the first degree on complaints number two through seven. So say you, Mister Foreman?"

The foreman adjusted the knot of his tie, cleared his throat, and said, "Yes."

"So say you all, members of the jury?"

More or less in unison, eleven voices said, "Yes," from the jury box."

Judge Waste then hammered his gavel a couple of times to quiet the chatter in the courtroom and said, "Members of the jury, I told you in my instructions that the verdicts in this case were your responsibility and your responsibility alone. For that reason, I never comment to juries on the verdicts they reach. I will say to you, though, that it is clear you took your responsibilities very seriously, and that you approached your decisions carefully and conscientiously.

"Your jury service is now complete. On behalf of all the people of the State of California, as well as the parties involved in this case, I thank you for your public service. This court will reconvene at nine tomorrow morning for the sentencing of the defendant. Court is now adjourned."

Throughout the session, both Charlie and I had been busily scribbling on legal pads. Slipping my pencil back into my inside coat pocket, I handed her my pad and said, "Here's the story. Please call Chicago and give it to Jack's team so they can get it on the air."

Standing, Charlie said, "Will do."

"Thanks. I'll stick around in the lobby downstairs until you're done. Then we'll get Don to buy us lunch."

As she rushed out to find a vacant telephone booth, Don said, "Buy you lunch, huh? You're sure milking this for all it's worth. Besides, you've got a big fat expense account now, so you ought to do the buying."

"Hey, Chambers, I made you a national hero. The least you can do is buy me a lousy sandwich."

Don grinned. "Okay, one lousy sandwich coming up."

On our way out of the courtroom several prominent officials stopped us to shake Don's hand and congratulate him on a job well done. One of those officials was Chief Davis. It seemed Don's status was on the rise.

I also noticed that Davis made no effort to toss me in his slammer and throw away the key. Yet another politician's promise goes unkept.

Tuesday—November 1, 1938—9:00 A.M.
Los Angeles County Hall of Records—320 West Temple Street

The crowd turning out for the sentencing was, if anything, even larger than that on hand for the verdicts. The only noticeable differences in the courtroom were the empty jury box and Kendall, who appeared haggard and distraught. Apparently he had a rough night, but not so rough he couldn't manage to send another menacing glare in my direction before he took his place at the defense table.

When everyone was finally seated, the clerk of the court again announced, "Hear ye, hear ye, the Superior Court of California in and for the County of Los Angeles is now in session, the Honorable William H. Waste, presiding. All rise."

Judge Waste wasted no time in getting down to business. "Is there anyone present who wishes to be heard by the court prior to sentencing?"

The judge allowed about ten seconds for a response, and when there was none, he gave the court clerk a "get on with it" gesture. The clerk said, "The defendant will rise and face the bench for sentencing." This time he didn't say, "Please." I guess court etiquette doesn't require being polite to convicted felons.

The defense team's chairs scraped the floor as they stood. The scraping sounds were almost deafening in the silent courtroom. The big moment had arrived and the air was dripping with tension.

When Kendall and his lawyers were standing, Judge Waste said, "Arden Kendall, Junior, you have been found guilty by a jury of your peers on six counts of murder in the first degree. For the first of these murders I hereby sentence you to execution in the gas chamber at San Quintin State Prison. I order that the sentence be carried out on a date no more than ninety days from today."

The tension instantly drained from the room. The suspense was over. The State of California intended to kill Kendall and that news set off a chain reaction of chatter throughout the room.

Judge Waste must have expected the crowd's response. He waited several seconds before hammering the courtroom back to order and finishing the sentencing.

"Additionally, for the remaining five convictions of murder in the first degree, I sentence you to five terms of imprisonment in a state penitentiary lasting ninety-nine years or until your death. These sentences are to be carried out consecutively beginning November Second, 1938."

The judge stared intently at Kendall for several seconds and the courtroom turned deathly silent again. Finally, Waste said, "Mister Kendall, considering the cold-blooded and heinous nature of your crimes, I would gladly sentence you to six deaths in the gas chamber if it were possible to do so. Unfortunately, one such sentence will have to suffice." In a tone completely devoid of sincerity, Judge Waste added, "May God have mercy on your soul."

With that, the judge banged his gavel once and left the courtroom. The clerk of the court rose and announced, "This session of the Superior Court of California in and for the County of Los Angeles is now adjourned."

Once again a racket erupted as reporters dashed out to call in their stories. I hardly noticed the noise, though, because I was hastily scribbling the conclusion to my own story on the legal pad in my lap. Jack Carpenter requested that I read my sentencing report over the telephone so he could get it on a transcription for distribution to the network. That's also why I didn't anticipate what happened next. My only warning was a gasp from Charlie.

I looked up just in time to see Arden Kendall, Junior flying head-first over the railing behind the defense table. He landed on top of me with his hands clasped tightly around my neck. I heard shouting and from the corner of my eye I saw Charlie beating on Kendall with clenched fists. Then the room began to darken as Kendall tried his best to choke the life out of me.

I had a fleeting impression of bailiffs reaching for Kendall over the railing, but it was Don Chambers who saved my life. He grabbed Kendall by the hair, yanked his head back, and smashed a fist into the killer's face. Blood spurted from Kendall's nose and the pressure around my neck ended just as I passed out.

When I rejoined the living a minute or two later, Charlie was leaning over me and Kendall was nowhere to be seen. I heard Don's voice say, "You gonna be okay, Park?"

In a voice that sounded like I'd swallowed a truckload of gravel, I said, "Yeah, I think so."

The next thing I noticed through the haze in my head was that the courtroom was nearly empty. The bailiffs were forcibly shoving people out the doors. I blinked a couple of times and Judge Waste appeared. He was standing on the other side of the railing where Kendall had been. I guessed he heard the commotion and returned to see what the fuss was about. Looking him in the eye, my hoarse voice asked, "I suppose there isn't much purpose at this point in charging Kendall with attempted murder, is there?"

The irony I'd intended was not wasted on Waste. He said, "No, son, I don't suppose there is, but I can darn well make sure you get a personal invitation to attend his execution in a few months."

Managing what I'm sure was an anemic smile, I replied, "I'll take you up on that, Your Honor."

As I stood, Charlie, who was holding on to my arm, sounded both worried and a little panicky, said, "Are you sure you're okay, Park?"

I said, "Yes." Then noticing that some of the hoarseness was clearing from my voice, I added, "Let's find a telephone so I can read my story for Jack's recorder."

Apparently some of the reporters heard about what happened in the courtroom after they left. When we got out into the hall, several of them clustered around me demanding a statement, among them Tommy Ebert from the *Tribune*. He gave me a face full of bad breath and said, "What happened in there, Atkins? What's the story?"

Looking him straight in the eye, I said, "Go to hell, Ebert. The rest of you can hear the story on the eleven o' clock news over KHJ."

With Don's help, Charlie and I pushed our way through the crowd to the row of telephone booths down the hall. I stepped into an empty one and closed the door.

I got Jack Carpenter on the long distance line, and on his cue, read the part of the report I had time to write down. Then I adlibbed the conclusion about Kendall attacking me. I delivered it with all the drama I could muster and concluded with, "This is Parker T. Atkins reporting over the Mutual Broadcasting System from Los Angeles, California."

Jack let his recorder hear a few moments of silence before he said, "Wow, Park! That was one hell of an ending! You sure earned your pay today. We'll get this out to the affiliates for the next hourly news and I'll talk to you later. Thanks for a great job!"

I told him he was welcome and stepped out of the phone booth. By then Don and Charlie were about the only ones left in the hallway. Charlie gave me a hug and the sort of kiss she usually reserved for less public places. Fortunately, Don just shook my hand and said, "Okay, Atkins, I saved your life this time, so lunch is on you."

Over lunch the discussion eventually turned to business when I asked, "So I take it Kendall never disclosed his source of information for selecting victims?"

The way Don looked at me shot holes in his answer before he even gave it. "Not a word. Fortunately they didn't need that to convict him. He's protecting someone and we didn't offer him any incentive to give us the guy, so he didn't see any reason to do it."

I looked Don in the eye for a few seconds. The expression on his face was a silent plea to accept his answer without question. His expression also told me I was paying a price for becoming a national network news reporter. I decided Don's friendship was important enough for me to drop the matter.

"Well," I said, "That's one Kendall will take to the grave with him. What about the guy with the European accent who answered his telephone the night I called?"

"After I returned from your neck of the woods, I got search warrants for both of Kendall's houses and sent them up to that Frisco homicide cop, Baily. Among other things he confirmed that the fellow with the accent was Kendall's butler and the guy didn't seem to have any connection with the killings.

"The warrants paid off, though, because when they searched the room Kendall used for an office in the Sea Cliff house, they found receipts from the Biltmore Hotel confirming Kendall was in Los Angeles for every date on which the Mob Avenger killed a victim. Fitts was happy to get his hands on those, I can tell you."

I nodded. "DA Fitts ought to be happy about a lot of things, especially the convictions he got from the jury."

"Yeah, he seemed unusually cheerful when I saw him leaving the Hall of Records. Oh, and speaking of our DA, you'll be interested to know that Fittsy won the battle of Santa Monica Bay. The jury upheld his argument that those gambling ships were in waters subject to state law. Cornero is appealing the decision, though, and word is he's got a good chance of getting it overturned."

Laughing, I said, "Good for Tony. I'd hate to see him have to turn away all those squirrels."

Rather than starting north after lunch as we'd planned, Charlie and I checked into a room at The Breakers Hotel in Long Beach. It's a classy joint on the beach and staying there was pushing the expense account to its limit, but I figured we deserved a treat.

I was leaning on the wall next to our window in my shirtsleeves watching the endless lines of surf roll in over the sand far below. The scene gave me a feeling of contentment, in effect, recharging my battery.

Charlie chose that moment to stand alongside me. "How are you feeling now, Park?"

Smiling at her, I said, "I'm feeling peachy keen. How 'bout you?"

She kissed me and said, "I'm feeling much better now than I was in that courtroom this morning. I thought sure that . . . so and so, Kendall, was going to kill you. It scared the wits out of me!"

"Me, too. By the way, thanks for helping Don subdue Kendall."

"I didn't do much. I don't think he even noticed me."

"It's the thought that counts, kiddo."

Looking a little coy and very sexy, Charlie said, "In that case, my thought is that you should lay down for a while before we go to dinner. I'll even keep you company."

"Good thinking, kiddo."

THE END

Meet H. P. Oliver

H. P. Oliver began his career with a degree in journalism from San Jose State University and spent the next thirty-some years writing award-winning entertainment and educational media. Now he applies his creativity and imagination to writing historical mysteries.

About mystery writing, Oliver says, "To be truly engrossing, a mystery needs a little meat on its bones—something more than just figuring out who done the evil deed. Taking a story back in time or even basing it on actual historical events is a great way to endow a good yarn with even more color and depth. Historical periods and locations give the writer an opportunity to take most readers where they've never been before."

H. P. Oliver lives in northern California and spends much of his time working on projects throughout the western states. In addition to his love of history, Oliver's interests range from vintage film to restoring classic cars.

For information about H. P. Oliver's books, including synopses, previews, video trailers, and purchase links, visit his fan site at www.HPOliver.com, where you will also find free illustrated history articles, video shorts, and other fascinating features. Plan to stay a while!

Books By H. P. Oliver

CLASSIC MYSTERIES IN HISTORY

THE TRUTH BE TOLD
(E-book)

AND THE ANGELS SING
(E-book)

SILENTS!
(E-book & Paper)

GOODNIGHT, SAN FRANCISCO
(E-book & Paper)

SO LONG, LA
(E-book & Paper)

WINGING IT
(E-book & Paper)

JOHNNY SPICER CAPERS

JOHNNY SPICER: THE FIRST CAPERS
(E-book)

PACIFICA
(E-book & Paper)

REVOLVER
(E-book & Paper)

TEMBO
(E-book & Paper)